PRAISE FOR

LITTLE GIRL GONE

"Readers will be at the edge of their seats." —*Crimespree Magazine*

"The energy in this chilling debut of the Afton Tangler novels mounts to a fever pitch." —*RT Book Reviews* (Top Pick)

"*Little Girl Gone* is taut and tense, a great tale to jump-start the Afton Tangler series." —*Minneapolis Star Tribune*

"Schmitt fills her thriller with numerous twists and builds it to a heart-pounding conclusion." —*Richmond Times-Dispatch*

LITTLE GIRL GONE

GERRY SCHMITT

BERKLEY

NEW YORK

BERKLEY
An imprint of Penguin Random House LLC
375 Hudson Street, New York, New York 10014

Copyright © 2016 by Gerry Schmitt
Excerpt from *Shadow Girl* copyright © 2017 by Gerry Schmitt

Berkley Trade Paperback ISBN: 9780425281772

Library of Congress Cataloging-in-Publication Data
Names: Schmitt, Gerry, author.
Title: Little girl gone / Gerry Schmitt.
Description: First edition. | New York : Berkley Books, 2016.
Identifiers: LCCN 2016004359 (print) | LCCN 2016015978 (ebook) | ISBN 9780425281765 (hardcover) | ISBN 9780698197473 (ebook)
Subjects: LCSH: Kidnapping—Fiction. | Police—Minnesota—Fiction. | Afton (Minn.)—Fiction. | Suspense fiction.
Classification: LCC PS3603.H56 L58 2016 (print) | LCC PS3603.H56 (ebook) | DDC 813/.6—dc23
LC record available at https://lccn.loc.gov/2016004359

Berkley hardcover edition / July 2016
Berkley trade paperback edition / June 2017

Printed in the United States of America
1   3   5   7   9   10   8   6   4   2

Cover art by James Osmond/Getty Images
Cover design by Anthony Ramondo
Book design by Tiffany Estreicher

1

MARJORIE Sorenson turned hard, flat, snake eyes on the young woman in the fox fur parka who strolled toward her in the Skylark Shopping Mall. And instantly pegged her: *rich bitch.*

This blond woman who walked so casually, who cast her eyes about the doll show booths with a certain air of entitlement, had long, flaxen hair like you saw in TV ads; a fancy purse with a bunch of initials littered across the fabric; and ripe, round hips that swayed enticingly.

Marjorie, on the other hand, had stringy, dishwater hair; coarse, pock-marked skin; and a stomach that hung down in a limp, bloated pouch. Once, when she was listening to an early morning radio show, she'd heard the DJs howling and making jokes about women who had gunts. Tuba sound effects had accompanied their hoots and nasty comments. Marjorie had stabbed murderously at the radio dial with the paring knife she held in her soapy hand and made it a point never to listen to that station again.

A delighted smile had spread across the blond woman's face now, as Marjorie continued to track her. The woman had just passed an enormous pink-and-white candy-striped banner that proclaimed DOLL SHOW TODAY, and found herself wandering through a maze of tables and booths that displayed the most intriguing array of dolls. Ballerinas, fairy dolls, Cabbage

Patch Kids, Barbies, Strawberry Shortcake, small porcelain collectibles in diminutive costumes, even antique dolls.

And one perfect little doll in Marjorie's booth that literally took the woman's breath away.

Life-sized, with fine blond hair, plump cheeks, and cupid-shaped lips, it had the perfect look, coloring, and complexion of a newborn. And just like a newborn, this doll was nestled in a white wicker basket with a pink floral blanket tucked around her.

Marjorie watched the woman as she continued to gaze at the baby doll with complete and utter fascination. Then she slipped her glasses on and stood up, a genial, practiced smile suddenly softening her coarse features.

"Isn't she beautiful?" Marjorie cooed, her voice struggling to convey a breathy excitement.

"She looks so real, it's positively eerie," the blond woman marveled. "As if she could wake up at any moment and start cooing."

Marjorie broadened her smile, revealing crooked teeth and pale pink gums. "Her name is Tiffany Lynn and she's a reborn."

"So precious," the woman murmured as Marjorie edged closer. "And you called her . . . what was that?"

"A reborn," Marjorie said. She reached down and snugged the blanket closer to the doll's tiny round chin.

The blond woman giggled nervously. "That's what I thought you said."

Marjorie smiled kindly, as though she'd already explained the reborn concept several times today. "I'm Molly Miller," she said, extending a hand.

"Susan Darden," the woman said, shaking hands with her. "Nice to meet you."

Gathering up the doll with all the care you'd accord a real live baby, Marjorie gently passed it to Susan.

"Reborns are a customized form of doll making," Marjorie said. "Reborn artists start with a commercial doll, often from Berenguer Babies or Secrist Dolls, and then do a complete transformation. For example, this doll was stripped of all factory paint, as well as hair and eyes. Then she was repainted with ten coats of paint, human hair was micro-inserted, and a tiny electronic device was implanted in her chest to mimic a heartbeat."

Susan's eyes widened. "She really has been remade."

"Reborn," Marjorie said. "Airbrushed both inside and out to capture the subtle coloring of a newborn." Her index finger indicated the doll's closed eyes. "This little sweetheart's eyelashes are genuine fox hair that was dyed and hand-inserted."

"I take it you're the artist?" Susan asked.

Marjorie nodded, allowing herself a modest smile.

Susan gazed tenderly at the little doll that lay in her arms and her heart lurched. The doll, Tiffany Lynn the woman had called her, had been weighted in such a way that it possessed the heft and feel of a real baby. Her eyes were closed and her tiny lashes brushed delicately against chubby cheeks. Susan could see that the baby's skin color had been fastidiously done, replicating the slight bluish-pink tint of a newborn.

"A reborn," Susan said, obviously in awe of the painstaking skill that had gone into creating this doll. "This is amazing craftsmanship. She really does look like she's only two or three days old."

"Thank you," Marjorie said. She gestured at the yellow-striped shopping bag from Ciao Baby that dangled from Susan's arm. "I'm guessing you might have a new baby yourself?" She'd noted the woman's slightly swollen breasts and still-rounded tummy, which peeked out from between her coat's lapels. Pegged her instantly as a new mommy.

Susan nodded as one hand moved absently down to touch her stomach. "I have a baby girl. She'll be three months old tomorrow."

"Do you have a picture of her?" Marjorie asked. She knew that almost all new mothers carried pictures of their offspring. On their cell phones or in a brag book. Babies always took center stage in a new mother's life, so this photo log was probably the only bright spot once they became lost in a fog of 3:00 A.M. feedings and a swirl of postpartum emotions.

Susan handed the doll back to Marjorie and pulled an iPhone from her handbag. She thumbed to her favorite picture. "Here she is. Elizabeth Ann."

"Ahh . . . precious," Marjorie said. She gazed at the snapshot, her mind clicking into overdrive. "But clearly not a newborn anymore. She's probably already growing and changing and wriggling with independence."

A shadow flicked across Susan's face. An emotion that Marjorie instantly picked up on. It said: *But what if I could recapture that special moment? What if I could have a doll that always looked as precious and wonderful as my own daughter did when she was just a day or two old? What if I could preserve forever that incredible moment in time?*

"Molly," Susan said, "do you ever do special orders?"

"Oh, sure," Marjorie replied, working to maintain a casual tone. "Lots of times I do that."

Susan flipped to another photo of Elizabeth Ann, one where she couldn't have been more than two days old. "Can you work from a photo?"

Marjorie peered at the screen and nodded. "Such a little angel. She's your first?"

Susan nodded.

"You and your husband must be filled with joy."

"We are," Susan said, obviously more than a little intrigued by Marjorie's hand-wrought reborns. "Are these babies . . . your reborns as you call them . . . are they expensive?"

"Depends on how lifelike you want to get," Marjorie said. "With Tiffany Lynn, I used wefts of unprocessed European hair and inserted magnets inside her mouth so she could simulate using a pacifier."

Susan gazed at the reborn, her face telegraphing the fact that she'd already made up her mind. "I'd love to have one. Of course, I'd have to talk it over with my husband first."

Marjorie smiled knowingly. Caught up in the flush of new baby excitement, the average husband could be talked into just about any kind of push present. "You think your husband would approve?" she asked.

"Oh, absolutely," Susan said. "Besides . . ." She smiled, almost to herself. "I have ways of convincing him."

Marjorie nodded. She hadn't known a man, really *known* a man, for almost twenty years. Her ex-husband, may his stultifying soul roast on the coal-encrusted back burners of hell, had pretty much soured her on the notion of men. Bill Sorenson, or Billy as the ex had preferred to be called by his friends down at Riney's Bar, had been the poster child for dumb-ass behavior. Billy had never seen a 7-Eleven he didn't want to rob, which was probably why Billy had been in and out of jail so often, he'd been on a first-name basis with the booking officers. Probably, they could have just installed a damn revolving door for Billy.

As far as Marjorie was concerned, the only redeeming thing Billy had ever done was pound away at her one besotted night and given her Ronnie. Now, nineteen years later, Ronnie had grown into a fairly decent young man. He kept things ticking around the old farm and, under her watchful supervision, kept his partying to a tolerable level; a few beers at the local strip clubs, maybe a couple of joints on weekends.

And wonder of wonders, the more Ronnie matured, the better looking the kid got. Friendly smile, curly brown hair, good in the height department, and fairly well built. And if a girl didn't ask too damn many snoopy questions, and failed to notice there wasn't substantive gray matter behind those distant blue eyes, then Ronnie was in business. *They* were in business.

Taking great care, Marjorie laid the Tiffany Lynn doll back down in its basket, then reached into her apron pocket and pulled out a pad and pencil. "Tell you what," she said, a thoughtful note creeping into her voice. "Why don't you jot down your name and phone number? Once I get back home and unpacked from this doll show, I'll give you a jingle. It doesn't cost anything for an estimate, right?"

"That would be wonderful," Susan said as she scribbled out her information. She handed it over to Marjorie, but seemed unwilling to pull her eyes away from Tiffany Lynn.

Marjorie's crooked grin stretched across her face like a leering jack-o'-lantern. She was already thinking ahead. Had to find Ronnie and get the boy moving. After all, there was work to be done.

A few minutes later, Marjorie found Ronnie lounging at the food court. He was sucking down an Orange Julius and trying to make time with the slutty teenage girl behind the counter. She cast a baleful glance at her son and crooked a finger.

Ronnie saw her watching him, gave a resentful look, and sauntered over. "What?"

Marjorie jerked her chin. "That one. Follow her." She pointed to the back of Susan's blond head as she drifted toward the exit. "Find out where she lives, then get your ass back here. I'll get this shit packed up."

Ronnie stared at her for a long moment, his faded blue eyes taking on a crazy gleam.

"Will you *move* it!" Marjorie put some real venom into her voice to finally get Ronnie moving. Then she went back to her doll display and got busy. Wrapping her dolls in tissue paper, she hummed as she worked. She decided that things often had a funny way of working out. She didn't think it was going to happen today. And then, praise the Lord, Susan Darden had come strolling along like an entitled little princess. Almost like she'd been dropped into her lap by the hand of God. And wasn't that something?

2

THAT'S the house," Ronnie said. They were hunkered in their rumbling, rust-spotted Chevy Malibu on Kenwood Parkway, one of the fanciest addresses in Minneapolis. Enormous homes of red brick and yellow sandstone, most of which dated back to the days of the timber and lumber barons, sprawled out around them. Bright lights glowed in lead pane windows and afforded them small peeks at wood-paneled libraries, lush living rooms, and dining rooms lit by crystal chandeliers.

"Shit," Marjorie said, clearly impressed. "This is big time." By *big time*, she meant big money. She wasn't easily roused from her normally angry, turgid state, but this kind of wealth was a whole new ball game. Gave her a little tingle right there in the pit of her stomach.

Compared to these people, the rich assholes who actually lived in these mansions, Marjorie knew that she and Ronnie looked like refugees. Just like those poor, sad people you saw in old black-and-white newsreels clumping down the gangplank from some tramp steamer. People who were at the back of the line, who would always be *kept* at the back of the line.

"You want me to go take a closer look?" Ronnie asked. He was slumped in the passenger side, eating cold French fries and dripping ketchup on his yellow sweatshirt.

"Don't be a dummy," Marjorie snarled. "We gotta wait." Her eyes squinted greedily at the twinkling lights that filtered through the panes of glass like some kind of picture-perfect postcard. Marjorie could imagine sterling flatware being laid out just so on pristine white linen. A cook, or a housekeeper at the very least, puttering around a warm kitchen, where pots steamed and bubbled. A sophisticated, elegant couple sitting down at their dining room table. Maybe being served soup from a tureen. Whatever the hell a tureen was.

An hour later, the numbing cold was getting to them. Marjorie shifted uncomfortably, pulled her thumb out of her mitten's thumb spot, and nestled it with the rest of her fingers. Their breath had created a thin skim of ice on the inside of the car windows.

"Maybe they ain't going out," Ronnie said. He was starting to get bored and his voice had taken on a whiny tone.

"It's Saturday night," Marjorie said. "Rich people go out Saturday night. That's what they do."

Periscoping her head up, Marjorie scratched off a small patch of ice with a ragged fingernail and pressed a watchful eye to the cold glass. Upstairs, on the second floor of the Dardens' grand home, a light winked off.

"Say now," she said to Ronnie.

Ten minutes later, Susan Darden and her husband came waltzing out the front door. Susan was bundled in a sleek black mink coat that was so long, it grazed the sidewalk as she walked. Her long blond hair was pulled snugly into a low chignon, the better to show off the size and sparkle of her diamond earrings. Her husband, tall, and radiating businessman confidence, had his arm circled protectively around Susan's waist. Halfway down the walk, he leaned down and whispered something to her, causing her to throw back her head and laugh. Marjorie imagined she could hear Susan's high, tinkling notes hanging like icicles in the frozen night. Then Mr. and Mrs. Darden climbed into a sleek jet-black Volvo and slowly pulled away from the curb.

Marjorie sat there for a few minutes. She just knew they were off to some-place fancy, an expensive restaurant or a party where people would eat crab puffs and drink French wine. Then she pulled her thoughts away from the Dardens and turned inward, thinking, mulling over their next move. As she mumbled to herself, neon dollar signs seemed to glow with an urgent, bright intensity right before her eyes. Then a wolfish smile crept across her face and she cranked her head toward Ronnie. "Let's go," she whispered.

ASHLEY Copeland stared silently around the empty house. It was blessedly quiet now that the Dardens had finally taken off. Mrs. Darden had yammered on with all sorts of picky instructions, while Mr. Darden just plain gave her the creeps. But he was her mom's boss, so she was careful not to kick him between the legs every time he leered at her.

This was Ashley's second babysitting gig this week, and she was desperate for cash. Winter Prom was right around the corner, and her dipshit boyfriend still hadn't saved enough money to spring for the kind of limousine and hotel room she'd always dreamed of. Then there was the matter of her dress. She intended to absolutely *crush* it in a hot pink strapless number that would put all the cool girls to shame.

At least this gig seemed like a no-brainer. The Dardens' baby was asleep upstairs and, according to Mrs. Darden, would probably remain asleep. So it would be a relaxing night of watching cable TV and doing some Face-Time on her iPad with her friends, Trish and Bella. It could be the easiest forty bucks she'd ever earned—as long as the privileged little brat stayed asleep.

Ashley walked through the dining room, trailing one hand on a high-gloss table. The furnace rumbled beneath parquet floors, and a few flakes of snow had started to *tick-tick* against the windows. She'd never been in a house this big before. What was really obscene was that only two people lived here. Well, actually three, but the baby didn't really count.

Flopping down on a bouncy leather sofa, Ashley pulled out her iPad and logged in as GoldyLox131. She tried to FaceTime several of her friends but no one answered. Bummer. She pursed her lips, blew out a glut of air, and looked around, already feeling bored.

But she wouldn't be for long. In the familiar children's story, Goldilocks has a very harrowing encounter with a group of marauding bears. For Goldy-Lox131, two wolves already lurked outside the front door.

THE kidnapping of Baby Darden was your basic piece of cake. Ronnie walked up to the front door, a battered Pizza Hut box balanced in his left hand, and rang the doorbell. Marjorie hung back in the shadows, watchful and listening. A few seconds later, a chime rang out deep inside the enormous house. *Bing, bang, bong.* Just like church.

Not thirty seconds later the babysitter opened the front door. Ronnie's first impression was of a skinny blond teenager with a tentative smile and a thin band of blue braces stretched across her upper teeth. Puzzlement flickered in her eyes when she spotted the pizza box. Then she gave a disdainful snort and said, "Nobody here ordered—"

Ronnie didn't waste a single precious moment. He straight-armed the girl in the face with his right arm, shattering her nose on impact, and sending her sprawling backward onto the Oriental carpet.

Terrified, screeching like a scalded cat, blood flowing copiously from her busted nose, the babysitter struggled to right herself. *"Eee . . . pyuh!"* she babbled as her feet paddled helplessly on the rug, unable to gain traction.

Ronnie was on top of her like a rabid pit bull. "Shut up!" he snarled as Marjorie slipped in behind him and kicked the door shut in one fluid motion.

"Stuff them socks in her mouth," Marjorie ordered. "Then blindfold her and snare your rope around her neck."

"I know what to do," Ronnie cried. He was caught up in the moment now, feeling totally enraptured. His blood was pulsing hotter, his synapses were firing more crisply than ever before. Struggling with this little piece of quiff was really turning his crank.

Scared out of her mind, Ashley begged and pleaded with him as she blew gluts of snot and bubbles of blood out of her shattered nose.

Ronnie grinned at her and hooked a thumb into the waistband of her jeans. He felt the button pop, the zipper start to go down. A narrow piece of hot pink silk, the girl's thong, stretched across her flat belly.

"Jesus Christ," Marjorie said. She was a little surprised by the violence of his attack. "Don't kill her. And don't do . . . that."

Illuminated under a French chandelier, Ronnie ground his teeth together in frustration and stuffed a dirty tube sock into the girl's mouth. He slapped on a hunk of silvery duct tape, then wound a hunk of rope around the girl's neck, stretched it tight, and looped it around her ankles. Hog-tied her nice and neat like a goat, just like he'd seen a 4-H guy do at the Pepin County Fair last summer. *Good*, he thought to himself. *This feels so good and the bitch deserves it.* He glanced around to see where Marjorie was. *If only there was time to really have fun.*

Marjorie took a few moments to scope out the downstairs, just in case there was a live-in housekeeper or a prowling dog. When she decided they were safe, safe enough anyway, she charged up the curving staircase. Expensive silk carpet whispered underfoot as she wondered what it must be like to live in a fancy house like this. A house with real oil paintings and custom leather furniture, and where you had actual carpeting instead of dirty, crappy linoleum. She gnashed her teeth, seething with unrequited envy as she climbed up to the second-floor landing. She hesitated for a moment, her hand stretching out to rest on an elaborately carved newel post, and glanced toward what she figured was the front of the house. Master bedroom located there? Probably, she decided. Which meant the nursery would be right next door.

Marjorie padded down the dim hallway, pushed open a door, and peered inside. And there, lying in a frilly white crib surrounded by a plush zoo of polar bears and penguins, was the baby. Elizabeth Ann. Just like some kind of grand prize in a box of Cracker Jack.

Peering over the railing of the crib, Marjorie whispered, "Hi, baby."

The baby stirred and gurgled softly.

"Perfect," Marjorie said, reaching down to gather up the child. "You're a perfect little angel, aren't you?"

3

WINTER always looked more pristine outside the city. And the small village of Taylor's Falls, as well as the surrounding three hundred acres of state parkland and bluffs, sparkled like a glazed sugar confection after last night's snowfall.

With basaltic cliffs that towered almost nine hundred feet over the winding Saint Croix River, the entire area was a climber's paradise, offering frozen waterfalls, steep rock faces, and glacier-formed sinkholes. But ice climbing is both challenging and dangerous, especially with a diamond coating of fickle new ice and snow.

Arcing her right arm back, Afton Tangler swung her Petzl ice ax into the ice-coated cliff. She grimaced as the sharp metal bit in and her shoulder absorbed the harsh impact. *Here we go*, she told herself. *Let's carpe this friggin' diem and show this big boy who's boss!*

Spits of cold ice chips stung her face as Afton repeated the motion with her left arm, drove in her toes, and found purchase with her crampons. Beginning her ascent up the cliff known as the Dihedral, she fell into the familiar ice climber's pattern. Thwack, kick, pull herself up. Thwack, kick, do it again.

Recent snows and temperature drops had brought early season ice to the bluffs at Taylor's Falls. It was good ice this morning, hard and resilient, shiny as glass, and Afton was the first one to take a crack at it. Lean and compact, just a shade past thirty, Afton had the piercing blue eyes of a Siberian husky and blondish hair that sprang into an artichoke-like assemblage if she wielded her blow dryer too enthusiastically. Right now, none of that mattered. She was just praying that she was tough enough to handle this cliff.

"On belay," called Hazel, one of her team members from down below. Three hours earlier, their Women on the Ropes climbing club had driven up from the Twin Cities, picked out a likely climbing spot, and affixed a web of climbing and safety ropes. Now Hazel meted out some of that rope as Afton made her ascent.

Moving methodically but cautiously, Afton climbed to just around the midpoint without encountering any major obstacles. The only issue so far was the sharp wind. It froze her cheeks and stung her eyes, making them water.

Damn, she thought, ducking her chin farther down inside her anorak. *It's cold. Maybe having first crack at this hill isn't so great after all.*

Afton climbed on autopilot for another ten feet, then paused beneath a craggy overhang, what climbers called an ice mushroom. She studied it, chewed her lip, and tried to muster her bravado.

Okay, she told herself. *Blow by this baby and it's a quick ten-foot scramble to the top. Like they say in Nike-land, just do it.*

But the ice was thinner up here, with patches of loose rock like cat litter. If she could find a decent toehold, Afton was confident she could muscle her way over this monster.

Afton took a deep breath, scanning the route. *Something's here*, she told herself resolutely. *Has to be.* She had to trust her instincts and believe in her route. She closed her eyes, breathed deeply, tried to slow her heart rate. Instantly, she felt calmer; now she could do it. Opening her eyes, she searched the route again. Then a plan materialized.

Afton would try for a small lip, maybe fifteen inches out from her right hip. It was high; it would be a stretch. She exhaled slowly, drove in her ax, swung her right leg up, and caught the toehold.

There you are. Gotcha, you bastard.

She clung to the wall, in an unnatural, contorted position, feeling a modicum of triumph. Now it was only a matter of jacking her other leg up. But as she hung there, trying to shift a little more weight onto her right foot, her shoulder muscles began to burn and her right hand had the stirrings of a cramp.

Shit.

"You okay?" Forty feet below, Hazel peered up at her, aware Afton was hanging in a fairly miserable position. The rest of the team was clustered below, watching, patiently waiting their turns.

"Terrific," Afton yelled down. She gritted her teeth, trying to decide what to do. Her apprehension had distracted her, causing her to make a couple of tactical errors. Worst of all, her arms were blown and she felt like a stupid fruit bat hanging against this ice wall.

Push through the pain, she told herself. They were words that were fast becoming her everyday mantra. A messy divorce had turned her into a single mom again, and her job as community liaison officer for the Minneapolis Police Department meant she had to deal with people in the messy, tragic aftermath of their worst day ever.

If I were on a completely vertical frozen waterfall instead of this fifty-five-degree slope, I'd probably have fallen, she berated herself.

So what the hell was she doing here? A soccer mom trying to act like an eighteen-year-old kid at the X Games? She should be lazing around home with the kids watching *The Real Housewives* and snarfing a bag of Chips Ahoy. Or better yet . . .

"Hey!" one of the women called up to her, and then gave a slow-motion wave. "You got a phone call. Somebody named Thacker."

Saved by the bell, Afton decided. As community liaison officer for the Minneapolis Police Department, she was part victim's advocate, part social worker. The MPD sometimes phoned her on weekends to help with a case or finesse a referral. Or maybe her boss was just anxious again. In his job as deputy chief, Gerald Thacker was anxious a lot.

"I'm coming down," Afton called, and everyone stepped back to give her room. She flipped herself around, snapped a SpiderJack descender onto the rope, and prepared for a fast descent. This was the easy part, the fun part. Exercising a *glissade*. Which, of course, was really just a fancy French term for scooting down the hill on the seat of your pants.

Once Afton reached the bottom of the cliff, she peeled off her gloves and grabbed the phone.

"It's your boss," one of the women said in a hoarse whisper. "Sounds important."

"Hey," Afton said into the phone as she rotated her left shoulder to unkink a knot. "What's up?"

Gerald Thacker's voice crackled in her ear. "We need you back here. Pronto."

"Are you kidding?" She and the other women had driven up here to sample fine wines and local cheeses, do a little ice climbing, and enjoy a good gabfest in their rented chalet. Not necessarily in that order. A mini vacation away from the demands of bosses, kids, husbands, and household humdrum.

"Listen," Thacker said. "There's been an abduction. A bad one."

Afton sucked in air. *Bad* had to mean a child. "A child?" she asked, and the women around her fell silent.

"A baby," Thacker said.

"Dear Lord. How old?"

"Three months yesterday," Thacker told her.

"Taken from . . ."

"Her home in Kenwood," Thacker said. "Last night. Stolen right out of her crib."

"Oh, jeez," Afton said. She immediately thought of her own two daughters, Poppy and Tess.

"There's a shit storm going on down here at city hall," Thacker said. "And your presence is required. So what I want to know is . . . how soon can you be here?"

Afton squinted at her watch, an old Cartier that seemed to perpetually run five minutes slow. "Hour and a half if I really crank it." Six months ago, she'd gotten a Lincoln Navigator as part of her divorce settlement. It was a big honkin' SUV that could do ninety without breaking a sweat.

"Good," responded Thacker. "Do it."

He was about to hang up when Afton said, "How are the parents holding up?"

There was a pause, and then Thacker said, "They're not."

4

PUNCHING it as fast as she dared, Afton sped south on I-35 toward the Twin Cities. She was a fast, intuitive driver who'd honed her skills schlepping her two daughters and their myriad friends from school to T-ball to piano lessons to soccer practice. And she'd joined the ranks of single working parents yet again. She was recently divorced from her second husband, Mickey Craig, a man with a dazzling smile and a wandering eye, who owned Metro Cadillac and Jaguar out in the western suburb of Wayzata.

Afton had actually met Mickey when one of his Jaguars, driven by his secretary, Mona, had been carjacked right in the middle of rush-hour traffic in downtown Minneapolis. She'd been called in to help deal with the traumatized secretary, who couldn't stop blubbering and waving her arms in desperation.

When Mickey arrived at the scene, Afton had found him hunky, attractive, and sweetly charming. Traits she'd always thought impossible in someone who owned a car dealership. And in the end, it turned out her instincts had been right.

TRUE to her word, Afton made the drive in an hour and a half, forgoing the ritual stop at Toby's for a take-home box of their famous sticky rolls. She arrived at police headquarters in downtown Minneapolis by eleven o'clock, dumped the SUV at one of the curbside spots reserved for police officers, of which she was not technically one, and headed inside to meet her boss.

"About time," Thacker said as Afton strode into his office still dressed in black leggings, boots, and a neon green fleece pullover. He sucked down the final dregs of his coffee, grimaced, and depressed the button on an old-fashioned intercom. "Angel," he barked. "Is everyone ready for the briefing?"

"They're waiting for you," came his secretary's muffled voice. Even she had been pulled in this Sunday morning.

"Good," Thacker said, brushing past Afton. "Let's get to it."

THE Minneapolis Police Department was a perpetual hive of activity. Officers dressed in blue hurried between rows of desks and ducked in and out of cubicles. Detectives in weekend casual sucked cups of black coffee and pecked at computer terminals. Interview rooms, which lined the perimeter of the detectives' area, were used for interrogations and sometimes staff meetings during periods of high activity. Today, the high-profile Darden case dominated activity in the department.

Afton followed Thacker into a large, fluorescent-lit conference room, where the murmur of conversation throbbed like a beating heart. Two uniformed officers sat hunched at a table with four detectives. They were all shoving paper around, jotting notes, and looking generally stressed.

All heads jerked up when Thacker entered. Deputy Chief Gerald Thacker was dressed as if he were attending a shareholders meeting at a Fortune 500 company. Plaid Joseph Abboud sport coat, black slacks, and high-polished black oxfords. Once the detectives in their khakis and thermal pullovers had surveyed Thacker, their eyes turned to Afton. This wasn't unusual. She was used to their stares, and it was starting to get old. She just wished she could be looked upon as another member of the team, not as a little sister, chickie-poo, soccer mom, or forbidden fruit. Only Thacker and Max Montgomery, one of the veteran detectives, treated her as if she really belonged here, and for that she was grateful.

"Okay," Thacker said loudly. "To catch everybody up, here's what we've got so far." He stood at the head of a battered wooden table covered with cigarette burns in a stuffy room that had probably been painted pea green sometime around the end of the Eisenhower Administration. Probably the only thing that had changed in the room in seven decades was that you weren't allowed to smoke there anymore.

"We got the call around midnight last night," Thacker continued. "The Dardens had just come home from a charity event . . ." He snapped his fingers at Max Montgomery.

"Carrousel to Fight Cancer," Max said.

"Hosted by the Edina Country Club," Thacker said. "Anyway, they arrived home to find their babysitter hog-tied and hysterical, and their infant daughter missing. Two uniformed officers responded immediately and secured the scene. Then Montgomery and Dillon here"—he nodded toward Max Montgomery and Dick Dillon, who were sitting side by side across the table from Afton—"got the callout."

Detective Dick Dillon, a short man with a florid complexion, cleared his throat messily and paged through his notes. He popped a pair of bifocals on his rotund face and picked up the story. "So Max and I showed up at the scene, immediately separated the parents, and commenced with interviews. Crime scene techs arrived and worked over the baby's room, her crib, the front door, and hallway."

"Anything missing?" Thacker asked. "Besides the baby?"

"Pink blanket," Dillon said. "Anyway, our guys also grabbed the Dardens' computers and are mining the data down in the geek cave." He paused. "As far as the parents go, Mom is totally beside herself. Dad not so much. Guy seems guarded, but that could just be good old Nordic stoicism."

Like a good partner, Max Montgomery recognized his cue and stepped in with his own assessment. "The babysitter, Ashley Copeland, wasn't a lot of help. She was pretty freaked out and was able to give only a rudimentary description of her assailant."

"You don't think she knew him?" Thacker asked. "That she let him in?"

"Oh, she let him in, all right, but it's doubtful that she knew him. We talked to her in the hospital, but her nose was broken and she was on some kind of IV drip, so we didn't get much out of her. The girl's mom assured us we could talk to her later so she can give a formal statement."

Montgomery, who was silver-haired and handsome in a slightly grizzled sort of way, stood up and kicked back his chair. "But there are a couple of interesting things. One of the Dardens' neighbors was out walking his dog, a big slobbery brown malamute, around eight thirty last night. He said he saw a couple of people kind of bent over and hustling toward a junky-looking car. Said the only reason he remembered the incident at all was because the car had one of those yellow smiley face stickers pasted on the back bumper." Max shrugged, strolled to the back of the room, and dimmed the lights. "And, of course, we got this. Footage from a nanny cam."

"A lucky break," Afton murmured. She knew this could be a real help.

Max flicked on a ceiling-mounted projector that was connected to a laptop computer sitting on the table. He punched a few keys and the projector hummed to life. "Those of us who have been up all night have already seen the baby cam footage. But you all need to see this, too."

"It's not the best quality," Dillon put in. "Dad cheaped out on the equipment."

"Is there sound?" Thacker asked.

"Minimal," Max said.

On the screen, a jumpy black-and-white image of a baby nursery burst into view.

Afton leaned forward and saw that the time code in the right-hand corner read, 20:17:45.569641.

"We moved the video forward to the part just before the kidnapper enters the baby's room," Dillon explained.

The footage was grainy and dim, but Afton could see that the room was large by nursery room standards. The crib was frilly and elaborate and surrounded by stuffed animals. There was also a changing table, rocking chair, and of course, the sleeping baby.

The baby looked to be a few months old. A little girl. She was swaddled in a puffy quilt, her little cherub face looking peaceful and innocent in her slumber. The soft, easy breathing of the baby reminded Afton of the many nights she had stood in her own children's rooms, gazing at them with a mixture of tenderness and awe.

There was the sound of a muffled scream and the child seemed to stir in her sleep.

"Babysitter just got jacked," Dillon said. Then silence returned and the camera continued to roll as the baby slept on.

Two minutes later, a dark shadow fell across the crib. Afton and the others in the room held their breath. Then someone slipped directly in front of the camera. To Afton, it reminded her of a scene from that old movie *Nosferatu*, when the slithery, wispy figure of the vampire casts his shadow, then slowly oozes into the frame.

"Jesus," one of the uniformed officers breathed. "That could be a woman. But it's hard to tell."

"Nobody said that men had a lock on kidnapping," Afton muttered under her breath.

"So a woman? We're looking for a woman?" the officer asked. He sounded shocked and more than a little dismayed.

"We think maybe a woman working with a male partner," Dillon said. "That's what the babysitter seemed to indicate." He consulted his notes again. "And there was a dusting of snow last night, so there was a pair of tracks on the sidewalk. One large set, one a little smaller, just where the dog walker guy said they'd be."

"Are there any other leads?" Afton asked.

"I was just getting to that," Thacker said. "There are a few . . . interesting aspects to this case. It seems that Susan Darden, the baby's mother, attended a doll show yesterday at the Skylark Mall. From what she's given us so far, the only person Mrs. Darden spoke to was a woman by the name of Molly who makes what is termed *reborn* dolls."

There was a cacophony of grunts and mumbles around the table.

"What're those?" asked Andy Farmer, one of the detectives. "Retread dolls."

"Re*born*," Thacker said, making a disparaging face. "They're dolls that have been painted and reworked so they resemble real live babies."

More murmurs ensued. "Sounds like real fruitcake stuff," Max muttered. "Is this doll lady a suspect?" Afton asked.

"We're not ruling anything out at this point," Thacker said. "Especially since Mrs. Darden gave this woman her phone number. The other thing is, reborn dolls are apparently some kind of cult thing. Apparently, hundreds of these dolls are sold over the Internet for big bucks." He pulled a sheaf of papers from a manila folder and passed them around the table. "Here. I had Angel make printouts from some of the more popular websites."

"Plastic dolls," Afton muttered, studying the splash page of a website called Anita's Babykins. "Painted and molded and dressed so they resemble newborns." It was the first she'd ever heard of this kind of thing. An interesting concept, she decided, but with a slight creep factor.

"A lot of these reborn doll makers are very proprietary about their creations," Thacker said. "In fact, they're big on having buyers sign actual adoption papers. So that's another wacky, off-kilter aspect to this case."

"You said a mouthful," Max said.

"Are there security tapes from the mall?" Afton asked.

"We're working on that," Dillon said.

"Obviously, this doll lady is the first angle we have to work," Thacker said. "But there are a few other wrinkles, too. The husband, Richard Darden, recently resigned his post as VP of Marketing at Novamed. Now he's over at Synthotech with a big-shot job in their new products division. But the powers that be at Novamed have accused him of breaking his confidentiality agreement and taking trade secrets, certain proprietary information, out the door with him."

"Has Novamed filed suit against him?" Farmer asked.

Thacker sorted through his hastily gathered file. "Ah . . . yes, they have," he responded.

"You think this kidnapping could be some sort of retaliation?" Afton asked. The idea sounded off the charts to her, but she had to ask.

"I don't know what to think," Thacker said. He reached a hand up and scrubbed distractedly at his mop of curly gray hair. "It doesn't feel like it.

Corporate execs don't usually get their hands dirty by hiring someone to nick a baby out of its bassinette. But . . . we gotta look at them anyway."

"This could be a straight-out kidnapping for ransom," Max said.

"Maybe the Dardens will get a phone call demanding money," Afton said.

"Maybe they already got the phone call," Max said. He moved around the table and took his same seat across from Afton.

"No, no, we've already pulled their phone records," Thacker said. "There's nothing unusual. And we're currently monitoring all their lines. No calls like that have come in."

"Did you put out an APB to area hospitals?" Afton asked.

This time Max answered. "That's the first thing we did. Alerted area clinics, hospitals, and doctors' offices. Advised them to be on the alert for any newborns that are brought in under what might be suspicious circumstances. And we strongly advised them to ask for positive ID from any new parents whose children aren't current patients."

"Has an Amber Alert been sent out?" Afton asked. "Is the FBI involved?"

Max rolled his eyes. "Yes, and we've met with our local federal agents once already."

"I just hope those techno-turds have the decency to stay out of our way," Dillon said.

"Listen up," Thacker said. "Even if you feel their hot doggy breath on the backs of your necks, I don't want to see any territorial shit. Job one is to retrieve that poor little baby and put her back in her crib or jolly jumper or whatever the hell. Okay? Is that understood?"

"Sure," Dillon said, looking unhappy.

Andy Farmer tapped the end of his pencil against the table. "If there's a nanny cam," he asked, "is there also a nanny?"

"There was," Max said. "A woman by the name of Jilly Hudson. She worked for the Dardens for about two months, starting the week before the baby arrived. Now Hudson is currently studying for her master's degree in early childhood development at the University of Minnesota." He pressed his hands together and steepled his fingers. "Hudson says she was staying at her parents' home last night and her story checks out."

"So there you have it," Thacker said. "I want you people to get out there, rip these twin towns apart if you have to, and find that kid."

"Yes, sir," Dillon said.

"What I want from you," Thacker said, turning toward Afton, "is to do what you do best. Function as a liaison between the Dardens and MPD. Work as closely as you can with Max, since he's going to be lead detective." Thacker paused and cocked an eyebrow at her. "Just remember, you're not doing any detecting. You're community liaison officer."

"Right," Afton said. Now she was the one who looked unhappy. The liaison thing hadn't really been her ultimate career choice. She'd much rather be an integral part of Max's team, sniffing around for clues, cowboying after the bad guys. But her masters in social work had made her a natural candidate for her current job, and she was lucky to get that at the time. Now she seemed stuck in limbo. But hope springs eternal and Afton harbored a secret plan. Do a superb job, continue taking classes in law enforcement, wow everyone with her investigating prowess, and sneak in the back door. If there even was such a thing.

"Everybody listen up," Thacker said, pulling himself to his full height and addressing the entire table now. "Any dealings with the Dardens, try to have Afton present. She's been specially trained for this. This is sensitive stuff and—"

"Women are sensitive by nature," Afton finished. Her voice carried a slightly acerbic tone. She was about to say something else, then stopped. Thacker had always been fair with her and she didn't want to piss him off too badly. He had, after all, taken a chance on her. Plucked her from the ranks of data entry clerks and elevated her to the liaison role.

"You got that right," Thacker said, looking annoyed. "So everyone make sure you're *damn* sensitive!"

SUSAN and Richard Darden were hunkered down in Thacker's office. They'd already spent hours with the FBI and the Minneapolis PD; now they were waiting for a visit with Afton before they headed home.

In the locker room, Afton shucked out of her fleece top and grabbed a navy blue blazer from her locker. It was a conservatively cut Talbots blazer that she kept for just such meetings. She struggled into it, and then, feeling a little breathless and unsettled, headed for her meeting.

"How are they doing?" Afton asked Angel Graham as she breezed into the deputy chief's outer office. Angel was Thacker's secretary and had been his right-hand counsel, confessor, and provider of homemade coffee cake for at least a dozen years.

"Not so good," Angel replied. She was seven months pregnant and looking fretful. "I feel so bad for them," she said, nodding at the closed door and absently massaging her stomach through a fuzzy pink sweater. "Guilty even."

"Don't be," Afton told her.

HELLO," Afton said. She tried to keep her voice sympathetic but calm as she eased into Thacker's office to meet Susan and Richard Darden. "I'm Afton Tangler, community liaison officer for the Minneapolis Police Department." They shook hands, Richard looking stoic and somber, Susan leaking tears like crazy.

"This is our attorney, Steven Slocum," Richard said, indicating a tall, hawk-nosed man who hadn't bothered to stand up.

"Nice to meet you," Afton said, shaking hands with Slocum, wishing he wasn't here.

Afton sat on a straight-backed chair directly across from the Dardens and tried to focus every inch of her being on them. "I want to offer you my deepest concern and assure you that the department is doing everything possible to solve this case," she said.

"So is the FBI," Slocum said stiffly. "They already have a team in place at the Dardens' Kenwood home." He snapped open the latch on his briefcase as if to punctuate his sentence. "Have for the last ten hours."

"Obviously they're taking the lead in this," Afton continued. "But the MPD is working with them in complete concert, doing everything necessary to assist. I know our crime scene team is there as well. I want you to know, however, that if there is anything, anything at all, that you need, any question you want answered, any issue that needs to be resolved, I'm here to run interference for you. So please feel free to contact me." Afton handed each of the distraught parents one of her business cards. "Twenty-four/seven, day or night. Don't hesitate to call."

Richard Darden rubbed her business card with his thumb, then put it in his inside jacket pocket and nodded.

"The media," Afton said, "is going to hound you relentlessly. Your first instinct may be to shy away from them but just remember . . . if we use them to our advantage, they can reach millions of viewers and listeners."

"Got it," Richard Darden said. He looked like he was ready to get the hell out of there.

Susan Darden continued to leak tears. "Our baby," she began in a halting voice. "Elizabeth Ann. She . . . she took her own sweet time to arrive."

"You don't have to talk about this," Richard said, but Susan shook her head defiantly.

"Please," she said, "I want to, it's important to me."

Afton leaned forward, gently placed a hand on top of Susan's clasped hands. "Tell me."

"We tried for three years," Susan said. "Endured two miscarriages, had to go through three rounds of IVF. But I finally got pregnant with Elizabeth Ann. She was our own little miracle. When she was born, I never knew such happiness could exist." Her voice cracked and she sobbed quietly, defeatedly, for a few moments. "Please, she's everything to us."

"The FBI and MPD are pulling out all the stops on this," Afton said. "They're good people, smart people. They'll find her, I know they will."

"Bless you," Susan sobbed.

5

AFTON cracked open the door to the conference room and peered in. Max was sitting by himself at the table, looking somber and a little tired "Hey, Max," she said. "Got a second?"

Max glanced up. "Sure." Manila folders and pages of notes were spread out around him. Max was old-school, not always in sync with technology. Case in point: He had a perfectly good HP laptop sitting on his desk, but claimed to prefer actual paper and handwritten notes.

Afton slipped into the chair across from Max. She was feeling edgy after her meeting with the Dardens. She figured that talking to him might help alleviate some of the pent-up anxiety and fear that had spilled over into her psyche.

Max seemed to read her mind. "You talked to the Dardens?" he asked.

Afton nodded. "And their lawyer."

"Yeah," Max breathed. "I heard they brought their lawyer along. Slocum." He said the man's name like he was referring to a steaming heap of manure. "The one who got that crazy football player off on the rape charge."

"I remember that," Afton said. "The so-called Love Boat Incident." She hesitated. "So you've huddled with the FBI?"

"I talked to Keith Sunder and Harvey Bagin from the local field office late last night. And Don Jasper, one of their top guys, a couple of hours ago. Jasper flew in from Chicago. Apparently he has a shit load of experience when it comes to child abductions."

"Sad," Afton said. "That he's garnered so much experience, I mean."

"Yeah," Max agreed. "It's a tough deal."

Afton gazed at Max. She liked him and had worked briefly with him six months ago. When two young Hispanic boys had been shot to death in a gang-related incident, she'd been brought in to help break the news to their mother. That had been a rough one. Martina Alvarez, a single parent working two jobs, had been devastated by her sons' deaths. Afton had stuck close to Mrs. Alvarez for several weeks, helping her notify family back in Juarez, making funeral arrangements, and always lending a sympathetic ear. In the end, she'd even managed to convince Mrs. Alvarez to join an advocacy group consisting of parents of murdered children.

Of course, what Afton had secretly wanted to do was track down the miserable bastard who shot Mrs. Alvarez's boys and put a bullet though his worthless skull.

But no, she had to be content to sit on the sidelines and make nice like a social worker.

"What's your next move?" she asked Max. He had been making jottings when she came into the room. Little scratches on a yellow legal pad.

"The FBI are the big dogs," Max said. "They're going to interview the Dardens some more, follow up on pizza places, run through their database of known and suspected kidnappers, and canvas the Kenwood neighborhood. I've been reviewing my notes from a phone conversation I had with the lady who organized the doll show. Muriel Pink. I'm probably gonna go pay her a visit."

"When?"

Max glanced at his watch. "Now."

"Can I come along?"

Max shrugged. "She lives over in Wisconsin."

"Where in Wisconsin?"

"Hudson."

Hudson was just across the state line. Straight east on the other side of the Saint Croix River. "No problem," Afton said. "It's practically a suburb. I'll even drive if you want."

"In the Jag?" Max asked, suddenly interested.

Everybody in the department seemed to know that Afton had gotten a Jaguar XKE and a Lincoln Navigator as part of her divorce settlement. She lived in a tiny house in South Minneapolis with her two kids and her sister, but she owned two luxury cars. How was that for crazy?

Afton nodded. "Sure," she said amiably. "We can swing by my place and pick up the Jag."

"Okay," Max said. "But maybe don't tell Thacker that I let you come along, okay?"

Afton nodded as she watched Max gather up his stuff. He was a grade one detective, married and divorced twice, who now had sole custody of his two sons. The scuttlebutt around the department was that Max was probably on the lookout for a third ex–Mrs. Montgomery. And Afton could see why women found him charming. Max was in his mid-forties, easygoing, and still attractive in a roguish kind of way. Silver hair, hooded dark eyes, still in pretty good shape. The proverbial silver fox, albeit Minnesota's version.

"Just out of curiosity," Afton said, "have any other babies been reported missing?"

Max's head was bent again. Studying his notes or just resting his eyes?

"Not in recent months," he said.

"But babies have gone missing?"

"Not here in the metro." Max touched the eraser end of a pencil to his forehead and scratched distractedly. "There was one in Rochester last year. Another one over in River Falls ten months ago."

"River Falls is maybe fifteen miles from Hudson," Afton said.

Max shrugged.

"Were the babies ever found?"

Max closed his notebook and focused his attention on Afton. "Rochester yes, River Falls no."

"If that reborn lady also lives in the Hudson area, there could be a connection."

Max cranked back his chair and stared at the ceiling. "Doesn't appear to be. The Rochester baby was a family squabble. Kid was recovered and put into foster care. The River Falls baby never did turn up, so who knows?" He indicated a handful of pages. "That's the faxed report from the River Falls PD and the Wisconsin DCI."

Afton knew the Department of Criminal Investigation was Wisconsin's equivalent to Minnesota's own BCA, or Bureau of Criminal Apprehension, which had statewide jurisdiction.

Max pushed the pages toward her. "Have a look if you're interested, and it sounds like you are."

Afton took a few minutes to skim the reports. Then she tilted back in her chair and asked, "What makes somebody snatch a baby?"

The venerable detective gave her a long look. "Some reproductively challenged fruit loops can't stand the cards they're dealt so they take matters into their own hands. That's one scenario. Then there are the scumbag baby brokers out there who take *orders* for babies, for Christ's sake, right down to hair and eye color." Max paused. "Then there's the worst possible reason of all."

"What's that?" Afton asked, not sure she really wanted to hear what Max had to say.

"Sport."

MAX was hungry so they swung into a Wendy's to grab a late lunch.

"One Baconator," Afton ordered into the speaker. When Max snorted, she added, "Hold the onions." And to him, "Hold the judgment, please."

"You can eat a big-ass burger like that and still stay skinny?" Max asked.

She ignored his comment. "What do you want?"

"Double cheeseburger," Max said. "Man cannot live by bread alone; sometimes he needs a little grease."

"There you go," Afton said.

They nibbled their way along I-94, blotting drips and drops of mayonnaise, talking about the Darden case, Afton asking a million different questions.

Max had to hand it to her. Afton had some interesting theories and insights. Maybe a few too many, but her heart was in the right place. She was persistent and dedicated, traits that generally made for a good investigator. And she was fairly decent company. Especially on an errand that would probably prove to be exactly that, an errand.

"Is this pretty standard?" Afton asked. "That you would cross jurisdictions like this without clearing it? I mean, what's the protocol?"

"I'm part of MPD's newly formed squad. It's called the Mutual Aid and Multi-Jurisdictional Squad. MAMJS. Gives the MPD a little more leverage in investigating outside our boundaries."

"So you've got free rein to chase down bad guys outside of Minneapolis?"

"Something like that."

"Bet the BCA hates that."

"That'd be about right."

They were cruising along at seventy miles an hour, just passing the Highway Patrol weigh station, when Afton asked, "How old are your sons?"

"Fourteen and seventeen," Max said.

"At that age they must be . . . a handful." Afton figured princess parties and My Little Pony were infinitely preferable to filthy sneakers and stinky hockey jerseys.

Max rolled his eyes. "You have no idea."

They drove for another ten minutes, both mulling over their own thoughts. Wondering about the missing Darden baby, formulating questions to ask this doll lady.

"How come you got two luxury cars?" Max asked suddenly. He'd cranked back the passenger seat in the Jag until it was fully reclined, then fiddled with the heater until he'd achieved the absolute perfect temperature. For him.

"It all came down to Mickey having cash flow problems, but owning a large inventory," Afton explained. Mickey had been the kids' stepfather but had never formally adopted Tess and Poppy. Thus, he was off the hook for any child support.

They spun across the Interstate bridge that arced over the Saint Croix, the river looking icy and turgid beneath them.

"I was always going to sell both cars and buy something more practical," Afton said. "Maybe a Ford or Honda . . ."

"But you like driving what you got," said Max, a Cheshire cat grin spreading across his face.

"Yeah," Afton admitted. "I guess you could say that."

MURIEL Pink, the woman who'd organized the doll show, lived on Flint Street, a couple of blocks up the hill from the main drag in Hudson.

Afton and Max turned down a tree-lined boulevard where each two-story house was practically identical to the next. As if they'd been given an allotment, each house had two trees in the front yard and a driveway leading neatly up to a double garage.

Afton pulled to a stop in front of a tall, narrow house and checked the address. Yup, this was it. Another white, two-story house with a slightly American Gothic vibe to it. Still, the sidewalk was shoveled, the slightly tilting bird feeder was stocked with oilseed, and the place looked well maintained.

"You ready to do this?" Max asked as they climbed out of the car.

Afton nodded as they approached the house. The front yard was a mash-up of animal tracks—dogs, squirrels, birds, maybe a raccoon or two. At the base of an evergreen tree a pile of feathers marked the scene of the crime where a neighborhood cat or marauding raccoon had murdered a bird.

Afton and Max knocked on the door and were greeted by Mrs. Muriel Pink herself. She was a small, frail-looking woman with a tiny waist and pouf of white hair. Probably in her late seventies, she wore a belted housedress and a pair of white slip-on sneakers.

"Are you the FBI?" Pink asked them in a high, thin, agitated voice.

"No, ma'am," Max said. "We're from the Minneapolis Police Department. I'm Max Montgomery and this is Afton Tangler. You and I spoke on the phone about an hour ago?"

Pink barely glanced at Max's ID as she ushered them into a tidy little house that felt like it was heated to around ninety degrees. Afton thought it was like walking into a thermal underground cavern.

"Would you like something to drink?" Pink asked. "Coffee? Tea?"

"Ice water would be great," Max said. His forehead was already beading up with sweat.

"Second that," Afton said.

Pink puttered about her neat little fifties-era kitchen, where dolls were displayed everywhere. On top of cabinets, on doll stands, posed on the counter, sprawled on the radiator. Afton wondered why the radiator dolls hadn't melted into a sticky, rubbery mess.

"You have an impressive collection of dolls," Afton said, peeling off her jacket. If it was one degree hotter in here, she was going to have to rip off her sweater and strip down to her camisole.

Muriel Pink set their glasses of water on the table in front of them. "Oh my," she said, laughing. "This is nothing. You should see my piano room and bedroom. Dolls everywhere."

"I can just imagine," Max said. Afton kicked him under the table.

"So," Pink said, finally easing herself into a kitchen chair. "You wanted to talk about that kidnapping?" She gave a little shiver. "Although I don't see how something like that could be tied to yesterday's doll show."

"Mrs. Pink," Max began. "As I mentioned on the phone, a three-month-old baby was kidnapped from her home last night. Interestingly enough, one of the last people the baby's mother spoke to was a woman by the name of Molly who had a booth at your show."

Sadness reflected in Muriel Pink's eyes. "Such a terrible, sad thing."

"Which is why we're following up on every possible lead," Max said. He pulled out a hanky and mopped his face. "You mentioned to me on the phone that you had an exhibitor list?"

Pink's brows knit together. "It's more of a partial list," she told them. "We had a couple of walk-in exhibitors."

Afton and Max exchanged glances. "Does that happen often?" Afton asked.

"More often than you'd think," Pink said.

"Do you have their names?" Max asked.

"Better than that, I've got their checks," Pink said. "I haven't deposited them yet."

"Do you remember a woman by the name of Molly?" Afton asked. "She was displaying some reborn dolls?"

"Molly," Pink repeated. She stood up, shuffled over to a highboy stuffed with dolls, and picked up a black notebook. "Let me take a look." She thumbed through a few pages and glanced up. "I'm sorry, I don't have anyone on my exhibitor list by the name of Molly."

Max looked startled. He reached a hand out. "May I see that?"

"Certainly," Pink said, handing the notebook over to him.

Max pursed his lips as he searched Pink's list. "Just to make sure," he said, "this is the list of exhibitors for yesterday's doll show at the Skylark Mall."

"Yes." Pink nodded.

"But Molly isn't listed here." Max directed his statement to Afton.

"Is one of your checks from someone named Molly?" Afton asked.

They went through all of Mrs. Pink's checks, one by one, but couldn't find one that had been written by anyone named Molly.

"She could have used a fake name," Max said.

"This might sound like a strange question," Afton said. "But could an exhibitor have just walked in and sort of set up shop?"

Pink looked startled. "I never thought about that. It's very unlikely."

"But it could have happened?" Max asked.

"I suppose so," Pink said. "I never . . ." Her voice trailed off.

"Were you present the entire day?" Afton asked.

"No," Pink said slowly. "I was there at setup, collecting money, and showing exhibitors where to place their tables. And then I had a dentist appointment and did some shopping. I was back there at seven o'clock to pay the mall people. They charge a fee, you know. I have to give them a percentage."

"Yes, I'm sure you do," Max said. He hesitated. "These shows are big business. I mean, you arrange a lot of them?"

Pink smiled. "Almost every other month. Sometimes more in summer, when people are more apt to travel."

"And you don't have a computerized list of your exhibitors?" Afton asked.

Pink shook her head. "No computers, just my notebooks."

"Is it possible to make copies of some of your pages?" Max asked. "I mean, we'd go to the nearest Kinko's or whatever and bring your notebooks right back."

"Surely," Pink said. "If you think that would help."

"It might," Afton said. "You never know."

"This woman, Molly," Muriel Pink said, looking more than a little nervous. "You think she's a suspect?"

Max pursed his lips. "Let's just say she's a person of interest."

6

THE farmhouse was quarantined on twenty acres of ninety-year-old cottonwoods perched on the edge of a cliff. And like the trees that feebly sheltered it, the house was nearing the end of its life. Once upon a time, long before the First World War, the enormous two-story house with its carved finials and finely turned balustrade had been built as a showcase to boom times. Wisconsin settlers, newlyweds, flush from a pre-income tax inheritance, had lived there and raised a large family.

In the nineteen thirties, Alvin Karpis and his bank robber gang, anxious to escape harassment from both the Chicago and the Saint Paul Police Departments, had leased the place and found it perfect. It was centrally located, but still off the beaten track, perfect for a little gangster R and R.

Dull and homely now, thanks to wind, rain, snow, termites, and old age, most of the home's exterior had been worn down to bare, gray wood. And not the silvered elegance of old barn wood, but the dowdy, gritty look of zinc.

The fields surrounding the house had been fallow for nearly twenty years, choked with an overgrowth of buckthorn and thistles. The skeletal remains of a large grain bin stood as the only testimony to this having once been a working farm.

Still, on this dark and frosty January night, people called it home.

Inside a large farm kitchen with outdated Kelvinator appliances, two women and a man sat at a battered wooden table under a heavy wrought iron light fixture. They sipped coffee, poked at pieces of meat that rested, gray and well done, on an oval platter, and ate Oreo cookies directly from the bag. Perched atop the refrigerator, overlooking this scene of tragic domesticity, was an enormous stuffed woodchuck, all flashing teeth and claws.

While Marjorie Sorenson crafted reborn dolls, Ronnie worked at his beloved taxidermy projects. And he was good at it, almost as skilled as Marjorie at breathing a startling reality into inanimate objects.

Ronnie's girlfriend, Sharice Williams, known as Shake to all her friends and anyone who'd ever stuffed a dollar bill down her G-string, sat at the table with them. She was eyeing the two of them carefully, trying to read the temperature in the room.

Finally, after a few minutes of noisy chewing, Ronnie said, to no one in particular, "Shake and me was gonna go hang out at Judge's."

Flat, cobra eyes suddenly drilled into him. "This girl's not going any-where," Marjorie told her son. "Especially not to some dimey bar like Judge's. In case you hadn't noticed, she's due to have a baby any day now."

"I'm bored," Shake whined. "There's nothin' to do here."

Shake was Ronnie's latest girlfriend. He didn't bed many women, but those he did seemed to share some common traits—they tended to be dirt poor, estranged from their families, and pretty enough, but in a worn-out, used-up way. Shake had been forced to give up pole dancing some five months ago when Buddy Yaruso, the manager at Club Paradise out on County Road A-2, had touched a hand to her distended belly, stuck a twenty-dollar bill in her panties, and fired her on the spot. He'd told her that a pregnant exotic dancer wasn't good for business. It just reminded his club patrons of what they were trying to forget about at home.

Shake had cried a river of tears, thinking how unfair it all was. Still, she wasn't about to score a job as Kim Kardashian's personal stylist, and that chief financial officer job at Coca-Cola just wasn't on the horizon. So hang-ing out with Ronnie and his old lady for a while seemed to be all right. Not good, just all right.

"Waaaaaah!" came a loud, demanding wail from down the hall.

"I wish that thing would shut up," Shake said. She looked at Marjorie, who pointedly ignored her as she lit another Kool cigarette. She turned her gaze toward Ronnie. "Where'd that kid come from anyway?"

"I told ya," Marjorie said. "She's my cousin's kid. Picked her up when we was in The Cities yesterday." She flicked a piece of hardened food gunk off her sweatshirt. "Gonna watch her for a while."

"Yeah?" Shake said. Suspicious eyes flitted across the table. "You got cousins in The Cities?" she asked Ronnie.

Ronnie pushed limp green beans across his plate and into his watery gravy. "Sure." He hadn't been much interested in Shake lately, now that she was all fat and swollen and crabby. Right now his brain was occupied with someone else. All day long he'd been replaying his encounter with the skinny blond babysitter. That bitch had been . . . unbelievably hot. He shifted in his chair, practically overwhelmed by feelings of lust and need.

Marjorie focused on Shake. "It wouldn't hurt you none to practice with that baby," she said. She was busy sawing at a piece of overdone strip steak with a dull steak knife. The broiler in the damn stove was on the blink again and she'd had to pan fry the meat. Now it tasted more like liver than steak.

"Practice?" came Shake's derisive hoot. "What for?" One of her hands was drawn unconsciously to her swollen belly. "I'm gonna give this baby up for adoption anyhow." She massaged the mass under her stretched-out Pantera T-shirt. "So what's the harm if we go over to Judge's and have a couple of drinks?" Shake was particularly fond of Crapple Bombs, a lethal concoction of Red Bull, Crown Royal, and Apple Pucker. "Who's gonna be the wiser?"

"Don't get smart with me, girlie," Marjorie snapped. "You're a guest in my house. Your old man disowned you and threw you out on your scrawny ass, remember?"

Shake gave a mirthless laugh. "Only because your precious son knocked me up." They'd played this blame game before. Always going round and round in an endless loop, never coming to any sort of resolution.

"If it's even mine," Ronnie said.

Hurt showed in Shake's eyes. "It is. You *know* it is."

"What the hell did you think was gonna happen?" Marjorie asked. "Prancing around onstage with shiny sequins pasted over your titties, wearing hooker heels, and bending over to show your cooch?" She snorted. "Exotic dancer. Hah."

Shake had been a crowd favorite at Club Paradise. Unhappy men from all over the North Country had come, flashlights in hand, to sit at the bar and shine their wavering beam at Shake's moneymaker.

"Go see if the baby's wet," Marjorie ordered Shake. The kid had been in their house for less than twenty-four hours and already things were in an uproar.

"Babies are always wet," Shake said, toying with what was left of her unappetizing dinner. "Besides, I gotta get changed if we're going out." She threw a hopeful glance at Ronnie. Unfortunately, he could be a real limp dick when it came to standing up to his mother. In fact, if she'd known how much of a momma's boy he really was, she never would have moved in here in the first place. Shake regretted that she hadn't just run away. Taken a bus to Chicago and figured *something* out. Now it was too late. Now she was due any day, fat and waddling, unattractive, a prisoner of her unborn child.

"*Waaaaaah!*" A shrill cry echoed from down the hallway again. The kid was persistent.

"Baby's still crying," Marjorie said. Her thin, penciled brows rose in a mild challenge as she worked on staring down Shake.

Ronnie's hands smacked down flat and hard on the table, jouncing the dishes and silverware, upending his cup of coffee. "Damn it," he snarled. "I'll go."

He stormed out of the kitchen and down the hallway, into the living room, where the baby was lying in an old plastic bassinette. He placed a hand on the side of the bassinette and shook it, jostling the baby and causing it to cry that much harder.

"Shut up," Ronnie whispered.

The upturned pink face was turning almost purple now as the baby wailed away, her shrieks piercing the air.

Ronnie stared at it impassively. His mind was beginning to drift, blocking out the squalling noise. He wondered idly what the baby would look like stuffed?

Probably, he decided . . . just like one of Mom's stupid dolls.

FIVE minutes later, Ronnie was out the door and on his way. Shake had pleaded with him to take her along. His mother had yammered after him like some goddamned little ankle biter dog. But Ronnie was on a mission.

When he pulled his car up in front of Judge's, he was happy to see there were still a couple of newspapers left in the green metal box that sat out front. He dropped in four quarters, grabbed a paper, and went inside, his guts prickling in anticipation.

Ronnie shoved two dollars across the bar and ordered a Leinenkugel draft beer. Then, as all around him music thumped and beer bottles rattled, he pulled out the news section of the Sunday paper. He was starting to feel a little anxious now, hoping he'd be able to find what he was looking for.

The story was right there on page one, just below the fold. The headline said, INFANT KIDNAPPED FROM KENWOOD HOME. He read the story slowly, his lips moving along as he read. When he got to the fourth paragraph, he smiled to himself. Ashley. The hot little babysitter chick's name was Ashley. And the story said that she'd been taken to a hospital, some place called HCMC.

Setting down the paper, Ronnie took a long sip of beer. He liked that her name was Ashley. It sounded classy and reminded him of a character on one of those teen reality shows. He dug his hand into a bowl of popcorn that sat on the bar. Popped a handful into his mouth, chewed, and hawked the hulls out onto the floor. Hadn't he and Ashley shared a moment together last night? Hadn't she stared into his eyes and given him a glimmer of encouragement? Sure, she had. Like most girls, she'd wanted it pretty bad. *Needed* it. He could tell.

Ronnie took another sip of beer and the liquid slid down his throat, cool and malty. "Ashley," he murmured. "Ashley baby."

7

I'M sorry you had to cut your climbing trip short," Lish said. Not ten seconds earlier, Afton had pushed open the back door of her home and tromped into the kitchen. Lish, Alisha Larkin, was stirring a pot of bubbling spaghetti sauce, steaming up their little kitchen in a nice, homey way. Afton had called her sister earlier in the day and told her about the change in plans. Told her she was back in town and would probably be home for supper.

"Mommy, Mommy!" Two eager voices blended into one as Poppy and Tess, Afton's two daughters, came careening around a corner to greet her. Poppy was six and serious, dressed in an oversized SpongeBob sweatshirt. Tess was ten going on fifteen, already into lip gloss and celebrity gossip, lobbying for her very own cell phone.

"I'm glad you came home, Mommy," Poppy said. She pattered across the kitchen floor and favored Afton with an enormous bear hug. "Even if it was because of that kidnapping."

Afton's and Lish's eyes met and Lish gave a little shrug that said, *Who knows?*

"How did you hear about the kidnapping, honey?" Afton asked. She made no secret of the fact that she was employed by the Minneapolis Police Department, but had always tried to spare the girls from any grisly details of the cases she worked. It was better, she'd decided, to focus on the positive role she played.

"It was on the five o'clock news," Poppy told her. "The lady was crying. A lot," she added with emphasis.

"Is the baby dead?" Tess asked. She sounded blasé but looked a little scared.

"No, of course not," Afton said. "The police and the FBI are working very hard to find her and bring her home."

"That's good," Tess said. She edged over to the counter, where Lish was busy grating a hunk of Parmesan cheese, and smiled at her impishly through masses of tangled blond hair. "Want me to set the table?"

"More than anything," Lish said.

"Mommy," Poppy said as Tess stood on tiptoe to gather plates and glasses from the cupboard. "How come you changed your name? How come you have a different name than Daddy?" It was sweet that she still referred to Mickey as her daddy, even though they'd only been together as a family for little more than a year.

"It's all about identity, honey," Afton said. "When you're a little older, you'll understand."

But Poppy wasn't about to drop the subject. "What if *I* want to change my name someday?"

"Honey," Afton said, bending down. "*Do* you want to change your name?"

A grin split Poppy's mischievous face. "I want to be Rapunzel!" she declared.

"Poppy Rapunzel," Afton said, gathering her daughter up in her arms. "It has a nice ring to it. Presidential even."

BY eight o'clock the kids' eyes were growing heavy as they sprawled on the sectional sofa eating popcorn and watching a DVD of *Finding Nemo*. Lish was upstairs, trying out Clairol's Ravenous Red hair color and singing along to an old Van Halen album. Afton was planted firmly in front of her computer.

She'd been curious about what Thacker had told them about Richard Darden, the missing baby's father. Wanted to see if there was anything in the business section of the newspaper that might shed some light on the lawsuit against him. She didn't think it possible that a reputable company would get so outraged about pilfered business secrets and that they'd retaliate by kidnapping a man's child. Then again, you never knew. In more than a few countries, kidnapping was commonplace.

Afton found two archived articles on the *Tribune* website. One was a short sidebar detailing Richard's move to Synthotech. The second was a lengthier article in which the *Tribune* business reporter, B. L. Aiken, interviewed Bruce Cutler, the CEO of Novamed, Richard Darden's former company, as well as Richard Darden himself, and Gordon Conseco, the CEO of Synthotech, Richard's new place of employment.

Cutler had only harsh words about Richard's defection; Conseco had only praise for his new employee.

But Conseco can't be that happy, Afton decided, *especially if Richard Darden was bringing questions of impropriety down on their heads.*

Afton found a few more articles, but they were just routine business press releases. A new product, yadda, yadda, yadda.

Bored now, she clicked over to her Facebook page and scanned a few posts from her friends. Ah, there were her neighbors, Deana and Bud, looking happy and sunburned on Waikiki Beach. It was difficult sometimes, to look at pictures of perfect couples. Even though it was a relief to be divorced, she sometimes felt like a screwup. Her first husband, the kids' father, had been a disaster. Then she'd met Mickey and struggled to make that marriage work. But it had quickly become obvious they weren't destined to be together. When collection agencies started calling, when the zone manager from GMAC came knocking on her door, she knew it was over. Slammed shut. There wasn't anything that Dr. Phil or Dear Abby could have done. Like Humpty Dumpty, their marriage had slipped off the wall, cracked wide open, and couldn't be put back together again.

Afton lifted her fingers from the keyboard, ready to shut it off. Then, on a whim, she Googled the word *reborn*. And watched in amazement as hit after hit spun out.

Curious now, feeling a tingle of apprehension, she perused the website for Marcy May's Reborns. Then Sarah Jane's Beautiful Babies. And then

Kimberly's Kuddle Kids. All these sites featured the extremely realistic-looking reborns that seemed to be growing in popularity with a cultlike following of doll lovers. All the dolls pictured either looked like newborns, or were a few months older. None went up to the age of a toddler.

Clicking on one of the reborn message boards, Afton read through a glut of messages. And found some of them strangely disturbing.

> LauraGrace@wynwood.com
> I just bought a beautiful reborn but have been unable to bond with her. Would love to trade for baby boy Berenguer.

> VeraM@lol.com
> Have an OOAK made by Emily K. Human hair, side-sleeping pose, simply breathtaking! Will e-mail photos.

> StephanieT.@fracas.com
> Greetings all. I have 3 foreign fashion dolls for sale, but would seriously consider trading for reborn—preemie preferred.

The phone rang just as Afton was printing out a list of sites that were advertising reborns. She snatched the receiver up, fully expecting it to be Mickey, the ex, wanting to chat with the girls. Mickey was a real champ at waiting until it was too late in the evening to have more than a superficial, hey-kidlins-how-ya-doin' type of conversation.

But it wasn't Mickey at all. It was Max Montgomery.

"I hate to interrupt," he said, sounding slightly out of breath, "but we just got a flash from Saint Paul Metro."

"What?" Afton asked, her antennae suddenly up and buzzing like crazy.

"A couple of guys were jogging along West River Road, down by Hidden Falls," Max said. "And they thought they heard a baby crying."

"Dear Lord," Afton said. "I'm on my way."

8

THE room was too quiet. It should have been filled with cries, coos, and little wet gurgles from the most beautiful baby ever conceived. Now it felt hollow and empty. As if a death had taken place.

Susan Darden scrunched her knees up closer to her chest. She was sitting on the floor, crouched deep in the corner of her daughter's nursery, wishing she could pull herself together so tightly that she'd just pop out of existence. Because the harsh reality of Elizabeth Ann being gone was simply too painful to bear. She wanted to die.

And Susan felt cold, cold as ice. She'd draped a white wool baby afghan over her knees to ward off some of the chill, but she still shivered almost uncontrollably, the tips of her fingers turning white. She knew that deep down inside herself, in the barely rational part of her being that was only just hanging on, her chill had nothing to do with room temperature. She was cold on the inside, deep within her heart.

As Susan let loose a low keening sound that she was only vaguely aware of, she realized that she'd somehow managed to acquire everything she'd ever wanted—a house, money, designer clothes, a nice car. And yet she had nothing. She *was* nothing without Elizabeth Ann.

Gazing dully at her fingers, at what had been a seventy-five-dollar gel manicure, she saw that her nails and cuticles were chewed and ragged.

Had she done that? She must have. She barely remembered.

No matter. She reached down and touched the fringe of the afghan, and began to shred it, methodically tugging and unraveling each thread. She worked patiently, thoughtfully, trying hard to make her mind go completely blank. To stop the pain. Except for a small pile of shredded fuzz that was building up beside her, the room was immaculate. She'd insisted on it. The room had to be absolutely perfect for when Elizabeth Ann came home.

Because she would return home. Susan had prayed for it. Whispering desperate prayers, her own self-composed mantras, over and over again.

"Susan?" Richard called out. His voice was muffled. He was down the hall, looking for her in their bedroom.

Susan's fingers stopped working, but she didn't answer him. She wouldn't answer him.

Sitting on the floor, gently pressed against her left hip, was her phone. It was her lifeline to the police. And she was expecting a call anytime now. Maybe any minute. She would answer calmly, and the police, with joy barely masked in their voices, would tell her that Elizabeth Ann was safe. That she'd been found.

Then Susan would drive to the police station and, once her baby was put back in her arms, would never let her out of her sight again. She would fulfill her destiny of being the perfect, nurturing, loving mother. There would be Mommy and Me classes, Montessori school, Disney movies, and princess birthday parties with real live purple ponies. She had it all planned out. There was no way this was not going to happen.

"Susan, where are you?" Richard called again. He sounded shaken and angry, and had been storming around the house, doling out threats she knew he couldn't make good on.

A fresh wave of despair swept over Susan like a swift, incoming tide. She was vaguely aware of more tears and her own mutterings.

"Sweetheart?" Richard stepped into the nursery and saw her huddled in the corner. "Sweetheart, what are you doing down there? Who are you talking to?"

Susan buried her face in her hands. She didn't want to talk to Richard right now. She only wanted to think about the bright future. Music lessons and family vacations and little pink dresses with ruffles.

Just the other night she had read a book to Elizabeth Ann—*Oh, the Places You'll Go!* by Dr. Seuss.

Of course, she had no idea of the places Elizabeth Ann would go. Or where she was right now. She choked hard, tasting pain and bitterness, feeling that her heart was about to shatter.

And then the phone rang . . .

9

WEST River Road was a winding, tree-lined boulevard that snaked along the Saint Paul side of the Mississippi River. The University of Minnesota stood at its northernmost point, the Ford Bridge and Lock and Dam No. 1 at its southern tip. Strung out like elegant pieces in a Monopoly game were large mansions, a slew of contemporary-looking homes, and one exclusive high-rise condo.

A perennial favorite of bikers, hikers, and dog walkers, River Road and its accompanying pathway veered precipitously close to the edge of the four-hundred-foot-tall sandstone bluffs that hunkered above the turgid, half-frozen Mississippi River.

Hidden Falls, usually a trickle of spring water that oozed from a cut in a limestone deposit, was located in a steep gorge that sliced directly down to the river. It was frozen now, iced over completely. Across from the falls, on mocha-colored bluffs crusted with snow, stood historic Fort Snelling.

When Afton arrived on the scene, an ambulance, a half dozen police cruisers with light bars flashing, and a Newswatch 7 truck were already convened. A cluster of bright vapor lights, running off a sputtering generator, lit the chill night. Exhaust fumes from the multitude of vehicles created a noxious cloud that hovered above the frozen ground and wafted through the crowd of onlookers, creating a near-psychedelic atmosphere of strobes and haze.

High above, a jetliner arced its way toward the airport just off to the southeast. The deafening engine noise overwhelmed the shouted orders from law enforcement superiors as the Tactical Rescue Squad busied themselves with more ropes and cables in case they had to lower a second team over the steep cliff.

Afton's feet crunched across the snow. Giant yellow snowplows had chopped and spit the most recent snowfall into hard little chips, then the bitter wind had swept it onto the boulevard and turned it into hardpack. Weeks of exhaust fumes spewed from passing cars had painted it a dirty gray. Now it was snirt, Minnesota's dreary combination of snow and dirt.

So cold, Afton thought as she pushed her way through the crowd of police officers, FBI agents, Fire and Rescue people, and neighborhood folks who'd donned their North Face parkas to come out and watch the spectacle. They whispered and wondered among themselves. If it was the Darden baby, how long had it been down there? And what shape was the poor thing in? Faces were grim and stretched tight, knowing the baby might have suffered terrible frostbite after only a few minutes of exposure.

Afton spotted Max, bundled up in a dark green parka, standing right at the edge of the steep, wooded cliff. She jogged down to meet him.

"The Tactical Squad is already down there," Max said. They both leaned forward and gazed down into the deep chasm, though it was so dark, there was nothing to see.

"Any word yet on whether it might be the Darden baby?" Afton asked. She stared at the array of ropes that led over the lip of a rocky cliff, wishing she had police clearance to rappel down and help in any way she could. She figured she was just as experienced with ice climbing as any of the team. And she was a certified Outward Bound instructor to boot.

"No word yet," Max said. "We're still waiting." He dug the toe of his boot in the snow. "Problem is . . . it's so damn cold."

Afton knew it was an oblique reference to the baby's chance of survival, which wasn't good. "I wish I could . . ." Afton was itching to scramble down there, but she knew Thacker would burst a blood vessel if he found out she'd clipped in and rappelled down the hill.

She also prayed that whoever had stolen Elizabeth Ann had simply thrown up their hands, scared off by the tremendous hue and cry set up by the FBI, police, Amber Alert, and frenzied media. Often, that's how child abduction cases were resolved. The abductor was just too terrified by the tsunami of angry police and citizens chasing after his sorry ass or on the lookout for his car. Once word was broadcast, abductors often hit the panic button and abandoned the captive child.

"Any word yet?" a smooth, female voice asked. Portia Bourgoyne, a features reporter for Channel 7, had edged her way into the fray. She was a cool-looking blonde with slightly almond eyes and a pale complexion. Despite the freezing temperature, she wore a very haute couture fringed tweed suit with a pussycat bow tied at the neck, and an impossibly short skirt that showed off her long legs. Afton wondered how Portia had managed to maneuver the slick slope in four-inch-high stilettos.

"They're coming up!" yelled one of the Fire and Rescue Squad members who was manning the ropes on top. An excited buzz rose up as everyone shuffled closer to the dangerous precipice.

A bright light suddenly flashed on, illuminating the entire area, and Afton realized it was Portia's gaffer, holding up a column of lights while her cameraman crouched in position and adjusted the focus on his lens.

Then a grim-looking man in a black neoprene suit clambered up over the edge, and a firefighter, who'd also been manning the ropes, said, "Damn."

Dear Lord, please don't let this child be dead, Afton prayed.

There was a cry and a high squeal and then, as the second climber scrambled up, someone from the rescue squad said in a disappointed voice, "It's a dog."

There was a cacophony of groans and the crowd took a collective step backward.

"A dog?" Max snorted. "I crawled out of a warm Barcalounger for a damn dog?" He wasn't angry at the dog; he was frustrated with the situation.

The second climber from the Tactical Squad who'd rappelled down into the gorge was up on top now, the head of a small dark dog peering out from between the folds of his jacket. Disappointment was palpable on the man's face.

Portia Bourgoyne dropped the carefully arranged look of concern on her face and ran a painted red index finger across the front of her throat, indicating for her cameraman to cut. "Nothing here," she said, sounding infinitely bored. "Just a stupid dog." Then Portia was hurrying up the slope to the street, where her nice warm TV van was parked.

"Abandoned," said an ambulance driver who was standing at Afton's elbow. "People do that all the time. Just toss out animals to freeze to death when they don't want them."

Afton moved through the crowd, toward the two rescuers. "What are you going to do with him?" she asked the man who still held the big-eared puppy in his arms. The dog uttered another squeak then squirmed around as if trying to figure out what all the fuss was about. For a little dog that had been tossed down a rocky hillside, he was certainly giving lots of attitude.

The rescuer shrugged. "I don't know. Probably drop him off at the nearest animal shelter."

"Here," Afton said, reaching her arms out. "Give him to me."

Max's big shoulder nudged hers as she gently accepted the dog. "You want to take the dog? I thought you once told me your husband was allergic to dogs."

"He is," Afton said as one of the paramedics slipped her a blanket. "But we're divorced now, remember?"

"Still gonna cut down on the number of visits to the kiddies," Max said, staring at the dog. "Jeez, look at the ears on that thing. Like a freakin' bat. What kind of mutt is that anyway?"

"Not a mutt at all," Afton said. "This happens to be a French bulldog." She'd seen one at a dog show once and been impressed by the big personality that was packed into such a small-statured animal.

"Ah," Max said. "Then you're probably going to name him Marcel or Jacques."

"Something like that," Afton said, thinking a small dog with this much attitude should rightly be called Bonaparte. "Anyway, the girls will love him. They've been asking for a dog." Cuddling the little dog close to her chest, Afton was suddenly aware of a commotion at the top of the hill. She and Max turned at the same time to glance up there and see just what the hell was going on.

"Shit," Max grunted. "It's the parents. They showed up."

"Oh no!" Afton gasped as Susan Darden's face suddenly appeared, a pale oval, looking scared and strained amid the too-bright lights.

"Is it my baby?" Susan pleaded. Her voice was high and tremulous. "Dear God, will someone please tell me what's going on?"

"They found Elizabeth Ann?" a frantic Richard Darden asked. They were standing on the sidewalk at the top of the hill, clinging desperately to each other.

"Somebody's got to set those poor people straight," Afton said.

"I'll do it," Max said. "You've got your hands full with the dog."

Max nodded and hastily scrambled up the slope, desperate to head them off. But Portia Bourgoyne, who was already up top with her camera crew, knew a heart-wrenching sound bite when she saw one and immediately sprang into action. Bright TV lights flashed on again as Portia stuck her microphone in the Dardens' startled faces before they knew what was happening.

"My baby, my baby!" Susan shrilled. "Is she here?" She was in the throes of a full-blown panic attack.

"We're standing on a rocky precipice overlooking the Mississippi River in Saint Paul," Portia Bourgoyne began. "Waiting to see if the plaintive cries coming from below this steep embankment could possibly belong to Elizabeth Ann, the three-month-old baby girl who was snatched from the Kenwood home of Susan and Richard Darden as she slept in her crib last night."

"Oh shit," Afton said as disgust rose up inside her. "Portia's running a con on the Dardens," she said to one of the paramedics. "She knows damn well that we hauled up a dog."

Max was already up top now, trying to break up Portia's phony, highly staged interview. Afton heard a babble of angry, high-pitched voices, heard Portia scream something about first amendment rights. Then the gaffer, the kid who was wearing a battery pack around his waist and muscling a rack of heavy TV lights, was shoved out of the way and the lights flickered off.

"It's not her," Max tried to explain to them in a soothing voice. "It's a mistake, there's no need for you to be here. Please, go home. We'll call you as soon as we know something."

Susan Darden's face collapsed. "This is all your fault!" she screamed at her husband. "It was your idea to drive over here!"

Richard Darden looked stunned. "I thought for sure it was Elizabeth Ann," he said. "I wanted to be here, to be able to put her back in your arms where she belongs!"

"Please," Max said, trying to interject himself in their conversation. "Everybody just calm down."

But Susan Darden continued to rail against her husband. "You told me it was her! You *promised* me."

"This is bad," Afton muttered. "We need to have these people working with us, not against each other." She scurried up the hillside as fast as she could, still carrying the dog wrapped in a blanket.

"Oh my God!" Susan Darden cried when she caught sight of Afton. "Is that her? Did you find her? Is that my Elizabeth Ann?" Hope flooded Susan's face as she rushed up to Afton and clawed frantically at the blankets before Afton was able to stop her. Then the little dog's head popped out and he gave a sharp yip.

Susan Darden reacted as if she'd been slugged. Her jaw went slack, her eyes flooded with pain, and she staggered backward. Flailing and stumbling, she nearly fell down. But when Max shot out a hand to steady her, she frantically batted him away.

"A dog?" Susan cried. "A filthy mutt?" Her face had become a mask of horror and rage. "How cruel can you be? Is this some kind of sick joke, taunting me like this?"

Afton knew the situation had suddenly turned bad. She'd had no intention of upsetting Mrs. Darden. She couldn't believe someone would have even told the Dardens to come here. But now it had turned into an absolute fiasco, and there didn't seem to be any way to back out delicately. Unless she . . .

Richard Darden suddenly stepped in front of his wife to accost a stunned Afton. He thrust his arms out, punched her hard on both shoulders, and shoved her backward.

"Get away from us," Darden said, his voice a mixture of cold rage and despair. "Do you see how much you've upset my wife?" He licked his lips and then came at her again. "This will be the end of your career. I'll see to that. No matter how long it takes, I'll make sure you pay for this ridiculous stunt."

Susan Darden darted in to land a final punch. "We don't need your kind of help," she cried. "In fact, we don't ever want to *see* you again!"

10

SOMETIMES the night is never long enough. Morning comes crashing in like an unwelcome guest that shows up at a party two hours early—and doesn't even bring a decent bottle of wine.

When the alarm did its 7:00 A.M. *briiiing*, Afton fought her way to consciousness. And as the fog lifted, tried to remember why she was feeling so tense and worried.

Then she remembered. The Dardens. The dog. Definitely not her finest hour. Would there be repercussions? Oh yeah, probably.

Stumbling out of bed, she slowly made her way to the kids' room. Tess was curled up in Poppy's bed, their identical blond hair tousled together on a single pillow. The little French bulldog, Bonaparte, lay snoozing at the foot of the bed in a pile of old blankets the girls had arranged as a cozy dog nest.

Sleepy moans and groans ensued as the girls stumbled down the hall—Bonaparte padding after them—so they could brush their teeth and get dressed for school.

After helpings of Cap'n Crunch and a quick dash into the backyard for Bonaparte, each girl solemnly kissed the dog on the nose and bade him good-bye. Then, in a flurry of red-and-yellow nylon parkas, they dashed outside to meet the yellow school bus that came lumbering down the street.

After a bowl of kibble and a slurp of water, Bonaparte looked expectantly up at Afton as she shrugged into her coat and gathered up her keys.

"I'm not kissing you good-bye, too," she told him. Then, "Oh, okay. If you insist."

The dog had been the only good thing to come out of last night.

DESPITE having her Lincoln stashed inside the relative comfort of her garage, the car's engine struggled to turn over in the bitter cold. And once she navigated the ruts down her back alley and swung out onto the street, she became intimately familiar with the sensation of the car's back wheels sliding ominously on ice.

Nasty day, Afton thought. She shivered as the heater spewed out chill air. With ice-glazed streets and a windchill that was off the charts, she passed three stalled cars on her way downtown, their bundled-up owners looking anxious as they waited for AAA to show up with an industrial-strength battery charger.

The parking garage attached to the precinct building was nearly full, so Afton was forced to park on the exposed top floor of the ramp. Frigid wind whipped her hair and scarf into streamers as she hurried to the building entrance. The elevator down to the third floor was a morass of wet slush.

Once inside, Afton was immersed in a frenzy of activity. Phones jingled, voices rose amid a din of noise, and people rushed about importantly. Hoping to avoid a walk of shame, praying she could remain relatively anonymous until last night's mess blew over, Afton kept her head down as she hurried to her desk. She turned the corner, slipped off her coat, and sat down.

The Force was not with her today.

There on her desk sat a stuffed Beanie Baby, a floppy-eared brown-and-white bulldog. A sign taped to her computer screen said, ROOM FOR ONE MORE?

Great.

As if someone had given a silent cue, loud, yappy barking suddenly broke out all around her. *"Arf, arf, arf."* Then the jerk three cubicles down from her broke into an off-key rendition of "Who Let the Dogs Out."

Afton felt her stomach start to sink. She'd worked hard to try to fit in here and this was the crap she got? Jeez. She hadn't screwed up on purpose. And they couldn't just leave the dog out there to freeze to death.

She heard a noise behind her and spun around. It was Max, looking tired and worn-out as he clicked his tongue and said in a mild tone, "Don't look so worried. It's just a little friendly departmental hazing."

"Really?" Afton said.

Max shrugged. "It means you're part of the gang."

She loved him at that moment. Would've walked across hot coals for him.

Max squeezed into her cubicle and wedged himself into an uncomfortable metal side chair. "You know, I've been with the department for twenty years, and the most important thing I've learned is that as long as you can meet your own eyes in the mirror every morning, you're doing okay."

"It sounds as if you're perilously close to being a glass-half-empty kind of guy," Afton said.

"Maybe I'll see if I can balance that out," Max said.

Afton crooked an eyebrow at him. "What's up?"

"I just spoke to Thacker. He wants to see you in his office."

"Oh boy." Afton's heart, which had suddenly felt hopeful, plunged again. She grabbed a notebook and pen and hurried down the hall to Thacker's office. This was one guy who didn't like to be kept waiting.

His secretary, Angel, was nowhere in sight, but his office door was open halfway. Afton peered inside and saw that Thacker was wearing the same clothes he'd been wearing yesterday. It must have been a long, exhausting night for him again. Lots of explaining to higher-ups, damage control with the media, and dealing with the distraught Dardens as well as the ever-snarky FBI.

Afton gave a tentative knock. She was half hoping he wouldn't hear her.

"Come in," Thacker said. He was sitting at his desk, staring intently at his computer screen. When he looked up and saw it was Afton, he said, "Close the door behind you."

Definitely not a good sign.

Afton took a seat across from Thacker in one of his two rump-sprung leather chairs. She instantly felt eight years old again, back in elementary school, sitting across from Mr. Murphy, the school principal, after she'd gone postal at recess and smacked Corey Miller in the face with an ice ball as retribution for sticking gum in her hair. Hopefully, the punishment meted out today would be the equivalent of one week without recess. A small price to pay.

Thacker grunted, removed his reading glasses, and stretched back in his chair. He looked exhausted.

"Last night wasn't exactly our department's shining hour," Thacker said. "But I want to be clear on this. I don't believe you did anything wrong. That said, I'm probably in the minority. Richard Darden has some fairly powerful friends, one of whom sits on the City Council. So if I appear a bit bedraggled, it's because I've been up all night fielding calls."

"Sir . . . I . . ." Afton stammered. Her heart was a pounding metronome.

Thacker held up a hand. "I said I've been fielding calls; I didn't say I was taking them to heart. Most of the knee-jerk bureaucrats who made any kind of stink were chin deep in their down comforters last night and got the story secondhand. Hell, Richard Darden isn't really mad at you. He's mad at himself, his wife, the situation, the FBI, and most of all the kidnapper."

Afton felt the wire that had been strung around her chest loosen a degree. "Where does that leave me, sir?"

"For one thing, you're to have no more contact with the Dardens."

"I understand."

"And I'm putting you back on desk duty."

Afton's knuckles flashed white as her hands crimped into tight fists. She'd been afraid this would happen. It *was* a kind of punishment.

Thacker held up an index finger. "I want you to work backup for Max. We're pathetically shorthanded, so I need you to go through that list that you and Max—yes, I know you went to Hudson with him—got from that doll show organizer. What was her name?"

"Muriel Pink," Afton said in a humbled tone. Did nothing get past Thacker?

"Right. Pink. We've got detectives and FBI agents out there interviewing a number of these so-called doll people, the ones who make the reborn dolls, as well as the Dardens' friends, acquaintances, and coworkers. While they're doing that, I want you to go through Pink's list. Run it against DMV, arrest records, real estate, divorce, adoption, anything you can think of. See if you can find any sort of connection, no matter how tenuous. You got that?"

"Yes, sir," Afton said. "That's it?"

"That's it for now," Thacker said.

Afton got up and started for the door. Then she paused and turned around. "Sir?"

Thacker was back staring at his computer screen. "Yes?"

"Thank you for sticking up for me."

"You don't have to thank me for doing the right thing," Thacker said. He lifted a hand to shoo her. "It's my job."

BACK at her desk, Afton found that someone had removed the dog and the note. Either they were destroying evidence or had grown tired of the joke.

Afton wasn't thrilled about being assigned to do research, but it was better than being flung down to the basement to work in the property room, amid a bunch of overweight, semiretired cops. Besides, Thacker had stuck his neck out for her and she didn't want to disappoint him. Max had once told her that real detective work was done in the shadows. Answers were usually gutted out by staring at a flickering computer screen or poring over notes. That's where she was now.

Two and a half hours later, the clock on her computer said 11:35. Afton could hear chairs squeaking and people filtering down the row of cubicles, heading toward the exits. The first lunch shift was under way, but there'd be no lunch break for her. She was only a quarter of the way through Muriel Pink's list, and not much had turned up. Only two exhibitors on the list had an arrest record, and only one of the two was serious—a DWI. Another exhibitor ran a licensed day care center out of her home. She made note of these three, though none of them had been exhibitors at the Skylark Mall. They'd all exhibited at a place called Sundown Shopping Center over in Eau Claire, Wisconsin.

Still, Afton plugged ahead. She wanted some nugget of information to emerge from all this drudgery. There was a missing baby out there, a set of grieving parents, a teenage girl who'd been assaulted, and a community that was nearly rabid for answers.

She wondered again how a baby could be snatched from her parents' home. And in Kenwood yet. Was careful planning involved, or was it just a spur-of-the-moment crime? Being a parent herself, she could feel the stab of paralyzing panic that was starting to creep through the Twin Cities of Minneapolis and Saint Paul. A predator was out there, one who was bold and crazy enough to break into a private home and steal a baby. If Elizabeth Ann hadn't been safe in her crib, then no one's child was safe.

Knuckles wrapped on her outer wall.

Afton turned to find Max standing outside her cubicle. Most of her coworkers simply barged in unannounced and started barking orders at her. But Max carried himself in an old-fashioned, almost dignified manner.

"May I come in?" Max asked.

"Sure," Afton said. As he eased himself in, she noted that his khakis didn't have the razor-sharp pleat that Thacker's dress slacks always had, and it was obvious that his shirts were machine washed and not dry-cleaned. Max was rumpled, but comfortable.

"I've been working on that list we got from Muriel Pink," Afton said.

"Whatcha come up with?" Max asked.

"There are three names that might be worth checking out." Afton handed him her notes and the partial list with three names highlighted in yellow. "One's a DWI conviction from back in 2012, another was busted with some of those Occupy Wall Street protesters that camped out in Loring Park a few years ago, and the third one runs a day care center."

"Day care," Max said.

"I thought maybe her contact with kids . . ." Her voice trailed off.

"I never considered that angle. But it's good. Okay."

He started to leave, but Afton said, "I appreciate your trying to make me feel better. I felt like a bit of a screwup today, so thanks. You made me feel . . . well, normal again."

"Why would you want to feel normal?" Max asked. "I've seen how you operate. You're definitely not civilian-type normal. You've got fairly good instincts that can probably be honed a lot sharper, so you're selling yourself short if you just want to be normal."

Max gave an abrupt nod of his head and left. He seemed to have a knack for getting in the last word. But that last word had inspired Afton to keep working.

AT 3:09, Afton looked up blurry-eyed from her computer. Except for a quick trip to the break room for a granola bar and a Diet Coke, she'd been working steadily for well over six hours. And she'd still only come up with three names, the same three she'd given Max earlier today. All her fancy data mining had turned up a big fat zero. The rest of the people on her list appeared to be upstanding citizens, organ donors, and careful drivers. None had been arrested, declared bankruptcy, been foreclosed on, or landed on Homeland Security's watch list. Heck, maybe they were all eligible for sainthood.

Afton pushed back in her chair, trying to stretch out the kinks. Her back felt knotted and sore—a result of hunching over her computer terminal since early this morning. Or maybe it was from that crappy ice booger she'd tried to skitter around yesterday.

Had it really been just yesterday that this entire scenario kicked off?

Yes, it had. Even though she felt like she'd been working this case for a week.

Groaning, she raised both arms over her head and stretched carefully. Sighing deeply, she relaxed into the stretch. And felt instantly better.

She'd just finished checking the last half dozen names on the list—again nothing—when Max once again ghosted in. Seems he was going to be her only real visitor today.

"You still hard at it?" he asked nonchalantly. He'd tugged on a bulky, army green snorkel parka over his equally bulky sweater and slacks.

"Almost finished," Afton said.

"How about a field trip?" He twisted a pair of suede gloves, what folks in the Midwest called choppers, in his hands.

Afton's eyebrows shot up. "Huh? Sure. What's up?" He was clearly going *somewhere*. Somewhere important?

"I'm heading over to Novamed, Darden's old employer. See if they're in the mood to dish a little dirt on him. Anyway, long story short, Dillon's not feeling up to snuff. I suspect it was the tamales *du jour* that he wolfed down for lunch at Taste of Salvador. That place is always high on the health inspector's naughty list, but Dillon keeps hoping for the best."

"I'd like to go," Afton said, buoyed by the fact that he'd actually invited her along. "But I've been grounded by Uncle Thacker."

"That's old news, because I just cleared it with him," Max said. When she started to say something, he said, "Hey, cheer up. Your sentence has been commuted. You've paid the price for your heinous crime."

11

MAX insisted they take his car, since he'd just been out driving and the car's engine and heater were still tepidly warm. So Afton found herself scrunched into the passenger seat of his Hyundai Sonata, amid a clutter of Red Bull cans, McDonald's wrappers, and assorted tube socks. A hockey puck was half wedged between her seat and the seat back, so she dug it out and tossed it behind her, where it clunked against a trio of hockey sticks.

"Hockey season," Max said as he shot past the new Vikings stadium and slid down an icy freeway ramp. He punched his defroster button, which had the reverse effect of clouding the interior of his windows with a thin skim of ice.

Afton grabbed a plastic ice scraper and attacked the windows, as Max, a notorious speeder, hurtled north on 35W at seventy-five miles an hour. He passed traffic and wove in and out of lanes like he was lounging at home in his sweatpants playing *Grand Theft Auto*. Afton felt a different kind of worry creeping up on her. The kind where you feared you might end up in a ditch waiting six hours for a tow truck to arrive.

"If you're going to survive in Minnesota," Max said as he hammered down on the accelerator, "you have to have seat warmers. In fact, you have to have—at a minimum—front-wheel drive and seat warmers."

The car exited 35, looped around an on-ramp, and swerved onto 694 West. When they finally slowed behind a line of cars that were clogging the left lane, Afton let out her breath slowly. A thermometer on a sign read 15 below.

"Legally, the guys at Novamed may not be able to say much," Max said. "Even if Darden really did steal their company secrets and jump ship."

"Do we know that for a fact?" Afton asked as tiny ice pellets began to beat fiercely against the windshield.

Max turned on the wipers, swore when the entire windshield smeared horribly, and then cut over into the right lane. His defrosters sputtered and the interior was starting to ice up again. "Scrape off that gunk right in front of me, will you?"

Afton scraped.

"Good," Max said as ice chips flew. "Thanks. Anyway, Darden as traitor. That's been the party line so far at Novamed." He shrugged, the shoulders of his parka rising and making a swishing sound. "We'll see if they've changed their tune."

They turned off at the 129th Street exit, and then wove their way down Larch Lane. After slip-sliding for a mile or so, they passed a stand of birch trees that was too perfectly geometric to be natural, then turned at a large silver sign that said NOVAMED, and into a driveway that was surprisingly clear of snow. In fact, Novamed's entire parking lot had been scraped clean. There was barely a glimmer of any snow or ice at all, which probably accounted for the two large piles of snow, pushed to the side of the lot and towering almost twenty feet high.

Novamed's large ochre-colored building was built in the form of an immense letter U. Though invisible now, the grounds were spectacular in summer—a large pond buttressed against a cobblestone patio, crab trees that flamed pink and red in spring. Large silver placards on the side of the building listed the various entrances: VISITOR ENTRANCE, DELIVERIES, EMPLOYEES ONLY. It looked to Afton that one entire wing was designated as offices, while the other wing consisted mainly of laboratories. Probably for R&D, research and development.

They parked and, ducking their heads into the wind, headed for the front door. Once inside, it was like entering a pristine art gallery of some sort. White marble floors, white walls, a white modular seating arrangement—not really couches, not really chairs—and a wall of windows that looked out over the grounds. No artwork, no area rugs, nothing but a large white front desk staffed by two young men in dark suits. Everything sterile, cool, and clinical.

Max flipped out his badge to show the two receptionists, who might, or might not, double as a security detail. "Max Montgomery and Afton Tangler," he said. "We have a three thirty appointment with your CEO, Bruce Cutler."

One of the men glanced at his computer screen and said, "Yes, we have you here. And you're right on time." He seemed pleased at their punctuality. The other man slid a black leather book across the counter and asked them to sign in and note the exact time of day. Then he gave each of them a plastic visitor ID badge to clip onto their clothing.

The computer screen guy said, "Andrew will show you to your meeting."

"Thank you," Afton said.

They followed Andrew down a hallway, where he badged them through a set of sturdy-looking security doors.

"As you might have guessed," Andrew said, "we're in a secured area now, with this hallway running past our outer ring of bio-labs. Clean rooms, as they're more familiarly known to the public."

They stepped along and passed a row of rooms that were white, brilliantly lit, and filled with complex-looking instrumentation. Inside, workers moved about purposefully. All were clothed in Tyvek jumpsuits, latex gloves, booties, and head coverings.

Afton wondered how anyone could work that way. The starkness of everything was intimidating and put her on edge. It was like staring into an impossibly brilliant void. If there had been a cold metal table with an alien autopsy going on, it wouldn't have surprised her.

"All our clean rooms are class one hundred," Andrew said. "That means we allow only one hundred particles—point five microns or larger—per cubic foot of air."

"That's good?" Max asked.

"Compare that to a typical office space that has between five hundred thousand to a million particles per cubic foot of air," Andrew said.

"In other words, no dust," Afton said.

Andrew smiled faintly. "No dust."

"And you manufacture what?" Afton asked.

"Medical test kits," Andrew said.

"So you do animal testing?" Afton asked.

Andrew ignored her question.

"Human testing?" Max asked.

Andrew led them through another set of doors. "Almost there."

Underfoot, the hard marble floor changed to carpet and they suddenly found themselves in the executive wing. But unlike the lavish wood-paneled offices typical of law firms or Fortune 500 companies, this was still relatively Spartan. All white with a modular reception desk at the center of what was a hub of offices and meeting rooms.

"And this is our conference room," Andrew said, stopping abruptly in front of an elegant beech wood door.

"Take notes," Max whispered to Afton. "I'll do most of the talking, but you pipe in wherever."

Andrew pushed on the conference room door and it opened with a slight *whoosh*. Three men in expensive suits with equally expensive haircuts were already seated around a bare, glass-topped conference table. No coffee, tea, bottles of water, or elegant French pastries awaited them. It was fairly clear that Novamed wanted this meeting to be over and done with as quickly as possible.

"Good afternoon," Max said, striding in with confidence. With his height and bulk, he loomed over the seated men. "I'm Detective Max Montgomery, and this is my assistant, Ms. Tangler." He tossed one of his business cards onto the table. "We're here to ask some questions."

The man sitting nearest to him popped up quickly and stretched out a hand. "Bruce Cutler, CEO." Cutler was tall and trim with short gray hair and piercing blue-green eyes. He radiated a subtle vibrancy and looked as if he'd be equally at home in a boardroom, crewing on a sailboat, or swanning around a black-tie charity function. Afton could see why Cutler had made it to the ranks of CEO. He just *looked* the part.

With the minimum daily requirement of mumbled pleasantries, the other two Novamed executives introduced themselves as well.

Shou Vang, the chief financial officer, was a wiry-looking Asian man with a placid expression. Afton figured a CFO probably needed to have a good poker face. Edmund Nader, a rotund man with florid cheeks and nervous, slightly damp hands, was their chief information officer.

Max and Afton took seats across from the men, and Max began. "So you know we're here on a fact-finding mission concerning Richard Darden. We're investigating the recent kidnapping of his young daughter."

Vang gave a sympathetic nod. "We've been following the news." He looked pointedly at Afton and she wondered if he'd caught her on TV last night with the dog. From his disapproving expression, she guessed he probably had.

"Our hearts go out to Richard and Susan," Cutler said. "They were part of the Novamed family for a number of years."

"I admire your collegiality," Max said in a slightly sarcastic tone. "Yet you have a major lawsuit pending against him."

Cutler's jaw tightened. "That's correct." It was clear he didn't want to talk about it.

Max frowned. "If I'm to believe the news stories, you accused Richard Darden of reneging on his confidentiality agreement and walking away with trade secrets. It would help if you'd elaborate on that."

"I'm afraid our hands are tied," Nader cut in. "Anything that deals with the lawsuit is proprietary information. You'd have to clear it through our attorneys."

Max glanced at Afton.

"And those attorneys would be . . ." Afton asked, her pen poised to write.

Cutler blanched. "We retain the firm of Baden, Barton, and Kronlach. They handle all our legal matters."

Afton jotted it down, thinking that Baden, Barton, and Kronlach sounded like a steamer trunk falling noisily down a flight of stairs.

Max leaned back in his chair and crossed his legs. "But this isn't exactly legal business that I'm asking about. I'm simply trying to get a bead on Richard Darden. How long did he work here, was he well liked, that sort of thing." He offered a thin smile. "It's much more comfortable to talk here than in a stuffy interview room downtown."

Cutler sighed and tapped a manicured index finger against the glass table. "I suppose," he said.

Max proceeded to ask questions for the better part of ten minutes. While the Novamed execs were hesitant and sometimes bordered on snappy, he never lost his cool. Afton sat there, jotting the occasional note, fascinated by Max's low-key interrogation, because, surely, that's exactly what he was doing.

When everyone seemed to relax, when they sensed that the meeting was coming to a logical conclusion, Max gave a slow, reptilian blink and asked, "Did Darden have any enemies?"

Cutler tensed. "If you're asking if someone here might have wished ill of him or his family, I would have to say no."

"Nobody was unhappy because Darden hopscotched them on his way up the corporate ladder?" Max asked. "Or because his departmental budget was larger than theirs? Or because someone on his staff got canned?"

The three men looked at one another, then Cutler steepled his fingers. "Not that I can think of," he said.

"Richard was well respected," Vang said.

"He was beloved by everyone?" Max asked. "Because that would probably rank as a major first when it came to interoffice politics."

Nader, the information guy, cleared his throat. "There was the issue of Bob Binger last year."

"Do tell," Max said.

Nader looked across the table at Cutler, seemed to get the go-ahead, and then proceeded. "Richard Darden was unhappy with Binger's job performance. With his research methodology."

"And how was the issue resolved?" Max asked.

"Binger was fired," Cutler said.

"By Darden himself or someone else?"

"Obviously HR handled it, but everyone knew it was Darden's decision," Vang said.

"Is this Bob Binger still in town?" Afton asked. She'd been scribbling notes like mad.

"As far as we know," Cutler said.

"I'm assuming your HR people can give us some basic information on Binger," Afton said.

Cutler waved a hand dismissively. "I'm sure there's nothing your department can't find on its own."

"But you could probably do it a lot faster," Max said. "Faster than you can say *subpoena* anyway."

"Fine," Cutler said. "We'll provide you with that information." He stood up and the two others followed suit. "If you'll wait here for a few minutes, I'll have someone pull Binger's records."

"Thank you," Max said.

When the last footfall was heard on the carpet outside the closed door, Max turned to Afton and said, "I wonder if Darden is still employed here."

"What?" He'd caught her completely off guard.

"Novamed wouldn't be the first company to try to sneak a skunk into the woodpile."

"Corporate espionage? Interesting theory."

"Ain't it?"

"If you're right," Afton said, "then how does the kidnapping fit in?"

"I don't know," Max said. "Not yet anyway. Or maybe it doesn't at all. Maybe it's two different things."

Time was ticking away and Afton could hear a hint of desperation edging into Max's voice. She was feeling it herself. "We have to huddle with those FBI guys," she said. "Keith Sunder and Harvey Bagin. They were the ones who interviewed the execs at Synthotech, Darden's new employer."

Max glanced at his watch. "Yeah, we gotta do that." He pulled out his phone and punched in numbers. But it wasn't the FBI he was calling; it turned out to be his home. "Everybody okay?" he asked. "Roof's still on the place?" The answer must have been yes, because he chuckled then winked at Afton. "Okay, looks like I'm gonna be late again. Think you can handle that, maybe order out for a pizza?"

While Max talked, Afton decided she'd better make that same call herself. But just as she pulled out her phone, a blond woman in a black skirt suit entered the room. She smiled at Afton, carefully set a sheet of paper down on the table, and said, "I believe this is the information Mr. Cutler promised you."

"Are you from HR?" Afton asked. The woman was in her late forties, polished, and exuded a tight HR look. A look that said, *I can fire your ass if and when I feel like it.*

The woman offered another thin smile. "That's right. I'm Betty Randle, director of Human Resources."

Afton glanced at the printed sheet. It looked sketchy at best. "This isn't very much." She let her dissatisfaction show through.

"Well," Betty said. "Mr. Binger is no longer employed by our company, so we don't exactly keep tabs on him."

Max, meanwhile, had hung up his phone and pulled the paper across the table so he could read it. "This is it?"

The woman pursed her lips. "I'm afraid so."

"We'd appreciate it you could scrape together a few more details," Afton said.

Max pulled out a business card and handed it to Betty. "E-mail the poop to me when you get it done, okay?"

"I'll try," Betty said. "But I'll have to clear it first."

"Do that," Afton said.

"I'll send Andrew to get you." Betty was clearly anxious to make her getaway.

When Andrew showed up, he was even less chatty than before. "This way," he said, giving a cool, perfunctory smile.

As they backtracked their way past the labs, Afton caught up to him and matched him stride for stride. "Do you like working here?" she asked.

"The benefits are excellent," Andrew said.

"But do you *like* it?"

"Who wouldn't?"

Five minutes later they were out the door and back into the cold. For some reason, it suddenly felt refreshing to Afton.

"What a creepy place," she said.

"Bunch of tight-asses," Max said.

"It's like they all have a great big secret they don't dare let out."

"Maybe they do," Max said.

"Or maybe they're all just terrified of losing their jobs. Or their excellent benefits."

Max checked his watch as they crossed the parking lot. "What we should do if we have time is stop by Hennepin County Medical Center and talk to that babysitter."

Afton nodded. "Ashley something."

"FBI talked to her yesterday, but it wouldn't hurt to check in again."

"I heard she was strong-armed pretty hard," Afton said.

Max's phone hummed and he hitched up his parka to unhook it. "She sustained some cracked ribs, a broken nose. She's supposed to undergo surgery tomorrow." He held the phone up to his face. "Montgomery here."

"Maybe I should drive on the way back," Afton mused to herself, then saw that Max had suddenly stiffened and hunched forward, as if he was trying to concentrate more fully. Something was cooking. And it probably wasn't a pepperoni pizza for his kids.

"Just now?" Max asked, and then fell silent again. He was starting to nod and his eyes fluttered nervously. "Okay, I'm maybe twenty minutes out." He listened some more. "Yeah," he said, his voice terse. "Will do." He clicked the Off button on his phone and turned toward Afton, looking grim.

"What?" she asked.

"That was Thacker. He just got a call from the Goodhue County Sheriff's Department. Two hunters reported finding the body of an infant in a stand of woods just east of Cannon Falls."

Afton felt her heart lurch into her throat. *Oh no.*

"Thacker wants me to jump on it immediately," he continued. "There's a helicopter waiting at Holman Field."

Afton made a split-second decision. "Can I ride along?"

Max jabbed a finger at her. "You think you're up to it?"

"Of course I am." Afton felt a trickle of excitement mingled with dread. A dead infant. Was it Elizabeth Ann?

Max popped the doors on his car and they tumbled in.

"I guess Portia Bourgoyne's hysterics shook something loose after all," Max said as he cranked the engine over hard and rocketed out of the parking lot.

"God help us," Afton said.

12

HOLMAN Field, also known as the Saint Paul Downtown Airport, lay in a low area, bordered on the north and the east by the Mississippi River, which flowed through downtown Saint Paul and then hooked south. Prone to flooding, the airport had only three small asphalt runways, which were used mainly for private aircraft. But the Minnesota National Guard did training runs there and a few government craft were stored in its hangars, since the airfield was barely two miles from the state capital and its surrounding legislative buildings.

Afton stepped out of Max's car onto the frozen tarmac and was immediately greeted by a man in a brown snowsuit emblazoned with a yellow Minnesota State Patrol patch. He gestured for her and Max to follow him and hastily ushered them around the side of a squat green building and out to a waiting helicopter, which looked like a big flying bubble. Two people of unknown gender, dressed in insulated suits, facemasks, and white helmets, were busy prepping the helicopter for its journey south to Cannon Falls. As Afton and Max approached, the copter's rotors began turning, churning up swirls of snow devils and creating a deafening racket.

Afton felt a tug at her sleeve and turned to face a nervous-looking Max.

"What?" she yelled over the noise.

"I'm not the best flyer in the world," he shouted back. A hand crept across his stomach. "Sometimes I get airsick."

"Why are you telling me this?"

"In case you want to sit on the other side of the cab, so I don't throw up on you," Max said.

She dug in her handbag and pulled out a plastic baggie that held two peeled carrots. "Here," she said, handing it to him.

"Carrots help fight air sickness?"

"No," she said. "Barf into the baggie."

He nodded. "Good thing it's a short trip."

Afton couldn't possibly have felt more differently. She'd never been in a helicopter before, and even with the possibility of a very bad outcome, she was eager to hop aboard for the flight. Maybe it was the daredevil in her DNA, but the one lesson she'd learned from rock climbing was that the best views, the most spectacular views, were always seen from above.

A technician quickly helped Afton and Max don chunky helmets and gave a brief orientation on how to work the headsets. Feeling like she'd suddenly joined the Special Forces, Afton climbed into her seat and buckled in. Max took a seat across from her, raised a fist in solidarity, and buckled himself in, too.

A voice crackled through Afton's headset: "Welcome aboard, Detectives." She smiled when she heard that title even though it was inaccurate. The voice continued: "My name is Captain Mark Travers. Myself and Lieutenant Shoney will be flying you today." His hands were flipping switches and his head swiveled back and forth even as he continued his preflight talk. "We'll take a path down the Minnesota River until we're just east of MSP International. At that point we'll head due south to Cannon Falls." The communications snapped off, then came on again briefly. "Sit back and relax and we'll have you there in no time at all."

Afton grinned from ear to ear when she felt the skids lift off the tarmac and they began their wobbly ascent. Soon, they were climbing higher, nose up, rotors screaming, as they lifted over the airport and flew out over an open expanse of snow. It appeared that the scrub of trees ahead were going to scrape the bottom of the helo as the gray, turgid river came into view, but they blasted over the naked branches unscathed.

The helo headed downstream over the partially frozen water. Below, large chunks of ice and floating trees bobbed along in the river's swift, unbreakable current. Each year, a handful of people were swept into the river and pulled beneath the great expanses of ice, never to escape. Afton couldn't imagine the horror of being trapped with no way to break free, hypothermia setting in, lungs screaming for a sip of air that would never come.

Banking left, the helo left the river flyway and moved south across a vast urban expanse consisting of straight-line streets and freeways, new housing developments, shopping centers, and golf courses, all looking soft and puffy under six inches of fresh snow.

Strong winds buffeted the helicopter as they gradually left the outer ring suburbs behind and eased into the rural area between The Cities and Cannon Falls. Afton watched as small forests, red barns with silver silos, and vast open spaces spun by below.

Max groaned loudly as a gust of wind shook them and they swayed and dipped like a fishing bobber on a lake filled with whitecaps.

"You doing okay?" Afton asked. Up front she could hear faint chatter as the pilot conversed with someone in ground control.

Max nodded. "Yup. No problem."

Yet, Afton thought.

Despite the turbulence, the flight felt way too short for her. Cannon Falls was only thirty-five miles south of Saint Paul, so they were already riding lower, beginning a gradual descent. Just when she was wondering where they were going to set down, the helicopter swung around and she saw a sheet of undisturbed snow, and then metal bleachers and a scoreboard that announced, HOME OF THE BOMBERS.

A web of power lines zigzagged around the perimeter of the football field, and in order to make the landing, the pilot would have to fly dangerously close to some of those lines.

"Ho boy," Max said and closed his eyes.

The wires were growing larger and larger in the cockpit's window, and

Afton was beginning to wonder when and where the pilot would set down. There was a sudden, stomach-lurching drop, as if they were hurtling down forty floors in an elevator. The wires spun by, almost too close for comfort, and then the helicopter bumped once and landed with determination on terra firma.

Afton tore off her helmet and looked around. Across the football field, two Goodhue County sheriff's cruisers sat on an adjacent road, red and blue lights pulsing. She could just make out two men standing in front of the cars in what was fast becoming a murky blue-gray dusk.

"Our next ride is here," Afton said to Max. She'd been bumped back to reality. Back to investigating a dead baby.

Max pivoted his head around, looking slightly unsettled. He seemed to be trying to take stock of where they were, and if they'd actually landed safely. "Okay," he said.

Afton handed her helmet and headset to the pilot and said, "Thanks for the lift."

"I wish it were under better circumstances," the pilot replied. "But we'll be here waiting for you when you get back."

Afton and Max plowed through ankle-deep snow toward the waiting deputies, the warmth of their cruisers, and the sadness they would probably find at the end of this journey. As they neared the cars, the taller of the two men walked out to greet them. He was an imposing figure, rangy and tough-looking in his khaki winter uniform, a Colt .45 stuck on his hip. He offered a gnarled hand.

"I'm Sheriff Jed Burney," the man said with a deep growl. "This is my deputy Bill Gail." He shook hands first with Afton and then Max. Then Afton and Max introduced themselves to Gail.

"Sorry to call you down here like this," Sheriff Burney said. "On such short notice."

"No," Max said. "We appreciate it." He cocked an eye at Burney. "You've been briefed on our case? The Darden kidnapping?"

The sheriff's Smokey Bear hat dipped forward. "We have."

"That's why we called you guys first," Deputy Gail said.

Max looked like he was about to say something, but didn't.

The sheriff hitched at his belt. "I suppose we best get to it."

Afton and Max piled into the sheriff's cruiser—Max in front and Afton forced to ride "perp" in the backseat. Sheriff Burney began an immediate rundown of what he knew so far as Deputy Gail followed behind in the second cruiser.

"The baby was found by a couple of hunters in a woods just north of town," said the sheriff as they spun down a two-lane road, the snow-covered farm fields stretching out on either side of them. "We got the call maybe an hour and a half ago."

"There are deer around here?" Max asked. He was a city guy.

"Oh, sure," the sheriff said. "There're still corncobs laying around in the fields. The deer come out, paw around, and uncover 'em."

"Corn-fed venison," Afton said.

Sheriff Burney chuckled. "Except deer hunting season is over. These boys were out after smaller stuff. You know, raccoons, badgers, opossums."

"Are your hunters still at the crime scene?" Afton asked.

"Right nearby anyway. I have another deputy waiting out there with them. I have to say, the hunters were pretty shaken up."

"Have you checked all the area hospitals to see if any babies have gone missing?" Max asked.

"All babies are accounted for so far," Burney said.

"We were told that the baby was found inside a hollow log," Max said. "How did the hunters stumble on that?"

"Just dumb luck," Burney said. "They stopped to light a cigarette, saw a piece of something—blanket or fabric, I suppose—kind of sticking out, and they took a closer look."

"These are okay guys?" Afton asked.

"I've known them both for fifteen years," Burney said. "I'm positive they're not involved." He tapped his brakes as they swung around a curve. "Of course, we still have to follow procedure."

Lights flashing, the cruiser flew past farm fields that expanded all the way to the graying horizon. A purple bruise of encroaching night was already settling around them, while a small blob of orange descended in the western sky.

Sheriff Burney turned off the main highway and onto a gravel road. He slowed a little, but not much. These back roads were obviously familiar to him.

"I've been sheriff here for almost nineteen years and things just keep getting worse," he told them. "When I first came here, my kids were little and we were looking for that hometown feel. My wife and I fell in love with this place. It's got great people, good schools, amazing scenery. There are places along the Cannon River, gorgeous little green groves of aspen and spruce, where you'd swear you found a little sliver of heaven." He sighed heavily. "Now we've got dead babies in our woods. A couple weeks ago we had to bust a meth lab just south of here."

"Times are changing," Max said.

Burney nodded. "And not for the better."

A mile up the road, Afton could see two cars and a beige pickup truck. Blue and red lights flared like strobes in a dance club against the mass of foggy exhaust that enveloped the vehicles. As they rolled closer, a sense of dread began to build within her. This was it. The investigation was about to get as visceral as it could get.

"Martha's here," Sheriff Burney said.

"Who's Martha?" Afton asked.

"Local doctor and part-time county coroner," he said as they crunched to a stop.

Afton gazed across an expanse of field toward a dense-looking stand of woods. It was going to be cold out there. She pulled up her collar, snugged her stocking cap down over her ears, and climbed out. The cold bit into her hard and she regretted that she wasn't dressed properly for this kind of work. Her boots were more fashion than function. Fine for a day at the office, but not nearly warm enough to walk a half mile in what was probably knee-deep snow. If only she had snow boots and a pair of goggles. And truth be told, an ice ax wouldn't be bad either. Max at least had his parka and a pair of Sorels.

As Afton hurried around the car, one leg slid out from under her and she nearly plunged into a steep drainage ditch. Knee-deep in snow and struggling, she muscled herself up, then hobbled around to the other side of the car, where hasty introductions were made. The two hunters sat quietly in their pickup truck, looking worried behind steamed-up windows, clearly not eager to get out and mingle with the newly arrived contingent of law enforcement.

Then Sheriff Burney pointed toward a distant tree line and Afton fell in line as he led Max, Deputy Gail, and Martha the coroner toward the woods. Nobody spoke a word as they followed a trail of footsteps across a snow-covered field, where bits of pale yellow corn stubble poked through.

When they were halfway there, another deputy emerged from a copse of trees and waved a hand at them. He shouted something, but the words were indistinct and lost to Afton, who was walking at the back of the pack.

Sheriff Burney turned around and hollered over the wind, "Deputy Seifert says the FBI and their crime scene team called. They just hit town and should be here in ten minutes."

They continued walking while, all around them, snowdrifts grew and receded, formed at the whim of the ever-insistent wind.

Afton was used to the cold. She'd grown up in Minnesota, where cold was always a factor. In her early twenties she'd been an Outward Bound instructor, even leading some winter campouts in the Boundary Waters Canoe Area. She was a skier, a neophyte snowboarder, and thrived on the challenge of ice climbing. Even with all those years of outdoor acclimatization, her feet began to feel numb in the subzero cold. Then the unwelcome sensation settled in her face. Each broken snowflake that struck her forehead and cheeks was a tiny pinprick of pain. She put her gloved hand over her mouth and nose to shield herself and kept slogging. Ice beads began to form on the tips of her eyelashes from each foggy breath.

But the trees were drawing closer and closer. They were almost there.

Five steps into the forest, into a grove of sheltering oaks and cottonwoods, and it felt as though Boreas, the Norse god of the north wind, had suddenly decided to hold his breath. The wind died to a whisper; the cold seemed to ease off a touch. Huge black crows scolded from the treetops as Deputy Seifert pointed out a trail of blue spray-painted footsteps.

"Stay in the blue prints," Seifert warned everyone.

Afton stepped out of line and saw a second set of prints leading deeper into the woods. "The other prints are from the hunters?" she asked.

"Yes," Burney said. "We marked our trail, but tried to keep everything else as uncontaminated as possible."

"Smart," Max said.

They trudged along another twenty feet into a small clearing. Just as Sheriff Burney had told them, there was an old log. It was large and smooth and silvered, as if it had fallen a long time ago and had lain there ever since. Bare trees overhead formed twisted patterns in the dying sun.

"Okay now," Burney said. "It's over here."

Afton tiptoed carefully through the blue prints. Moving toward the scene was almost like playing a monochrome game of Twister.

Right foot blue. Left foot blue.

Afton crept up next to the log, where a fragment of pale green blanket stuck out. The sight of that blanket, frozen stiff and smudged with grime, made her heart pound faster.

Who could do this? she wondered. Then the answer swam up to her. *A monster.*

All five of them stood in a semicircle and gazed at the fallen log, which had done its job in sheltering the tiny little body, probably keeping it safe from woodland predators. The sheriff pulled out a heavy-duty Maglite and aimed the beam at the open end of the log.

"Go ahead," Martha said. "I already took a look."

Max took a step forward and bent down on one knee. He peered in for a good couple of minutes, then shook his head and stood up.

Afton was next.

13

AFTON sank down on both knees into the soft snow and put her face as close to the end of the log as possible. The shadows formed a light and dark chiaroscuro, playing faint tricks on her, but she could definitely make out the body of an infant swaddled tightly in a blanket. Anger and shock flared within her, and her initial reaction was to beat a hasty retreat. Fighting to push down that impulse, she forced herself to absorb every detail of the scene. There was the dirty, frayed blanket that appeared to be woven from cheap polyester. And though she couldn't see much of the infant, she noted a few hairs. Dark hairs. Wasn't the Darden baby supposed to be towheaded? She thought so.

Finally, Afton stood up and brushed snow off her knees. She turned to Martha and asked, "From what you could make out, could you get any sort of fix on the baby's age?"

Martha shifted from one foot to the other as wind moaned through the treetops. She was a little chubby and older than the rest of them, like someone's slightly hip grandmother. She'd dressed well for the cold, too—red snowsuit, thick fur gloves, and boots. A few strands of gray hair poked out of her stocking cap.

"I can't tell from just looking at this baby," Martha replied. "I'd need

X-rays of the skull to tell how far along the anterior and posterior fontanelles have solidified. We can also tell age by how advanced its cranial sutures are."

"But it's not a newborn," Afton said.

"No."

"And it could be older than three months."

"It probably is."

Sheriff Burney cleared his throat. "We shouldn't be calling that poor baby an *it*."

Martha held up a finger. She wasn't finished. "What I can do is give you a guesstimate of how long that baby's been out here."

"How long?" Max asked, stepping in closer.

"More likely months rather than days," Martha said.

"So it's not the Darden baby," Afton said.

"It's not her," Martha said.

Sheriff Burney grimaced. "I don't know if that's a good thing or a bad thing."

"Maybe bad for you," Afton said. "This is your problem now."

Max shrugged. "We've still got the FBI's crime scene guys coming to take a look." He turned toward Martha. "If it doesn't put your nose out of joint, they could probably take the baby back to Minneapolis, get some lab tests going, do a DNA analysis. Maybe even put their guys on the hunt for the parents."

"Or the killer," Afton said.

"That's fine with me," Martha said. "We've got a contract with the ME in Minneapolis anyway. I'm not really trained in forensics; my specialty is pediatrics."

"Minneapolis PD and the FBI have better equipment and more manpower than we have down here," Burney said. "So I definitely think that's the best thing to do, considering the circumstances."

It was full-on dark now as Afton stared into the woods. A strange thought capered through her brain—trolls stealing babies.

Now where did that come from?

Maybe she'd read about it in one of Poppy's storybooks. *No trolls here, though*, she thought to herself. *Just a stone-cold killer.*

"Here they come," Sheriff Burney said. He looked past their group at a pair of white-clad techs and a man in civilian garb who were pushing their way toward them. "They made good time." When they got closer, he called out, "You made good time."

Afton immediately recognized the man walking in the lead. It was Don Jasper from the FBI's Chicago office. She'd met him yesterday afternoon in a fleeting introduction outside Thacker's office. Today he was wearing a nice-looking shearling jacket and a navy stocking cap that said FBI in yellow letters.

The two techs deposited their cases and immediately began securing the perimeter and setting up lights. Once the crime scene resembled an outdoor photo shoot, they readied their cameras and began shooting stills as well as video. One of the techs pulled Martha aside and began discussing protocol for the removal of the body.

"Hey, fella," Jasper said to Max as they shook hands. Then he turned to Afton and stuck out a hand. "Don Jasper. FBI." He was tall and lanky with steel gray hair and warm brown eyes the color of precious amber. They seemed to twinkle when he spoke.

"Afton Tangler," she said. "We met yesterday. Briefly."

"Oh sure. And you are . . ."

"Minneapolis Police Department liaison." Afton decided the man was not unattractive. On a scale of one to ten, he was a . . . well, he was definitely up there.

"A liaison on a crime scene when there are no victim's family present?" Jasper said. "They must think highly of you."

"It's more happenstance," Afton explained. "I was out with Max when he got called down here."

Jasper cocked his head at her. "So you're working on the missing Darden baby case, too."

Afton nodded. "We were just interviewing the execs at Novamed, Richard Darden's previous employer."

"Learn anything?"

"Nothing beyond the usual boilerplate bullshit," Afton said.

"Ah," Jasper said. "I see you have the proper amount of irreverence and disdain for civilian corporate culture. You'll fit right in with us."

"Trying to," Afton said. *Hoping to.* She took a step back as Max and Sheriff Burney joined the conversation.

"Did you talk to the two hunters still quarantined back in their truck?" Max asked Jasper.

"There's an agent interviewing them right now," Jasper said. "But I don't think . . ."

"What?" Afton asked.

"I don't think anything will come of it," Jasper said.

"They're just a couple of regular old hunters," Sheriff Burney said. "Stumbled upon a bad thing and made the right call." He glanced toward the log. "Oh boy."

The four of them watched silently as Martha and one of the crime scene techs gently slid the baby out of the log and placed it inside a black vinyl body bag. The bag was then placed upon a child-sized stretcher.

Sheriff Burney slid his hat off his head. "I feel like we should say a prayer or . . ." He stopped and glanced up as the sounds of helicopter rotors split the air.

"What the hell?" Max cried. Now he was looking up, too. "Did our ride just take off?"

The roar was absolutely deafening as a helicopter suddenly appeared over their heads. It hovered above them, swaying slightly, creating a tremendous updraft that turned snow, ice, and bits of leaves into a swirling maelstrom.

Afton gazed up as a bright beam of light suddenly flashed on, encompassing all of them in its glowing circle. Then she saw the red letters that spelled out CHOPPER 7. The unwelcome intruder was Channel 7 News.

"Go away!" Sheriff Burney yelled as the technicians scrambled frantically to try and salvage what was becoming a messed-up crime scene. "Get the hell outa here!" But his words were drowned out by the frantic beating of the rotors.

High overhead, Afton could see a man with a camera poke his head out the side of the helicopter and begin filming the scene below. Now their entire group was trying to wave the news chopper away, but it held firm. The cameraman continued to film as the coroner and one of the crime scene techs leaned over the stretcher to hopefully protect the baby's body from the swirling wind.

Afton looked around at the angry faces, the shiny black body bag, and the helicopter hovering overhead like some kind of dark angel. And thought, *What a terrible ending to a terrible day.*

BUT it wasn't over yet. There was the technical matter of a debriefing at police headquarters. Don Jasper and Harvey Bagin, also with the FBI, huddled with Max and Afton in Deputy Chief Thacker's office. It was an "I'll show you mine, if you show me yours" type of meeting. The FBI guys had a laundry list of completed tasks and an even longer to-do list. Then it was Max's turn to sketch out the meeting at Novamed and their findings in Cannon Falls. He did it quickly and efficiently, as if he'd already written the report in his head.

"This Cannon Falls baby isn't related to the Darden baby kidnapping, is it?" Thacker asked.

"Doubtful," Max said.

"Okay then," Thacker said. "Write it all up and give it to me in triplicate." He looked across his desk at Jasper. "Better make that quadruplicate. We have a lot of different agencies working on this."

THANK goodness you can type," Max said. He and Afton were squashed into his cubicle, finishing up the last of their report. He yawned, did a slow neck roll, and said, "Long day."

"You look like you're badly in need of a decent night's sleep," Afton said.

"I'm okay." Max pulled a jingle of keys from his pants pocket. "I'll be home in . . ." He stopped, frowned, and said, "Damn."

Afton looked up from the computer. "What's wrong?"

"I was gonna stop over at HCMC. Talk to that kid."

"Ashley Copeland. The babysitter."

"Yeah, but it's probably too late now," Max said. "They probably gave her a sleeping tablet or something."

"I drive right by that hospital," Afton said. "I could pop in."

Max looked mildly interested. "Yeah?" Then he shook his head. "It's probably a bad idea. If Thacker got wind . . ."

"You don't trust me? To interview her, I mean."

"She's already been interviewed. I was just gonna make a casual inquiry."

"Because you're wondering if she might have remembered something else," Afton said. "Something new."

"That'd be about it."

"I can handle that."

Max continued to stare at her.

"Really," she said.

Max considered this for a few moments and then nodded. "After the kind of day we just had, I suppose you can."

14

AFTON eased her Navigator up to a meter on the street outside Hennepin County Medical Center. The glowing clock on the courthouse tower two blocks away said nine o'clock. Late to be visiting someone. Then again, she knew that hospitals were much more lenient about visiting hours these days. And she did carry a police ID.

Inside, the gift shop had just closed, its wooly sheep, plump teddy bears, and tethered balloons keeping their silent vigil in the dark. Afton rode an elevator up to the fifth floor and crept down the hallway looking for Room 522, Ashley's room. The overhead lights had been dimmed and the floor was quiet but not yet deserted. Nurses floated past on rubber-soled shoes, a patient shuffled along pushing an IV pole down the hall. As Afton passed a few open doors, she heard snatches of quiet conversation, the hum and hiss of machines, and the rattle of privacy curtains being pulled.

Room 522 was at the very end of the hall. Afton stopped outside the door and listened. Nothing. No TV, no talking. Maybe Ashley Copeland was asleep already? Maybe, just as Max had figured, she'd been given a pill to carry her away to dreamland.

Well, she'd come this far. Besides, she knew that Ashley was just a few years older than Tess. Which meant the girl could be huddled under the covers, playing possum and texting like mad.

Afton pushed open the door and stepped into the room. A dim nightlight was on somewhere, but a flimsy privacy curtain had been pulled across one half of the room, blocking her view. Behind the curtain a shadow quivered.

"Ashley?" Afton said. "Are you still awake, honey?"

She put a hand out and slowly pushed the curtain aside.

"My name is Afton Tangler. I'm with the . . ." Afton's eyes suddenly registered the dark apparition that loomed up on the other side of the sleeping girl's bed.

"Ashley?" she choked out again. But she knew it wasn't Ashley. Whoever this dark, menacing person was, they were suddenly lunging directly at her!

Spinning as fast as she could, Afton raced for the door and pulled it open maybe half an inch.

Quick as a snapping turtle's bite, a hand shot out and smashed the door closed.

Too late! Her escape was cut off!

Afton twisted her body around to face her attacker, determined to make a stand and defend herself. She jabbed toward the darkness that was his face, intent on poking a finger into his eye. But the man—whose face was completely obliterated by a wool ski mask—heaved himself hard against her and flattened her against the door.

Afton opened her mouth to scream, but he quickly clapped a hand across her mouth. She squirmed as she felt his pelvis bump up against her. His closeness, his almost indecent intimacy, made her skin crawl. Terrified, forcing her frenzied brain to recall her self-defense training, Afton fought like a wild woman. She wiggled and bit and struggled until she managed to rip her right arm free of his clutches. Mustering all her strength, she drove a fist up, hard, directly under the man's chin.

He let out a *woof*, drew back an arm, and swatted her with an open hand, as if she were a bug. Afton's head flew back and cracked hard against the door. Before she could regain her bearings, his fist slammed into her jaw.

Afton literally saw stars. Miniature constellations that spun sickeningly inside her head. She sagged into him and when he took a half step back, she gathered what strength she had left to jerk her chin downward and head-butt him in the chest. Two seconds later she was tossed to the floor. Pain flared in her lower back as the man crawled on top of her, trying to capture her arms and legs, as if they were contestants in a high school wrestling match.

He was so strong! And the sickening odor that came off him smelled like a wet animal.

Slowly, Afton stopped struggling until she lay completely still. He didn't seem to have a weapon, so what was he going to do? The man was breathing hard now, like an overwrought teakettle. Was he excited by their struggle? Was he enjoying himself?

A terrifying thought rose like a bubble in Afton's brain. Oh no! Was this the same boy who'd strong-armed Ashley the other night! Had he come back to finish things with Ashley? To rape her? Or worse, to kill her?

As Afton felt the man lift up slightly from where he had her pinned, she brought a knee up hard, aiming for his groin. She wasn't on target, but she wasn't all that far off either. As her knee connected, the man groaned and partially loosened his grip.

That was all she needed. Elbows and knees pumping like pistons, Afton spun away from him and clambered to her feet. Catlike, the man sprang up after her, blocking her chance for a getaway. With her options dwindling, Afton sprinted toward the bathroom. Just as her feet hit tile and she struggled to pull the door closed behind her, he landed a roundhouse punch and she felt a stabbing pain in her right shoulder. Afton stumbled as he hit her a second time, and this blow sent her reeling across the bathroom and crashing into a second door.

The impact of hitting that second door popped it wide open and catapulted Afton into the adjoining hospital room. She fell against an empty bed and slid awkwardly to the floor. She had two seconds to gather her wits and then he was on her again, this time hooking an arm around her neck. Afton gasped for air as he squeezed her hard, putting tremendous pressure on her airway. Blind panic began to set in. Her arms and legs flailed furiously, hitting an IV stand in the process. The metal pole crashed down on top of them, striking her assailant in the head. As his grip suddenly slackened, Afton scrambled on hands and knees toward a silver medical cart. She grabbed frantically for the boxy metal cart and wrenched it toward her. The medical cart swayed for a few moments, and then slowly tipped up onto two wheels. The drawers flew open, shooting its hodge-podge of contents toward them.

Afton grabbed the first thing she saw—a syringe for drawing blood. She clutched it in her hand and used her thumb to flick off the orange plastic tip, unsheathing the two-inch needle. Growling in anger, Afton spun around as fast as she could and cocked her arm. Like a picador attacking a bull, she lunged forward and rammed the syringe deep into the man's neck.

The man let loose a bloodcurdling scream and flew backward. He stumbled and landed hard on his butt. One hand flailed and batted frantically at the syringe, which was stuck deeply in the side of his neck.

That was the break Afton needed. She ran for the door, yanked it open, and plunged down the dim hallway toward the nurses' station. She spun around the tall Formica desk, sending a stack of file folders tumbling to the floor, banging her hip on the corner. She spotted a phone and grabbed it. A nurse, a small, dark-haired woman in a pink smock, who had just emerged from a storage room, gaped at her in surprise. "You're not supposed to be back here," she scolded.

"Call hospital security!" Afton cried. Then she punched in 9-1-1. And then she called Max.

TEN minutes later, Thacker himself showed up, looking both visibly shaken and quivering with outrage. He was accompanied by a scrum of eight uniformed officers, who immediately searched the area and huddled with hospital security. They looked everywhere, up and down the back stairway, ripping open janitor's closets and storage rooms, but found no one.

Max showed up some twenty minutes later, ashen-faced and practically frothing at the mouth. "He was here?" he cried out when he caught sight of Afton. "You think it was the kidnapper guy?"

"We don't know it was him," Thacker said. He sounded calm and controlled, though he'd been furious when he'd first arrived.

"I think it was him," Afton said. "I mean . . . for Christ's sake, he was right there in Ashley's room."

"Does she know?" Max asked.

"No," Afton said. "Amazingly, she slept through the entire thing. Even when the nurses moved her bed to a different room so crime scene could get in there, she never woke up once."

"Sleeping pill," Max said.

"Where do I get one of those?" Afton asked.

FINALLY, thankfully, when all the talking was done, when all the gentle reprimands had been doled out, Afton went home. Max had insisted on following her in his car and offered to park a cruiser at the curb to keep watch for the night.

Afton had declined his offer. She just wanted this day to be over and done with. Now she was at home, snuggled in her own bed under a pile of warm blankets. Poppy and Tess were asleep in their rooms; Bonaparte snored loudly from where he was curled up at the end of her bed. The TV was on, but it was just flickering images, something to occupy her wonked-out brain.

Afton was mentally reviewing her day, which had seemed to unfold like some kind of weird time warp. Chastisement followed by the trip to Novamed, followed by a nail-biter helo ride, followed by the discovery of the dead infant, and then the attack at the hospital.

Had it been one of the kidnappers that she'd tangled with tonight? Had the boy come back for Ashley Copeland? To do what? See her again? Kill her?

Afton had read the transcript of Ashley's interview with the FBI. And the girl really hadn't told them anything of value about her attacker.

Hell, *she* had been face-to-face with a crazy person who was probably the very same guy and she didn't have much of a takeaway. Barely a description, really more an impression.

They would have to talk to Ashley tomorrow. Push the girl a little harder, try to ascertain if the girl knew more than she'd let on.

Afton fumbled with her pillow, struggling to get comfortable. She was having trouble trying to erase the image of the poor baby who'd been stuffed inside the log. Was that baby lying on a cold metal laboratory table right now? She knew the answer was yes. Max had even told Don Jasper that he planned to attend the preliminary autopsy tomorrow morning. The notion didn't thrill Afton, but she supposed it was part of the case. And if she wanted to stay on this case, then an autopsy was part of the package deal.

Shivering, Afton picked up the remote control and flipped along until she hit Channel 7. It was eleven o'clock and she was curious—and a little fearful—to see what kind of footage the TV station had actually shot down in Cannon Falls. She drew a deep breath, amped up the sound, and watched as the somber face of the Channel 7 news anchor appeared. His blow-dried hair was camera ready, his diction was precise, even his demeanor was appropriately solemn as he said, "Good evening. Tragedy struck in Cannon Falls today when the body of a dead infant was discovered in a hollow log. And only Newswatch 7 was live on the scene to bring you this exclusive footage . . ."

Afton watched, wide-eyed and disbelieving, as the film footage played out just as she remembered it. The fields, the clearing in the woods, the tracks spray-painted blue. And there, in the middle of their little law enforcement huddle, she saw her own pale face staring quizzically up at the camera as everyone around her waved and shouted.

The anchorman blathered on. ". . . calls placed from our newsroom to the Sheriff's Department in Goodhue County, as well as to our local FBI office, were not returned. A spokesperson for Susan and Richard Darden had no comment. So now we wait with bated breath to find out if this missing baby turns out to be the recently kidnapped Elizabeth Ann Darden—or if this is the body of yet another missing child."

"Oh my God," Afton whispered. She couldn't believe they could be so callous as to speculate on the dead infant's identity. She wondered if poor Susan Darden was watching this. She hoped not.

15

SUSAN Darden scrunched her knees up to her chin and stared disbelieving at the TV screen. There she was, that dog woman again. Right in the center of the screen, staring up at the helicopter. Lady cop or liaison or whatever she claimed to be—she would never forget that face.

But as the Channel 7 News continued, her horror was suddenly compounded. A baby had been discovered in a desolate woods near Cannon Falls? Out in the cold with animals roaming around? Was it her baby? Was it Elizabeth Ann?

Panic gripped her. Why hadn't the police called? Should she call them?

But still Susan didn't throw back her blanket and jump off the couch. Her eyes were riveted on the TV screen as the camera panned from the stupid woman over to two people who were huddled together, obviously trying to shield something. Oh no, it was a body bag! She felt a rip inside her, a flash of pain that felt like she was on fire. Bitter tears welled up and she began to scream. Loud, pained howls, like a wild animal with its leg caught in a trap. She wanted to tear and claw and draw blood. In fact, if that dog woman were here right now, she'd rip out her eyeballs.

Deep within her rational mind, Susan knew she should try to pull herself together, call the police, and find out what had happened. *Demand* to know what had happened. But still she screamed, a bloodcurdling scream that trailed off into a raspy hiss. As the pain welled up like a balloon that would burst inside her, she grabbed a pink pillow and held it to her mouth.

Make it stop, she told herself. *Make it all go away.*

"Susan! Susan!"

She heard a familiar voice as she gasped and whimpered into her pillow. She felt as though she was being pulled into a deep morass, a nightmare from which she would never wake up. Now there were hands on her shoulders. Was someone trying to hurt her? She struggled, dropping the pillow, flailing her arms and throwing punches without bothering to open her eyes.

"Susan!" Richard Darden shouted. "Calm down, baby. Calm down."

It took all her strength to pull back from the brink of despair. Exhausted, unable to move, she brushed a damp tangle of hair off her face and slowly opened her eyes.

Richard was standing over her, his expression a mixture of concern and panic.

"Susan?" he said.

The familiarity of his voice helped pull her out of it.

"The baby," she whispered. "I just saw it on TV."

"It's not her," Richard said. "It's not our baby." He said it slowly, enunciating carefully in his patient, paternal voice. The one he sometimes used when he was trying to cajole her.

She sat up and blinked. "Are you sure? Swear to me that you're sure."

"I already talked to the police on the phone."

"They called? When?"

"An hour ago, maybe a little more. They said it's definitely not Elizabeth Ann." He reached out and snapped off the TV, as if to add emphasis to his words.

Susan put a hand to her heart, unsure whether to be grateful that her child had been spared, or even more fearful that Elizabeth Ann was still out there in the hands of . . . a crazy person.

"You're sure?" she asked again.

"Positive," Richard said. "I spoke with that agent, Don Jasper, from the FBI. He was most emphatic. It's definitely not her. The baby they found was older, almost a year old. And it had been in the woods for several months."

"Oh." Susan looked around her family room with its matching cream leather sofas, swags of draperies, and antique cribbage table. After the flurry of the past two days, the intrusion of law enforcement officials with their badges and averted glances, the place suddenly looked forlorn and empty. "The FBI, the police. Are they here?"

"No," Richard said. "I sent the one officer home a couple of hours ago." He patted her shoulder gently. "You've been sleeping."

She sat up a little more. "I had terrible dreams."

"I can understand that you're having trouble . . . coping. But, sweetheart, you've got to start making an effort."

"I am. Really I am." Susan fumbled for a tissue and blew her nose. "How are you holding up?"

"Terrible," Richard said. But Susan thought there was something in his voice. He didn't *sound* terrible.

"What have you been doing?" she asked.

Richard lifted both hands as if in supplication. "Nothing. Hoping. Praying, I guess." He dropped his hands and took a step back. "Maybe you should take one of your pills. Go upstairs and crawl into bed, try to get some more rest. Just . . . zonk out." He managed a smile. "Doesn't that sound better than lying around down here?"

She wanted to scream at Richard and tell him that getting Elizabeth Ann back was what sounded better to her. Instead, she said, "I suppose." After all, he was just trying to be helpful. She sighed. Men were never emotionally supportive in a crisis. Of course, she wasn't exactly a model of female courage either.

"Want some help?" Richard offered a hand.

She stood up and gave a shaky smile. "No, I can manage."

"Atta girl."

Susan wobbled down the hallway and into the kitchen. She needed a sip of juice or water to soothe the rawness in her throat. But a fresh onslaught of grief came flooding over her when she opened the refrigerator. Lined up on the middle shelf were four bottles of baby formula. Just sitting there. Waiting for her baby to return.

Susan slammed the door. She couldn't even recall mixing them. She must have simply been acting on autopilot, fixing a bottle every few hours. *For a baby that isn't even here.*

Susan stared at the refrigerator for a long ten seconds, then pulled it open again and grabbed a bottle of mineral water. She unscrewed the top and pitched it aside—she didn't care where—and carried the bottle back to talk to Richard.

He folded the newspaper down as she came into the room. "Feeling a little better?"

She made a broad gesture. "We have, what . . . five thousand square feet of house? Four bathrooms? A sewing room even though I've never managed to sew a stitch? A pool table even though you've never shot a round of eight ball? Guest rooms even though we've never seen an overnight guest? What's it all for?"

Richard stared at her, pain flickering in his eyes. "What do you mean, what's it all for?" He was suddenly on his feet, ready to confront her. "I don't remember you having a problem when we picked out this house. You loved the Kenwood address, said it would impress all of your friends. And you were perfectly enthralled with hiring decorators and wall mural painters, and scouring art galleries for the perfect paintings and antiques. You even ordered monogrammed guest towels, for Christ's sake. Seems to me you were completely on board at the time. Am I right about that?"

Susan nodded slowly. "Yes, I was. I'll admit that, I wanted the dream lifestyle, the perfect home. But now our bubble has been completely burst. I mean, what good is all this if we don't have Elizabeth Ann?"

"Susan, I hear you," Richard pleaded. "And my heart aches just as much as yours does. But what do you want me to do? Go outside and drive around? Look for her like she's some kind of lost puppy?"

"I just want . . ." Susan flapped an arm and said, "I don't know what I want." Then her face tightened and she said, "No, I *do* know. I want our baby back."

"And so do I," Richard said, firmness in his voice. "And I believe, deep down in my heart, that we *will* get her back. I have to believe that. It's the only thing that keeps me moving forward, the only thing that keeps me from going absolutely freaking insane."

"Richard," Susan said. She touched a hand to his cheek and stepped in close. "I'm sorry. I'm acting like a shrew, a crazy lady. We have to stick together, we have to *get through this* together."

Richard put both arms around her and pulled her close. "Then let's forget these last ten minutes ever happened, okay?" He kissed her gently on the nose. "Just go upstairs, take your bottle of water with you, and swallow one of your pills. Hop into bed and try to get some rest. God knows you need it."

"What are you going to do?" Susan asked, yawning. She really did feel completely exhausted.

"I'm going to wait right here. Keep watch. Keep the home fires burning."

"Bless you," Susan said. She turned and trudged over to the staircase. As she climbed each step, she felt like she were moving through molasses. She could even see faint traces of black powder—latent powder, they'd called it—the stuff police used to obtain fingerprints. To gather evidence.

Susan let out a low groan at the bitter reminder. Because the other horrible thing that crouched at the back of her mind like some kind of evil praying mantis was the fact that her home had been invaded. A crazy person had violated the sanctity of their home. They'd stolen in under cover of night, gone into Elizabeth Ann's nursery, and snatched her from her beautiful little crib.

Unable to resist, Susan tiptoed down the hallway and pushed open the door. She stepped into Elizabeth Ann's room, fighting back tears now, and collapsed on the familiar pile of pillows and plush animals.

What had she been thinking? A two-thousand-dollar crib? Hand-painted bunnies capering across the walls? A fancy, high-tech baby monitor so she could sing Elizabeth Ann to sleep from practically any room in the house?

They should have put their money into better locks, an armed response security service, and a really nasty German shepherd. Screw the nanny cam. A lot of good that had done.

Twenty minutes went by with Susan lost in thought and deep regret. Then she pulled herself up and crept over to the crib. Reaching in, she picked up a plump black-and-white penguin. It had bright beady eyes and a little yellow felt beak, and it had been Elizabeth Ann's favorite stuffed animal. As Susan cradled the fuzzy toy against herself, half humming a nursery rhyme, she heard a faint ringing sound.

Telephone?

She frowned, momentarily confused. And then it dawned on her that she was hearing the phone ring through the baby monitor. The monitor was switched on, able to broadcast back and forth from four different rooms in the house.

But who's calling at this time of night? Maybe the police?

Her jitters returning in a rush, Susan leaned forward and cocked an ear at the baby monitor. And heard Richard say, "Now's not a good time."

Not a good time for what?

Then, "No, I'm not angry at you, Jilly. Of course not."

Jilly? Jilly Hudson, our former nanny?

Susan decided that Jilly must have been seen the latest news report and called to offer support. Still . . . it seemed awfully late. She cranked up the volume control, but all she could hear was Richard saying, "Uh-huh, uh-huh." Not very interesting. Then again, neither was Jilly.

She was about to turn away when she heard Richard's soft laughter.

What? How can he be laughing at a time like this?

Then came the damning words.

"No, of course she doesn't know," Richard said. "Haven't we always been discreet?" There were a few moments of silence and then Richard said, "Definitely not tomorrow, I'm totally jammed as you can imagine. But maybe I can pry myself away for an hour or two on Wednesday." Jilly obviously responded to his suggestion because he chuckled again.

Susan felt the sudden pounding of blood in her ears. Her mouth had gone bone-dry, and there was the faint taste of bile at the back of her throat.

Richard and Jilly? Oh my God!

Susan stared icily at one of the painted dancing bunnies on the nursery room wall. And for the first time in two days, she felt a cold and rational intensity steal its way through her. She clenched her jaw in a bitter smile. She was suddenly dry-eyed as the cobwebs began to clear.

Now Susan knew exactly what she was going to do.

Tiptoeing silently down the hallway to their bedroom, she found her Gucci bag and pulled out her cell phone.

Before Richard's last laugh died on his lips, Susan was dialing the police.

16

_____

CRAP! Why won't this stupid thing stay on? Why won't this stinkin' tape hold? Why didn't we get some *decent* diapers?"

It was late at night and Shake was feeling tired, angry, and completely overwhelmed as she fussed with the baby and muttered to herself. All day long her stomach had been painfully bloated and the skin above her ankles puffy and swollen like donuts. There was a new sensation, too, a gnawing, stabbing pain deep within her gut that hadn't been there before. The pain made it impossible for her to concentrate or even eat and she had a sickening feeling that her baby might be arriving sometime soon.

And here she was, up late at night, getting zero to no rest, trying to change yet another diaper on a kid she didn't even know.

This wasn't what she'd expected. She'd always thought babies were mostly pink wiggles and soft coos, adorable little bundles of joy. But this screaming, squalling, demanding, red-faced thing was way more than she'd ever bargained for. Even the diapers were a disappointment. The ones she'd wanted in the grocery store had cute little pictures of puppies and baby ducks on the labels. This crappy brand had nothing—just a series of legal disclaimers and the word NEWBORN on a stupid white box.

Marjorie had told her that babies were easy—"Shit, sleep, and eat. It's not rocket science," she had said.

But to Shake, it seemed a lot more complicated. In fact, everything in her life had gotten pretty dang twisted up lately. And here she was, alone, pregnant, and in pain, confined to a dilapidated house way out in the middle of nowhere.

The worst part of her current living arrangement was that Marjorie was constantly monitoring her every move. She padded around the house in her robe and stupid, backless slippers, watching out the corner of her eye, always judging and finding subtle ways to humiliate her.

It was no secret that the old bitch scared Shake. But what could she do about it? She had nowhere to go. Her dad wouldn't take her back, and she hadn't been in touch with her friends for months. Even Ronnie seemed cowed by his crazy mother, so he was spending more and more time downstairs. Every night after dinner, he'd disappear into the basement to work on one of his precious taxidermy projects. And when he wasn't down there stitching up an animal carcass and picking out the perfect glass eyeballs, he was out procuring new animals.

Dear Lord, when would she and Ronnie ever escape? They needed their own place, far away from Marjorie's taunts and evil glances.

Shake taped the diaper as best she could, gathered up the crying baby, and cuddled her to her chest. "Why won't you stop crying?" she whispered. "I've changed you. I've fed you. Please stop . . ."

"How did you ever think you'd manage one of those on your own?" came Marjorie's taunting voice.

Shake glanced around. Marjorie was hunkered in the doorway, staring at her. Her eyes glittered and she was smoking one of her Kool cigarettes.

"You shouldn't smoke," Shake said. "It's bad for her."

Marjorie exhaled a long stream of smoke. "Like you give a shit," she said, and walked away.

Shake carried the baby into the living room and sat down in a rickety rocking chair. She shifted her bulk and adjusted the baby in her arms, trying to cradle its head as best she could. The baby had actually stopped crying and was watching her now. She wondered if maybe her own baby would be born this week. She hoped so, because she'd been making plans.

Once she was out of the hospital, once she had her former dancer's body back, she would convince Ronnie to clear the hell out of this place. She knew he was a poor excuse for a boyfriend, but if she could get him away from Marjorie, maybe things would be okay. *Okay* being a relative term since she would pretty much settle for an apartment with hot running water, no roaches, and a landlord that wasn't a grab-ass.

Bending over the little baby, Shake began to sing softly. "Hush, little baby, don't say a word, Papa's gonna buy you a mockingbird." The baby closed its eyes. "And if that mockingbird don't sing . . ."

"It's a good thing you know how to shake your fat ass," Marjorie chuckled. "Because Christina Aguilera you ain't."

Marjorie was back. All crooked teeth and wild eyes, watching her carefully.

The baby started crying again.

"Looks like your caterwauling woke her up," Marjorie said.

"I'm trying my best," Shake whimpered. "She was almost asleep before you came in."

"So you're saying it's my fault?" Marjorie said. Her laugh was like a chain saw. "You know all about babies now? Did you get so smart reading those books by Dr. Spock? You know he's not the guy on *Star Trek*, right?"

"Why don't you just leave me alone," Shake hissed.

Marjorie lifted her head and jabbed her chin at Shake's stomach. "Because I'm waitin' for your baby to come out."

"What if I decide to keep it," Shake said, challenging her. Holding an actual baby had got her to thinking, had awoken a tiny flicker of maternal instinct that she didn't know she had.

Marjorie was unfazed. "Too late, cupcake. You already signed the papers for the adoption to go through."

"Maybe I could still arrange for a private adoption," Shake said. "Make sure my baby goes to a nice young couple that I approve of."

"Honey," Marjorie said. "You ain't never gonna get that chance." She reached out for the baby. "Give her to me. I'm gonna take her upstairs."

Shake handed the baby over to Marjorie. Part of her was glad to be rid of the fussy baby, and another part of her wondered if she was doing the right thing in giving her own child away. Her eyes misted over, and tears rolled down her face.

"That's right," Marjorie said. "Cry about it."

Marjorie's taunting voice followed Shake as she ran down the hallway and thundered down the creaking wooden steps to the basement.

As dirty and dilapidated as the upstairs was, the basement was even worse. Flagstone walls had crumbled in some spots, leaving craggy, damp fragments in small piles (like dead animals?) on the earthen floor. Just coming down here set Shake's teeth on edge.

How can Ronnie stand to spend so much time down here?

But she knew the answer. This was where he worked on his beloved taxidermy animals. Right here in what looked like Freddy Krueger's boiler room. Ronnie's macabre hobby only made the place scarier; the smell of formaldehyde, borax, and death was nearly suffocating.

Shake moved quietly across the floor. Ronnie's workbench was set up just to the right of the stairs. His back was turned to her as he worked on sewing up the underside of a large black bird.

"Ronnie?" He'd come storming into the farmhouse a half hour ago. She thought he'd been out drinking, but his eyes were rimmed with red and his face was tight and angry, looking like he was about to pop a blood vessel. Had he been in a fight? She could only guess.

"Ronnie?" Shake tried again. "I really need to talk to you."

Ronnie lifted his head and looked at Shake, as if he had suddenly woken up from a dream and was surprised to find her standing there. "Shake," was all he said.

Shake knew Ronnie wasn't good at focusing his attention, that his mind had all the staying power of a steel ball inside a pinball machine. But when he was working on his critters, a nuclear bomb could explode outside the back door and he wouldn't notice.

"We gotta talk," Shake said.

"What?" Ronnie asked. He reached for a scalpel that was hung on a brown pegboard, along with his collection of razors, knives, and large sewing needles.

"Your mother's on my ass again."

Ronnie unfurled a length of nylon fishing line, cut it neatly with the scalpel, and then threaded the line through a large needle. "So what? She's always been a little bug-shit."

"She scares me," Shake said. "I don't trust her."

Ronnie didn't reply. His mind was still . . . elsewhere.

"I think the smart thing for us to do would be to get out of here." Shake bit her lip. "Like . . . now."

"Why would we do that?" Ronnie asked. He was listening to her, but Shake could tell he wasn't really *comprehending* her words.

"Because we don't have any kind of *life* here. What if we just . . . took off and drove south? Got out of this brutal, cold weather. Tried to start a life someplace else."

Ronnie swiveled in his chair and frowned at Shake. "You want to just up and leave? What about the baby?"

"I'll deal with the baby."

Ronnie shook his head. "*She'll* deal with the baby. That's what she does."

Shake narrowed her eyes. She'd picked up just a whiff of something that felt oddly tainted. What was it? A lie? Danger lurking somewhere? "Is there something going on?" she asked. "Something you're not telling me?"

Ronnie turned back to his workbench and resumed stitching his bird. "No."

"That kid upstairs? You never really did explain that."

"Cousin," Ronnie said. One eye fluttered, almost out of control, as he jerked the thread tight.

"There's something else we need to talk about," Shake said. She hesitated. "Everything inside me has started to hurt." She cupped a hand protectively beneath her belly. "Really bad."

"That's because you're pregnant." Ronnie picked up a long knife, hefted it with a smile, and then set it back down. "Because you're going to deliver your baby in a week or so."

"I think it might be something else," Shake said. "Ever since I got up this morning, there's been a new kind of pain. Sharp . . . stabbing." She considered this. "What if something's really wrong?"

"You're fine," he mumbled.

"But what if I'm *not* fine?" Shake said. "Like what if the baby is upside down or something?" Her voice was shaky now, her mind racing as she considered the awful possibilities. "Ronnie, I think maybe I should go see a doctor." She wanted to kick herself for being so callous about her pregnancy. No checkups, no prenatal vitamins, just smoking and drinking and eating crappy fast food. What had she been thinking? What was wrong with her?

"You've got Mom."

Shake's lip curled. "She ain't no doctor."

Ronnie took another stitch and pulled it tight. "But she's had plenty of experience. She's helped a bunch of girls from that Amish community down near Lockport."

"You mean, like, she's some kind of midwife?" Somehow Shake couldn't picture Marjorie whispering gentle encouragement to a terrified woman who was in the throes of hard labor.

Ronnie swiveled in his chair again, tried for a smile, and then reached out and circled his arms around Shake's waist. "C'mere, you." He pulled her tight, praying that she'd stop her endless yammering.

Grateful for his attention, Shake sank against his chest.

Ronnie eyed her with a smirk. "Maybe you just need to . . . you know."

Shake pulled away from him. "Ronnie, no. I can't have sex now."

His face hardened. "You never want to have sex."

"Is that why you go out at night?" Shake asked. "To be with other women? To have sex with them?" Her heart felt like lead. "Is that where you were tonight?"

"No, of course not." Ronnie reached out and his hands made soothing little circles on her back. "You think I'd cheat on my girl? No way." As he stroked her, his eyes darted back to his dead bird and his mind was a million miles away.

"Oh, Ronnie," Shake sighed. She wished with all her heart that she could believe him.

17

NOW she has to stay on the case," Max said.

Thacker countered. "She's not a trained investigator."

They were sitting in Thacker's office this Tuesday morning. Max was pleading his case for keeping Afton on the job, while Thacker scratched his head, looking dubious.

"Doesn't matter if she hasn't come up through proper channels," Max said. "She's got all the right instincts. Last night proved it."

"Hey," Afton said. "Do I get to say something here?"

"No," Thacker said. He leaned back in his chair, grabbed a yellow pencil, and twiddled it like a drummer would.

"Just let Afton stick with me for a couple more days," Max said. "Until we talk to the babysitter and huddle with this Binger guy who got fired by Darden."

"Farmer can handle that," Thacker said.

"Okay, then just until Dillon gets back," Max pushed.

"Which might not be any time soon," Thacker said. He blew out a glut of air. "On top of full-blown food poisoning, he's flirting with pneumonia. He's tossing down antibiotics like they're Pop Rocks."

"So where does that leave us?" Max asked.

"Maybe send flowers?" Afton asked. She was only half joking.

Thacker glowered at her. "Are you really okay?"

"Yeah. Hell, yes," Afton said. She wasn't really, she was sore beyond belief, but she wasn't about to tell either of them that.

"No ill effects?"

Afton forced a cheery smile. "None."

"Okay, well . . . okay," Thacker said. "Afton can stay. But only because we're so damn shorthanded. Between this kidnapping situation, the Bloomington Avenue double homicide, and that pharmaceutical heist, we're all chasing our tails like a pack of wild monkeys."

Afton had been holding her breath. Now she let it out slowly. She'd just noticed a little wooden sign on Thacker's desk that said, WHEN YOU CHASE TWO RABBITS, BOTH GET AWAY. She wondered if that was a Thackerism or an ancient Chinese proverb?

"Anyway," Thacker said, hunching forward, "as long as Afton's going to hang around, I need to bring you both up to speed. There's been a new twist in the Darden case . . ."

Max and Afton exchanged glances. "What?" Max asked.

"Susan Darden called the Homicide desk last night just after eleven o'clock," Thacker said. "She was in a full-blown panic. Seems that Richard hasn't exactly been a good and faithful husband."

Max let loose a low whistle.

Afton perked up. "What'd he do? Have an affair?"

"Apparently Mrs. Darden overheard her husband talking on the phone," Thacker said. "He was whispering sweet nothings to their former nanny."

Afton fished for the name and came up with it. "Jilly Hudson?" She knew the FBI had interviewed the former nanny, even though Hudson hadn't been considered a suspect. Now she wondered if the girl's status might change. Sure it would. Of course it would.

"Isn't she just a kid?" Max asked.

"She's twenty-three," Thacker said. "Old enough to know better."

"So is Darden," Afton put in.

"Anyway," Thacker said, "Darden's apparently been enjoying a full-blown, class A, convenient, extramarital love affair with Miss Hudson for a couple of months. And it started right there in his own little love nest."

"Not anymore he's not," Max said.

Thacker continued. "Mrs. Darden was so off-the-chain furious when she found out that she demanded we send over a cruiser. By the time the responding officers arrived, she'd tossed her husband out on his ass. Apparently his shit was lying all over the front yard, too. Suits, shirts, underwear, golf clubs . . . everything scattered in the snow."

Max scratched his nose. "Sounds kinda crazy. Like a scene out of an Adam Sandler movie."

"Susan kicked him to the curb," Afton said softly.

"I guess," Max said. He patted his jacket for his notebook, didn't find it, and said, "Don't we have Richard Darden scheduled to come in for a second round of questioning this morning?"

"One o'clock," Thacker said. "I can't wait to hear his explanation about this—or maybe I can." The phone on his desk suddenly shrilled. "Hang on." He picked it up. "Yes, Angel?" He listened intently. "What? *Now?*" He straightened up in his chair and frowned. "Okay. Well, put her in Conference Room C. That's right, the one that looks like a big orange Creamsicle puked its guts out." Thacker hung up and shifted in his chair. "Change of plans."

"What's up?" Max asked. "Is the FBI stepping on somebody's toes?"

"No. It appears that Mrs. Darden just showed up *here*. I mean right now this minute. And she's asking to talk to the person in charge of her daughter's investigation." He cocked a finger at Max. "That would be you, my man."

"Okay." Max made a motion to stand up.

"Not so fast," Thacker said. "Susan Darden also wants to see your sidekick here." This time he pointed at Afton.

"Me?" Afton squeaked. "Why?"

"Damned if I know," Thacker said. "But I'm betting that, between the two of you, you'll wring it out of her."

SUSAN Darden wasn't so much sitting in an uncomfortable orange plastic chair as she was crouched in it. Every muscle was tensed, her normally flawless complexion was red and blotchy, and her fingers drummed relentlessly against the Formica table. Even though she was a hot mess, Afton noted that she wore a spectacular winter white pantsuit with gold braid trim.

Max held the door open for Afton as they shuffled into the room. "Hello," Max said, nodding at Susan Darden. He was according her the distant respect a mongoose might give a cobra.

"Hi," Afton said. She wasn't sure what to expect either. Would the woman go postal and start hurling invectives at her? Would she remain calm but seething? It looked like they were about to find out.

Afton and Max slid into chairs across the table from Susan.

"I appreciate your meeting with me like this," Susan said. Her lips barely moved and her voice was low and contained.

Max tipped a hand as if to say, *Go on.*

Susan cocked her head. "Obviously you heard what happened?"

"Just briefly," Afton said. Her face was fixed in a neutral position, but deep down she was dying to hear the full story.

"Why don't you tell us what happened," Max said. He was staying cucumber cool, too.

"That asshole was *cheating* on me," Susan spit out. Then, wraithlike, her face twisted with pain, she lurched forward in her chair and barked, "Richard was planning to see *her*. Our precious daughter's been kidnapped, I'm a complete basket case, and all he can think about is that little *tart*."

"We're sorry about that," Max said. "We really are. But how exactly do you think your husband's, um, extracurricular activity affects this particular situation?"

Susan paused to gather together her thoughts, and then said, "What if it's a plot?"

"A plot against you?" Afton asked.

"I don't know," Susan said. "What if Jilly took the baby? Or the two of them conspired and are holding the baby somewhere?"

"And they would do that . . . why?" Max asked. He wasn't buying the conspirator theory, but he was giving her the benefit of the doubt.

"To drive me crazy," Susan said. She twisted the ring on her right hand, an enormous moonstone set in gold. "It *is* driving me crazy. I can't eat, I can't sleep, I can't focus. All I can think about is Elizabeth Ann."

"You know we're doing our best," Max said. "We've been working in concert with the FBI, following up on a number of leads."

"I get that," Susan said. "I saw the two of you on TV last night. You were down in those woods checking to see if that poor frozen baby was Elizabeth Ann." She hesitated and then her voice grew softer. "That's when I knew that both of you cared deeply. I finally comprehended that finding my baby is important to you, too."

"We understand your pain," Afton said. "We're parents, too."

Susan pulled a hanky from her purse and dabbed at her eyes. "I thought for sure that little baby was Elizabeth Ann."

"But it wasn't," Max said. "Which really is a blessing of sorts."

"Know this," Afton said, leaning forward. "If it *had* been her, we would've called you immediately."

"Really?"

"Absolutely," Afton said. "We wouldn't have let you spend one extra second worrying if it was her or not."

"It's always better to have an answer," Susan said.

"Yes, it is," Afton said.

Everyone was quiet for a moment, and then Susan gazed at Afton and said, "You're a mom, too?"

"Yes, I have two girls," Afton said. "And Max has two boys."

"So then you know," Susan said.

"I do and I don't," Afton said. "I know the love a mother feels for her children, but I've never experienced the terrible pain you're going through right now."

"It's awful," Susan whispered.

"Tell us more about the plot," Max said.

Susan waved a hand. "I don't know that it's a legitimate plot. On the other hand, I wouldn't put it past Jilly. She's a strange girl. Very focused and driven. When she sees something she wants, she doesn't hesitate to go after it."

"And you think Jilly went after Richard?" Afton asked.

"Well . . . yes, I do," Susan said.

"You're thinking she stood a better chance with the baby out of the way?" Max asked. Susan winced at his words and Max said, "I'm sorry, but we need to be absolutely clear about this."

Susan picked at an invisible piece of lint on her lapel. "Yes, I think Jilly would stand a better chance without the baby. It's . . . The baby served an important part in keeping our marriage together."

"Okay," Max said. "That's all we need to know."

"What's that supposed to mean?" Susan asked.

"It means," Max said, "that we're going to severely sweat the two of them."

"That's the best news I've heard yet," Susan said. "But Richard is . . . well, let's just say he's honed his skills at being evasive."

"Of course he has," Max said. "He's a corporate big shot. Still, we're fairly skilled in our interview techniques. And there's always the threat of incarceration."

"That sounds good to me," Susan said. She showed a faint smile. The first one they'd seen from her.

"While we have you here," Afton said, "would you mind if we went over a few things?"

"I guess," Susan said.

Afton consulted her notes. "Are you familiar with the Wee Ones Day-care Center on France Avenue?"

Susan shook her head. "No. Why?"

"The woman who owns it had some trouble recently," Afton said.

"Concerning a child?" Susan asked.

"Actually, it was a tax issue," Afton said.

"Oh," Susan said. She looked thoughtful. "You know, I never considered taking Elizabeth Ann to day care." She curled her lip. "But I was pretty darned hot to hire a nanny. Although I hesitate to call Jilly Hudson that now. Considering . . ."

"I doubt she'll be putting nanny duties on her résumé for a long time," Max said.

Afton leaned forward and said, "If you can manage it, I'd like to hear a little bit more about the doll show lady. The one who called herself Molly."

"There's not much to tell," Susan said. "I was at the Skylark Mall buying a pink snowsuit for Elizabeth Ann and I kind of stumbled upon this doll show."

"And you met a woman named Molly who created reborn dolls," Afton said.

"Yes," Susan said. "At first it seemed a little weird, but when you see one of them, when you actually hold one in your arms, there's something . . . kind of compelling about it. Something magical."

"So you'd say this Molly was fairly polished at sales," Max said. "At drawing in customers."

"She drew me in," Susan said bitterly.

"What else can you remember about her?" Afton asked. "I know you sat down with a police artist and did an Identi-Kit sketch, but the one I saw was fairly generic. It could have applied to a lot of females in the forty-to-fifty-year age range."

"I'm sorry about that," Susan said. "My memory . . ." She touched a hand to her head. "It's terrible."

"Don't apologize," Max said. "At least it's a starting point. But what we'd really love is some little detail or snippet of information that might be lurking in your memory. Something you picked up, but haven't shared with us yet."

"I have no idea what that might be," Susan said. "I mean, I've been over this about a dozen times with the FBI. I even looked at that nanny cam footage, but it was too dark and grainy to really see anything."

"We know that," Afton said. "And we appreciate it. But if you could just scrape up a little bit more information on this Molly person. Even if you just shared your impressions, it would help us."

"Well," Susan said. "She was a thin woman and not all that attractive."

"How'd she wear her hair?" Afton asked.

"Kind of mousy and straggly. Brown, with little touches of gray."

"So your general impression was . . ." Afton prompted.

"That she'd lived kind of a hardscrabble life," Susan said slowly. "She had this careworn look about her. And her hands . . . they were rough and raw, as if she'd done a lot of hard work. Like maybe she'd worked in a factory or on a farm."

"What about her speaking voice?" Max asked.

"Fairly smooth," Susan said. "But now that you mention it, she was doing the nicey-nice thing. You know, like salesclerks do? Pretending they're your friend?"

"Did you get the impression that this woman was educated?" Afton asked.

"Just the opposite," Susan said. "In fact . . ." She stopped, tilted her head, and said, "She had that Midwestern dialect going. Kind of like those people in the movie *Fargo*. Like, when she finished a sentence, her voice kind of went up at the end. As if she was asking a question, even though she wasn't. Hmm, it's funny how I just remembered that."

"You did good," Max said.

"You did great," Afton said.

Susan gazed at them, her eyes suddenly turning red and moist. "Are you going to find my baby?"

Afton never hesitated. "Absolutely we're going to find her."

18

SPITS of ice and snow pinged the windshield of Max's car. Car exhaust boiled up around them, making it look as though they were navigating a field of hot springs in Iceland. Instead, they were blasting through the heart of downtown Minneapolis on barely plowed streets, headed for the Medical Examiner's Office.

"You shouldn't make promises like that," Max said. He reached over and turned on the radio. Taylor Swift's "Bad Blood" blared out. He curled his lip unhappily and clicked it off as they slewed wildly around a corner.

"We have to give Susan some hope," Afton said. She held a cup of coffee in her hand and was alternately trying to warm her hands, sip from it, and avoid a catastrophic spill.

"Why?" Max asked. He switched lanes and ended up directly in front of an enormous sixty-foot-long articulated bus. When the driver blasted his horn, Max simply ignored him.

"Because *we* have hope. We still believe that baby can be found."

"Maybe," Max said. They were on their way to meet with the ME about yesterday's Cannon Falls baby. Neither of them was looking forward to it. In fact, Afton was dreading it.

"Do you think this is really necessary?" she asked. "Wasn't this Cannon Falls baby case already kicked over to the FBI?"

"Yeah, I guess," Max said. He had a big plastic Super America travel mug that he was sipping from. Afton figured the coffee had to be stone-cold. "But you never know what we might find."

"You think the two cases are connected?"

"Not really."

"But you have a hunch."

"Not exactly," Max said.

"A twinkle?"

"Whatever." Max aimed the nose of his car at the opening of an unmarked parking ramp. "Here we are." They bumped into the darkness and sped past a row of dark blue state cars, then circled up two floors and found a spot.

"I was wondering," Afton said, "if I could sit in on your session with Richard Darden this afternoon?"

Max kicked open the driver's side door and frigid air swept in. "Not possible," he said. When he saw the look of disappointment on Afton's face, he added, "But I could probably arrange for you to watch the interview from behind a one-way mirror."

CROWDED into an anteroom just outside the morgue, Afton and Max grunted as they struggled with disposable gowns, gloves, and masks, trying to pull them over their street clothes. The morgue attendant, a tiny Hispanic man who seemed to speak in a perpetual hoarse whisper, supervised their transformation.

"Booties," the attendant rasped. He pointed at Afton's uncovered loafers and handed her two blue puffs of crinkly paper.

It was, of course, a wise precaution until the medical examiner got a firm handle on the cause of death. Or in case the maniac who'd murdered this poor child had transmitted any sort of communicable disease.

As the two of them shuffled awkwardly into the morgue, Afton gave an involuntary shudder. Cold, clinical surroundings never failed to depress her. And this place had it all—stark metal tables and cabinets, the inevitable sound of running water, unholy plumbing that kinked down into floor grates.

"Good morning, I'm Marie Sansevere." The medical examiner gave a perfunctory smile as she introduced herself.

Afton noted that Dr. Sansevere had a body that was beyond thin, almost bordering on anorexic. Her green scrubs hung loosely on her spare form and her pale, translucent skin looked as though she'd never seen the sun's rays, an indulgence Afton still allowed herself. Dr. Sansevere's short, cropped, Scandinavian white-blond hair was the type seldom seen outside Minnesota or Wisconsin. Afton decided the good doctor was as pale and ethereal as the bodies she worked on.

Once they'd gathered around the autopsy table, Dr. Sansevere said, "You know we only have time for a cursory look this morning?"

"Understood," Max said.

The baby lay on a waist-high aluminum autopsy table that sloped gently from top to bottom and featured drainage holes much like a kitchen colander.

"This is awful," Afton whispered to Max. He nodded back.

Dr. Sansevere began with a visual inspection of the body, dictating her observations into an overhead microphone. "Rigor mortis is well developed and livor mortis is dorsally distributed," she said in a monotone.

Afton and Max followed Dr. Sansevere around the table like a pair of ducklings as she took various swabs and blood samples. Then she put on a pair of magnifying glasses and examined the infant carefully.

"See anything?" Max asked. "Hairs or fibers?"

"A couple," Dr. Sansevere said. She touched a tweezers to the baby's right hip and extricated a strand of something. Then she turned off all the lights in the autopsy suite and switched on a black light. She focused the light about six inches from the body and moved it slowly across, then up and down. Where a few areas glowed a ghostly phosphorescent white, she stopped and took smears from those areas.

"What causes that weird glow?" Afton asked.

"Not sure," Dr. Sansevere said. "Until we run tests."

"Do you know what the cause of death was?" Afton asked.

"Not until I open her up," Dr. Sansevere said.

Max grimaced. No way did he have the stomach to stick around for that.

"She looks underweight," Afton said.

"She is," Dr. Sansevere said. "This child was malnourished." She shook her head, took a step back, and pulled off her mask. "A few months ago, I autopsied two children. The mother and the boyfriend, both crack users, had kept them locked in a closet for almost a year. The older one, the five-year-old girl, should have weighed at least sixteen kilos, but she was just under twelve. Died of starvation and pneumonia." She busied herself with her instruments. "Absolutely inhuman," she muttered.

Twelve kilos, thought Afton. That translated to about thirty-five pounds. It was heartbreaking to think that two children had been kept in a dark closet, starved to death, and never given medical attention. But over the last couple of years, she'd come to know and understand firsthand the harsh realities of the world. Terrible beasts roamed the earth, killing and wrecking havoc at will, leaving carnage in their wake. In a little cottage in North Minneapolis, she'd come face-to-face with a woman who'd fed rat poison to her sick and aging parents. Sitting handcuffed in her cheery harvest gold kitchen with matching café curtains, the woman had matter-of-factly explained to police that her parents had simply become too much of a burden for her.

YOU ready to go back to the scene of the crime?" Max asked. They were ripping off their paper suits and hastily stuffing them into a bin that was labeled, HAZARDOUS WASTE.

"What?" Afton said.

"I mean go over to Hennepin County Medical Center to talk to that babysitter, Ashley. HCMC is, like, two blocks away. We can walk there through the skyway."

"I guess," Afton said. The truth of the matter was she was dreading it. All night long she'd had troubled dreams where she'd struggled with a faceless attacker, fighting him off as his hands crept around her throat to choke her. And when she finally pushed him away and reached out to rip off his mask, there hadn't been any head at all. Just a bloody neck stump.

"It's been a couple of days since the girl has talked to the FBI," Max said casually. "Lots of times it takes that long for a witness to calm down and start remembering critical details. Look at Susan Darden, how she was able to dredge up a few impressions of that doll lady. It all helps, you know. Solving a kidnapping, a homicide, is like putting together a big fat jigsaw puzzle."

"Okay," Afton said. "But you don't want to be late for Richard Darden. You're supposed to talk to him at one."

Max squinted at his watch. "We got time. Darden can sit and spin for all I care."

ASHLEY Copeland was in a horrible mood.

"Who are you guys?" she spat at them. "And why is there a fat cop sitting outside my room?" She was ninety-six pounds of quivering rage packed into a teenage girl's body.

Afton and Max quickly introduced themselves, and then Max said, "There was a small incident here last night. We didn't want you to feel like you were in danger."

"That's the same excuse my mother gave me about being moved to a new room," Ashley said. She tossed her head, and her blond hair swished back and forth. "I want to know what kind of incident? And should I be scared?"

Afton chose to ignore her questions. "How are you feeling?"

Ashley had a small white splint on her nose and was sitting up in bed in her private room. She was covered in a paisley down quilt that was probably more Martha Stewart than standard hospital issue. Surrounding her was a clutter of gossip magazines—OK! *Magazine*, *Life & Style*, and *People*—as well as candy bar wrappers, Coke cans, an iPad, an iPhone, and a pink Hello Kitty notebook.

"That's such a stupid question," Ashley said. "Look at me. I've got three cracked ribs and I was supposed to have surgery today on my nose. Now it's been postponed." She touched a hand to the splint she was wearing.

"Everything hurts like hell and I look like the biggest freaking dork that ever walked the planet."

"It's not that bad," Max said.

"You think I'd post a selfie looking like this?" Ashley asked. "Boy, are you ever stupid."

Max threw Afton a helpless look. This wasn't going as planned. Then again, Max had two boys. He'd never dealt with the vanity, insecurities, fluctuating hormones, self-centeredness, and angst of a teenage girl.

Afton knew she had to steer the conversation onto a more manageable plane. "Other than your ribs and your nose, how are you feeling?"

Ashley touched a hand to her neck, where pink welts showed above the neckline of her flannel T-shirt. "My neck still hurts. Where that asshole lassoed me."

Afton smiled. She could relate. "But you're obviously feeling feisty."

"I guess," Ashley said. "I asked my mom if I could have my boobs done at the same time they fix my nose. You know, while I was under anesthesia. But she said no." She picked up a magazine, riffled through it hastily, and then hurled it across the room, where it smacked against the wall. "It's not fair."

"No," Max said. "None of this is."

Ashley stared at them. "My mom says you didn't find the baby yet."

"Not yet," Afton said.

"I bet you won't find her," Ashley said. "Those were really mean people who broke in and took her. They're probably going to *do* something to her."

"That's why we need your help," Afton said. "Because we're running out of time."

Ashley's brows puckered together. "What do you want from me? I'm a victim here, too."

"You certainly are," Afton said. "So we thought if we could just talk to you, ask a few questions, you might be able to nudge us in the right direction."

"But I don't *know* anything," Ashley whined.

"You were there," Afton said in what she hoped was a soothing voice. "Maybe you could kind of fill us in on what you remember."

Ashley let loose a heavy sigh. Afton and Max waited. Hoped.

Finally she said, "The pizza guy."

"Yes," Afton said. "The one who came knocking at the door that night." *And probably tried to attack you again. Only he ended up attacking me.*

"That guy was bat-shit crazy," Ashley said. "He came crashing in and smashed my face with his fist. I fell down and started bleeding really bad. It hurt like hell. I've never been in so much pain in my entire life!"

Afton nodded.

Tears filled Ashley's eyes. "I could hardly breathe, but he still climbed on top of me and tied me up. Stuck a gag in my mouth." She lowered her voice. "I think he wanted to, you know, have sex with me, 'cause he started to pull down my pants. But thank God he didn't."

"Did he say anything to you?" Max asked.

"Not really," Ashley said. "At least I don't remember anything." She frowned. "Not actual words anyway."

"But there was something," Afton prompted.

"Kind of," Ashley said. "The whole time he was tying me up, he was making this weird low-level sound. Like he was humming or something."

"You mean like a song?" Max asked.

Ashley shook her head. "No, no. More like an angry . . . insect. It was weird. Scary."

"Do you think you could identify him if we showed you a picture?" Afton asked.

Ashley shook her head. "No."

"You did an Identi-Kit, right?"

"That stupid computer drawing thing? Yeah, I did it. But I couldn't remember much about the guy. He was, like, this generic dude."

"But you were face-to-face with him," Afton said. "So you must have gotten a fleeting impression. What do you remember most?"

"Maybe his eyes," Ashley said. "They were blue, but they looked kind of vacant. Like . . . blue marbles. Just rattling around inside his head."

"Anything else?" Afton asked.

"I think he had a tat."

"A tattoo?" Max asked. "Where was it?"

"Like, on his neck."

"Could you make out what it was?"

Ashley shook her head and her hair swished back and forth like a golden curtain. "Not really."

"Part of it maybe?" Afton asked.

"I'd be guessing, but maybe an angel's wing? Or a cloud?"

"What about the other person who came in behind him?" Afton said. "Can you recall anything about her?"

"Not really," Ashley said. "I was pretty out of it by then."

"Is there anything else you can tell us about that night?" Max asked.

"Yeah," Ashley said. "Mr. Darden was a creeper."

"How so?" Afton asked.

"You know, like a lech," Ashley said. "Like he wanted to *do* me."

There was a sudden hubbub outside in the hallway, voices raised in excitement and a scramble of footsteps. Afton got up to see what was going on. She came back into Ashley's room a moment later and looked pointedly at Max. "Channel 7 just showed up."

"Oh my God!" Ashley exclaimed. "Are those the TV people? Do they want to talk to *me?*"

"I suppose," Max said. He didn't sound happy.

"I can't go on TV looking like this," Ashley squealed. "It's impossible. Wait a minute." She reached over and grabbed a hand mirror off her nightstand. Then she held it up in front of her face and carefully peeled back the bandages that held her nose splint in place. She pulled off the splint in one smooth move.

"Do you think you should be doing that?" Afton asked.

"Whatever," Ashley said, frantically combing her hair and arranging her coverlet. "Okay. Now they can come in."

Portia Bourgoyne and her camera crew brushed past Afton and Max as they came into the room.

"Try not to screw this up, too," Max said. He was in a snarly mood.

Portia blew him off royally. "Are you kidding? This kidnapping story is the best thing that ever happened to me. You think I want to work in a mid-market, jerkwater town doing fluff pieces on food shelf volunteers and polar bear plunges? This is my ticket to a network job where I can do hard news."

"Like Ebola and suicide bombers?" Afton asked. "Good luck with that."

"If you think this kid's gonna make you a network star," Max said, "you're sorely mistaken. She can barely remember her own name."

Portia just smirked. "Don't worry about me, sweetie. I've got more than one trick up my sleeve."

19

JUST as they popped out of the parking ramp, ready to head back to the department, Don Jasper, the Chicago FBI agent, called. And he sounded frantic.

"I'm over here in Woodbury," Jasper said, his voice high-pitched and strangled amid all the static. "At Synthotech. I need you to run something down for me."

"What's that?" Max asked.

"Our field office just received an anonymous tip. Somebody saw a man toss a bundle into a Dumpster down behind Rush Street Pizza at Twenty-fifth and Lyndale. You know where that is?"

"Yeah. A bundle, you say?"

"The caller thought it looked like a baby." Jasper's voice was so loud and insistent that Afton could hear his words blaring from Max's cell phone. "They're sending a black-and-white to the scene but if you could . . ."

"We're on our way," Max said. He cranked his steering wheel hard, executing a skidding U-turn right in the middle of Marquette Avenue. Cars honked, a bus jammed on its brakes and swerved, and Afton hung on for dear life. It was like being in the middle of a NASCAR race. Or if somebody really had dumped the Darden baby, it might just be a life-and-death race.

* * *

HOLY shit!" Afton cried. Skidding into the pizza restaurant's back parking lot, Max almost plowed headlong into a black-and-white cruiser as it also converged on the scene, its light bar pulsing red and blue.

"Easy, easy," Max said as he twirled the steering wheel hard and slid, nose first, into an enormous pile of plowed snow. They were still moving, in fact, as Afton flung open the passenger side door and jumped out.

She was focused on only one thing—the dark green Dumpster that was shoved up against the back of the building. It was stuffed to capacity with bags of trash, and big hunks of wet, floppy cardboard spilling over the sides. The words DARREL'S SANITATION were stenciled on the front.

Max caught up to Afton and then the two uniformed officers caught up to him.

The officer, whose name tag read PINSKY, had a hangdog face and a worried expression. "The information we got said a child might have been stuffed inside?" he asked, his breath pluming out in the cold air. "A baby? Is this the . . ."

"We hope it's not the Darden kid," Max said. He put a hand on the Dumpster and glanced around. "Somebody want to give me a boost?"

But Afton had already stuck her toe on a protruding handle and, with an agile leap, landed on top of the one metal flap that was closed. A dull clang resonated in the cold air.

"Be careful up there," the second cop cautioned her. He was younger and looked more athletic.

"Studer, get up there and help her," Pinsky ordered.

But Afton was single-mindedly focused on her mission. "I got this," she said as she bent forward and yanked open the second metal flap. The pungent odor of stale beer, rotten tomatoes, mouse droppings, and dirty socks assaulted them. Your basic sickly-sweet aroma.

Studer made a face. "Jeez."

"See anything?" Max asked.

Afton stared down at mounds of black plastic garbage bags, hunks of frozen pizza, assorted beer bottles and cans, and stacks of ripped cardboard. "Not yet." Her heart was filled with dread but she steeled herself.

This was too important to wimp out now. "I'm gonna have to . . . uh." She grabbed a fat garbage sack and tossed it out onto the snow. It landed with a heavy splat. Cardboard, beer cans, and bottles followed in quick procession as the smell got progressively worse. "I still don't see any . . . Oh shit."

"What?" Max asked. He was standing on tiptoe now, trying to peer into the Dumpster.

Afton bit down on her lower lip. Right under her right boot, stuck below a pizza box, was a dirty white blanket. *Please no.*

"There's something here," she said.

"Careful," Pinsky cautioned.

Afton reached down and gathered up the bundle. As she straightened up, her foot slipped on something slimy and one leg started to slip down into the unsteady pile of trash. She hurriedly passed the bundle to Max and caught herself on the lip of the Dumpster.

"Let's get you out of there," Studer said. He reached up to give her a helping hand.

But Afton was focused on one thing. "Is it the baby? Is it Elizabeth Ann?" she asked as she scrambled down the side. "Should we call an ambulance?"

Max carefully unwrapped the dirty blanket.

"Holy crap," Studer said, his face going slack.

They all stared wordlessly at a huge pair of blue eyes that had sunken into a cracked plastic face.

Pinsky was the first to find the words. "Holy shit, it's a broken doll. I really thought it was gonna be that dead kid."

Studer's mouth worked soundlessly for a few moments and then he croaked out, "But it almost looks like it's alive."

"That's because it's a reborn doll," Afton said.

Studer frowned. "A what?"

Afton and Max stared at each other.

"Cameras," Afton said.

Studer stowed the doll in the backseat of his squad car while Afton, Max, and Pinsky took turns ducking into the pizza place, a pet grooming business, the Pressed for Time One Hour Dry Cleaner, and the Cut &

Curl. In talking to the managers in all the businesses, they found only one shop that had a camera positioned outside. The dry cleaner.

The manager, actually the owner, was a harried-looking man who introduced himself as Joey Debow. He was skinny, had dark slicked-back hair, and looked to be in his early fifties.

When they gave him a quick rundown, and told him what they'd just discovered in the Dumpster behind the pizza place, Debow said, "This is about that missing baby, isn't it? You thought it might be that kid."

"We did," Afton said. "But now we'd like to figure out who dumped the doll. Because it's . . . well, strange."

Debow nodded and ushered them past racks of plastic-bagged clothes into his back office so they could all view his surveillance tapes.

Which really weren't tapes at all.

"It's just a motion-activated camera," Debow explained. "Duane, my sixteen-year-old, was the one who set it up for me. It just records for a couple hours, pauses, then records again over the old stuff." He sneezed hard, said, "This damn sinus drip, excuse me," then pressed a button on a small monitor. "I don't know if this will help or not, but you're more than welcome to look."

"Can you take it back to about a half hour ago?" Max asked.

Debow fiddled with some more buttons and a picture came up immediately. They watched patiently for ten minutes as a couple dozen people streamed by, and cars and buses zipped past on the street. Finally, lo and behold, there was a man dressed in an old brown coat with a ratty fur collar, a coat like immigrants sometimes wore when they came trooping through Ellis Island back in the thirties. The man was walking down Lyndale Avenue and clutching a bundle.

"Holy crap," Pinsky said. "That's gotta be your guy."

"It could be," Max said.

"The question is, why is he doing that?" Afton asked. She wondered if it was supposed to be some kind of ruse or decoy. Or, God forbid, a practice run?

Max looked at Debow. "Can we have this tape?"

"It's a CD. Go ahead and take it," Debow said, trying not to sneeze again. "Hope you find that poor baby."

* * *

WHEN they returned to the parking lot, Studer had already looped black-and-yellow crime scene tape around the Dumpster and between two light standards to cordon off the premises. "Already called in the crime scene guys," he told them.

Now they all stood around blowing out plumes of steam, stomping their feet to stay warm, and fending off a half dozen looky-loos who seemed to enjoy the leisurely pace of not having a day job.

"You realize," Afton said, "this place is, like, twelve blocks as the crow flies from Kenwood."

"Yeah," Max said, "but look around. It's a whole 'nother universe."

And he was right. This stretch of Lyndale Avenue was populated by Vietnamese green grocers, loan offices, Mexican restaurants, and thrift shops. Whereas Kenwood was old-world stone mansions clustered around picturesque Lake of the Isles, this area was strictly working class. Mom-and-pop businesses were interspersed with fading apartment buildings, duplexes, and small bungalows. It was, as a sociologist might say, still in the process of gentrification.

Max thanked the two officers, who said they'd wait there with the doll for the crime scene techs to arrive.

"Now what?" Afton asked.

"Climb in," Max said. "I got an idea." He turned down Lyndale then suddenly sliced right onto Twenty-fourth Street.

"We're taking a detour?" Afton asked.

"I want to take an extra five minutes." Max nosed along slowly, then turned down a narrow alley that was basically two churned-up ruts in six inches of packed snow.

"What are you looking for? *Who* are you looking for?"

Max pursed his lips. "Aw, just this guy I know. He's a kind of . . . contact, I guess you'd call him."

"A snitch?" Afton said.

Max lifted a shoulder. "Something like that."

"Does this guy have a name?"

"He's just known around town as The Scrounger," Max said. "Here." He slowed to a crawl and then stopped. "This is his place."

The Scrounger lived in what looked to be a shabby duplex with a falling-down three-car garage out back. The backyard was heaped with junk—tires, old bicycles, snow blowers, lawn mowers, rolls of metal fencing, railroad planks, old oil barrels, and a pile of demolished swing sets.

"This is his place of business?" Afton asked. And then, "What exactly is his business?"

"Scrounging," Max said. "He drives around in this beat-up old black pickup truck looking for stuff."

"Stuff."

"Junk that people toss into the alley. Or that's been left on the street. You name it."

"What does he do with it?" Afton said.

"I don't know, he repurposes it."

"Isn't that just a fancy name for selling scrap metal?"

"I suppose," Max said.

"How do you know this guy, or shouldn't I ask?"

"Popped him a couple years ago on a B and E. But the thing is, he's kind of a charming guy. Well spoken, reads a little William Carlos Williams, sneaks into Orchestra Hall when the good conductors drop into town."

"You took pity on this Scrounger guy because he's got taste?" Afton gazed at the junk-strewn backyard again. "Well, maybe he does when it comes to the arts."

"Let's just say we have a well-oiled quid pro quo going on."

"And you think The Scrounger might know something about that doll we just found?"

"Not that specifically," Max said. "But he's connected, he knows this neighborhood." He nodded to himself. "And maybe even the whack job who planted the doll."

20

SITTING behind a battered wooden desk at the Family Resource Center in New Richmond, Wisconsin, Marjorie Sorenson was hardly recognizable. In her long black wool skirt and prim white blouse, with her hair combed neatly back and held in place with a crisscross of bobby pins, she looked like a nun. Or at least one who'd recently kicked the habit.

Not only that, Marjorie had cleverly appropriated the demeanor of a nun. No longer the caustic, tough-talking kidnapper, she spoke to the young woman sitting across from her in a measured and thoughtful tone of voice.

At the same time, Marjorie noted that the girl was clearly frightened out of her wits. She'd come creeping into the Family Resource Center looking like a tentative rabbit, all hunched over, her face a mask of pain. She'd asked to speak with one of their counselors, and Libby Grauman, the director of the center (which was really not about family resources at all, but distinctly pro-life) had directed the girl to Marjorie.

Marjorie volunteered two mornings a week. She typed (badly), filed (haphazardly), and helped counsel the pregnant, unwed teens and twenty-somethings who came tiptoeing in. The ones who had nowhere to turn, whose boyfriends had skulked off at the mere hint of a bun in the oven.

She'd been given her role at the center because of her professed belief in the sanctity of life. But Marjorie thought of herself as a kind of wolf on the prowl. Someone who was smart, cunning, and had a discerning eye for the weak and easily manipulated. In other words, those particular young women who were more than willing to put their names on a hastily produced document and sign away their babies.

"How far along are you?" Marjorie asked. She was filling out a form as she spoke soothingly to the girl.

"Three months," said the girl, who'd identified herself as June. Just June. She wore a dowdy dress, scuffed brown boots, and a coat that was definitely of the thrift store variety.

She probably didn't have two nickels to rub together, Marjorie thought, as she kept up her gentle patter.

"And you're living at home?" Marjorie asked.

"For now," June said. "After this . . ." She patted her stomach. "I'm gonna go live somewhere else."

Marjorie didn't ask where because the girl probably hadn't figured that out yet. Maybe never would.

They'd been talking for twenty minutes and Marjorie suspected June was going to be one of the easy ones. She had that trapped-animal look about her. All she wanted was to be done with her pregnancy problem and get rid of the evidence.

"I'm so glad you found your way to us," Marjorie said, giving her a smile and revealing pink gums. "If you sign an agreement to carry your baby to full term, the Family Resource Center can guarantee that we'll find a wonderful loving home for it."

"That sounds . . . good," June said. Her boyfriend had already left for Afghanistan and her parents were ready to disown her. Living in a small farming community didn't give her a lot of options.

Marjorie dug a file folder out of her desk drawer. "Let me show you something." She pulled out a glossy color photo of an eager-looking young couple. "These are the kind of people who would love your baby as if it were their own, and give it every opportunity in the world."

June bit her lower lip and studied the photo. "They look nice."

"In fact, this particular couple," Marjorie said, "own a lovely home in Evanston, Illinois. They're both college graduates and hold down good jobs. The husband is a VP at Wells Fargo bank and the wife is currently working at an interior design firm." Marjorie smiled. The stock photo she'd pulled out of a frame from the Ben Franklin had served her well. "But as soon as they adopt, the wife wants to quit her job and devote herself to being a full-time mother."

"They sound perfect," June said as tears glistened in her eyes.

Marjorie fingered a sheaf of papers, and then slid them across the desk to June. A pen followed. "Why don't you sign this agreement right now and I'll get things rolling."

The young girl suddenly shivered, as if an ill wind had just swept in and chilled her to the bone. She paused, considered her predicament for a moment, and then slowly signed the papers. After all, what other option did she have?

MARJORIE hummed to herself as she typed up her report. Across the room, Libby Grauman stood up from her desk and slipped into her coat. She headed for the door and paused.

"I'm going to run over to the Hamburger Hut and grab some lunch. You want me to bring something back for you?"

"No thanks," Marjorie said. "I brought a bologna sandwich from home."

"Okay then." The director was gone, closing the door firmly behind her.

Marjorie waited a full five minutes. Just in case Libby came back for something. When the coast seemed to be clear, she quickly dialed a long-distance number.

After wheedling her way past two different gatekeepers, her contact came on the line. "Yes?"

"I've got three," Marjorie said.

"You've been busy. I hadn't heard from you in a while so I wondered if maybe . . ." Then, "How old?"

"I've got a three-month-old girl, one that's due any day now, and another in six months or so."

There was a long hesitation. "Three months, you say? Is this another kid from that Amish group you're hooked up with?"

"Not this one, no," Marjorie said. "In fact, she's special. Blond hair, blue eyes. The perfect baby for those fancy-pants clients of yours." When her contact didn't reply, she said, "Hey, I ain't got all day here. You want her or not?"

"A girl." There was a sharp intake of air and then her contact said, "Jesus, Marjorie. Do you really think I'm that stupid?"

"I think you're in this as deep as I am," Marjorie said, putting a touch of venom in her voice.

More breathing on the other end of the line. "It's the Darden baby, isn't it? Christ, are you crazy? It's been all over the news. The FBI was brought in to investigate!"

"So what?" Marjorie said.

"Damn it, you did this to me once before and I warned you—never again. This just leads to big problems."

"Big money, too," Marjorie said. "This is one cute kid."

"But a terrible risk." Another pause. "I don't know that our arrangement from here on is going to work out all that well."

"Then try harder," Marjorie snarled. "You have clients, I deliver. No questions asked."

"You really are crazy, you know that? You take way too many chances."

"That's my problem. I'll deal with it."

"Ah, but now you're making it *my* problem. This isn't just some abandoned kid from a crack whore. Or some bastard kid that a bunch of religious fruitcakes don't want. This is dangerous business. There could be major repercussions."

Marjorie's voice came out in a low hiss. "Don't you *dare* try to dime me out. You're just as complicit as I am. Maybe more." She thought her contact might hang up on her, but they didn't. She knew they were still on the line because she could hear wheezy breath sounds.

"Okay, okay. I want 'em," came the response. "The two little ones anyway."

"Good. Start lining up your people," Marjorie said. "Tell 'em the three-month-old is on the way, and the other one, the baby, is due any day now.

And don't forget to put a nice fat wad of cash in the mail for me. You remember the post office box number?"

"Yeah, yeah. I got it. So . . . when do we meet? When can we make the exchange for the, uh, three-month-old?"

"Soon," Marjorie said. "No more than a couple of days. I'll call you."

"Use a pay phone, okay?"

"Still don't trust me?"

"It's just the smart thing to do, Marjorie."

"Sure, whatever."

HANDS clenched, jaw working like crazy, Marjorie's contact hung up the phone.

This was the last time. Just these two private adoptions and then it was over and done with forever. The money was good . . . well, actually, the money was tremendous. It was amazing what upper-crust white-bread couples would pay for a baby. But dealing with Marjorie simply wasn't worth it. She was too unstable. Too crazy. The one time she'd set foot in the office, she'd scared the crap out of everyone.

On the other hand . . . there might be a clever way to handle this. A way to make a final bundle of money and then step away from this dirty business for good.

Yes, there was more than one way to skin a cat.

21

RICHARD Darden looked considerably different from the last time Afton had seen him. For one thing, the man had aged. Worry lines etched his face, undermining his chiseled features. And his cocksure, aloof attitude seemed washed away under the harsh, fluorescent lights of the interview room. Dressed in a pair of khakis and a wrinkled Macalester sweatshirt, Darden looked positively bedraggled, a far cry from the primped and polished business executive that he'd been a few days earlier.

Afton suspected that Darden's wardrobe malnutrition was a result of Susan Darden not allowing her husband back into the house for the rest of his clothes. Then again, the woman could hardly be blamed for drawing such a hard line. Less than a week ago, Susan had been blissfully unaware of her husband's affair with the nanny. Now his pitiful weakness had been exposed.

It was hard to fathom how Darden could possibly think of anything other than his missing child. But in Afton's limited experience, she'd noticed that high-powered, testosterone-fueled type As weren't typically tethered by the same empathic constraints that were felt by the rest of the world.

Afton sipped her coffee slowly as she stared through the one-way glass. Darden and his snake-eyed lawyer, Steve Slocum, sat on one side of a wooden table; Max was on the opposite side. Slocum had launched a pro forma protest at being kept waiting for forty-five minutes, but Max had brushed it off, remaining cool and relaxed. Still, Slocum didn't bother to mask his disdain and contempt for every question his client was asked.

Admiration swelled within Afton. She didn't think she could maintain the same confidence that Max did when faced with constant scrutiny from Slocum. Every single question Max asked was met with a curled lip and a barrage of lawyerly protests. Some of them were even in Latin.

Even now, while Max scribbled notes on his yellow legal pad, Slocum was leaning back in his chair, scrolling through his phone messages, trying to look bored, probably hoping to gain a cool upper hand.

Max reached into a file folder and pulled out a black-and-white photo. Afton recognized it as one of the stills the techies downstairs had hastily pulled from the security camera DVD they'd gotten from the dry cleaner.

"Do you know this guy?" Max asked. He held up the photo for both of them to see.

Darden barely glanced at the photo. "No, I've never seen him before in my life."

"Take another look," Max said. "Take a good look."

"My client already gave you his answer," Slocum said. "He said he doesn't know the man."

"Indulge me," Max said. "Trust me when I say this is important."

Darden glanced up and studied the photo for a few moments. "No, I . . ." Then his brows pinched together as he scanned the entire photo. "Wait a minute . . . what's that man carrying in his arms?"

"This is quite enough," Slocum said.

Max lifted a hand. "Just give your client a minute."

Darden shook his head as if he were processing the information. "Is that Al? It *can't* be Al!"

"You know him?" Max asked with some urgency.

"You *know* him?" Slocum said, surprised.

Darden shot Max a fearful glance. "Did Al take Elizabeth Ann? Is this bundle he's carrying supposed to be her?" He tapped the photo hard with an index finger. "That son of a bitch. I can't believe it." Darden clenched his fists as his face flushed pink with rage.

"Who's Al?" Slocum asked, clearly confused.

"He's our handyman," Darden said. "Well . . . really a gardener that Susan hired last fall. He raked and bundled leaves, that sort of thing." He sat back in his chair, looking shaken. "Where did you get this photo? My God, is he the one who kidnapped Elizabeth Ann?"

"We don't know that yet," Max said. "We're still pursuing a number of leads. Do you know this man's last name? Or have his address?"

"No, I don't have any of that information. But Susan probably does. Damn it! I told her never to hire scum like that. I told her. She was always so trusting and naïve, never met a stray dog she didn't want to drag home." He pounded the table with his fist. "If this is the guy, you've got to get out there and find him!"

"We will," Max said. "I promise."

"This could be *something*," Darden said, turning toward Slocum.

"Did this Al person work for you on a regular basis?" Max asked. "It would help if we had dates. If we could pinpoint exactly when he might have been at your home."

"I don't know," Darden said. "It was just that one time, I think. A couple of months ago."

"How was he referred to you?" Max asked.

Darden rubbed his eyes and said, "You can thank Susan for that. I think the guy was part of a charity that Susan was connected to. You know, like hiring ex-vets or something."

"And you don't know where he lives?" Max asked.

"I told you, no. If I did, I'd be on my way over there right now to wring his neck," Darden cried. He paused. "But if you call Susan, I'm positive she'll remember the name of the organization. It's called Graceful Nation or something like that."

"We'll do that." Max glanced at the one-way mirror.

* * *

AFTON got the message immediately. She pulled out her cell phone and called Susan Darden.

Susan Darden answered on the second ring. "Hello?" she gasped. Her breathless voice broadcast her obvious distress.

"Mrs. Darden?" Afton said. "Something's come up."

"You found her?" Susan said.

"No, I'm afraid not. But we do have a lead."

"Oh, please let this be something."

"You had a handyman, a gardener, working at your home a few months ago. A person named Al?"

"Oooh!" She let out a hoarse moan. "Al Sponger. Is he the one who took Elizabeth Ann?"

"We don't know that. But we do want to locate this person for questioning. We were hoping you might provide an address for the organization Al worked for."

"Of course!" Susan said. "Just a minute. Let me grab my . . . address book."

Afton could hear a frantic pawing of pages. Then Susan came back on the line.

"Yes, I have it right here. It's called Grateful Nation. Their address is twenty-eight fourteen Girard and . . ."

Afton carefully wrote down the name—Grateful Nation, not Graceful Nation—as well as their address and phone number. "Thank you, Mrs. Darden. We'll contact them immediately."

"And you'll let me know?" She sniffled. "As soon as you can?"

"Absolutely."

Afton thanked Susan Darden again and hung up. Then she walked out of the small room and handed the slip of paper to the uniformed officer who was stationed outside the door of the interview room. She would have loved to follow up on the lead right away, but knew Thacker would skin her alive if she did.

When Afton returned to her spot on the other side of the glass, Max was just pocketing the note and about to switch gears.

"Okay," Max said. "Tell me about Jilly Hudson."

"Detective," Slocum sighed. "I hardly think this is relevant. Unless my client is a suspect, this line of questioning is completely inappropriate. Mr. Darden is a victim here and you're attempting to compound his misery with a foolhardy line of questioning."

"Not at all," Max said. "But I've been sitting here, listening to you scrutinize every question I've asked. We have a missing child and time is running out. So unless you want to prolong this session, I suggest the two of you start answering my questions."

"No," Slocum said. "We simply can't go there."

Max shuffled a stack of papers. "It would be unfortunate if some of the local TV stations sniffed out this information on their own. This kind of shit happens, you know? They've got that relentless twenty-four-hour news monster to feed."

"Don't you threaten us!" Slocum said.

Max kept right on going. "The six o'clock news might even lead off with a picture of the lovely Jilly Hudson with a juicy story about how your poor, innocent client happened to be banging the nanny."

"Stop it," Darden said. He looked miserable.

"And how long do you think Synthotech will keep your client on staff when that shit storm starts to fly?" Max leaned back. "No, I think Richard better start explaining himself." He stared stolidly at Slocum and then at Darden.

"He's bluffing, Richard. I advise you not to answer," Slocum said.

Max flipped a hand. "Up to you, Richard. Ball's in your court."

Darden broke. "It was just a thing, okay? It didn't mean anything. It was just . . . convenient."

"Richard," Slocum said. "I have to insist—"

"Shut up!" Darden hollered. "I've lost my child, I'm losing my marriage, do you want me to lose my job, too?"

Slocum sighed and set his mouth in a grim line.

"What?" Darden said, staring at Max. He sensed there was more to come. He was right.

"Did you ever hear of new baby syndrome?" Max asked. "The baby arrives and suddenly Daddy isn't getting his REM sleep anymore. He gets tired and cranky, starts to resent all the bottle feedings and diaper duty. Then you've got people dropping in all the time to see the new baby, so it's no longer all about you. Finally, the house smells like poop from all the diapers, wifey is chronically exhausted and doesn't have time for her husband anymore, and the alpha male in the house has been permanently dethroned. Hell, it's almost justifiable when you think about it . . ."

Richard hung his head. "It wasn't like that. I love Elizabeth Ann. And Susan, too."

"Sure you do," Max said. "That's why you found yourself a new squeeze who was younger, cuter, and—"

"Where exactly are you going with this?" Darden demanded.

"That maybe you got rid of the kid yourself," Max said.

"What?" Darden's face drained of all color and he practically choked on his own tongue. "Are you serious?"

"It wouldn't be the first time something like this has happened," Max said.

"I wouldn't do that!" Darden blustered. "I *couldn't* do that. My wife and I were at the Edina Country Club with two hundred other people eating rubber chicken and drinking wine that probably came in a cardboard box on the night Elizabeth Ann was kidnapped. Why, I could give you the names of fifty people I talked to that night."

"I have no doubt you can," Max said. "You're a very smart man, Mr. Darden. And your bank account has more commas than a James Joyce novel."

"So then . . ." Darden began.

"You could have hired kidnappers," Max said.

"What do you think?" Darden said. "That I went on Craigslist so I could steal my own child? Be serious!"

Max lifted a shoulder. "You could have hired this guy Al."

Darden placed both hands flat on the table and stared earnestly into Max's eyes. "No," he said. "I didn't mastermind this kidnapping. You have to believe me."

"I want to," Max said. "I really do."

* * *

AFTON watched Max with open admiration. He was doing a masterful job. Drawing Darden out, cutting off Slocum, asking the tough questions. She was actually taking notes, writing down his sly techniques that . . .

The door to her darkened room suddenly flew open. Thacker and three of the FBI guys, Keith Sunder, Harvey Bagin, and Don Jasper, walked in. Silently, like shadows, they took their places along the window.

"How's he doing?" Jasper whispered.

Afton wasn't sure whether he meant Max or Darden, so she said, "They identified the handyman and just finished a discussion regarding the girlfriend."

"How'd all that go?" Thacker asked.

"Not very well for Darden," Afton said.

Jasper nudged Keith Sunder. "You want to go in there and make a move? Like we talked about?"

Sunder nodded. "Sure."

"What move?" Afton asked after Sunder had left.

"Just watch," Jasper said.

THE door to the interview room opened, and Keith Sunder casually strolled in.

"Excuse me, Detective," Sunder said. "I hope you don't mind if I sit in for a few minutes."

"Be my guest," Max said. If he was surprised that the FBI agent was joining them, he didn't show it. "You all know Special Agent Keith Sunder, don't you? From our local FBI office?"

Darden and Slocum grudgingly bobbed their heads.

"Good," Max said. "We were just about to move on to Mr. Darden's job status."

"Past or present?" Sunder asked.

"Let's focus on the past," Max said. "Novamed. You had a nice salary there with plenty of fancy benefits and stock options. A pretty sweet deal." He paused. "Why'd you leave?"

Sunder leaned forward in his chair. "And why is your ex-employer so closemouthed about your departure?"

Darden didn't answer. He just stared at the floor and unconsciously jiggled a foot. Afton recognized it as a classic stall pose.

"We're waiting, Mr. Darden," Max said.

The silence in the room was palpable. Even Afton could feel it through the glass. She wondered if there'd been mismanagement of funds or too many golf junkets on company time.

Finally Darden said, "It was time to move on."

"And it's blatantly obvious that you did," Max said. "The question remains, *why* you chose to move on."

"What happened over there?" Sunder asked. "Were you caught stealing proprietary information?"

Darden gave a disdainful snort. "I wouldn't do that."

"Help us out here," Max said.

Darden lifted his head and said, "There was sexual misconduct."

"An affair," Sunder said.

"There was no affair," Darden said. "Just an implication of sexual harassment."

"Who'd you harass?" Max asked. "Who was the woman?"

Darden cocked his head and gave Max an incredulous look. "What? No, you've got it all wrong. It was a woman who was pressuring me!"

"What?" Max said. Now it was his turn to look surprised. "What woman? Who?"

At which point Slocum interceded. "That's not relevant," he said smoothly. "The issue is over and done with and there are sealed documents for both parties. Mr. Darden has cooperated with you voluntarily. Now, if you need any more information, you're going to have to obtain a subpoena."

"We can do that," Max said pleasantly.

"Richard?" Slocum said. He stood up and cocked his head toward the door. But Darden remained seated.

"You're going to find this guy, Al, right?" Darden asked Max. "You're going to bring him in and question him like crazy?"

"Right away," Max said.

"If he dared to take Elizabeth Ann . . ." Darden clenched his fists and got to his feet. As he stumbled toward Slocum, he looked like a man who was completely defeated.

CRAP on a cracker," Thacker burst out from where they were seated. "He was carrying on with another woman? What is this guy, some kind of modern-day Don Juan?"

But Afton was studying Darden as he shuffled out of the room. "I don't think he stole his own baby," she said softly.

"What?" Jasper said, turning toward her. "What'd you say?"

"I think Darden's a lech and an arrogant jerk," Afton said, with more assurance in her voice now. "But he's no kidnapper."

"He *looks* guilty enough," Thacker said. "He could have hired this guy Al to do the job for him. Maybe Al was the guy you tangled with last night."

No, Afton thought. Darden's demeanor and posture told her he was a broken man. Though he was floundering in an ocean of self-pity, she doubted that he'd masterminded the kidnapping. Or had a hand in last night's attack.

"We gotta huddle with Max," Thacker said. "See if he wants us to send in a SWAT team to grab this guy Al."

"Al Sponger," Afton said.

Thacker and Bagin filed out, leaving Don Jasper behind. He fixed Afton with an inquisitive look.

"What?" she asked. She was afraid he was going to lay a mild flirt on her, hit on her. Or did a part of her *want* him to hit on her?

"Try not to lose that empathy," Jasper said. "The best investigators retain their humanity despite having to endure a daily trudge through the mud. As long as you can wipe your feet off at the end of the day and remain human, you're doing okay. Better than okay."

"You think?" Afton said. She was feeling a little forlorn. None of this had been pretty.

Jasper gave her a wink. "I know."

22

THE drive down Hennepin Avenue was sloppy and slow. Slush spattered the windshield as Afton navigated her Lincoln past a hodgepodge of mom-and-pop businesses set alongside slick national chain stores. She was glad she'd offered to drive, even though she was feeling tense. Max had decided that the two of them would go in and talk with Al Sponger. SWAT would hang back and keep their distance unless needed.

"Has Sponger been popped before?" Afton asked. She meant arrested.

Max shook his head. "No. But he did six months at Saint Peter." Saint Peter was a state mental institution.

"And now he's at a halfway house."

"Yup. It's our lucky day."

They'd just crept across Twenty-sixth Street when Afton saw flashing lights up ahead.

"Accident," she said. "I'm gonna turn left at the next street."

"Huh?" Max grunted. He'd been busy reviewing notes from the Richard Darden interview. "Okay . . . sure."

"The SWAT van's still behind us?"

Max glanced back over his shoulder. "Yes."

"Good." Afton wasn't as confident about confronting Al Sponger as

Max was. If Sponger had, in fact, kidnapped the Darden baby, then it was possible that he was the man who'd attacked her last night.

Heading into what was known as the Wedge, that slice of pie-shaped real estate between Hennepin and Lyndale Avenue, Afton sighed at the shrinking roadway. As snow continued to accumulate, each pass from the city's snow-plows left more and more snow piled up along the curb. By the time March rolled around, the streets would be as narrow and carved as a bobsled run.

"What's the address again?" Afton asked. Her nerves were fizzing, her stomach turning flip-flops.

Max fumbled for the note Afton has passed on to him earlier. "Twenty-eight fourteen Girard," he said. "It's some kind of halfway house for vets."

"You think Sponger still lives there?"

"When I called fifteen minutes ago, the director said so. Or at least the guy showed up for supper two nights ago."

"But you warned the director not to tell Sponger that we were gonna drop by."

"That's right. Always nice to have the element of surprise on your side."

Afton swung right on Girard and crawled along for a couple of blocks. "I think that's it up ahead on the right."

"Drive slow," Max said.

"If I drive any slower, I'm gonna get a parking ticket," Afton said.

"Okay, okay."

Max was keyed up, too, and Afton knew it. This could be the break they needed. Thacker had wanted to go in with full SWAT, but Max had persuaded him to hold off, to have them stand by. The SWAT team with their bang sticks and smoke bombs could always come later.

"This is it," Max said.

Afton turned into a semicircular drive outside a three-story white stucco house with two dormers that overlooked the street. Ahead of them, a large white passenger van with DEAN'S HOUSE stenciled in red on the side blocked the rest of the drive.

"Here we go," Max said. His right hand crept unconsciously to the Glock G43 he wore in his shoulder harness.

They climbed the front steps, pulled open a rickety door, and found themselves inside a screen porch. There were three battered lawn chairs and a tippy-looking table that held half-filled disposable cups of coffee and an overflowing ashtray.

Softly kicking snow from their boots, they pushed open the main door of the halfway house and went in. The place wasn't exactly homey, but it wasn't terrible either. Directly ahead was a wooden front desk with a honeycomb of open mailboxes behind it, like you might see in an old European hotel. Off to the left was an empty parlor with a circle of folding chairs, presumably some kind of meeting room. To the right was a large room with two overstuffed sofas, various mismatched easy chairs, and two dilapidated wheelchairs. A TV was on and three men were huddled in front of it, watching a reality show where two women snarled at each other over the paternity of their "baby daddy."

Max walked up to the front desk and rang an old-fashioned bell. "Anybody home?" he called out.

A door opened and a skinny guy emerged from a small, messy office. He was mid-fifties, balding, wore gold wire-rimmed glasses, and was dressed in a pair of green army slacks and a 1991 Twins World Series T-shirt. "Help you?" he said.

"Minneapolis Police," Afton said, while Max held up his ID.

"Tom Showles?" Max asked.

Showles nodded and tugged at his pants, which seemed to be slowly slipping down around his hips. "That's me. I'm the director." He lifted a hand in a cautionary gesture and said, "We don't want any trouble."

Afton thought Showles looked underpaid, underfed, and under pressure.

"Neither do we," Max said.

"Is Aldous Sponger here?" Afton asked. "We need to speak with him."

Showles looked worried. "May I ask why?"

"Like I told you on the phone, it's just a formality," Max said. Which was copspeak for, *Get his sorry ass out here.*

"He was seen disposing of a package in a Dumpster off Lyndale Avenue," Afton explained.

Now Showles looked confused. "You're here because Al was involved in clandestine dumping?"

"Just point me toward his room, okay?" Max said.

"Room 303. Top of the stairs," Showles said. "But I'm not sure he's here."

"Where is he?" Afton asked.

Showles shifted from one foot to the other. "I don't keep strict tabs on the men. We operate on the honor system here."

"Yeah?" Max said. "How's that working out?"

"Mr. Sponger maintains fairly well when he stays on his meds."

"What meds is he on?" Max asked.

Showles looked nervous. "I believe he takes chlorpromazine and Risperdal."

"Heavy duty," Afton said. This was not good news.

"He's only experienced two psychotic breaks that I know of," Showles said. "Since he's been here anyway."

"Is this guy dangerous?" Max asked.

"I don't think so."

"But you don't really know," Max said.

Afton and Max clumped up two narrow sets of stairs, Showles deciding to huff along behind them. They stopped outside Room 303 and Max wiggled a finger at Afton.

She knocked on the door and said in a pleasant, lilting voice, "Mr. Sponger? Are you in there?"

No answer.

Max stepped in and rapped harder on the door. "Mr. Sponger. Sir, we'd like to talk to you, please."

Again nothing.

"Like I said, he might not be here right now," Showles told them. "Sometimes he's gone for a while. Hanging out at the library or down by the old railroad track."

"The railroad track?" Afton said.

"Sponger used to live down there," Showles said. "Before they paved it over and turned it into a bike trail. Back when he was drinking, before we took him in here. He'd hunker up under one of the bridges. Sometimes Al . . . well, he gets the urge to go back."

"Let's take a look in his room," Max said. He reached for the doorknob and turned it. It was locked.

Afton gazed at Showles. "I presume you are the keeper of the master key?"

"I'm still not sure if I should let you people in," Showles said.

"If you think we need a warrant," Max said, "just say the word."

Showles sighed and pulled out a ring of keys. The first key he tried didn't work; the second one did.

As the door swung open, Max reached out and grabbed Showles by the shoulder, muscling him aside. Then Max stepped into the room, swiveled his head around, and waved Afton in after him.

The small white room was no larger than an eight-by-ten jail cell, but it was neat and clean. The narrow bed was made and covered with a threadbare white chenille bedspread, the folds razor-sharp. A small desk held a stack of old *City Pages* newspapers, a mug filled with pens and colored markers, and a small plastic Batman figure, the kind you'd get from a fast-food place.

"Tidy," Max said.

"Monastic," Afton said. There was a small closet but it was minus a door. A dozen articles of clothing dangled from wire hangers.

"Not much to see," Showles said. "He lives a fairly quiet existence. Which is why I'm surprised you . . ."

Afton moved swiftly toward a series of pictures pinned to the wall and tapped one with a finger. "Is Mr. Sponger religious?"

Showles thought for a moment and then shook his head. "Not particularly. We have prayer circle, but . . ."

"Whatcha got?" Max asked.

"These pictures," Afton said. She was slowly recalling the one art history class she'd taken at the University of Minnesota. "They're bits and snips from Renaissance paintings. In fact, they look as if they were probably cut from an art book."

Max stared at the pictures and frowned. "Angels. Huh."

"They're actually cherubs," Afton said. "Painted by Raphael." She was starting to get a bad feeling in the pit of her stomach.

Max sucked in air through his front teeth as he studied the pictures a second time. "They're babies, really. Little blond babies." He shifted his gaze to Showles. "Where'd you say Sponger liked to hang out?"

"It's cold, so he might be at the library . . . a few blocks over."

"Walker Library," Afton snapped. "Let's go."

WALKER Library wasn't the most popular spot this Tuesday afternoon. They pulled into one of a dozen empty parking spots, next to a bicycle outfitted with studded tires and chained to an iced-up drain spout.

Their footsteps were loud and determined as they crunched across a layer of rock salt that the library's maintenance staff had probably laid down to melt the ice.

"SWAT is still backing us up?" Afton asked. Her nervousness had turned to fear. Tom Showles's mention of Sponger's psychotic breaks didn't sit well with her.

"I told 'em to stay back," Max said as they muscled their way into the newly spiffed-up library. "Unless I make the call. Then they'll come running." Two men and a frizzy-haired woman were huddled at the front desk sorting books. They barely afforded them a glance as they breezed past.

Afton figured this was good. Get in, find their man, and get out. Let the chips fall where they may. And if they had to bring in the SWAT guys, so be it.

"You circle right, I'll go left," Max said. "Be careful."

"I will."

Afton slipped off to the right, edging between the outside wall and the first set of tall, metal bookshelves. She decided she'd do a methodical search, up one aisle, then down another. She stepped along briskly, got to the end, turned a corner, and glanced at a small sign. She was in nonfiction, in a section that went from Relationships to Zoroastrianism.

Not surprisingly, nobody was browsing books in this particular aisle. No problem. This was a sprawling library and she still had lots of aisles to cover. She ghosted along, covering two, then three more aisles. No sign of Sponger. Turning a corner, she emerged into a common area. One man in a suit sat with his back to her, doing a hunt-and-peck number on his laptop computer. A young mother paged through a magazine while her toddler slept in a stroller. Another young woman, a student perhaps, read a Joan Didion novel, making occasional notes.

Sponger wasn't here.

Okay, just keep going.

Afton was in fiction now, moving along, a few book titles that she'd always wanted to read catching her eye. She turned the corner and . . . boom.

Sitting on the floor, bent over a large book, was a man in a ratty gray parka, brown stocking cap, and dirty Sorel boots. He was frowning and muttering to himself. Was this Sponger? Had to be—he looked an awful lot like the guy from the photo. She just hoped he'd remembered to swallow his little pink pills this morning.

Afton backed out of the aisle slowly and went off in search of Max. She found him lurking in the Business section.

"Sponger's here," she told him. "Maybe ten rows over. In Fiction."

Max's eyebrows rose in twin arcs. "Show me."

They dodged around shelves and tiptoed down a row of books just one aisle over from where Sponger was sitting. Afton pulled a book off a shelf and Max peered through the empty space. He nodded when he caught sight of Sponger's face. He recognized him, too.

"Wait here," Max whispered. He walked to the far wall, paused for a moment, and then dove around toward Sponger.

Sponger saw him coming and exploded like he'd been fired from a cannon. He leapt to his feet, squirted away from Max, and almost ran smack dab into Afton, who had headed around the other way.

"Hey!" Afton cried as Sponger skittered past her, wild-eyed and screeching, his arms flapping like an angry bird. She flailed out, trying to grab hold of him, but her fingertips only brushed the tail end of his coat.

"Noooo!" Sponger screamed as he raced through the common area.

Chairs flew, stacks of magazines toppled, a row of CDs went down like dominoes. Sponger grabbed a metal chair, tossed it back at them.

Afton leapt over the fallen chair, but heard a crashing sound and then Max swearing behind her. He hadn't cleared it.

"Call SWAT!" Afton cried. She pounded out the front door after Sponger and skidded to a stop. Her eyes darted up and down the street, trying to figure out which direction he might have run. Finally, she caught sight of him.

Sponger had dodged his way across Hennepin Avenue through fairly heavy traffic and was on the far sidewalk running north.

"Police! Stop!" Afton shouted, but Sponger ignored her. Scared but determined, she dove into traffic, was almost bullied back by a big black SUV with an aggressive driver and a honking horn, but managed to skitter across the street anyway. Sponger might have had a running start, but Afton had something to prove. If this was the guy who attacked her last night, she was out for revenge. *Gonna run this asshole down,* she told herself, *kick him in the balls, grab him by the throat, and not let go no matter what.*

Pushing herself, Afton sprinted after him. Up ahead of her, Sponger might have looked awkward and gawky, but he was setting a blistering pace. No problem. She was prepared to chase him forever. All the way into downtown Minneapolis if need be. Or until the guys in the black van showed up to take him down.

Which was why Afton was completely shocked when Sponger suddenly squirted off to his right and fled down a narrow, barely plowed alley that looked like a cul-de-sac.

Afton pumped harder, raggedly sucking cold air into her lungs, her legs driving like pistons as she followed him.

Sponger stumbled, turned to look back over his shoulder, and saw her coming. That's when things went a little crazy. He zigzagged toward a pile of snow, seemed to hesitate for one frozen moment, and then tumbled forward and disappeared completely.

What?

Ten seconds later, Afton pulled up short and stared down a steep, snow-covered embankment. There he was, running below her on a trail. Like a fox who'd gone to ground, Sponger had slithered his way down into the deep trench that was known as the Midtown Greenway. Dug over one hundred years ago as a railroad corridor, it was now a paved road for bicycle and pedestrian traffic. But this time of day, in the dead of winter with the sun making an early descent, the roadway was deserted, icy, and cold. It yawned into the distance for miles, snaking under dozens of old bridges and offering myriad places to hide.

Still, Sponger didn't have that much of a lead on her. Afton hurled herself over the side in what she hoped would be a controlled descent down the fifty-foot-high embankment. Feet set wide apart, she kicked up twin rooster tails of snow that blew back into her face and mouth. Slipping and sliding her way down the hill, she mentally prepared herself for a hard landing. As she hit bottom, she slewed to one side, rolled once, then recovered and bounced to her feet. Within seconds, she took off down the trail after Sponger.

"Sponger!" Afton shouted. She was cold and wet and angry as hell. She also knew this was a terrible place to be stuck. Even though she was running through the heart of the city, the hostile landscape felt more like something out of a nuclear winter. Enormous dark trees rose up on each side of her, their bare branches rattling in the wind like old bones. There were huge piles of snow-covered rubble everywhere, and the sheer depth of the trench deadened all sound.

Sponger heard her call out. He half turned, flapped his arms, and promptly fell down.

Afton renewed her efforts. "Stop!" she cried. "Minneapolis Police!"

Sponger struggled to his feet and headed directly for one of the old bridges that arched over the trail. When he disappeared into the shadows, Afton slowed her pace. She pulled out her cell phone and punched in Max's number.

"Where are you?" His voice was urgent, angry.

"Down on that Midtown Greenway trail," she told him. "Sponger just went under the Fremont Street bridge." She fought to catch her breath. "I've been chasing him."

"Keep an eye out," Max said. "But do *not* try to apprehend him. SWAT's on its way."

"Hope so," Afton murmured as she clicked off. She continued to walk slowly toward the bridge, shivering a little now. Her shot of adrenaline had worn off and the jitters had taken over. She stopped just short of the bridge and peered in, hoping to catch sight of him.

Damn, she couldn't see Sponger lurking anywhere in the shadows. She crept under the bridge, where it was dark and the cold seemed even more brutal. Had he found a hidey-hole up among the stones and network of wrought iron? Or had he clambered all the way to the top of the embankment and found a sneaky way out of this old corridor?

Afton was debating what to do when she heard a low hiss, like an angry alligator. She spun around just in time to see Sponger pop out from behind a jagged hunk of stone.

"What do you want, girl?" Sponger snarled.

There was murder in his eye, and a hunting knife clutched in his right hand.

Afton felt her guts tighten. She backed away from him. "Take it easy. I'm not here to hurt you."

Sponger turned the blade sideways and said, "I hurt *you*."

Afton turned on her heels and ran. Without hesitation, she scrambled up the steep stone abutment that reinforced the old bridge. The stones were slippery and icy, but she moved carefully, knowing any misstep could cost her.

Hurry, hurry! Her brain beat out an urgent mantra as she heard him panting and scuttling noisily behind her.

When Afton was at the very top of the abutment, tucked way under the span of the bridge, she twisted around. Sponger was some twenty feet below her, doing his best to climb after her, but picking his way tentatively. Like some kind of crazy-ass pirate, he held his knife in his mouth as he clung to stones with his bare hands, pulling himself up, struggling and grunting to find basic toeholds.

Overhead, traffic rumbled on the bridge. Down here there was nobody around.

And Afton had no weapon.

Fear welled up inside her as she searched for something . . . anything to defend herself with. Her eyes caught sight of a narrow piece of rusted metal just above her. It was a bent piece of the bridge's framework that stuck out about three feet.

Could she grab it in time? Could she even work it free?

Afton sidestepped her way across the narrow stone platform and grasped hold of the metal bar. One end was still loosely riveted to the struts of the old bridge. She jerked at the metal bar and pulled hard. Nothing doing. She glanced down and saw that Sponger was getting closer. She didn't have much time. She could ditch out of here, try to slide down, and then make a run for it. Or she could stay here and make her stand.

Grasping the metal bar with both hands, she wiggled and seesawed it back and forth. It remained attached with only one loose weld. If she could just pop it free . . .

Sponger moved closer, growling, scrabbling upward, as Afton worked frantically. She had one eye on the metal bar that was bending much freer in her hands now. But Sponger had stuck a tentative foot on the cement shelf and was moving toward her, crab-stepping like a demonic circus performer in some high-wire act.

Metal flakes flew into her eyes as Afton gave the hunk of rusted metal one last tug. And it suddenly came loose!

Like Buster Posey swinging at a fastball, Afton whipped the metal bar at Sponger's head. And connected hard. Hit him dead center in the forehead.

Thwock!

There was the sickening sound of ripping flesh, a light spray of blood, and then Sponger let loose a high-pitched scream as the knife flew out of his mouth and his eyes rolled back in his head. He dropped to his knees, managed a clumsy half twist, and then lost it completely. His fingernails fought for purchase, but it was too late. He went sliding down the bridge embankment on his belly, his chin bumping every rocky protrusion along the way. Thin, reedy cries shattered the silence. His knife clinked and clattered its way down the ragged stones alongside him. Then Sponger hit bottom and cartwheeled to a stop.

That's when the cavalry finally showed up. The SWAT team was suddenly there in full force, garbed in black, wearing protective armor. They scrambled all over Sponger. They hoisted him up, shook him like a rag doll, and then forced him to his knees. One officer wrenched his hands behind his back, another bent over and picked up the knife.

"You okay up there?" one of the SWAT guys called to Afton.

She was crouched on her heels, trying to still her quaking heart and quiet her breathing. Yeah, she thought she was okay. But talk about your on-the-job training.

"I'm fine," Afton called out. "I'm coming down." She dropped into a crouch, lifted her heels, and bumped her way down on her backside.

Then Max was there, angry and apologetic all at once. "I had no idea," he sputtered. "We should have gone in full force."

Afton held up a hand. "It's okay." Max seemed more upset than she was. Or maybe she was just getting used to having close calls. "Really, I'm just fine."

Sponger was whimpering and straining to pull himself into a tight little ball.

"Don't hurt me," he cried. "I didn't do nothin'. I didn't hurt nobody." His eyes rolled pitifully in his head and his chin quivered as if he were about to cry. Blood streamed from his nose, his lips were scuffed and bleeding.

"Then why'd you run away from us?" Max asked.

"Why'd you pull the damn knife?" Afton barked at him. She had to restrain herself from smacking him upside the head. "All we wanted to do was ask you some questions."

"You're from the military?" Sponger blubbered. He tried to press his hands against his head. "You'll put metal clamps on my head to read my thoughts."

Max snapped his fingers in front of Sponger's face. "Hey. Dude. Pay attention. We're Minneapolis Police."

"What?" Sponger shook his head, still looking mistrustful. "Why?"

"Why?" Max said. "He wants to know why."

"It's not him," Afton said to Max in a low voice.

Max frowned at her. "What?"

"It's not the guy from last night."

"You're sure?"

"That guy was a maniac," Afton said. "Sponger just seems . . . deficient."

"Damn."

Sponger looked miserable. "Don't hurt me," he whimpered again.

"Oh, for shit's sake," Afton said. She kicked a hunk of ice and sent it flying. "We just want to ask a few questions."

"We want to know about the doll," Max said.

"Doll?" Sponger said. He glanced around, blinking like mad, working his mouth soundlessly. He seemed to be hoping that the SWAT team guys would jump in and lend a hand. They didn't.

"We caught you on a security camera dumping a doll in the trash outside Rush Street Pizza," Max said.

"The doll?" Sponger's eyes seemed to focus a little better. "That's what this is about?"

"Now you're catching on," Max said.

"Where'd you get it?" Afton asked.

Sponger ducked his head. "I bought it. I got money."

"Where?" Max said.

Sponger sniffled, then said, "This guy I know over on Chicago Avenue. I knew him from before, when I lived in a different place."

"And this guy sells dolls?" Max asked.

"He sells secondhand stuff."

"You mean stuff that's hot?" Max asked. "Stolen?"

Sponger's eyes shifted away from him. "I don't know," he mumbled.

"Okay," Afton said. "You bought the doll because . . ."

"I got a little girl," Sponger said. His face softened until he looked almost normal. "I haven't seen her in . . . hell, I don't know how long. Her mom and I had problems." He bit his lower lip and then said, "Okay, the problems were mostly me." He tapped an index finger against the side of his head. "You know?"

"Keep talking," Afton said.

"Anyway, I bought the doll as a present for my kid . . . her name is Jennifer. Jennie. I got all cleaned up and went over there to see her."

"Then what happened?" Max asked.

"I get to the door and Holly, that's my ex-wife, she says I should have called first. She gets all pissed off and says that I can't see Jennie right now. I told her I brought my little girl a nice present and couldn't I just see her for a couple of minutes." He shivered. "But Holly laughed in my face." Sponger dropped his head and his eyes welled up with tears. "Same old shit, same old Holly. Nothing's ever good enough." Fat tears coursed down his cheeks.

Afton sighed deeply. Sponger wasn't making up his story. This had really happened. She gazed at the western sky, which had darkened into a palette of purple and gray-blue.

"So why'd you pitch the doll?" Max asked.

"What the hell was I supposed to do? I don't know, I just tossed it away. Pitched it in the Dumpster. Just like my life. Just . . . garbage. It's all freaking garbage, man."

"Why do you have pictures of cherubs on your wall?" Afton asked.

"Cherubs?"

"Angels," Afton said.

Sponger gazed at her with red, puffy eyes. "Because they're pretty. I found 'em in an art book somebody threw out."

"Take him downtown," Max said. He sounded profoundly disappointed. "Book him."

"What's the charge?" one of the SWAT team officers asked.

"I don't know," Max said. "Figure something out."

23

HE'S definitely not the guy from last night," Afton said on the drive back downtown. "That guy was stronger and more aggressive, always on the attack. Sponger was angry but pathetic."

"Another lost soul," Max said. "Or asshole, depending on which side of the fence you're on."

"So what happens now?"

"Sponger spends the night in jail, probably gets released tomorrow. We put him under surveillance for a couple of days, just to make sure. Ah . . . let me make a couple of calls to let everybody know what the hell just happened." Max pulled out his phone and growled into it as they cruised past Walker Art Center. Just off to the right, Afton could see two cross-country skiers gliding along, making fresh tracks in the snow as they rounded the pond in Loring Park. A picturesque scene set against the stark gray Minneapolis skyline.

Back at police headquarters, Don Jasper had called a hasty meeting to brief everyone on his second interview with Jilly Hudson. Afton stopped by her desk, hung up her coat, downed two Tylenol, and retrieved the yellow notepad she'd been using since the start of the investigation. To the outside eye, Max may have looked like the epitome of the tough-talking, running-on-gut-instinct-alone detective. Truth was, Max was detail-oriented to the point of being OCD. He kept painstaking notes that he pored over relentlessly. He'd made her take the same notes, even if their observations overlapped. It was Max's firm belief that it was the small, obscure facts that often broke an investigation wide open.

Afton stepped into the conference room and saw that Max, Thacker, Don Jasper, Andy Farmer, and Keith Sunder were already there. She took a seat next to Max, as the third local FBI agent, Harvey Bagin, hurried in to join them.

"So I understand Mr. Sponger is over in booking?" Thacker said to Max.

"That's right," Max said. He'd done a little tap-dancing concerning their story, hadn't told Thacker how much Afton had really been involved.

"But you don't think there's anything there?"

Max shook his head. "Doubtful." He was barely hiding his disappointment. "Maybe something you can throw to the media."

Thacker glanced at Farmer. "You take a run at him, too, okay?"

"I'll give it a shot," Farmer said.

"Then everybody write up their reports all nice and neat," Thacker said. "The mayor's office is starting to exert a ton of pressure."

Max glanced over at Afton, who immediately began jotting notes.

"The media is keeping pressure on, too," Bagin said. "They want to know if we're any closer to finding the kidnapper."

"Screw the media," Thacker said. "When we know, they'll know."

"All right," Jasper said, glancing around the table. "Let's get to it. Bagin and I just did a second interview with Jilly Hudson."

"How'd that go?" Thacker asked.

"This time she was lawyered up," Jasper said. "We showed up at her parents' house, a humongous Cape Cod overlooking a thousand feet of rip-rapped shoreline on Lake Minnetonka, and her lawyer was there to greet us."

"Actually," Bagin said, "it was her father's lawyer. Her father is some big muckety-muck vice president with Randall Manufacturing."

"Did she admit to the affair with Darden?" Max asked.

"Admit to it?" Jasper said. "The girl thinks they're going to get *married*.

She did everything but show us her trousseau. I don't know if she's delusional or . . ."

"In love?" Afton said. When they all turned to look at her, she said, "Face it, Darden led her on." Jasper cleared his throat, a noise that may or may not have been meant as commentary, so she continued. "Look at the facts. She's a young grad student who Darden hired as a nanny. He brought her into his home, flirted with her, and probably made all sorts of promises."

"And he slept with her," Max said.

"Exactly," Afton said. She tapped her pen against the cover of her notepad. "Beside the fact that Jilly's tearing pages out of *Brides* magazine, what did she say about the baby? About Elizabeth Ann?"

"The thing I found most interesting," Jasper said, "aside from the fact that Ms. Hudson was unapologetic about her affair, was that she seemed genuinely fond of the baby. In fact, she was horrified that someone was able to waltz in and kidnap the child."

"And we still don't see Hudson as having a hand in that?" Thacker asked.

"It doesn't seem like it," Jasper said. "She's still going to school, gets good grades, and lives with two other roommates over near the university."

"And she has an alibi," Bagin said. "She was with her parents the night the Darden baby was kidnapped."

"The three of them were home alone?" Max asked.

"No," Bagin said, "they were having dinner at Somerset's out on Lake Minnetonka." He sat back in his chair. "This is the second interview we did with Jilly Hudson and she still comes up a big fat zero."

"And the first time was?" Thacker asked.

"Sunday afternoon, right after the Dardens gave us a list of all the people they'd been in contact with for the past six months."

"But two days ago you didn't know about the affair," Afton said.

"No, we did not," Bagin said. "Nor did we suspect it. Ms. Hudson expressed shock at the kidnapping but could offer no information at all."

"What about her relationship with the baby?" Afton asked. "If she genuinely liked the child, she probably felt naturally protective of her."

Bagin stared at her. "By that you mean . . ."

"Did she take the baby out for walks? Did she notice anyone giving them an unusual amount of attention? Was there a creepy neighbor or a UPS guy who got a little too chummy?"

Don Jasper smiled at her. "You've got kids."

"Two kids, yeah," Afton said.

"Sounds like you should have been along today," Jasper said.

"I'd be happy to take another run at Hudson if you want me to," Afton said. She'd pin Jilly Hudson's ears to the wall if it meant helping to find that baby.

Thacker held up a hand to interrupt. "No, no, we still have a number of other people to interview. And Farmer has to brief us on Binger."

"Binger . . ." Jasper said.

"He's the guy Darden fired over at Novamed," Thacker said. He nodded at Farmer. "Okay, you're on."

Farmer droned on about Bob Binger while Afton thought about Richard Darden and Al Sponger. She was fairly confident that neither of them had anything to do with the kidnapping, yet she knew they would continue to be scrutinized. No, there was someone else out there who had that poor baby in their clutches. Was it the man who'd attacked her at the hospital last night? Who, she assumed, had really come to attack Ashley Copeland? Or was it the woman from the doll show? Those were the two people who plucked at the strings in her mind. But how . . . how in hell were they going to find them?

When the meeting finally broke up, they'd worked out a sort of strategy. The FBI would continue to pursue the people on the list that Susan and Richard Darden had given them this past Sunday, as well as reinterview the babysitter, Ashley Copeland, and her mother, Monica Copeland, who worked as an administrative assistant to Darden. Max would keep an eye on Sponger and swing back to Novamed to see what he could find out about Darden's harassment case.

"That could be something," Thacker said.

"What do we know about this woman?" Afton asked.

"She lives in Woodbury and she has a teenage son," Thacker said.

Teenage son, Afton thought. *Interesting.*

If there was time and it seemed warranted, Thacker also wanted Max to make a second run at Binger. Afton, who'd seemingly reestablished good rapport with Susan Darden, would stay on as Max's assistant. For now anyway.

Thacker seemed generally displeased with how little they'd all come up with, and seemed stretched thin with honchoing several other investigations.

"How's that pharmaceutical thing coming?" Max asked him as they walked out of the room.

Thacker shook his head and blew out a glut of air. "Morelli's either working his ass off, or he's already solved the case and is kicking back on twenty milligrams of black market Valium."

"Sounds like a plan," Max said.

SUNSET during a Minnesota winter comes early. So with just a thin red line banding the horizon, Afton pulled into her garage. She was tired from what had been a long day, but she was revved up, too. How often did a girl get to chase down an actual perp? Or sit in a brainstorming session with honest-to-goodness FBI agents? For her it had been never. Until today, that is.

Yes, she was sore from her chase with Sponger. Yes, her head was swimming from taking notes and asking questions. But a couple more Tylenol tablets and a hot cup of chamomile tea would help ease her aches and pains. And dinner with Poppy and Tess would clear her head and take care of everything else. After all, this was their burger and beans night.

Poppy and Tess were sprawled at the kitchen table doing their homework when Afton stepped through the back door. Then pens, tablets, and backpacks went flying as the girls threw themselves at her. And once Afton had administered a copious amount of hugs, kisses, and grins, she laughed to see that Bonaparte was crowding in, too. The little dog was prancing and dancing and not a bit shy.

How fast the little guy had fit into their family, Afton decided. How easy it was for dogs, how difficult it was for so many people.

"Where's Aunt Alisha?" Afton asked.

"Upstairs," Tess said. "Talking on her phone."

"Talking to a *man*," Poppy said, tugging at her sister's ponytail. "I hope she doesn't get any ideas in her head and run off and leave us." She sighed. "Then we'd just be latchkey kids. Coming home to an empty house."

"Poppy, sweetheart, wherever did you get that idea?" Afton asked.

Poppy shrugged. "That's what happens."

"That's not what's going to happen to us," Afton said. "We're a family. We're always going to be here for each other."

Poppy still looked nervous. "Still, sometimes little girls have to go away."

"Honey, are you still worried about that baby that was kidnapped?"

Poppy nodded.

"That could never happen to anybody here. You know why?"

Both Poppy and Tess were looking very serious now. "Why?" Poppy asked.

Afton put her arms around them both and hugged them tight. "Two reasons. First, because we now have a ferocious guard dog who can dance on his hind legs." That comment made the two girls giggle like mad.

"What's the second reason, Mommy?" Tess asked.

"Your mommy knows some very tough police officers and FBI agents," Afton said.

"Wow!" Poppy said. "Real FBI like on TV?"

"That's right," Afton said. She grabbed the big frying pan and pulled a pound of hamburger from the fridge. *And the third reason*, she thought to herself, *is if anybody ever lays a hand on my kids, I'll kill them. I'll do a double tap right in the middle of their forehead.* "Boom, boom," she said out loud.

"Boom, boom," Poppy echoed from her spot at the table.

WHILE Afton sautéed onions and patted out burgers and the girls set the table, she turned on the TV to catch the evening news. She half listened as the coanchors blathered on about winter storm warnings, odd and even side of the street parking, and snow emergency routes. Just when she was thanking the powers that be that Channel 7 had stopped running wall-to-wall coverage on the Darden kidnapping, Portia Bourgoyne's face filled the screen.

Oh crap, it's the Queen of Mean again.

The camera pulled back to reveal Portia standing in front of a small white house surrounded by trees. Afton recognized the house instantly. It belonged to Muriel Pink over in Hudson, Wisconsin. The woman who had organized the ill-fated doll show at the Skylark Mall.

Suddenly, there was a two-shot of Portia and Muriel Pink, standing in Pink's kitchen. Behind them, dolls seemed to grin and peek over their shoulders. Afton wondered if it was still so stifling hot in there.

"As the hunt continues for the missing Darden baby," Portia said, "Newswatch 7 has obtained an exclusive interview with Muriel Pink, the woman who organized the doll show at the Skylark Mall."

Then Portia went hot and heavy into the interview, rapid-firing questions at Pink, who looked a little deer-in-the-headlights stunned.

"I understand you were one of just a few people who talked to this mysterious doll lady who's the prime suspect in the Darden baby kidnapping?" Portia asked, enunciating carefully.

Pink gave an uncomfortable nod. "Yes, I suppose I am."

"Did she seem a little strange or off to you?"

"Now that you mention it, I think she might have been."

Portia gave an encouraging smile, so Pink continued.

"I've always had a sixth sense about people . . ."

Afton grabbed her phone and dialed Max's number. When he answered, she said, "Is your TV on? Are you seeing this?"

"Yeah," Max said. "Pretty unbelievable, huh?"

"How on earth did Portia find out about her?"

"Who knows? Portia's probably got paid informants in the MPD. In the FBI for all I know. A woman who looks like that, Lord knows how many guys are lining up to give her what she wants."

"You think we've got a leak in the department?" Afton asked. She was still half listening to Pink on TV.

"Hard to say."

"This is just not good."

"And it might not go anywhere either."

"Still," Afton said, "Muriel Pink seems to be remembering a lot more. A lot more than she told us anyway."

"You've got to let this thing go for a while," Max said. "Or else you're gonna drive yourself nuts and burn out. Take a bubble bath or whatever you ladies like to do. Or better yet, hug your kids and read 'em some Dr. Seuss."

"You're right," Afton said with a certain reluctance. "I hear you. See you tomorrow."

Afton tried, she really did. She piled up their burgers with pickles, onions, and cheese, wiped bean spatter off the stove, and joked with Lish about her date this coming Saturday night.

Finally, she sprawled on the living room rug with Poppy and Tess and played a game of Clue.

But she still couldn't let it go. Because trying to resolve the Darden kidnapping just wasn't as cut-and-dried as discovering Professor Plum in the Billiard Room with a candlestick.

24

MARJORIE feathered her brush just so against the baby doll's face, creating a perfectly arched brow. She'd always had a steady hand. Even as a child, she'd been able to trace her letters perfectly. Her teachers always told her that she was gifted, advised her parents to send her to art school. Those teachers were so stupid—they didn't know her father. They didn't know what he was capable of, or what a sadistic bastard he really was. But that was then, this was . . . years later.

Blessed with a photographic memory, Marjorie required no pictures of babies to provide her with inspiration. She knew what appealed to mothers the most—big blue eyes, cherubic lips, masses of silken hair. So she created baby dolls that were so impossibly beautiful that women were driven almost delirious when they saw them.

Now, as she labored over her latest creation in her workroom, Marjorie gently placed the doll in a silk-lined holder and wheeled her chair sideways. She pulled open a plastic drawer that contained bags of fox fur in dozens of brown, auburn, and red tones. This baby boy she was working on had chestnut hair with a few auburn highlights, so she needed just the right color for his eyelashes. She inspected one of her plastic bags. It wasn't quite right. She tried another bag. Finally, she found just the perfect color. She took a small bit, just what she needed, and sealed the bag up tight again, rolled back to her workbench.

Wearing a pair of Bausch & Lomb magnifier glasses, Marjorie leaned in close and began the painstaking process of inserting each individual strand of fox hair. She worked steadily, humming as she went, and was halfway through the second eye when she was interrupted by a loud pounding on her door. She ignored it.

The pounding came again, this time more insistent.

"Go away," she called. It had to be Ronnie.

"Ma!" he shouted. "Ya gotta come see this!"

"What?"

"Ma! Come quick!" He pulled open the door, his face a mask of excitement and concern.

"Okay, hold your water, hold your water," Marjorie said. She got up from her chair and followed Ronnie into the living room, where the TV set was blaring.

Ronnie gestured frantically at the television. "It's that lady," he cried. "The same one who organized the doll show last Saturday. She's on TV!"

"Shit." Marjorie sat down hard in one of the chairs.

They both watched, a little stunned, as Portia Bourgoyne posed with Muriel Pink in the woman's neat-as-a-pin kitchen in Hudson, Wisconsin.

Portia was doing a quick recap: "Mrs. Pink is the woman who organized the doll show where Susan Darden supposedly met the vendor who is suspected of abducting little Elizabeth Ann Darden."

"Shit, shit, shit," Marjorie said.

Portia peppered Pink with questions, and as the interview progressed, Pink seemed to remember more and more. She even seemed to be intimating that she definitely *did* remember seeing Molly, the doll lady, who was the prime suspect in the Darden baby kidnapping.

Ronnie thrust out his chin. "This ain't good, Ma. You really screwed up."

Marjorie held up a hand. "Shut up." She wanted to hear the rest of the interview.

The Pink woman blathered on as Marjorie watched with growing rage and ever-narrowing eyes. *This woman could be trouble*, she thought to herself. *If the police come back and question this woman, it could be the end for us. For me anyway.*

"Ma, don't ya think . . ." Ronnie started.

Marjorie tuned him out as the camera moved in close on Portia Bourgoyne. "Here at Newswatch 7," Portia said, looking smug, as if she'd already scored a network anchor job, "we feel this information will be critical in helping solve such a horrific crime."

"That's what you think," Marjorie said to the TV.

The TV cut back to the anchor desk, where a blow-combed anchorman gazed steadily into the camera and said, "On a related note, the baby found in the woods outside of Cannon Falls . . ."

Marjorie's heart was jolted for the second time in two minutes. "What!" she exploded. "What did I just hear?"

Ronnie frowned as Marjorie extended a hand toward the television set and listened to the story. When it was over, she grabbed the first thing she could lay her hands on—an amber glass ashtray with a Budweiser logo—and hurled it at Ronnie's head. Cigarette butts exploded everywhere as it caught him squarely in the right temple.

"Ma!" he yelped.

"You left that baby in the woods near Cannon Falls?" Marjorie shrieked. She was on her feet and screaming, hopping up and down like a crazy person. "What the hell were you *thinking*? You were supposed to *bury* it!"

Ronnie held up a hand. "I can explain everything."

She folded her arms across her scrawny chest. "This better be good."

"Do you remember when I went to pick up that bobcat carcass from that hunter down in Red Wing?"

"Not really, but go on. I want to hear your whole stupid story."

"It was just a couple of months ago, right after that other baby died. You wanted me to bury her, but it was too cold. We had that early ice storm and the ground was already frozen. Even the pickax would just, like, bounce back at me."

"Lazy," Marjorie said. "You stupid lazy boy. So you're telling me you took the kid along with you? To Red Wing?"

Ronnie was nodding now. "I thought I was just being, you know, practical. But Red Wing is kind of . . . populated. More populated than here anyway. So I drove farther west, until I came across this woodlot. How was I supposed to know that a couple of dumb-ass hunters would stumble upon the thing? I couldn't, right? I mean, I couldn't know that."

"Huh," Marjorie said. She didn't want to hear any more of his excuses. She had too much to think about.

Ronnie touched a hand to his forehead and winced. "Jeez, Ma. You really clobbered me."

"Shut the hell up, Ronnie. You're the one who screwed things up. Now I gotta think for a while." Marjorie got up and walked out of the room. Her voice trailed after her. "I have to figure out what to do."

Retreating to her craft studio (if you could even call it that), Marjorie grabbed her tweezers and resumed working on the doll's eyelashes. She nipped and poked for another ten minutes until she had them just about perfect. The whole time she worked, her brain skittered along, planning, scheming, trying to calculate the odds. She knew the Cannon Falls kid probably wouldn't present that much of a problem. If Ronnie had left it in the woods like he said he had—and she had no reason to doubt him—they should be fine. Animals, rain, wind, and snow would have erased any little bits of telltale evidence.

No, the real problem, the major dilemma Marjorie faced right now, was talky old Muriel Pink. Muriel Pink, who had started flapping her lips once they poked a TV camera in her face. Because as sure as God made little green apples, the cops were gonna go back and talk to that old bitch again.

BY nine o'clock that night, Marjorie had devised what she figured was a pretty smart plan. It was dangerous, even daring. But executed properly, would surely put an end to all their worries. They'd be safe again. And Marjorie, just like a little brown spider who'd administered its lethal bite, would be able to scuttle back into her snuggle hole again. Because she wanted to, *needed* to, be safe.

Ronnie was standing in the kitchen, refrigerator door wide open and drinking milk directly from the carton, when Marjorie said, "We're going out. Just get your car and don't ask any questions."

Ronnie wiped his mouth. "Can't," he said. "My battery's fried. I tried putting a charger on it but it wouldn't hold worth shit. Probably gonna have to go to Fleet Farm and buy a new one."

"Can you take the battery out of my car for now?"

"Yeah, I guess," Ronnie said.

"Do it."

Marjorie knew that Ronnie's car, a two-door lowrider from the late eighties, was the perfect crime car. Painted a dull brownish burgundy, it had been stripped of any make or model insignia, and a bystander would be hard-pressed to give an exact description of it. Besides, the car was registered in Ronnie's name. If things really went off the rails tonight, if Ronnie got caught red-handed and hauled down to the police station, it might give her the break she needed to get away. She still had five grand in cash stashed in a lockbox in Eau Claire. After that . . . well, she'd just have to improvise.

Five minutes later, Ronnie came stomping back inside. "Done," he told her.

"What's done?" Shake asked. She'd heard doors opening and closing and had crept in to investigate.

"None of your beeswax," Marjorie said. That's all she needed was Shake nosing around. She didn't trust the girl as far as she could throw her.

"Ronnie?" Shake said. But Ronnie was focused only on Marjorie.

"How bad's the weather?" Marjorie asked. She'd already looked up Muriel Pink's address in an old phone book.

"It's sleeting like a bastard out there," Ronnie said. "Really coming down."

"What are you two up to?" Shake asked. She clutched at a ratty pink cardigan that barely stretched across her belly. "Where are you guys going?"

"Just some business," Marjorie said. "I have to run over to the Family Resource Center."

"At this time of night?" Something didn't feel right to Shake. But she was dog tired and her ankles were sore and swollen again. All she could think about was crawling back into the lounger and settling into a restless sleep.

"We won't be gone long," Ronnie assured her. "You take it easy. Get some rest."

"I guess," Shake said. She stared at them again, then waddled out of the room.

Marjorie turned anxious eyes on Ronnie. "Do you still have your night vision goggles?"

"Yeah, sure I do." Ronnie had bought a set of Sightmark Ghost Hunter night vision glasses that were his pride and joy. He'd earned the money to pay for them by doing taxidermy jobs for local hunters. Sometimes he even hit the jackpot and got to work on something really great, like the bobcat he'd done for the guy over in Red Wing. A great big cat the man had shot when he was hunting out in Wyoming.

"And you need to bring your hunting knives, too."

Ronnie stared at his mother for a full fifteen seconds before comprehension finally dawned. "Oh shit," he said. "You wanna do that old lady, don't you?" He was suddenly both aroused as well as struck with an almost paralyzing case of nerves. Was this what he wanted to do? Was this all he was good for?

"We can't do nothing about that Cannon Falls baby," Marjorie said. "That's a done deal." She was pulling on her coat, fumbling with her mittens. "But we can sure as hell do something about Muriel Pink."

THE drive through the countryside was dicey at best. Sleet pelted down, icing the windows and turning the blacktopped county roads into a skating rink.

"This is really getting bad," Ronnie said. He snuck a sidelong glance at Marjorie. "You think we should turn around?"

Marjorie just stared straight ahead. Her mind was made up; there was no turning back.

They crawled along County Road BB, finally came out on Carmichael Road, and then, four miles farther, hit the Interstate. Finally, they slid down the hill, the Saint Croix River a wide swath of darkness below them, and turned off into Hudson. As they cruised through the downtown area, they didn't see a soul out walking. Just lights burning in a couple of bars.

"They really roll up the sidewalks in this town, don't they?" Marjorie said. "That's good." She peered out, silently mouthing the names of the street signs. "Turn here. Locust Street." They drove up a slight hill, past the police station, and then hung a left on Third.

They cruised past the Octagon House at Myrtle and Third and then turned right on Oak. A couple more turns and Ronnie slowed the car as they glided past Muriel Pink's house on Flint Street.

"That's it?" he asked. The house was dark, save for a dim light that glowed somewhere. Maybe in the kitchen.

"Keep going," Marjorie said. "Go on past her house a little ways."

Ronnie drove to the end of the block and stopped. Put the car in Park, left the engine running. "You sure you want to do this?" he said. Ronnie didn't mind a little rough sex when he needed to get his gun off, but killing a woman? Then again, it might be interesting. Sort of a new . . . diversion.

"She's gonna be a problem," Marjorie said, sounding almost philosophical. "Sooner or later. You saw the way she talked on TV. All puffed up and certain of herself. With a little more coaxing, she could probably identify me. You, too."

"I don't think she saw me."

"Don't get smart."

Ronnie hunched forward over the steering wheel.

"I need you to man up and take care of business," Marjorie said.

"What do you mean?" Ronnie snapped back. "Exactly?"

"I want you to go in there and use your hunting knife. Take care of that woman nice and quick, just like you would an ordinary whitetail deer."

Ronnie smiled crookedly in the darkness. "You mean kill her?"

Marjorie stared at him.

Ronnie was sweating in the faint warmth being spewed out by the car's heater. He'd worked with a butcher once, a guy named Hofferman over in Martell. Helped him butcher and process more than fifty deer during hunting season. Skinned 'em, carved out the front shoulders, backstraps, brisket, sirloin, and hindquarters. Quick and efficient, assembly-line style. He'd found the work thought provoking.

Finally Ronnie said, "I never did a person before."

"There's a first time for everything, my boy. Besides, you've gone after women before, don't play dumb with me."

He gestured back toward Muriel Pink's house and shrugged. He was still undecided. "But not like this. She's an old lady."

"Listen to me." Marjorie reached across the front seat and grabbed hold of his collar, showing surprising strength for such a birdlike woman. "If that old lady ID's either one of us, we're cooked."

"Maybe she—"

"Shut up and listen to me. Do you want to go to prison?"

Ronnie shrugged his shoulders. "Of course not."

"If that Pink woman identifies us, we'll sure as shit go to prison, no questions asked. And you, my boy, will never survive that experience."

Ronnie felt his guts practically turn to water.

"When women are sent to jail, they get to live in cottages and cook meals in a real kitchen," Marjorie said. "Guys go to hard-core prisons with cement cells, twenty-foot walls, and guard towers with automatic rifles. You've seen that prison over in Stillwater, haven't you? You want to call that place home for the next thirty years?"

Ronnie shook his head.

Marjorie continued to pound away at him. Finally, she turned the tide by asking him one simple question: "Do you want nasty old men to use you like they would a woman?"

That was when Ronnie heaved a knowing sigh. He gathered up his knives, his night vision glasses, and the battered pizza box in the backseat. Then, without a word to her, he climbed out of the car and slunk toward what would soon become a charnel house.

* * *

MARJORIE waited in the dark. Anxious, quivering like a frightened Chihuahua. Biting her nails down to almost nothing. Then, finally, to bloody stumps. With the engine off, it was getting colder and colder and she sank into her coat, pulling up the collar and shivering. As the night yawned on, the windows began to fog. Still, her hands and feet jiggled with nervous energy.

After what seemed like an eternity—but was probably no more than twenty minutes—Marjorie was delirious with worry and ready to jack the key into the ignition and take off without him. She glanced into the rearview mirror and caught barely a hint of shadow creeping around the corner of the house. Ah, Ronnie. Now the boy was moving more quickly, his head swiveling to see if anyone was watching.

No one was.

As he neared the car, Ronnie broke into a staggering lope. Then he ripped open the car door and flung himself into the backseat.

"Did you do it?" Marjorie asked, turning to look at him.

Ronnie sank back, a stupid smile on his face. "What do you think?"

In the dim light from the overhead bulb, Marjorie could make out telltale bloody splotches. "Watch your clothes," she warned. "Watch your clothes and stay on top of that old army blanket."

"Shut up and drive."

Marjorie slid across the front seat and took her place behind the wheel. She drove back through Hudson slowly and carefully. When she finally gazed into the rearview mirror, Ronnie was sprawled across the backseat and snoring softly. He might have been unnerved by his actions tonight, but he was sleeping like a baby.

Marjorie allowed herself a tight smile. *The kid came through*, she told herself. *He pulled it off. Which means one big problem is solved. Now, knock on wood, we're home free.*

25

MAX, Afton, and Andy Farmer were sitting in the conference room, watching the tape of Portia Bourgoyne's interview.

"The TV station sent this over?" Max asked.

Farmer nodded. "Not because they were particularly interested in doing a public service. There was, shall we say, pressure?"

"Good. Have the FBI guys seen this?" Max asked.

"We sent a copy over to them," Farmer said.

"I still can't believe Bourgoyne got to this woman," Afton said.

"Leaks," Farmer said. "They're what can kill an investigation."

"Or bog it down," Max said.

Afton looked at the paperwork strewn about the table. "Are we bogged down?"

"You tell me," Max said. Then, "Maybe."

Afton furrowed her brow. She wished she could be of more help.

"Or maybe not," Max said. "Sometimes you can't see the forest for the trees."

"You gonna go through all those notes again?" Farmer asked Max. "You got copies of all the interviews? The stuff Dillon and I did? The ones the FBI handled?"

"We got it all," Max said.

AFTON and Max were twenty minutes into their analysis when the phone rang.

Max didn't look up, but instead aimed a pen at the phone. Afton snatched up the receiver. "Yes?"

"I thought you and Max might be in there," Angel Graham said. "I have a call holding from a Dr. Sansevere at the ME's office. Do you want me to put her through?"

"Please." Afton punched the button to turn on the speakerphone. "Dr. Sansevere is calling," she told Max. "I think she might have something for us."

"Dr. Sansevere?" Max said. "This is Max Montgomery. How can I help?"

"I've got some news for you." Her voice was brisk and businesslike.

"Go ahead. Sorry if this sounds like we're talking from the bottom of a garbage can, but we've got you on speakerphone. I want my colleague to hear this, too."

"The baby that was brought back from Cannon Falls?" said Dr. Sansevere. "There was a problem with her heart. What we call a VSD, a hole in the heart."

Afton felt sick to her stomach. "You mean somebody stabbed her?" she asked. "Shot her?"

"No, no," Dr. Sansevere said. "Nothing like that, not any kind of external injury. It was a congenital defect, something the child was born with. A ventricular septal defect. Lots of babies are born with it. It's basically a hole in the septum that separates the ventricles, the two lower parts of the heart."

Max locked eyes with Afton.

"Could it have been repaired?" Afton asked.

"Perhaps. If she'd had immediate medical attention. VSDs more often than not require open heart surgery."

"So that was the cause of death?" Max asked. "A bad heart?"

"Probably the defect was so bad that her heart simply stopped beating," Dr. Sansevere said.

"So she was doomed from birth?" Afton asked.

"I would say so, yes," Dr. Sansevere said. "That was the main issue we encountered in her autopsy. I found no petechial hemorrhages to indicate she might have been smothered, which is an insidious but common way to kill an infant. There were no ligature marks, no cuts or bruises. Her head hadn't been shaken, nothing abnormal showed up in her scan. The only thing abnormal about that little girl was her heart. And the fact that she was somewhat malnourished."

"I'll be damned," Max said.

"What about the phosphorescent stuff?" Afton asked. "The little bits and pieces that glowed when you ran the black light over her."

"Oh," Dr. Sansevere said. "Under electron microscopic testing, they appear to be crystals of oxalic acid."

"What is that, please?" Afton asked.

"It's an agent commonly added to water to reduce the pH balance."

"Is this something commonly found in baby products?" Max asked.

"Not that I know of."

"Just the name *oxalic acid* sounds fairly dangerous," Afton said.

"Yes, well, I suppose it could be."

"Any idea how it got there?" Max asked.

"None whatsoever," Dr. Sansevere said.

"You find anything else on her?" Max asked.

"Nothing that was atypical considering the circumstances of where she was found. Leaves, a few animal hairs."

"Has she been DNA typed yet?" Afton asked.

"We're still working on that."

"Okay, thank you," Max said. "I trust you'll contact us right away if you learn anything else?"

"Count on it," she said.

Max disconnected from her, then looked at Afton. "Thoughts?"

Afton shook her head. "I don't know what any of that means."

"Neither do I." Max blew out his cheeks, and then said, "But I'm feeling antsy. Come on, let's take a ride. Go blow out the carbon."

WHEREVER they were headed, Afton decided that Max was taking the long way around. They sliced over to Hennepin Avenue, right in the middle of downtown Minneapolis, and cruised slowly along the thoroughfare.

"This used to be appropriately tacky and mildly interesting," Max said. "All sorts of dimey bars, strip joints, rock clubs, magazine shops that sold dirty books in back, record stores, and waffle houses. Now it's all chain restaurants—Italian, Mexican, Chinese. If we ever patch things up in the Middle East, somebody will probably open a McFalafel."

They passed the Basilica, its dark green dome gleaming in the faint sunlight, slid under a bridge, and turned up Hennepin past the sculpture garden. Everywhere they went, traffic was either backed up or crawling at a glacial pace. Thanks to continued cold and two more inches of snow last night, there were also stalled vehicles, fender benders, and abandoned cars.

Afton was pleased that Max had dialed back on his aggressive driving and was exercising a bit more caution today. She could almost relax in the passenger seat and take a deep breath. Almost.

"Where are we going?" she asked, one eye still focused on the speedometer.

"Sampson's," Max said. He momentarily swerved into the oncoming lane, dodging a car that was stuck at the bottom of a steep grade. "Gotta look somebody up."

"Who?"

"A guy."

MAX drove past Sampson's Bar, made a U-turn, and then pulled in front of the bar, nosing into a no-parking zone. He threw an OFFICIAL POLICE BUSINESS card on the dashboard and said, "C'mon. We're gonna have us a little confab with The Scrounger."

Afton gazed at the cheesy red-and-yellow exterior of Sampson's Bar, which clearly announced, *I'm a dive.* The hand-lettered sign in the window advertising Dubble Bubble seemed to say, *Come on in, the drinkin's fine.*

"How do you even know he's here?"

"Couple of things tipped me off," Max said. "First off, there's his butt-ugly pickup truck held together with Bondo tape parked illegally in a spot marked 'Handicapped.'"

"Okay."

"Plus Sampson's is the crappiest bar in the neighborhood, which makes it his official stomping ground. Everything else around here is your basic fig and fern bar."

"I think fig and fern bars went out in the early nineties," Afton said.

"What do they call them now?"

"I don't know. Maybe craft beer bistros or wine bars. Something like that."

"Still," Max said. "It's the same old bullshit."

"Of course it is."

The interior of Sampson's was darker than pitch. Probably well under the regulation lumens required by the liquor licensing board. That was okay with Afton. This way she wouldn't have to look at the winos who were already slumped anonymously at the front bar, or the ugly orange carpet, or the studded red plastic lamps that dangled on bare cords.

Max paused to study the inhabitants, didn't recognize any familiar faces lurking at the bar, and turned his attention to what could loosely be called the dining room. Loosely, because it was basically three Formica tables and an unattended pull-tab booth encased in chicken wire.

Seated at one of the tables, eating peanuts and sipping an amber-colored drink, was a man dressed in coveralls, Red Wing work boots, and a red cap with the earflaps down. His chair was tipped back and he was watching a college hockey game on TV.

"There's our boy," Max said.

They strolled across a dark expanse of dance floor that felt sticky underfoot, and headed straight for The Scrounger's table.

"Whoa," The Scrounger said when he caught sight of Max. "Look who's out slumming."

"How do," Max said.

"Detective Montgomery," The Scrounger said. "What an unexpected pleasure." His eyes flicked over and took in Afton. "And I do believe you've made a serious upgrade when it comes to your choice in partners."

"Thanks," Afton said. "I think. Although I'm not technically a detective." The Scrounger had ginger-colored hair pulled back into a ponytail, a scruffy beard, and brown eyes that were pinpricks of intensity. He looked like a cross between a stoner and a University of Minnesota English professor.

"Mmn," The Scrounger said, smiling at Afton. "You must be a protégée then."

"Something like that," Max said. He sat down across from The Scrounger and Afton followed suit. "This is Afton Tangler. She's been working with me on the Darden kidnapping case."

"Ah," The Scrounger said. "Nasty." He crunched a peanut between his front teeth and smiled again at Afton. "I meant the case, not you."

"The FBI is working the case pretty hard," Max said. "Obviously, they would. But MPD is running its own investigation as well."

"It's been all over the news," The Scrounger said. "They think it might have been a woman who stole the kid?"

"It's possible," Afton said.

"I know that Kenwood Parkway, where the Dardens live, is one of your routes," Max said.

"Surely you don't think that I—"

Max held up a hand. "No, no, nothing like that. But I know you're familiar with that particular part of the city."

The Scrounger nodded. "Intimately."

"And I was wondering if maybe you'd seen or heard anything that was a little off?"

"You mean suspicious," The Scrounger said.

"Right," Afton said.

The Scrounger thought for a few moments. "Last week I found an entire set of encyclopedias dumped in a trash can in the alley that runs behind James Avenue. Can you believe that? A compendium of universal knowledge trashed along with the detritus of chicken bones and potato peels. The biography of Cicero, great battles of World War Two, and botanical miracles. What's the world coming to?"

"Digital," Afton said.

"But are we better off for it?" The Scrounger picked up his almost empty glass and tinkled his ice cubes.

"Probably not," Afton said. Though she did love her iPad.

"No, of course not," The Scrounger said. "But to get back to your original inquiry . . . I have not noticed anything unusual or out of place in that neighborhood. Except for an empty Ripple bottle tossed into the recycling bin of a home that generally prefers Château Margaux Grand Cru or, at the very least, a Mondavi Cabernet. Though perhaps it was an insensitive transient who deposited his refuse among that of the hoi polloi."

"So nothing at all," Max said. He sounded disappointed.

"Nothing, my friend," The Scrounger said. "Though I wish I could propel you in a more positive direction."

"Ever hear of a halfway house called Dean's Place?"

"Sure," The Scrounger said. "Bunch of ex-druggies and drunks."

"There's a guy lives there named Al Sponger," Max said. "Worked for the Dardens once. We brought him in for questioning yesterday and he's being released this morning."

The Scrounger nodded. "I see."

Max pulled a photo out of his pocket and slid it across the table. "It'd be worth your while if you'd keep an eye on him."

The Scrounger studied the photo. "Ah . . . a second level of surveillance. Your basic shadow-type investigation."

"Something like that."

"Consider it done."

Max slipped a twenty from his wallet and placed it on top of the photo. "In case you'd like another refreshing beverage."

"Always," The Scrounger said.

*   *   *

BACK in the car, Max seemed at a loss for what to do next.

"Maybe we should finish going through the interviews?" Afton suggested.

"Better than just twiddling our thumbs," he said, just as his cell phone rang. He grabbed it and swiped the On button.

"Detective Montgomery?" a voice blurted out. It was a man, his voice high-pitched and loud over a background of radio static and frantic voices. He was excited and speaking loud enough that Afton could hear him.

"Yes?"

"This is Sergeant Bill Hadley over at the Hudson Police Department?"

"What can I do for you, Sergeant Hadley?" Max hit another button and the phone was now on speaker.

"You'd better get over here fast," Hadley said. "One of the witnesses you guys interviewed in that missing baby case was killed last night."

Max didn't seem to register what Hadley had just said. He hesitated for a few moments and then he said, "What?"

"One of the witnesses . . ."

"No, I heard that part," Max said. "It's just that . . . Wait, are you saying that Muriel Pink has been killed? The woman who was interviewed on TV last night?"

"Yes," Sergeant Hadley said. "That's it. Muriel Pink."

"And she was . . ."

"It's a mess," Hadley cried. And this time he sounded anguished. "Worst I've ever seen!"

26

IF Max could hardly believe Muriel Pink had been murdered, neither could Afton. They both stared straight ahead as Max banged onto the entrance ramp to I-94, ignoring the speed limit as they sped across town heading for Hudson.

"How could this happen? How could this happen?" Max muttered.

Afton could only keep repeating, "I know, I know."

They flew through downtown Saint Paul's Spaghetti Junction, rocketed through Woodbury, flew past the Minnesota Highway Patrol weigh station, and finally crossed over the bridge that ran above the Saint Croix River. As they swerved onto the icy off-ramp, Afton said, "Easy, take it easy. You're gonna fly right off this curve and take us straight into the river."

"That damn Portia," Max seethed. His knuckles were white from his death grip on the steering wheel; his face was as red as a Roma tomato. "That interview aired last night and set somebody's whiskers a-twitching. God, somebody should have known. *I* should have known. We should have had somebody watching Muriel Pink. At the very least brought in the Hudson Police."

"You couldn't have known," Afton said.

"It had to be that damn doll lady," Max snarled. "She figured out where the old lady lived, then came back and finished her off. Murdered the poor old bat."

"You don't know that."

"That's the funny thing," Max said. "I *do* know that." He glanced over at her. "And so do you. Tell me you don't have the same gut feeling that I do."

"Okay," Afton said as they passed the local Dairy Queen, barely squeaking through a yellow light. "I do."

MURIEL Pink's neighborhood looked starkly different from the last time they'd been there. Squad cars with flashing lights, an ambulance, and several unmarked FBI vehicles clogged the street in front of the murder house. On the front walk and in the side yard, crime scene investigators marked, measured, and cataloged footsteps in the newly fallen snow.

Grim-faced neighbors stood in clumps of two and three, watching the spectacle. Their faces were as gray and shocked as Afton figured hers must be. Muriel Pink's murder was unforeseen. But yes, in hindsight, someone should have been worried about her and put some security precautions in place.

"Son of a bitch." Max swore under his breath as he stepped from the car. They'd been forced to park a block away. Now they were running the gauntlet of watchers and law enforcement.

Max badged both of them through two different rings of security. Then, rounding the corner of the house, they caught a glimpse of Don Jasper. The Chicago FBI agent was standing at the back door, talking to a crime scene tech in a navy jumpsuit. When Jasper saw them, he motioned for them to come forward.

"How bad?" Max asked as he and Afton crowded onto a sagging back porch.

"Bad," Jasper said. His affable nature and normally twinkly eyes seemed dulled by what he'd just witnessed. "See for yourself."

They pressed into the kitchen, where it was crowded and stuffy with at least a half dozen people jostling around. Cameras strobed wildly and Afton surmised that Muriel Pink must be lying in the middle of that maelstrom of activity.

Max elbowed his way through the crowd, Afton practically riding his coattails. He stopped abruptly and they saw her. Muriel Pink was lying on the linoleum floor, eyes staring blankly up at the ceiling, her face as yellowed and crinkled as old parchment paper. Her floral robe was flung open, revealing the fact that her torso had been slashed from sternum to stomach. An enormous pool of blood had congealed around her and soaked up into her clothing. An older white-haired man in green scrubs was leaning over her. Afton figured he might be a local doctor, doing his turn as county coroner.

"Who found her?" Max said to no one in particular.

A Saint Croix County sheriff's deputy turned to answer him. "Neighbor. When the old lady didn't come over for her usual cup of coffee, the neighbor got worried and peeked in the back window. Saw this."

"Damn," Max said. "Somebody really went to work on her."

The officer removed his Smoky Bear hat, as if in deference to the slain woman, and ran a hand over his blond brush cut. "Carved her up pretty good."

"You ever see anything like this before?"

"Not exactly like this," the deputy said. Then he paused. "Well, maybe once when I arrested a couple of hunters. They'd shot a doe, but didn't have a proper deer license. They were hurrying to . . ." He gestured futilely, not finishing his sentence.

AFTON stepped around the circle of onlookers and walked quietly into the living room. A brass clock over a small red brick fireplace ticked reassuringly. Dolls smiled out from the shelves of a bookcase. A pair of fuzzy white slippers were tucked next to a well-worn lime green easy chair. An AARP magazine was spread open on a nearby end table. But Muriel Pink was never again going to sit in here and enjoy her cozy little home and read her magazines.

Just who were they dealing with? Obviously, a person so callous they would break into a person's house, beat the crap out of the babysitter, steal a baby, and then double back and stab an old lady witness. Sometimes the world was a pretty sick place.

"Afton!" Max called. "Afton!"

Afton spun around to find Max huffing toward her. It was clear he hadn't cooled off. If anything, he seemed to have doubled down on his anger.

"We're not going to get anything here," Max told her. "Between the FBI, local law enforcement, and crime scene techs, they've got it under control." He drew a deep breath. "But there's only been one officer so far who canvassed the neighborhood." An expectant look filled his face.

"What are we waiting for?" Afton said.

BACK outside, the gawkers who had been standing on the front lawn had all but disappeared. Their absence was either a result of freezing temperatures, the fact that being on the fringes of an investigation was pretty boring, or the Saint Croix County deputies shagging them away. The only evidence that something unholy had taken place here was the string of law enforcement cars and vans snaking around the corner.

Max took one side of the street, Afton took the other. She knocked on the doors of three houses before she found someone who was at home. But when she introduced herself and asked the woman if she'd seen anyone walking around outside last night, the woman shook her head. No, she hadn't seen or heard anything until the police had shown up at poor Mrs. Pink's home a couple of hours ago. And wasn't that an awful thing?

Afton continued to plug away, but was having miserable luck. And by the set of Max's shoulders as he covered the other side of the street, he was striking out, too.

It wasn't until Afton hit her sixth house that a woman named Ellie Schroeder remembered seeing someone walking down the street last night.

"What time was this?" Afton asked her.

"Oh, pretty late," Schroeder said. "Maybe ten o'clock?" Schroeder was thin and mousy looking, wearing baggy slacks and a sweatshirt that said, WORLD'S GREATEST GRANDMA. "But I don't think the person I saw was your killer."

"Why do you say that?"

"Because he was carrying a pizza box," Schroeder said.

Inside her chest, Afton's heart did a slow-motion flip-flop.

Schroeder went on. "I just assumed it was Mr. Foster from down the block." She leaned in and squinted at Afton. "He's a divorced dad, and when his kids stay over, he usually buys pizza." She said it disapprovingly, as if Mr. Foster should be grilling a medley of organic carrots and broccoli instead.

"Mrs. Schroeder, wait a minute, will you?" Afton was excited. This was the same MO the kidnappers had used when they'd strong-armed the Dardens' babysitter. She ran across the street, grabbed Max, and pulled him back to Mrs. Schroeder's house.

"Tell him," Afton said to Mrs. Schroeder. "Tell Detective Montgomery exactly what you saw."

Max listened to her carefully, asked a couple of questions, and then said, "Could you identify this man again?"

"It was pretty dark."

"But if we sent a police sketch artist over, you'd give it a try?"

"Absolutely," Schroeder said.

"And which house does Mr. Foster live in?"

"That one." Schroeder pointed to a nondescript two-story home that was two doors down.

"I knocked on the door there," Afton said. "Nobody's home."

"Do you know where Mr. Foster works?" Max asked.

Schroeder gave a tight nod. "Certainly. He works at the Heartland Insurance Agency right down on Main Street. Next to the ice cream parlor."

Max threw his cell phone at Afton. "Get him. Get Foster on the line ASAP."

Afton did a fast Google search, located the number, and got Foster on the line. When she told him why she was calling, he sounded stunned.

"Mrs. Pink?" he said. "Dead?"

"Let me give you to Detective Montgomery," Afton said, passing the phone to Max.

Max did a little more explaining to the somewhat excited Foster, then said, "This may sound like an odd question, but did you order a pizza last night around ten o'clock? Did you pick one up and carry it home? Or have one delivered?"

Max's brows pinched together, and he shot a look at Afton. The answer must have been no. He thanked Foster, and then asked him to call either the FBI or the Hudson Police if he suddenly remembered anything that might be of help.

Max thumbed the Off button on his phone. "No pizza last night."

Schroeder's face went white and she touched a hand to her throat. "So that was the killer I saw?" She looked stunned.

"Could have been, ma'am," Max said.

IT had to be the same guy," Max told Jasper. "The same guy who cold-cocked the babysitter." Max and Afton had done a quick dog-and-pony explanation to a grim-looking Don Jasper.

That was the spark that lit the flame. Suddenly Jasper was snapping his fingers, gathering his posse. Radios crackled to life and backup was called for. More FBI, state police, and uniformed officers. Jasper was demanding backup for his backup.

As the furor boiled up around them, Max pulled Afton aside. "We gotta go talk to Susan Darden again. Now she's the only one we know who really got a decent look at this doll lady."

Afton was all for it.

"But who the hell *is* this doll lady?" Max chewed on this problem as they hurried to his car. "Do you think she knows Susan or Richard Darden?"

"Maybe she worked with Darden," Afton said.

"At Novamed? That thought never occurred to me."

Afton shrugged. "It's a possibility."

"So how does she relate to the pizza guy?"

"I don't know," Afton said. "Could be . . . his girlfriend? Or maybe, I don't know, his mother?"

27

IT was a subdued Susan Darden who opened the door for Afton and Max that evening. Dressed in a pale peach cashmere hoodie and matching pants, she looked the perfect picture of a young upscale mommy. Except, of course, for the swollen red eyes, missing husband, and kidnapped child.

"Come in," Susan urged as Afton and Max stomped snow off their boots and stepped from darkness into the flood of warm light that bathed her front hallway. "It's still so cold out." She closed the enormous door as a hiss of freezing air blew in.

Afton and Max shrugged off their heavy coats and hung them on a brass coatrack. Max did a little extra clumping to extricate the snow from the waffle weave soles of his boots.

"This way, please," Susan said.

She led them into her living room, a fairly grand space in Afton's estimation. Two enormous white tufted sofas faced each other across a red-lacquered Chinese-style coffee table. Drapery hung in artful swags on the windows. Oil paintings and framed prints hung on the walls and above the white marble fireplace. Afton recognized one, a contemporary graphic of pill bottles that she thought might have been done by the artist Damien Hirst.

"You have a lovely home," Afton said.

"Thank you," Susan said almost absently. "I suppose it is."

"Nice Oriental carpet," Max said. "Real springy."

"Silk, I believe," Susan said. "Persian. A kilim pattern."

They were standing in a semicircle, everyone a little on edge, until Susan finally said, "I'm sorry, where are my manners? Please come and sit down."

That made things a little better.

Once Max and Afton were settled on one sofa and Susan on the other, Max didn't bother to mince words. "You know about the woman in Hudson? That she was killed?"

Susan nodded ever so slightly. "The woman who was in charge of organizing the doll show, yes. Chief Thacker called me late this afternoon." She crossed her arms in front of her and hugged herself tightly. "I'm afraid I might be next."

"We're going to send some personnel over here to stay with you," Max said. "Since you don't have your . . . Since you're here by yourself."

"My sister is flying in tonight," Susan said. "From Denver."

"That's good," Afton said. "But we'll still have a female officer inside your home and park a cruiser on the street. Twenty-four/seven if that makes you feel any better."

"The officer and the police car," Susan said. "That would be excellent." She gave a little shiver and then said, "Are you going to tell me what happened? Chief Thacker didn't reveal much of anything when he called. Just that the doll show organizer had been killed and that you were going to drop by."

"We believe Muriel Pink was murdered sometime last night," Max said.

Susan wedged herself into the corner of her couch and pulled up her knees. "How?" she asked in a small voice.

"Stabbed," Afton said. "Someone broke into her home and stabbed her while she was fixing a cup of hot chocolate."

"We believe," Max said, "that Muriel Pink's murder was the direct result of a TV interview she did with Portia Bourgoyne from Channel 7.

Going on really just a raw hunch, Bourgoyne linked Pink with the doll lady suspect in your daughter's kidnapping. The interview aired on Channel 7's *News at Six* last night."

"I didn't see it. But I'm guessing that you believe the kidnappers saw Mrs. Pink being interviewed?" Susan asked. "And they got worried?"

"That's exactly what we think," Afton said. "Mrs. Pink seemed to be . . . *recalling* a few more details."

Susan's face crumpled, and her hand crept up to her mouth. "So the kidnappers are also killers?"

"It's beginning to look that way," Afton said.

"And you believe it's the same two people who broke in here that night," Susan said slowly. She seemed to be trying to orient herself. "The man who knocked Ashley down and tied her up, and the woman who stole Elizabeth Ann."

"That's right," Afton said.

"So the *man* is the killer?" Susan asked.

"We don't know anything for sure," Afton said. "It's all speculation so far. But we think that might be the case. There were some, um, *elements* to the Pink murder that looked amateurish."

"And it wasn't Al Sponger," Susan said.

"Highly doubtful," Afton said. "Unless he's got a doppelgänger twin running around out there."

"Sponger is under surveillance right now," Max said. "But we don't believe he's competent enough to mastermind a high-profile kidnapping. Or to commit murder."

"I never thought he was the kidnapper," Susan said. "Even when the FBI came over yesterday and asked me a whole bunch of questions about Sponger, I never really thought it was him."

"Sponger's not entirely off the hook," Max said. "After all, we're looking for two suspects."

"And he did toss out a toy doll," Afton said. The FBI had briefed Susan Darden on that as well.

"When Sponger was working here, did he ever come into the house?" Max asked.

Susan lifted a hand to her forehead. "Let me see . . . Yes, I believe so. I think he might have asked for a glass of water or something."

"Did he ever see the baby?" Afton asked.

"I think so. Seems like I was always in the kitchen warming a bottle. I'm sure I had the baby with me in her little bassinette."

Afton and Max exchanged glances.

"But Sponger's not in custody?" Susan asked.

"He was," Max said. "But we didn't have enough to hold him."

"But we're watching him," Afton said.

"In case he might . . . lead you to . . ." Susan broke off her sentence.

"That's right," Afton said. "But let's not fixate on Sponger right now. We've got him covered, and if he even itches his big toe, we're going to know about it."

"Okay." Susan's voice was thick but controlled.

"We'd like to ask you about the woman at Novamed," Max said.

Susan dropped her head and then peered up at them through a fringe of blond bangs. "You know about that?"

"It came up yesterday when we were talking to Richard," Afton said.

"I don't know who she is," Susan said. "Because I didn't want to know. All I know is that it happened."

"And you believed your husband," Afton said. "Believed him when he said there was no impropriety on his part."

Susan considered this. "I believed him at the time."

"We're wondering," Max said, "if there's a remote possibility that Molly, the doll lady, could be the same woman who harassed Richard at Novamed?"

"That would be an awfully big coincidence, wouldn't it?" Susan asked.

"Yes, it would," Max said. "But like I said, we're looking at all the angles. Trying to tear everything apart."

"Okay." Susan shifted on the couch and bounced her knees nervously.

"If the doll lady works or once worked at Novamed," Afton said, "then that could be where she first came into contact with Richard."

"Maybe she developed a thing for him," Max said. "Or saw you at one of their social functions—you did attend corporate functions, didn't you?"

"Yes." Susan wrinkled her nose. "A few. You're saying this doll lady might have become obsessed with Richard?"

"It's a possibility," Max said. "And if she's seen you in the past—and then she saw you that day at the Skylark Mall . . ." Max grimaced. "Maybe seeing you triggered something in her brain and she took advantage of the situation."

"Oh my God," Susan said. "But I . . . I don't know who the woman was that supposedly harassed him. Um, did you ask Richard?"

"His attorney advised him not to reveal her name."

"Slocum," she spit out. "What a weasel. I suppose he'll represent Richard in the divorce, too."

"We're in the process of obtaining a court order and will pay another visit to Novamed's headquarters tomorrow," Afton said. "So we can put a name to a face."

"If I saw her, then I could identify her," Susan said.

"That's right. So we'll interview her and snap a picture," Max said.

"This is like an endless nightmare," Susan said.

"I know it is," Afton said. "But you're doing well, you're holding up remarkably well. And we will get your baby back, I know we will."

"Bless you," Susan said, just as there was a muffled ring. She fumbled in the pocket of her hoodie and pulled out her cell phone. "Excuse me, this is probably my sister," she told them. She punched a button, said, "Hello?" and listened. Susan's face, which two seconds earlier had been filled with concern, suddenly clouded over with anger. "Richard," she spit out. "What do you want? If you're calling to . . . *What?*" Susan suddenly stiffened and her eyes filled with fear. "What are you saying? Uh, uh, uh . . ." She dropped the phone to her chest, trembling, looking as if she was about to have a seizure.

Sensing a disaster in the making, Max lunged to Susan's aid. But all she did was thrust her phone into his outstretched hand.

"Listen to this," she moaned. "Talk to him!"

"Richard?" Max said into the phone. "This is Detective Montgomery. What's the problem? What's going on?"

"Did she get the call?" Richard screamed. "Did she get the same call that I did?"

"Slow down, slow down," Max said. "What are you talking about?"

But Richard was in full-blown hysterics. "The ransom call! Did the kidnappers call Susan, too?"

"Ransom call?" Max said, which caused Afton to spring up off the sofa.

"Yes," Richard said. "Just now! Like, fifteen seconds ago."

"Who called you?" Max asked. He was making urgent motions for Afton to take notes. "Was it a woman?"

"It was a man," Richard said. "He asked for two million dollars in exchange for Elizabeth Ann."

"Two million dollars," Max repeated, more for Afton's benefit than Susan's.

"Oh my God," Susan breathed. "She's alive." She made a grab for the phone. "That means she's alive?"

But Max shrugged Susan away, trying to remain completely focused on what Richard Darden was telling him. "When are you supposed to deliver the money, did he say?"

"He said he'd call back tomorrow with explicit instructions as to time and place," Richard said. He gave a bitter snort. "He said he wanted to give me enough time to get the money together."

"Where are you now?" Max asked. He listened carefully, and then said, "Okay, you stay right where you are. I'm going to call Don Jasper and some of the other FBI guys to come over and get you. Don't make any more calls with that phone. In fact, just hang up and sit tight. Somebody's going to be there in about five minutes."

"Okay, okay," Richard said. "Tell Susan about this, will you?"

"Yes. Just hang up now," Max said. "And I'll see you shortly."

Max pressed the Off button and stood there, holding the phone.

Susan crawled across the sofa toward him. "There's a ransom demand?"

she asked, even though she'd heard everything Max had said. "That means she's alive, right? That my baby's still alive?"

"Yes," Max said. "It's probably a good sign." He handed Susan's phone back to her, and then pulled out his own. I've got some critical calls to make. But by the time I finish, there'll be an officer here to stay with you."

"Thank you," Susan whispered.

28

AFTON wiped a sleep crusty from the corner of her eye as she sat at the far end of the table in the big conference room. It was the room where the chief of police made major announcements and the mayor sometimes held press conferences.

As if things hadn't been crazy enough last night, with hastily assembled meetings that included Don Jasper, Richard Darden, and an entire cast and crew of law enforcement, things were really popping this Thursday morning as well. All the same people were back once again and the room fairly pulsed with a mixture of excitement, officiousness, and frayed nerves.

Thacker stood at the head of the table barking orders. Everyone scrambled as Angel Graham sat at his side, serenely taking notes. Richard Darden was back from spending the night at the Spencer Hotel, just one block from police headquarters, and he looked appropriately dazed. The big debate raging now was whether Darden should attempt the ransom exchange by himself, or whether a member of the SWAT team, duded up to look like Darden, should take care of it.

"No, no," Darden protested. "I've got to be the one to do it. They'll be expecting me."

"They may not even know what you look like," Don Jasper reasoned. "So why take the chance?"

"Oh, please," Darden said. "You can Google my name and get a dozen hits just from the *Tribune* alone."

"Then he wears a vest and we put a wire on him," Harvey Bagin suggested.

"And a tracking device," Keith Sunder said.

"A camera would be even better," Bagin said. "That way he can broadcast in real time."

Thacker wasn't so sure. "If the kidnapper's a pro, he'll spot that shit in a heartbeat."

"What if he's not a pro?" Jasper said. "What if it's who we think it is? That crazy doll lady and some guy?"

"We're still not sure who we're dealing with," Thacker said. "From what Mr. Darden has told us, the man he spoke to last night sounded older than the fellow who coldcocked the babysitter. Somebody a little more slick, a lot more rehearsed."

"It was a man," Darden said. "And fairly well spoken at that. I sure as hell didn't talk to any dumb kid."

"When's the kidnapper supposed to call back?" Jasper asked.

"He just said he'd call today." Darden cast a panicked glance at the cell phone that sat on the table in front of him.

Thacker gazed at him. "Did you get the money together yet?"

"We'll be doing that in two shakes," Jasper said. "Going over to First Federal. Talk to . . ." He looked at Darden.

"Bruce Billiard," Darden said. "VP of their Private Client Group."

"And you can get the full two million?" Thacker asked.

"Yes," Darden said.

Max glanced at Afton and wiggled his eyebrows.

"And please tell me we have Mr. Darden's cell phone carrier on full alert?" Thacker said.

"All that's been taken care of," said Dick Boyce, one of the techs.

"I don't care what anybody says," Bagin said. "I still think we need to track him."

"What if the kidnapper wants to make the exchange in the middle of a cornfield out in East Bumbleburg?" Thacker asked.

"Tracking is still tracking," Bagin argued.

The debates and arguments raged on, with Afton sitting next to Max, both of them following along as if they were watching a tennis match at Wimbledon.

Finally, tasked with technical, financial, and legal responsibilities, people began filtering out of the room until only a handful remained.

Thacker took off his glasses, rubbed his eyes tiredly, and glanced at Afton and Max. "You two still here?"

"What do you need from us, boss?" Max asked.

"Don't call me 'boss,'" Thacker said. "I thought you were going to pay a visit to that mystery lady over at Novamed."

"Just say the word," Max said. "But she's not a mystery anymore. Darden spilled everything."

"Okay," Thacker said. "Go now. It probably won't amount to much, but do it anyway. And keep in touch, okay?"

"Will do," Afton said. Though the stakes were high, she was tingling with excitement. The hunt was shaping up; the dogs were snapping their jaws.

THE reception area at Novamed was just as stark and antiseptic as Afton remembered it. Andrew and his same-cookie-cutter buddy were still officiously manning the front desk, though they seemed somewhat less cordial this time around.

Max, however, was enjoying himself. He dangled a piece of paper in front of their noses and said, "This piece of paper is a subpoena signed by District Court Judge Marsha Folbridge. It gives us complete and total access to Richard Darden's personnel records as well as to Eleanor Winters, the heretofore unnamed woman in the sexual harassment arbitration that took place here on corporate premises this past October."

Andrew sighed and punched a button. When his party answered, he said, "We have two detectives here who want to inspect Richard Darden's personnel records." He listened for a few moments, and then said, "Yes, they do. It seems to be in order." He hung up and said, "Sign in, take a badge, and please take a seat. Someone will be down to fetch you."

"Thank you," Max said.

Max signed his name, and then passed the pen to Afton.

They waited five minutes, then ten minutes. Afton sensed this might be carefully calculated. To give the Novamed folks a chance to collect their thoughts. Or, worst-case scenario, shred their documents.

Finally, a door opened and Betty Randle came bustling out. She was dressed in black once again, a severely tailored skirt suit, and had her blond hair done up in what Afton thought might be an old-fashioned French roll. Or maybe the style had swung back into fashion again as a hip, retro look.

"We meet again," Randle said. Then, "May I see the subpoena, please?"

Max handed it over and let Randle study it for a moment. Then he plucked it back from her and slid it into his leather folder. "Satisfied?"

"Follow me," Randle said. She led them through the door she'd emerged from, down a long white corridor carpeted in industrial gray fabric, and into a small conference room with a table and six chairs. A manila file folder sat in the center of the table.

Afton and Max sat down, and then Max pulled the file across the table and flipped it open. He took his time, going through the various papers, turning them over carefully. From the look on his face, Afton knew there wasn't much there. Maybe some shredding had gone on. Or at least some sanitizing.

"Miss Randle," Max said. "We also put in a request to talk to the employee involved in the Darden harassment issue."

"I'm not sure that's possible," Randle said.

Max glanced at Afton, who dutifully pulled out her cell phone. "Miss Randle, I'm going to dial the number of the state attorney general and let you speak with him directly."

Randle shrank back. And for the first time, her composure seemed to slip. "That won't be necessary," she said. "I'll bring Ms. Winters in."

"Thank you," Max said.

They heard Eleanor Winters's protestations even before she came through the doorway.

"This is ridiculous," Winters sputtered as she followed Randle into the conference room. She glared at them and reluctantly sat down at the table. "I had assurances that this absurd misunderstanding was over and done with."

Afton studied the outraged Eleanor Winters. She was pencil-thin and raven-haired with an almost unnaturally narrow face. The type of woman who might get labeled "high-strung" by the men she worked with.

"Miss Winters," Max said. He extended a hand, but Winters chose not to respond. She crossed her arms and fixed him with a steely gaze. Unfazed, he went ahead with cursory introductions.

Randle glanced at her watch and said, "Time is at a premium, Detectives. If you could please ask your questions?"

"You realize, Miss Winters, that Richard Darden's baby daughter has been kidnapped?" Max said.

"I read the newspapers," Winters said.

"Since you had a tertiary involvement with him, we'd like to ask you a few questions."

Winters's lip curled. "Then ask."

Afton and Max had rehearsed their questions on the way over. They started with gentle lobs, asking Winters how long she'd worked at Novamed, what her job entailed, like that. Then they moved on to the more hardball issues. That is, had she sexually harassed Richard Darden?

"Those allegations are utterly preposterous," Winters spit at them. "The whole episode was something his overachieving, macho male ego dreamed up."

"Yet your company took it seriously enough," Afton said, "that both parties were afforded arbitration. What was the technical term they used? Oh yes, a grievance committee."

"People file grievances around here when the water bubbler doesn't work," Winters snapped.

"But there *was* a grievance," Max said. "Between you and Richard Darden. Is that correct?"

"Yes," Winters said.

"Yet you say it was baseless," Afton said.

"Asked and answered," Randle said.

Max held up a hand. "You seem quite upset, Miss Winters."

"I am upset," she said. "You have no right to come in here and question my ethics or morality." She started to stand up. "In fact, I'm not about to—"

"Sit down!" Max shouted. "Sit down and listen to me."

Reluctantly, Winters sat back down in her chair.

"We can go over these questions in the comfort of this office . . ." He glanced around at the sterile white walls. "Well, relative comfort. Or we can go down to police headquarters and find a nice cozy interview room."

Winters stared at him, her eyes hard as obsidian. Then she turned to Randle and said, "Will you please call security?"

That was enough for Max. He slammed his hand down on the table, causing it to tremble and papers to scatter.

"Enough," he shouted. "There's been a kidnapping, a murder, and an extortion attempt, so everyone better start cooperating right now!"

"What is it you want to know?" Winters asked through tightly clenched teeth.

Afton and Max resumed their good cop, bad cop routine. They asked questions about Winters's relationship with Darden, and about the grievance he'd filed against her. Winters barely gave them one- and two-word answers.

Until they asked for her side of the story.

Then Eleanor Winters opened the spigot. Darden had come on to her, she claimed. Subtly at first, and then escalating his interest in her until it was no longer possible for her to comfortably get her work done. The grievance had been filed, arbitration ensued, and Novamed had resolved things by assigning her to a different department. She made it clear how unfair the resolution had been and how unhappy she was.

"But things are on an even keel now," Max said.

"Somewhat," Winters said. Then, "Yes, I suppose they are."

Max smiled evenly. "Thank you for your cooperation. We really appreciate it."

"Am I finished?" Winters asked. "I have work to do."

Max held up a hand. "We just need to tie up a few loose ends."

Afton looked up from studying Winters's file. "You live in Woodbury?"

"Yes," she said.

"With your son."

"Leave him out of this!"

"He's a junior in high school?" Afton said. "And the two of you live fairly close to Hudson, Wisconsin."

"What does that have to do with anything?"

The Max, speaking in a pleasant tone, said, "Tell us about the dolls."

Winters's head snapped in his direction, a puzzled expression on her face. "Dolls?" she said. She looked at Randle. "What does he mean by 'dolls'?"

Randle shook her head.

"I'm sorry," Afton said. "We were under the impression you had a doll collection."

Randle leaned forward in her chair, fairly seething. "Wait a minute, you think *I'm* the crazy doll lady they've been talking about on TV? Are you insane?"

"You don't collect dolls?" Afton asked.

"No!"

"Ever owned a doll?"

"Not for a long, long time," Winters said. She curled a lip. "What about you?" she fired back. "Do *you* collect anything? Stamps, postcards . . . teddy bears?"

"I think," Afton said, "that a collection is just a shopping addiction in drag."

Winters turned to Randle. "This conversation is beyond insulting. I'm not answering one more ridiculous question unless I have an attorney present."

Randle tipped her head. "You heard the lady."

Max held up both hands. "Hey, we're just trying to cover all the bases." He turned toward Afton. "Do you have any more questions?"

Afton shifted her attention to Randle. "How about you, Miss Randle? Do you have any connection with dolls? Any dolls lying around your house?"

Randle actually smirked. "I'm afraid I can't help you."

"Actually," Afton said, "you've both been a big help." She pulled out her cell phone and, as Winters seemed to relax, sensing the interview was about over, snapped a quick shot of her.

Winters went ballistic all over again. "Wha— You can't *do* that!"

"I just did," Afton told her.

THOSE broads are a couple of cold fish," Max said once they were back outside, crossing the parking lot.

"Don't call them 'broads,'" Afton said. "I don't like them any more than you do, but there's no reason to be disrespectful."

"You have an interesting way of phrasing things."

"Thank you."

They ducked into Max's car, grateful to be out of the wind and cold. He turned on the engine and flipped the heater on high. "You got Susan Darden's number?" he asked.

"Got it. I'm texting the photo to her right now. She knows it's coming; she'll be on pins and needles. Now all we have to do is wait."

They didn't have to wait long.

Susan Darden called a minute later. "It's not her."

"You're sure?" Afton asked.

"Positive. The photo you texted me, that woman is way too *chic* looking. The doll lady, she was more of a country bumpkin."

"It's not her," Afton told Max.

"She's sure?" Max asked. "She's positive? Tell her to take another look."

"I can hear him," Susan said in Afton's ear. "Tell Detective Montgomery that I'm sorry, but it's not the same woman."

"Okay," Afton told her. "Thank you."

"I'll talk to you later?" Susan asked.

"Count on it."

As they spun out of the icy parking lot, Afton glanced back at the white building, which seemed perfectly set against the snowy landscape, like an enormous pile of ice that had washed up onshore in the Antarctic. "That place is a dead end," she said.

"You don't know that," Max said.

"Yeah, I do. I've got that gut feeling, just like you do."

"Just because the harassment lady wasn't the doll lady—"

Afton cut him off. "The really tragic thing is we're running out of time. That baby's been missing for almost five full days."

"Maybe we wait for the ransom exchange," Max said.

Which made Afton feel even more disheartened. How rotten was it that they had to wait for the ransom exchange to see how this drama played out? And buried deep in her psyche was the burning question: Would there even be a ransom exchange?

29

SHAKE sat on the edge of her bed, gnawing her thumbnail. She had a decision to make and she knew she didn't have a whole lot of time. Ronnie and his crazy mother were acting more and more strangely. *Lunatics* was the word that kept rolling around in her brain. Ever since they'd come home with that baby last Saturday, they'd both been tiptoeing around on eggshells. And any time she asked a question about the kid, Ronnie's face took on this dumb, guilty look. She knew Ronnie wasn't a bad guy, certainly not the worst she'd known. But being under his mother's thumb . . . well, anything could happen.

And maybe it already had.

Shake still wondered where the two of them had lit out to on Tuesday night. Going to the Family Resource Center? No, she'd didn't think so. Besides, they'd fumbled around for a long time, with Ronnie getting all dressed up like some kind of damn commando in a Dwayne Johnson movie. And though she hadn't actually seen Ronnie with any sort of weapon, she'd had a feeling that he might have been sneaking out of the house with one of his knives.

Sneaking out of the house.

Like she was planning to do right now.

Shake folded a pair of jeans, tossed it on top of her meager stash of underwear, and stuffed it all in her purple nylon gym bag, what had once been her dancer's bag. Two sweatshirts followed, as well as her makeup case, hairbrush, and a box of panty liners. There. What else? Nothing else. She didn't own much. Well, that was all going to change. As soon as she had this baby, she was going to head south, maybe to Florida or someplace warm like that. She'd once heard one of the other dancers talk about how there were lots of gentlemen's clubs down in Florida. And they were frequented by rich older men who were willing to lay a ten spot on the runway so they could watch a cute girl work it and twerk it.

She zipped her bag closed and looked around the bedroom. The closet door was standing open and she saw Ronnie's Green Bay Packers jacket hanging there. She hesitated for a moment and then grabbed it. Felt absolutely justified in doing so. After all, she was trying to stay warm for two.

Tiptoeing out to the second-floor landing, Shake could hear the TV blaring downstairs. Marjorie was eating a tuna fish sandwich and watching *The Bold and the Beautiful*, her favorite soap opera. Ronnie was down in the basement, mixing up a batch of chemicals so he could tan a couple of deer hides.

Shake unzipped her boots and slipped out of them. Better to carry them downstairs and put them on once she was outside. If she *made* it outside. She was filled with trepidation and mumbling a prayer now, unconsciously reverting to the little bit of religion she'd been taught as a child.

Forgive us our trespasses . . .

Two of the steps creaked as she slowly eased her way downstairs. That made her hesitate for a few terrifying moments.

Deliver us from evil . . .

In her mind's eye, Shake imagined Marjorie popping out at her like some kind of menacing funhouse ghoul. But her luck held and it never happened.

For Thine is the Kingdom and the power . . .

In the kitchen, Marjorie's car keys sat bunched on the counter. Shake made a hasty sign of the cross as she snatched up the keys, hoping that

Ronnie had replaced the battery in his mom's car. She thought he had, since he'd been out there early this morning, fiddling with things.

The baby was gurgling away in a playpen near the stove. Shake thought about grabbing the little baby and taking her along. But no, that wouldn't work. It wasn't part of her plan. Breathless now, her heart hammering inside her chest, she kissed the little baby on the top of her head and stepped outside.

The raw wind sliced at her, taking her breath away as she hesitated on the side porch. Still, Shake knew she had to keep her eyes on the prize—her ultimate freedom! She stuffed her feet into her boots, zipped them up, and waddled toward the car.

Marjorie was a skinny little witch, so the front seat was jacked all the way forward, almost to the steering wheel. With her big belly, Shake had to partially squash her way in and then slide the seat back. She fumbled with the keys, missed the ignition slot, then jammed in the key and turned over the engine.

The car roared to life immediately. Thank God!

Desperation rising like bile in her throat, Shake threw the car in Reverse, gunned the motor hard, and promptly flew back into a snowdrift.

No!

She fumbled the car into Drive and hit the gas again, a little too hard. Now the wheels spun frantically. Damn, what was wrong with this car? She cranked the steering wheel hard to the right. Nothing, there was no purchase at all. She was stuck in an icy rut on practically bald tires!

What now? What to do? Her older brother had once shown her how to get out of a snowdrift by rocking the car, so that's what Shake did. She threw the car into Reverse, and then into Drive, trying to rock it, begging it to inch forward, pleading for it to move forward.

A face appeared in the frosted kitchen window. Marjorie. Fifteen seconds later the door flew open and Ronnie came running out. Shake tromped down harder on the accelerator, making the tires scream like a crazed banshee. Now her teeth were chattering so hard that her fillings ached. Was her escape ruined? No, it couldn't be. She was going to drive to Florida, after all. Have the baby and then just . . .

Ronnie ripped open the driver's side door and screamed, "What are you freaking *doing*?"

Shake's first thought was, *Caught like a rat in a trap.* Then she wondered, *Can I possibly reason with him?* If she could make Ronnie understand how terrified and upset she was, would he finally see her side of the story? Would he hop in and come with her?

"I'm getting out of here!" Shake screamed at him. "If you had any sense, you'd come with me."

"Stop it," Ronnie said, half climbing into the car with her. "Take your foot off the accelerator, you're burning rubber. You're gonna wear off any bit of tread that's left!"

"Huh? What?" Shake lifted her foot and the car quieted down. She started to cry helplessly.

"Shake. Baby," Ronnie said. "Where do you think you're going?"

"Anywhere," she sobbed. "Away from here." She lifted her eyes and saw Marjorie standing on the porch now, struggling to pull on her pink ski parka.

"Not her," Shake said through gritted teeth. "Not now."

Ronnie waved a hand at Marjorie. "Go back inside," he yelled. "She's fine."

"She fine?" Marjorie screamed. "Are you crazy?"

"I'll take care of it," Ronnie yelled back. "Just . . . get away."

Muttering loudly, throwing murderous looks at Shake, Marjorie finally retreated back inside the farmhouse.

Shake was jibbering now, scared out of her mind. "We. Have. To. Go."

"Shhh," Ronnie said. "Stop crying. We'll do it, okay?"

Shake was still crying. "What?" Had she heard him correctly? "You mean we'll run away? Together?"

"Yes, of course together. But not like this. After you have the baby. Then we'll pack up and go. Just leave this . . . place. I know it's not good for us."

Relief flooded Shake's brain. "Jeez, Ronnie, do you really mean it? You promise?" He'd jammed himself partway into the car and she was clutching at him now, as if he were her only lifeline.

"Cross my heart, I promise. Now just . . . come back inside, okay? This can't be good for the baby and I'm freezing my nuts off out here."

"We'll really go? Soon?"

"I think . . . maybe next week," Ronnie said. "Now come on . . ." He turned off the ignition, then reached a hand out and helped hoist her out of the car. "We'll go, okay?"

Shake clung to him, nodding. "Okay, okay."

She followed him back inside, but deep down, a tendril of fear lingered. Ronnie talked a good game right now—and she almost believed him. But what if he really didn't have the guts to run away? Then what?

30

AFTON felt beleaguered and nauseous. Her condition wasn't a product of Max's erratic driving, but of all the dead ends they'd been hitting in the search for Elizabeth Ann Darden. She'd felt certain that the interview with Eleanor Winters might turn into something, but it was just another false lead. How would they ever find that baby? Each road they went down seemed to lead nowhere. She was beginning to lose heart.

Now they were on their way to interview Bob Binger. Andy Farmer had already interviewed Binger, but now Thacker wanted them to take another crack at him. Maybe the man that Richard Darden had fired from his post at Novamed would be able to shed a small amount of light on the situation—or throw some dirt on Darden. Afton wasn't sure which.

As they bumped west on Highway 55, Afton's restlessness grew into irritation. The seemingly endless pods of slow traffic made the drive seem even more tedious. She slumped in her seat and stared out the window. As soon as they'd made the transition from urban to suburban, fast-food franchises seemed to spring up like errant mushrooms and towering office buildings loomed at each intersection.

Max read her frustration. "Almost there," he said. They turned onto

494, zipped past the Carlson Towers, took the next exit, and then bumped down a south-side frontage road until they hit a shabby-looking redbrick strip mall. There was a tax preparer's office, a Thai restaurant, an office furniture store, a veterinarian, and three other small- to medium-sized businesses. He pulled into a parking slot in front of a silver sign that said MEDIGAIN. "Some corporate office, huh?"

Medigain, Afton had learned, was one of a hundred upstart medical tech companies that had come on the heels of millions of dollars of venture capital money. Most of that money had long since dried up or been frittered away, but there were a few companies that had dug in their heels and hung in for the long haul. Medigain was one of these. It had recently received a government patent for a new type of heart valve and its stock was slowly beginning to tick upward.

Afton and Max entered the lobby and were pleasantly surprised. The reception area was neat and orderly with a half dozen bright red club chairs and dozens of healthy-looking green plants. Their front desk was staffed by a smiling twentysomething woman who was wearing a telephone headset.

"Welcome to Medigain," the receptionist said, beaming.

"Good morning," Max said. Then he caught sight of the clock over her shoulder. "Afternoon," he corrected.

"No worry," the woman said. "That clock just ticked past noon a minute ago."

Max fished out his badge and held it up for the woman's inspection. She seemed to experience a moment of indecision, then said, "How can I help you, Detective?"

"We have an appointment to speak with Bob Binger," Max said. "We called earlier."

"Then I'll let him know you're here." She hit a few buttons, connected with Binger, and announced their arrival. "Okay," she said into her headset. "I'll bring them right back." She stood up and smoothed her flowered skirt. "If you'll follow me, please?"

They were led down a narrow corridor between beige industrial-looking cubicles. A few of the cubes were empty, but most held staffers who were busy talking on their phones, texting, or eating lunch. The receptionist opened the door to a generic-looking conference room and ushered them in.

"Thanks," Max said.

"He'll be with you in a minute," the receptionist said.

Afton sat on one side of the table, Max on the other.

"Thoughts?" he said.

"I don't know," Afton sighed. "I understand why we're here, but I still think we should be focusing on the pizza guy. I think we'd do better if we were back in Hudson working the crime scene."

"The FBI has that covered. We're here to dot the i's and cross the t's."

"Bob Binger being one of the i's?"

"You never know."

"Hey," a man said as he huffed his way through the doorway. He had a sallow, pudgy face and a paunch that was barely restrained by his belt. He looked tired, overworked, and scattered.

Afton and Max both rose to shake Binger's hand and introduce themselves. His palm was damp and his face was florid. Maybe he was nervous, Afton thought. Or maybe he just had high blood pressure.

"I hope this won't take long," Binger said, plopping down into a chair.

"We'll try to keep it brief," Max said. "Like I explained on the phone, we're trying to gather background information on Richard Darden."

"This about his missing kid?"

"We're focusing more on him right now."

Binger snorted. "King Shit Darden, huh? Well, what do you want to know?"

"Richard Darden fired you, is that correct?"

A tiny vein in Binger's forehead pulsed and his nostrils flared. "That arrogant puke cost me everything. Fourteen years I put in at Novamed. I led a team of eight developers. Never had a bad word in my personnel file. Never. Year after year, my team was one of the most productive in the company."

"Then what?" Max asked.

"Darden, that's what," Binger said.

"Care to explain that?" Afton asked.

"Darden looked smart in a suit, played a good round of golf, and had enough smarm to spread around in the executive offices. He hopscotched his way up to head of R and D—that's research and development—and became my boss. Every time we came up with a new idea, Darden took credit for it. When I finally called him out, he fired my ass. Security came in, threw all my personal gear in a cardboard box, and escorted me out the front door." He mopped at his forehead. "Right in front of my team. God, it was embarrassing."

"So you were angry," Max said.

"I was livid. Plus, I was out of work for almost six months after that."

"Ever have any revenge fantasies?" Afton asked.

Binger looked startled. "What? Me? No." He stared at them. "I see where you're going with this, but it wasn't me who kidnapped that baby. Heck, I've got three kids of my own. I could never pull a stunt like that. No way."

"Do you know anyone who would?" Max asked.

Binger was slow to answer. "No, I can't say that I do. Oh, there were plenty of people who wanted to get back at Darden. But . . . I don't think they'd go about it that way. No, I can't think of anyone who's *that* crazy."

AN hour later, Afton and Max were back at the office.

"C'mon," Max said. "Let's grab a cup of coffee before we check in."

"Sure," Afton said.

"Got any change?"

She handed over her last three quarters.

Max popped them into the machine, gave it a hard kick, and got his cup of coffee. It spilled out oily and burned, just the way he liked it. They headed down the hallway just as two FBI agents, looking like on-the-job German shepherds, came jogging toward them and then passed by without saying a word.

"Keepin' us in the loop," Afton snorted.

They poked their heads into Thacker's office and were waved in.

"How did it go with Binger?" Thacker asked. He looked dapper today in a charcoal gray pinstripe.

"Not much there," Max said. "Guy's pissed off, but he's not that kind of pissed off. What's happening here?"

"We saw more FBI agents," Afton said, curious. "Out in the hallway."

Thacker leaned back in his chair. "There's still no word from the kidnappers. Darden is starting to lose it, so he's been calling anyone and everyone who's in a position of power."

"Which means you've been getting trickle-down pressure?" Afton asked.

Thacker's laugh was a sharp bark. "I've talked to more state senators, city council members, county sheriffs, and governor's aids today than I normally do in an entire year of operations. Unless it's an election year, and then they're calling to panhandle or ask for an endorsement."

"I'm sorry to hear that," Afton said. "I know you've got a lot on your plate."

Thacker grunted. "There's more."

"What?" Max asked.

"Richard Darden is thinking about offering a reward. One million dollars."

"Oh no," Max said. "That'll just bring out all the crazies. Tie up the phone lines. Exhaust our resources." He blew out a glut of air. "As if they're not exhausted enough."

"When the kidnappers hear about it," Afton said, "they'll just want him to add it to the ransom."

"I'm working hard to get him to hold off," Thacker said. His clenched hands flew open. "But . . . who knows?"

"Has the media gotten a whiff of this yet?" Afton asked.

"I hope not," Thacker said. He looked at her sharply. "Still want to be a detective?"

"Would it sound strange right now if I said yes?"

"Maybe a little," Thacker said. "But I kind of suspected that's what you'd say. You have to be a little out there on the edge to be able to handle this job."

Afton sat a little straighter in her chair. This was Thacker's version of praise. "You think I meet the minimum daily requirement of derangement?"

"Maybe," Thacker said. "You might be getting there." He was silent for a moment, and then said, "We've got things pretty well covered here. You two should head over to the Saint Croix medical examiner's lab. The ME is doing an autopsy on Muriel Pink this afternoon." When Afton looked squeamish, he said, "Yeah, I know. But it's part and parcel, so take off."

THE last person they expected to run into at police headquarters was Portia Bourgoyne, but there she was. Lounging in the hallway next to the file room, speaking in a low melodic whisper, her lips practically brushing the ear of a young uniformed officer.

Harry Affolter, Afton thought, when she caught sight of them. Was he the leak? Then she turned her attention back on Portia. The woman was wearing a black cashmere dress and black stilettos that showed off her rounded curves and shapely calves. It seemed fairly clear that the young officer was firmly under her spell.

"Is there something I can help you with, Miss Bourgoyne?" Max asked in a loud, authoritative tone. He'd not only caught Portia's attention, but sent the young officer scurrying away.

Portia cast a disdainful look at Max and said, "I was just checking in with your media relations officer."

"Trying to wangle some inside information?" Afton asked.

Portia ignored her.

Max suddenly advanced on Portia. "You killed that woman, you know that?" His mouth was an angry slash, and if Afton didn't know better, she'd say his ears were pulled back flat against his head. Like a jackal ready to attack.

Portia just stared at him.

"Muriel Pink," Max hissed. "You killed her just as sure as if you'd held a knife to her throat and slit open her jugular."

Portia's eyes blazed. "How dare you insinuate—"

"I'm not insinuating anything," Max said. "I'm stating a fact. You manipulated that poor, gullible old woman. You put her on TV and practically dared the killer to go after her. Well, that's exactly what happened. So now I'm asking you, how do you sleep at night?"

"Any issue of culpability can be taken up directly with my news director," Portia spit back. "And my station's attorney."

Afton had to hand it to her. Portia was good. She wasn't afraid to stand her ground. Or maybe she was just too dumb to know she might be in serious trouble.

Portia curled a lip. "With a two-million-dollar ransom demand, and now a possible reward in the making, you're going to have your hands full fielding calls from all the loonies out there."

Afton couldn't believe what she was hearing. How did Portia know about the ransom? And the fact that Darden might offer a reward? Was the department hemorrhaging information?

"Who'd you have to bribe to get that information?" Max asked.

Portia focused a cool smile on him. "A girl's gotta do what a girl's gotta do." She tilted her head and gazed up at him. Bit her lower lip and offered a sexy smile. "C'mon," she said, her voice a little breathier now. "Work with me on this, Max. When this case finally breaks—and I know it will—a lot of people are going to want to grab the brass ring and take credit. I can make sure the bright lights land squarely on you."

Afton watched Max carefully. She couldn't tell if he was angry or capitulating. Then he did something she never would have expected. He blinked and smiled at Portia. He hung his head and said, in an almost sheepish tone, "You know what? I give up."

"What?" Afton said.

"Excuse me?" Portia asked. Even she seemed startled by his change of heart.

"I may as well tell you the whole thing." Max gave a deferential shrug. "You're just going to find out anyway."

"No, Max," Afton said. "What are you doing?"

But like a great white shark, Portia had sensed a trickle of blood in the water. Her confident smile returned and she pulled out her smartphone to record Max's words.

Max waved his hands. "No, this has to be off the record. You didn't hear it from me, and Detective Tangler will deny all knowledge of this conversation." He glanced at Afton. "Correct?"

Afton stood in dumbfounded silence. She wasn't sure what to make of this. "Correct," she said finally. She wasn't sure what kind of game Max was playing.

"Okay, that won't be a problem," Portia said. "I can cite you as an anonymous source close to the investigation." She held up a finger. "But when this story breaks, I'll want you to go on record to corroborate my story."

Max appeared to consider this. Finally, he nodded his head and said, "Yeah, that works for me."

"So what?" Portia asked, drawing closer to Max. "What's going on? What's the latest on the Darden kidnapping?"

"We have a very strong lead," Max said. "But we're being stonewalled."

"By who?"

"Novamed."

Portia was watching Max like a lion might eye a zebra. "Explain, please."

"We've obtained information concerning a possible marital indiscretion between Richard Darden and one of their company executives, an Eleanor Winters."

"So she's a suspect?"

"Absolutely. Only problem is, Novamed is covering for her like crazy. They've got several new products coming on the market and they'd hate like hell to have any adverse publicity right now. Their stock is up and they don't want anything to upset the delicate balance."

Portia wasn't convinced. "Are you saying this Eleanor Winters is the kidnapper or that she has information relating to the case?"

Max spread his hands apart, palms up, in what looked like an outright appeal. "We simply don't know. That's what we've been trying to find out."

Portia eyed him carefully. "And you swear this is legit?"

"Absolutely," Max said with a straight face.

Portia reached for her black mink coat, which was casually draped over the wall of one of the cubicles. "If this turns into something, I'm gonna owe you big time. But if you burn me, watch out."

"I know," Max said. "Hell hath no fury and all that."

"You'd better believe it," Portia said. She pulled on her coat, leaned forward, and gave him a peck on the cheek. "Thanks, sweetie."

"You're welcome," he said as she scampered away. Then he turned and gave Afton a rueful look. "What do you think?"

"I think she's going to come back and slit your throat open with a dull letter opener is what I think."

"Maybe so," Max said. "But it was worth it."

"How so?"

Max pulled his mouth into an angry snarl. "Payback."

31

I feel like we live on this damn freeway," Max said. They were humming along, heading for Hudson again and what would probably be a not-so-nice meeting with the local medical examiner.

"You remember when all those college kids were disappearing, maybe ten years ago?" Afton asked.

Max nodded. "Yeah, I remember. There was a fellow down in La Crosse . . ."

"One in Eau Claire," Afton said. "And one in Minneapolis and another up in Saint Cloud. I always thought of the perp as the I-94 killer."

"Most law enforcement agencies thought the murders were isolated incidents. Local incidents."

"I know. But I always had a feeling it was either a long-haul trucker or maybe a traveling sales guy. Somebody who drove that stretch of I-94 fairly regularly. They'd stop in college towns where they knew kids would be drinking and hanging out in the local bars. Then they'd lure them away from their groups and murder them."

"Seems to me all the victims were dumped in water."

"Rivers and swamps," Afton said. "Yup, same MO for all of them."

"You did research on this?"

"It was kind of my hobby for a while," Afton said. "This case and that poor anchorwoman who disappeared down in Iowa."

"Some hobby," Max said. "Doing research on missing, murdered people."

"Somebody's got to do it," Afton said. "Somebody's got to try to take down the monsters."

AFTON and Max passed by the large blue Hudson water tower and made a quick turn into the oversized parking lot that fronted the Saint Croix County Government Center. The large brick structure housed several county government entities; few area residents realized that the morgue was located in the basement.

They badged their way in and then took a clanking elevator down to the lower level. A sign with an arrow directed them to the corridor on their right.

"Hate this smell," Max said as their footsteps echoed in the white-tiled hallway.

The smell that wafted toward them also made Afton's stomach lurch. Chemicals mingled with harsh cleaning fluids and a touch of something foul.

Max pushed open the crash doors at the end of the hall and they suddenly found themselves in a small anteroom. More Spartan than a reception area, not quite a lobby.

A young man in green scrubs looked up from a desk. "Help you?" With his earnest look and curly hair, Afton thought he looked like he was about fourteen years old. A medical student? Mort sci student?

"We're here to see Dr. Taylor," Max told the kid.

The young man stood up. "Got some ID?" He pushed his wire-rimmed glasses up his nose, squinted a careful assessment at their IDs, and then said, "Follow me, please." He guided them down a wide, green-tiled hallway, pushed aside a large vinyl curtain, and said, "There you go."

Afton and Max stepped inside a compact autopsy room that contained Muriel Pink's body. She was lying atop a metal table with a white sheet pulled up to her chin. With her eyes shut and her mouth closed, she looked like she was lost in peaceful slumber, so very different than the look of horror and agony that had marred her face earlier. A man they assumed was Dr.

Taylor backed away from her when he heard their footsteps and turned to face them. He was also young, maybe late twenties, and blond and blue-eyed, in keeping with the area's high concentration of Scandinavians.

"Detective Montgomery?" he asked.

Max nodded. "Dr. Taylor, how do. This is my associate Afton Tangler."

Afton gave a short nod. Taylor was gloved and gowned and made no effort to shake their hands.

"I just got through a few preliminaries," Taylor said. "But we'll have to wait until our director, Dr. Healy, runs a few more tests and makes a final determination. I'm sorry he couldn't be here, but his brother-in-law had a heart attack this morning."

"Sounds like a tough deal," Max said. "Any chance this could be kicked up to the State Crime Lab?"

"You'd have to take that up with Dr. Healy when he's available," Taylor said.

"So is there anything you found that could be of help?" Max asked. "Even though Pink isn't technically our case, she's somewhat pivotal to the kidnapping that we're working."

"I understand," Taylor said. "Our police chief already briefed me." He picked up his clipboard and read from it. "Weight: sixty-three point five kilograms. Height: one hundred fifty-seven centimeters. Based on the evidence at the scene and my examination of the body, it was determined that the victim sustained a class-four hemorrhage and lost over four liters of blood."

No shit, Afton thought. Anyone at the scene could have determined that the victim had bled out. It didn't exactly take an advanced degree in medicine.

"So what's the bottom line on all this?" Max asked. "How'd she die?" He was practically salivating for a little more information, too.

Taylor glanced at Pink's body. "Based on lateral bruising on her neck and the angle of the initial cut, we surmised that the assailant grabbed our victim from behind and stabbed downward into our victim's abdomen."

Our *victim*, Afton thought. *Yes, she was ours. She became ours and we let her down.* "So he grabbed her and slashed her?"

"It's a little more complicated than that," Taylor said.

"By 'complicated,' you mean gruesome," Afton said.

"Yes," Taylor said. "The entry wound only crippled her."

"So she was still alive after the initial cut?" Max asked.

Taylor nodded. "The assailant then made a second incision into the abdomen, slicing from the waist up to the terminus of the evisceration at the victim's third rib. Both the celiac artery and abdominal aorta were cut, so the victim bled out quickly." He looked up. "And of course, her inner organs spilled out."

"Like you'd gut a deer," Afton said. "Just like a hunter might."

"This guy *is* a hunter," Max said.

"Well, yes," Taylor said. "I suppose you could compare it to that. In fact . . ." He hesitated.

"What?" Max said.

"It's an odd thing that you should even mention hunting," Taylor said. "Because a couple of stray hairs turned up on her."

"Animal hairs?" Afton asked.

"Probably. I'm guessing fox or coyote perhaps? They've got that look of a canine coat, like guard hairs."

"But Muriel Pink didn't own a dog and I doubt she was out running around in the woods," Max said. "The woman was almost eighty years old and her neighbors said she hardly ever left town. Except for her doll shows."

"The hairs might have come from one of her dolls," Afton said. "Remember the reborn doll Susan Darden told us about? It supposedly had fox eyelashes that were hand-inserted."

"So that could be it," Max said. "It would make sense anyway."

They all stood there for a while in the unnatural cold and fluorescent lighting, the sound of heavy-duty fans rumbling above their heads.

Finally Afton said to Dr. Taylor, "Have you ever seen anything like this before? The stab wounds? The dumping of the organs?"

Dr. Taylor slowly took off his glasses and rubbed his eyes. It was as if he needed a minute to pull himself together. "Working here, I've seen a lot of bad shit," he said, in words that suddenly seemed out of character to his professional demeanor. "But nothing, *nothing*, quite like this."

ON the way back to Minneapolis, Afton put in a call to Dr. Sansevere. When she finally got the ME on the line, she asked one simple question.

"Dr. Sansevere," Afton said. "Can you check to see if there were any stray animal hairs found on that baby you autopsied? The Cannon Falls baby?"

"I can tell you the answer to that right now," Dr. Sansevere said. "There were. But I just chalked them up to her prolonged exposure in the woods."

"But the baby's blanket wasn't torn or mauled?"

"No," Dr. Sansevere said. "I found no evidence of that."

"So how do you account for the animal hair?"

"Probably the surrounding area was just animal habitat."

"Thank you. Thank you very much." Afton ended her call and rode in silence for a while.

"What was that all about?" Max asked.

Afton drew a deep breath. "What if it was the same person?"

"What?" Max sounded shocked. "What are you talking about?" He glanced sideways at her.

"What if the sick person who stuck the baby in that log in Cannon Falls was the same person who murdered Muriel Pink?"

"Why would you say that when there's no real connection?"

"But there is," Afton said. "Animal hair was found on both of the victims." Even as Afton said it, it sounded weak to her. No, it sounded preposterous.

"It's too far-fetched," Max said.

"I hear you."

Max tilted his head back, pursed his lips, and seemed to be working the notion through his mind. Finally he said, "You're grasping. You *want* there to be a connection."

"Yes, probably." *Go ahead and talk me out of it.*

"But it doesn't make any sense. We're pretty sure it was the doll lady who went after Muriel Pink. But how on earth would she tie in to the Cannon Falls baby?"

"I have no idea. Unless . . ." Afton stopped herself. "No, you're right. The whole thing is too preposterous."

"What were you going to say?" Max asked.

"Well, a baby was found. And another baby has disappeared."

"Okay," Max said. "I think I see where you're going with this. And the whole thing scares the hail holy shit out of me."

"Me, too."

"That'd be one hell of a nutty twist."

"The animal hair thing is what freaks me out," Afton said.

"All right," Max said. "Say we brought the animal hairs into the equation. Who would have something to do with animal hair?"

"I don't know. A hunter maybe?"

"Or a dog trainer?"

"Maybe," Afton said. "We've got samples of both hairs. We could have our lab do a DNA analysis. To see if they're related."

"I don't know. I'm still thinking the hair from Pink came from one of her dolls, while the animal hairs found on the baby are just that, from an animal."

"But if they are related . . ." Afton didn't want to drop it.

"Then we're really in deep shit," Max said. "Okay, so it's something to think about. When we get back, I'll run it past Thacker. See if it's worth doing the lab testing."

"Thank you," Afton said. She looked out the window as a stand of birch trees flew by. "Is Darden a hunter?"

"Not that I'm aware of. This is a guy who even gets manicures. I don't know too many guys with manicured nails who spend their weekend in a deer blind hugging a rifle and freezing their ass off." Max tapped the brakes and slid into the right lane, the slower lane. "Animal hairs. Shit."

"A zookeeper? A trapper?" Afton wondered.

"Hard to sift out the possible suspects from the regular Joes."

"What would you do normally?" Afton asked.

"Probably look for sex offenders, felons in the area."

"Should we do that?"

"Sheriff Burney is already doing that in his jurisdiction," Max said. "And we can try it, too, up to a point. There's protocol to follow and we can't investigate everybody. We don't have the manpower."

"What do we do in the meantime?" Afton asked.

"Keep working the case and wait for the kidnapper to call back," Max said.

"When do you think that will be?"

"Not sure. My experience tells me it's got to be fairly soon. Criminals usually like to grab their money and run."

"I wish I could be there," Afton said.

"You mean, to facilitate the exchange with the kidnapper?"

"No, to put a bullet in his brain."

WE'RE still missing something," Max said.

"What?" Afton asked. It was late afternoon Thursday and they were sifting through a pile of reports that had been slowly filtering in on missing children. "We're getting decent cooperation from—"

"No, I mean like a thread . . . a connection."

"Like the animal hair thing?"

"No," Max said. "I mean like a personal connection."

"Okay." Max was worrying something, tossing it around in his brain, and Afton decided the best thing to do, the smart thing to do, was let him chew at it until he came up with something.

"We need to go over to Synthotech."

"Darden's current employer," Afton said. "But the FBI guys already did all that." She shuffled some more papers. "I have their reports right here. First on their list was Gordon Conseco, the CEO of Snythotech."

"Was he standing firmly behind his new hire?"

Afton scanned the report. "Mmn, not so much. Conseco seemed more concerned with doing a slick PR job for Synthotech. Decrying any involvement with the kidnapping and offering law enforcement complete access to all their employees."

"So Don Jasper and his guys talked to everyone over there?"

"They conducted interviews with at least a dozen people," Afton said. "And there just wasn't much takeaway."

"For them. But maybe there would be for us."

"Because you think we're smarter?" Afton knew that wasn't the case. Don Jasper and his band of merry men were scary smart. If they couldn't pry anything loose at Synthotech, how could she and Max?

"The babysitter . . ." Max said.

"Ashley Copeland," Afton said.

"Her mother works there. That was Ashley's connection with Darden in the first place. Who talked to Mom?"

Afton looked through the papers. "She was interviewed by Keith Sunder."

"Our friendly local FBI guy."

"Yup."

"Maybe we should give it a shot, too."

Afton picked up a stack of papers and tamped them together. "Why not?"

MONICA Copeland wasn't enthusiastic about talking to them. In fact, she was just putting on her coat when Afton and Max arrived. She was one of two administrative assistants recently assigned to Richard Darden and claimed not to know him all that well.

"But you work with him," Max said.

"I started at Synthotech about the same time he did," Monica said. "So I'm fairly new. Sasha, the other admin assistant, is the one who works most closely with him."

"Did she train him in?" Afton asked. It was one of the dirty little secrets in corporate America. Secretaries often trained in their bosses; bank tellers often trained in loan officers and banking vice presidents.

"Well, I suppose Sasha showed him the ropes anyway," Monica said.

"And your daughter babysat for him," Max said.

"Yes. Unfortunately. Just that one time."

"Which is what we'd like to talk to you about," Max said. "Even though you've been over this before with the FBI."

Monica looked like she was ready to cry. "My poor Ashley. She was viciously attacked and tied up while that little baby was stolen. Then someone came after her again in the *hospital?*" Now tears streamed down Monica's cheeks. "It's like the bad things just won't stop happening. I feel like Ashley's completely lost her innocence."

Afton remembered the spoiled, petulant Ashley, who had demanded a boob job from her mother. Really not that innocent at all.

"Ashley was released from the hospital . . . when?" Max asked. "Yesterday?"

"That's right," Monica sniffled.

"Has she opened up to you about the night of the kidnapping? Confided in you?"

"Not at all. I think she just wants to forget the whole thing."

"Do you think she's remembered any more about the guy who strong-armed her?"

Monica shrugged. "She just told me that he was really strong. Said he reminded her of a wrestler."

"How so?" Afton asked. That was the exact impression that she'd gotten from the hospital attack.

"You mean like a pro wrestler?" Max said.

"No, more like a high school wrestler," Monica said. "Those kids with all the crazy, flailing arms and legs who try to pin their opponent. For the win, I guess."

"We know this has all been very frightening for Ashley," Afton said.

"She told me she's been traumatized," Monica said. She wrinkled her nose and made a face. "And that she felt repulsed."

"Repulsed," Afton repeated.

Monica lowered her voice slightly. "She said the man smelled horrible."

Max's brow wrinkled. "Was there anything about that in the report?"

Afton shook her head. "Not that I recall. Ashley never mentioned any sort of smell to us either."

Monica waved a hand. "It was just something she mentioned to me in passing. A fleeting impression she had. It probably doesn't mean a thing."

"Mrs. Copeland," Afton said. "It's all important. Every tiny little detail is important."

"What did Ashley think the boy smelled like?" Max asked. "Like . . . garlic breath or something? Bad BO?"

"No," Monica said. "She said she thought he smelled like a dead animal."

32

SHAKE shuffled into the kitchen in her stocking feet, opened the refrigerator, and stared with glassy eyes at their meager larder. All evening long she'd been having contractions. The pain would come in waves, first tight and twisting, and then bursting inside her as if someone had thrown an electrical switch in Hell. After a few minutes of agony, they would retreat to a dull ache. Like a bad, rotting toothache, only way deep down inside her.

Her hands shook as she reached out and grabbed a carton of milk. She hadn't eaten a thing all day and now she was feeling nauseous. Maybe some milk would help. Or maybe, she thought, having this stupid baby would help.

She opened the carton and tipped it back, guzzling greedily from it. Wasn't milk supposed to be nutritious for mothers-to-be? Sure it was. She thought it was.

Taking a step back, she felt something cool and wet trickle down her legs. She looked down at her chest stupidly, thinking she'd dribbled milk all over herself. But there was nothing on her T-shirt. Then what?

Shake finally noticed it. Not milk, but a clear liquid. Puddled on the gray linoleum floor right between her legs. Her eyes widened in surprise. This was what happened when you started to have a baby? *Oh no, oh no, oh no.*

"Help!" she screamed at the top of her lungs. "Somebody help me!"

Shake's piteous cries brought Marjorie pounding in from the living room. "What the hell are you—" She slid to a stop. Saw Shake standing there, looking down between her feet, with a terrified look on her face, and said, "About time."

"What's happening?" Shake cried.

"Water broke," Marjorie said. She took the milk carton out of Shake's hands and shoved it back inside the refrigerator. "Ronnie!" Now it was her turn to scream. "Get in here and clean up this mess. Your girlfriend is about to have a baby."

"It's . . . uh . . . You mean now?" Shake babbled. "It's started . . . now?" She was trembling so hard she didn't seem to be able to hold her thoughts together.

"Yes, now," Marjorie said. "When did you think it was going to happen? Next week? Next year?"

"Help me, please!" Shake implored. She stretched a hand out to the woman she feared the most. "We have to go . . . hospital."

Marjorie shook her head. "You're going to a private birthing center over in Pepin County. It's all been arranged."

Shake sank to her knees. "Hospital?" she pleaded in a small voice.

"This is cheaper."

"Please," Shake whimpered. "Don't let it hurt."

Marjorie gazed at her, and for the first time, a look of pity came across her face. "Oh, girlie, it's gonna hurt. Having a baby always hurts."

33

IN what felt like a serendipitous blip in the weather—in other words, a slightly milder temperature and no additional snow for the time being—Afton decided to take Tess and Poppy sledding.

So after all the chili con carne had been spooned up, the corn bread devoured, and the kitchen cleaned, they set out this Thursday evening pulling a sled and a flying saucer.

Powderhorn Park was just four blocks away and an easy walk. And Afton, Tess, and Poppy weren't the only ones out on this wintry night either. Snowblowers roared to life all around them as neighbors emerged from hibernation to clear their sidewalks and driveways. Impromptu snow forts sprang up amid all the piles. Some enterprising and highly territorial residents even cleared on-street parking spaces and then staked out their boundaries using yellow highway department cones.

"Let's go right to the big hill," Tess begged. "After all, we're not little kids anymore."

"It's okay with me," Afton told them. "But it's a lot more hill for you guys to climb. It's a lot steeper."

"We can do it," Poppy said with confidence.

"Okay, just be careful." Afton watched as the two of them scrambled up a slope where the snow had already been packed hard by sleds, tobog-gans, flying saucers, and inner tubes. The kids reached the crest, then turned and waved at her. Afton waved back, grinning at her little munch-kins. Then Tess flopped down on her sled and Poppy squatted on her flying saucer and they both flew down the hill.

The kids went back up the hill again and again. As the evening wore on, they were joined by dozens more kids, so there was a constant din of squeals and shouts as sled trains were formed and impromptu races took place.

Good for them, Afton thought. Her kids were having a ball. It was about time they got outside and breathed some fresh air. She was, she decided, a true Minnesota mom. She subscribed to the notion that winter should be embraced and that kids should be encouraged to get out there and enjoy winter sports. And even though sliding wasn't technically a win-ter sport, it would certainly help build their confidence for the skiing or snowboarding lessons that were yet to come.

"Look at me!" a child's voice shrilled, and Afton couldn't help grinning as a small boy shot past her on his sled. Then she turned her attention back to the top of the hill, where two dozen kids danced around, silhouetted in a bright patch of moonlight.

"Tess, Poppy," Afton called out. "One more time and then we've got to go home, okay?" She searched the hill, looking for an acknowledging wave, but didn't see a thing. In fact, she didn't see her kids anywhere.

No, that can't be. They were right there.

"Tess, Poppy," she called out again, this time a little more urgently.

Still nothing.

Where did they go?

Afton glanced at the crowd of kids and parents who were at the bottom of the hill, but didn't see them anywhere.

Her heart lurched inside her chest. *This is how it happens*, she suddenly thought. *This fast. You look away for one miserable second and your kids are gone.*

Afton was pounding up the sledding hill now, digging hard into the churned-up snow, slipping a little because of the stupid rubber soles on her stupid leather boots.

Hurry up. Faster.

She dodged a little girl in a pink-flowered parka who was balanced atop a yellow plastic runner, and sprinted the final twenty feet to the very top of the hill, her breath feeling ragged and labored.

"Tess! Poppy!" Afton was shouting now, the other kids looking at her with either bored or puzzled expressions. She was clearly a worrywart parent who'd shown up to spoil their fun.

Afton was panting heavily, spinning around as if in a daze, looking for her kids.

They're here, they have to be here.

And they were.

She found them just over the crest of the hill. Daredevil Tess had decided to slide down the other side. The dangerous, steep side that ended abruptly in a church parking lot. Poppy was hunkered in the snow, a few feet down, watching her.

"What are you *doing*?" Afton screamed at them. "What were you *thinking*? I couldn't *see* you guys."

Tess looked thoroughly chagrined. "Sorry, Mom, but we were—"

"I was so *worried*."

Afton's heart was still hammering inside her chest as she grasped their little mittened hands and dragged them back home.

AFTON made a conscientious effort to try to relax once she was back in the warmth and comfort of their own little dwelling. Nothing had happened; the kids were okay. She'd had a Nervous Nellie brain fart; that was all. Still, she felt pent up and restless. Every time she got up to do something, Bonaparte jumped up to follow her, like a friendly ambassador. She settled into an easy chair and tried to read the new John Sandford thriller, but like an old-fashioned stuck record, her mind kept skipping over and over the same sentence.

Finally, she set her book aside and decided there were just too many things on her mind. The kidnapping, finding the Cannon Falls baby, Muriel Pink's murder, the kidnapping. She felt both enervated and keyed up at the same time. Her head was working overtime, spinning various theories about the Darden baby, Muriel Pink's killer, and everything else. But nothing felt right. Nothing seemed to gel.

Afton stared at the TV, where flickering, dancing images captivated her girls, but couldn't seem to hold her own interest. Maybe if she made a phone call downtown? To see if anything had happened?

Afton slipped into her small office, Bonaparte padding after her, and called downtown. Asked Don Farley, the night Homicide guy, if there had been any word yet from the Darden kidnappers. He told her no—he'd just checked with the comm center a few minutes ago and they hadn't heard a damn thing.

"Where's Richard Darden?" she asked. "Is he still hanging out there?"

"He was wandering around here for a while," Farley said. "All wired up, ready to go, but nothing happened. No phone call. Now he's back at his hotel."

"Okay. Thanks." She reached down and scratched Bonaparte between his ears.

Damn.

Back in the living room, Afton flopped into a chair and tried to focus on what Poppy and Tess were watching. It appeared to be yet another movie about insect-looking aliens that had invaded Earth, only to be repelled by a small cadre of brave young teenagers. Afton wondered why the aliens had even bothered coming here? There were so many problems. Global warming, a disappearing rain forest, air pollution, wars, energy shortages, missing babies . . .

As the kids hooted and hollered like mad, Afton pulled herself up straight in her chair.

"Are you kids cheering for the aliens?" she asked suddenly.

Poppy raised a tiny fist above her head. "Yes. We love the little green guys."

"Turn that thing off. It's time for bed."

TEN o'clock at night. Afton lay sprawled on her bed in the dark. She ruminated over the fact that she was thirty-four years old, had never drunk a cosmopolitan, never worn a Wonderbra, and never vacationed at Club Med.

She knew she had a decision to make. She could back the hell out of this investigation right now and go back to being a community liaison officer. She could do her job diligently and with dignity. She could leave the horrors of the past week behind, take her kids to Disneyland over Easter vacation, and maybe even get around to pursuing her frivolous "want list."

Or she could keep bulldogging her way through the investigation, help find that missing baby, and nail the son-of-a-bitch kidnapper's ass to the wall.

It wasn't a difficult decision.

34

SHAKE lay trapped in the worst kind of hell she could ever imagine. Her belly felt like it was about to burst open, her lungs were unable to suck in enough air, and the pain between her legs was unimaginable. All she could do was lie on the narrow, padded table, drenched in sweat, helpless as a beached whale, praying for the baby to finally come.

Eight hours of labor had taken its toll and Ronnie hadn't been a damn bit of help. He'd crept in occasionally to stare at her with abject fear in his eyes, always looking like he was about to lose his lunch. Or his breakfast, or his Hostess Ho Hos, or whatever he'd last snarfed down. Marjorie hovered nearby, looking inquisitive but relatively unconcerned.

The midwife came rustling over to check on Shake again. She was a big-boned farm lady with a mop of curly brown hair and oversized hands. Shake understood that she was the certified nurse-midwife. That she owned this birthing center somewhere out in the country. She supposed the small cottage with its rough-hewn walls, rocking chairs, and handmade quilts tacked on the wall was supposed to inspire warmth and serenity. But for her, it just meant unrelenting agony.

"Painkillers," Shake gasped through clenched teeth and cracked lips. "I need something for the pain."

The midwife's disapproving face loomed between Shake's spread-eagled legs. "You're nine centimeters dilated," she said. "You're on a Pitocin drip. Try to relax; try to breathe." She shook her head. "Didn't you take the classes? Don't you remember the drill?"

Shake threw her head back against the pillow and groaned in desperation. Her world was one red blur of pain right now. She wished she could reach down and rip the baby from her womb and just hand it over to the adoption people.

"Ronnie," she whispered.

Floorboards creaked as Ronnie crept closer. "How you doin', Shake?"

"Hurt," she croaked. "Feel sick."

Ronnie was in the room with her, but Shake could feel him pulling away emotionally, felt his almost-resentment at being made to witness this birthing experience. At the same moment she realized he was never going to take care of her, was never going to take her away from the farmhouse. And wasn't that a big freakin' surprise? She almost chuckled maniacally to herself. He was a guy who still lived at home with his wacko mother and whose sole ambition in life was to own a new Ford Ranger Quad Cab. What did she expect, really?

The midwife was checking her again. She felt practiced fingers slip halfway inside her.

"It's coming," the midwife said. She put a hand on Shake's knee and squeezed. "When I say push, you bear down with everything you've got."

"Push? Now?" Shake was instantly filled with panic. She wasn't ready for this. Her heart was fluttering like a wounded dove inside her chest and all she wanted to do was run away. But there was this *thing* happening, right between her legs. Pain and blood, and oh dear God, what was happening to her? She was sick with fear and anxiety, and wondered in a bleary haze how things had even gotten to this point of no return.

"Are you ready?" came the insistent voice of the midwife. "Okay, now. Now push!"

Shake pushed and groaned and pushed some more. She sobbed, bit her lower lip until she tasted blood, and pleaded for the midwife to do a C-section, to cut this damn baby out of her.

Another long hour passed of pushing and pleading and screaming. And Marjorie hovering nearby, like some malevolent fairy lurking in the woods.

Finally, when Shake couldn't bear the pain any longer, when it felt like there was a burning ring of fire that the baby could never pass through, she let loose a bloodcurdling scream. She was dying. She was being split open and nobody cared.

"One more push," the midwife cajoled. She was panting like a steam engine herself from all the exertion. "Come on, you can do it!"

There was a rush of wet warmth and what felt like faint relief from the searing pain.

"It's a girl," the midwife announced, a touch of pride in her voice.

Shake heard its tiny cry.

"Baby," she moaned, and descended into a pit of darkness.

35

AFTON stared at her computer screen. Her cubicle was beginning to feel more like home than home did. Mornings seemed to be starting earlier and earlier. At least this Friday morning had. All the hours she'd logged this week made Afton worry about her girls. It wasn't often that she had to spend this much time away from them. At least she'd taken Tess and Poppy sledding last night. That had been exactly what they all needed. Until she'd let her imagination run a little bonkers anyway.

All the noise in the office, along with the usual cop horseplay, made it difficult to concentrate, so Afton fished her headphones out of her desk drawer and plugged into her phone. Sometimes a little background music was precisely what she needed to focus.

Okay. Now . . .

Sitting atop her desk was a single case file. The name ELIZABETH ANN DARDEN, NUMBER MP2134-16, had been affixed to the folder via an adhesive label. Every day the file's girth had grown as more notes, photos, dissertations, reports, faxes, subpoenas, and timelines were added. She'd just added the information about animal hairs and Monica Copeland's remarks about the kidnapper smelling like a dead animal.

Now the file was filled to near busting. They'd found no resolution yet, but Afton knew that somewhere inside was the germ of an answer. Information that would ultimately lead them to the Darden baby.

Afton's own notes, the ones she'd taken for Max, were scrawled on a large yellow legal pad. Scribbled across twenty or so sheets were names, phone numbers, addresses, and Max's candid as well as random thoughts.

Staring up at her from the first page was the information on Muriel Pink. She'd been the first person they'd interviewed, way back last Sunday when the case was still fresh.

Waves of guilt coursed through Afton. She should have known then that Muriel Pink might be in danger. And now . . . now the old girl was dead.

Afton circled Muriel's name with a red pen and swabbed the entire paragraph with orange highlighter. She didn't want to forget that name ever. It was a bitter lesson learned the hard way.

A dozen or so missing person reports, some recently faxed and some still warm from the copier, lay to the left of the file. These were the reports that, per Don Jasper's request, had been dribbling in all week long from law enforcement agencies all over the Midwest. There were a few new reports, too, ones that she had been tasked with going over.

It was sad, she thought, as she read through these new reports, that all these people—and some children, too—had simply vanished without a trace. There were families that were desperate for any word, for any information or closure, yet they'd probably never find it.

Midway through the stack of new reports, she found a missing person report on another baby. This baby was from Des Moines, Iowa, stolen from a day care center. Her name was Tiffany Lynn Matthews.

Afton worked her upper teeth against her lower lip. *How awful,* she thought. Stolen right out of a day care center. If your kids weren't safe at day care, where were they safe?

She set the report aside and concentrated on the next one.

Wait a minute. Something pinged deep inside her brain. Day care center? Something about that felt familiar.

Afton went back and read the report on the missing Des Moines baby.

Hmm. Day care center. And there was a day care center in question here. In Edina. But the FBI had already checked out that day care center, so that couldn't be what was bothering her.

With a faint ping still ringing in her brain, Afton scanned the report again.

Wait a minute . . .

She dug back through the notes Max had jotted down when he'd first interviewed Susan Darden. She tore through them, feeling there was something there, something that might . . .

She found it on the third page of a misspelled report that Max had typed himself and stuck in the file. "Tiffany Lynn" was the name of the reborn doll that the doll lady had proudly shown to Susan Darden.

Tiffany Lynn.

A missing child, a reborn doll. Both with the same name. What were the odds?

Afton grabbed the police report along with Max's notes and skittered down the hallway.

"Max!"

She found him sitting in the conference room, papers spread out around him, talking quietly to Don Jasper. They both looked up when she appeared in the doorway.

"What's up?" Max said. "Where's the fire?"

"Hey there," Jasper said, giving her one of his devastating smiles.

"Tiffany Lynn," Afton said, a little breathless. "We just received an old police report on a missing Tiffany Lynn Matthews from Des Moines, Iowa." She held up the report. "And Tiffany Lynn is the name of the doll that Susan Darden was so captivated by at the Skylark Mall doll show." She held up Max's notes. "It was in your notes."

"Lemme see that," Max said.

Afton handed over the paperwork.

"Sit down," Jasper said. "Don't just stand there lurking. You make me nervous."

"Son of a bitch," Max muttered as he read through the papers. "She's right." He slid everything over to Jasper, who did a quick read.

"My guys are going to plotz when I tell them about this," Jasper said. "This is a very good catch."

"So you think we should let Des Moines know about this?" Afton asked.

Jasper stood up. "I'll put somebody on it right now." He breezed out of the room.

"Oh," Afton said. "And here I thought I was already on it."

"You were," Max said. "It just got kicked upstairs. Happens all the time."

"I guess I'll have to get used to that."

"Or you'll learn how to keep a lead to yourself until you've taken it to the next logical step."

"Is that what I should have done?"

"Naw, you did the right thing." Max grinned at her. "Now get back to it. You done good."

Afton went back to her cubicle and sat down heavily. She wanted to march down to Don Jasper's temporary office and demand to be let in on the Des Moines case. But she knew that wasn't the smart thing to do; it wasn't the political thing to do.

"If it isn't Inspector Clouseau," came a man's teasing voice from behind her. "Taken in any stray dogs lately?"

Afton spun around in her chair. Richard Darden was standing there, a slightly condescending look on his face. "Any word?" she asked him.

Darden shook his head. "Not yet." He took a step toward her. "Still busy playing detective?"

Afton gave a delicate snort.

"I understand you're all hearts and flowers with my wife now," Darden said. "Charming woman, wouldn't you say? Now that's she's threatened to eviscerate my bank account."

"It really doesn't matter what I think."

Darden pressed closer to her. "You don't like me very much, do you?"

"Mr. Darden, I don't give a rat's ass about you or your friends in high places. All I care about is finding your daughter."

"What's going on?" Max asked. He was suddenly standing directly behind Darden.

"Just having a friendly chat," Darden said.

"Not so friendly," Afton said.

Darden cocked his head and held out his hands in a plaintive gesture. "Oh, excuse me. Community Liaison Officer Tangler wants to treat me as if I'm a suspect in the disappearance of my own daughter. If that's the case, why don't you guys slap a pair of handcuffs on me right now."

Max pointed a finger at Darden. "You," he said, "are wanted in Don Jasper's office." He switched his gazed to Afton. "And you're coming with me. Grab your coat and let's go."

"Where are we going?" Afton asked as she followed after Max. Once again, she felt like she was being called to the school principal's office. But no, they were headed for the elevators.

"Lunch," Max said. "I figured I'd better get you out of there before you tore that guy a new . . . well . . ."

"Brooks Brothers suit?"

"Whatever."

The elevator arrived and Max pushed *L* for the lobby.

"You're not mad at me?" Afton asked.

"*Moi?* If Darden rode me as hard as he's been riding you, I'd toss a saddle on my back and call myself Trigger."

AFTON and Max ended up at Richie's, a small diner on Fifth Street, a few blocks from their building. Richie's owner, Richie Novotny, was a former Marine supply sergeant who ran his diner like he was still running things in the Corps. The interior was painted a grim barracks green and the dining area sported bare-bones metal tables and chairs. Placards on the wall listed the rules and regulations that Richie's customers were expected to follow: NO SPITTING. NO SWEARING. NO FIGHTING.

"What kind of place did you bring me to?" Afton asked. "No fighting?

Does that mean a fight could actually break out here? And the place *is* a trifle short on ambience." Truth be told, it was way short on ambience, bordering on institutional.

"This place is a classic," Max said. "And Richie's not so bad once you get to know him."

Afton wasn't so sure she wanted to get to know Richie. She'd just spotted another sign that said, NO PEACE SIGNS OR OTHER HIPPY DIPPY CRAP.

"The food's real good here," Max said, handing her a menu. "Even though the menu is limited."

Afton scanned the menu. It offered a basic burger, a cheeseburger, a meatloaf sandwich, pot roast and gravy, macaroni and cheese, and something called chipped beef.

"Chipped beef?" she asked.

Max waved a hand. "It's a . . . kind of a Marine tradition from way back when."

"Uh-huh." At the bottom of the menu, she saw the words JARHEADS EAT FREE—NO EXCEPTIONS. All right, maybe Richie was an okay guy after all.

A waiter in a white T-shirt, white slacks, and a long white apron took their order, and then hustled off toward the clattery kitchen. Richie himself, a behemoth of a man with a barrel chest and a buzz cut, never seemed to budge from his chosen spot behind the cash register.

Max waited until they were both halfway through their macaroni and cheese before he said, "Has this been tough? I mean, being away from your kids so much?"

"It has been this week."

"I hate to tell you, but this is pretty much the life."

"I'm beginning to see that."

"It's not for everybody."

"But it works for you," Afton said.

"My kids are a little older than yours," Max said. "Jake will be graduating high school this year and Tyler is fourteen."

"And they're both hockey fanatics."

"Yup. That's why I'm broke and can't afford a fancy new car," he joked. "Our priority is new skates every year, as well as a half dozen new hockey sticks and breezers. I guess that's the price we pay for living here. It seems like everybody's kids are into hockey. What about your girls?"

"No hockey, thankfully," Afton said. "Tess enjoys acting in school plays and playing violin. Poppy is certain she's going to be the next Taylor Swift. So she sings in front of the mirror all the time. She'll probably be pretty good if she keeps it up."

Max paused. "Hell of a thing being a parent and working on a case with a missing baby. I don't think I could handle it if one of my boys went missing."

"Not sure I'd be any different," Afton said. She recalled her moment of panic last night.

"That was good work noticing the name of that missing Iowa baby, by the way."

"I was just the first one to go through the new faxes."

"No," Max said. "Detectives first grade and FBI agents with more experience and formal training might have missed that. I think you could make a good detective. I think Thacker might be on board for that, too."

"Not sure if I've got the right training," Afton admitted.

"You've been taking the criminal justice courses?"

"That's right."

"And you've got what? A degree in sociology or something?"

"Yup, I finally buckled down and focused on a degree after I got tired of hearing my parents complain about how I was wasting my life as an Outward Bound instructor."

"Jeez," Max said. "You were one of those? Does that mean you can start a fire using a compass or lash together a canoe out of pinecones?"

"No, but I can use my watch as a compass and start a fire using a bow drill or flint. I worked up in the BWCA for a couple of years. I love it up there. So gorgeous and peaceful."

"Is that where you started climbing?" Max asked. He waggled his head back and forth. "One of the guys mentioned you were a rock climber."

"I started my life on the rocks after going through a program offered by the Minnesota State Parks. There was a class on rock climbing and rappelling up at Tettegouche State Park. That's where I first caught the bug. Now I do most of my climbing at Taylors Falls, but once a year I try to get back up north." She grinned. "Of course, my dream trip would be El Capitan in Yosemite."

"Big dreams," Max said.

"And of course, the rock climbing led to ice climbing, which means you can enjoy the sport all year round."

"Yeah, but frozen waterfalls? I mean . . . that's pure crazy."

Afton shook her head. "I take a lot more precautions than I used to. I can't seem to rationalize hanging off a frozen waterfall a hundred feet in the air when I have two daughters waiting for me at home."

A chill wind suddenly blew across their ankles and Afton shivered, as if someone had just walked across her grave.

Over by the door Richie shouted, "Shut that door, asshole. Don't you know there's a blizzard on the way? We supposed to get thirteen inches by morning."

THE weather really had gone to shit. Steam curled from sidewalk vents; a bank's time and temperature sign flashed an icy white as it registered a chill 10 degrees. A woman in a down coat that made her look like an overblown Michelin man was walking a little schnauzer in a yellow coat and boots. Afton thought the dog looked embarrassed.

They were almost back at police headquarters when Max got the call. He listened on his cell phone for a minute, then said, "Send a squad, lights and sirens. We'll hoof it over there right now. We're three, maybe four, blocks away at best."

He dropped his phone in his jacket pocket, turned, and said, "C'mon, we gotta go."

Afton spun with him. "Where?"

"Call just came in about some guy taking photos of babies over at HCMC."

"What?" Afton shrilled. "At the hospital?"

"Yeah." Max coughed as he jogged along. "He's apparently taking pictures of newborns."

"Holy crap. That guy . . . maybe he came back!"

Max skidded out into traffic, trying to get a jump on the green light. "Come on, we gotta *move.*"

THE Maternity Center was located on the second floor at Hennepin County Medical Center. Max and Afton ran down Seventh Street, ducked in a side door, and caught an elevator.

"Come on, come on," Max whispered urgently as the elevator started moving.

"Is hospital security going to grab this guy?" Afton asked.

"No, they're just going to watch him. Busting him is our job."

The elevator doors slid open and Max burst out so fast, he practically collided with a rolling cart stacked with sheets and towels. "Shit," he cried, trying to sidestep it.

The female employee who was trying to hump the cart onto the elevator frowned her disapproval at him. "Hey," she said.

Max dodged past the cart and ran lightly down the hallway, Afton following in his footsteps.

Skidding up to a nurses' station, Max held up his ID and said, "Maternity?"

"Straight ahead," one of the nurses said. "You can't miss it."

They didn't miss it. And the man was still there. His face was pressed up against the glass, staring in at all the newborn babies in the nursery. A camera dangled in his right hand.

Max deliberately slowed his pace and crept up behind the guy. He clomped a hand down hard on the man's shoulder and said, "Stop whatever you're doing. Right now. Put your hands in the air. If you yell or make any sort of scene, I will for sure shoot you."

The man's mouth dropped open and he managed a startled, "What?" He tried to spin around, but was held firmly in Max's viselike grip.

"You heard him," Afton said. She reached down and, slick as you please, snatched the camera out of the man's hand.

"What the . . . You can't do that!" the man protested. He was thirtyish and wore a brown plaid parka over a pair of gray cargo pants. His dark hair was slicked back, he wore heavy horn-rimmed glasses, and had a distinctly pointed chin. Afton was immediately disappointed. This was clearly a different guy.

Max spun the guy around hard, placed one hand on his shoulder, and twisted his arm behind his back. Then he duck-walked the guy stiffly down the hallway. When Max spotted a small waiting room, he steered him into it. He frisked the man and, when he was satisfied that he wasn't carrying a weapon, pushed him down into a gray plastic chair. "You want to explain yourself?"

"Who do you think you are?" the guy demanded. "The photo police?"

"Minneapolis Police," Max said.

"So what do you want with me?" the guy asked.

Afton held up the camera. "You care to explain this?"

"It's a camera," the man snarled.

"Still or video?" Max asked.

Afton examined it. "Still."

"Delete everything he's got," Max said to Afton.

"Whoa!" the man cried. "Don't be doin' that!"

"Then maybe you really do want to explain yourself?"

The man sighed. "I'm gonna reach into my pocket and pull out my wallet, okay?"

"Sure," Max said. "Go ahead."

The guy pulled out his wallet, dug around in it, and pulled out a business card. Handed it to Max. "My name is Danny Kinghorn."

"So what?"

"I run a website called Bloody Blue Murder dot com. We're international."

"No shit," Max said.

"We do articles on true crime. You know, Jack the Ripper, Son of Sam, that kind of thing. The newer guys, too, like BTK. Plus we post book reviews on all the new thrillers and crime flicks."

"Why were you taking pictures?" Max asked. But he said it in a bored, tired manner, as if he already had an inkling of what might be going on.

"Because I'm working on a story about the Darden kidnapping," Kinghorn said. "And I needed some snaps to go with it."

"Of babies," Afton said. She was basically repulsed.

"Yeah," Kinghorn said as if it were the most natural thing in the world. "Sure."

"No," Max said. "That's not going to happen."

"You want me to delete everything?" Afton asked.

"Yeah, go ahead," Max said.

"No!" Kinghorn cried. "Don't do that. *Please* don't do that."

Max grabbed the camera from Afton and shoved it roughly into Kinghorn's hands. "You know what? You can have your stupid camera back. But I'm going to have our tech people watch your website like a hawk. If I find out that you've used even one of the shots you took, I swear I will have my guys deliberately burn your site. Then I will personally hunt you down and rip you a new asshole. You got that?"

"Yeah," Kinghorn said, cradling his camera. "You're a tough guy. I got that."

"Now get out of here."

A cagey look spread across Kinghorn's face. "You know, if you had a couple of minutes, we could do a quick interview. You're clearly part of the Darden investigation, so maybe you could give me your perspective on it. That'd make a great article. My readers would love it."

"Get out," Max said. "*Get out*."

36

SHAKE stretched out her legs and very gingerly pulled the white chenille coverlet up to her chin. She'd been shocked to wake up and find that she was back home, lying in the double bed she shared with Ronnie. It had seemed too much like a fuzzy, weird dream. But when she opened her eyes again and the cobwebs cleared, it was indeed where she was. Tucked in bed, propped up on a bunch of pillows like some kind of cripple or sick person. She guessed that Ronnie must have driven them all home early this morning and then carried her upstairs.

Was it only last night that she'd gone into labor? Was this Friday night? Shake guessed that it was. But it felt like an eternity had passed. Hell, her labor and the unrelenting pain had stretched on like all of eternity. Everyone said that once it was over, you'd forget all about the pain. But she could recall every single torturous moment. The sweating, the muscle cramps, the torment of her body heaving and fighting to push that baby out. And just when she'd hit her breaking point, just when she'd thought she couldn't endure another second, a miracle had happened. Her baby had slipped out and the pain had slowly receded.

Not all the pain had gone away, of course. She still felt like she'd been run over by a two-ton truck. And she still felt cramping in her back muscles and a dull ache in her gut. But it was a different kind of pain now. A pain that said, *You've been through the worst, girl, and you've finally had your baby. Now you're going to slowly get better.*

Her baby. Shake turned her head to look at her baby. Ronnie had miraculously produced an old wooden crib and Marjorie had found a tiny baby mattress and some sheets and blankets. Now her baby—goodness, she was going to have to figure out a name for this sweet little girl—was lying there asleep. Looking pink and perfect with tiny little eyelashes that brushed her chubby cheeks just like the softest snowflakes. Just like a tiny angel.

As Shake had been lying there, sipping water through a straw, she'd been rethinking things, trying to explore where her emotions were taking her. And she was pretty sure that maybe she'd experienced a change of heart. For one thing, she'd decided that she definitely did have feelings for her little baby. In fact, she might actually *love* her.

That realization had been shocking. Had come tumbling at her pretty much out of the blue and freaked her out. Humbled her even. But over the last couple of hours, she'd begun to embrace these new and conflicting emotions. And Shake had decided that she might have to formulate a whole new plan for her life.

Like dancing in Florida maybe wasn't such a great idea after all?

No. Not with a baby to take care of.

If she could get herself to a bigger city, maybe a place like Chicago, there would be a lot more opportunities. Then she could get herself a decent job, maybe as a waitress or even some type of office worker. She could almost picture herself, dressed in a nice skirt and sweater, taking notes, filing pieces of paper, maybe even sitting in a meeting. If she made enough money, she could even afford a little apartment.

It would be a struggle, of course, just the two of them. And she'd have to find some kind of babysitter for the days on which she worked. But it was a germ of an idea that had taken hold deep inside her heart. An idea that suddenly felt very right.

"Knock, knock," came Ronnie's voice. He was standing outside her door holding a tray. "I brought you some food." He came in and set the tray on the nightstand. "You hungry?"

Shake looked at the fried egg and toast and her stomach lurched. She shook her head. "Not really."

"How are you feeling?"

"Tired." She rubbed her belly. "Really sore." She looked out the window and saw that it was dark. "What time is it?"

"Mmn . . . about seven o'clock."

"What do you think?" Shake asked him. She needed to feel him out, needed to give him a chance.

Ronnie cocked his head. "About what?" He was looking thoughtful, more so than Shake had ever seen him look before.

Shake lifted a hand to indicate their baby. "Our baby girl."

Ronnie sat down next to her on the edge of the bed. "She's really something." His voice sounded like it was tinged with real emotion.

"You really think so?" Shake thought she was the most precious thing in the entire world.

"She kind of changes things, doesn't she?"

Shake's heart rose about half an inch. "That's what I've been thinking, too."

Ronnie picked up Shake's hand and slowly rubbed his thumb across the back of it. He'd never done that before. Never displayed that kind of tenderness toward her. Up until tonight, he either tended to joke with her, ignore her completely, or treat her as a sex toy.

"You know the other day? When you were trying to get away?" he asked.

Shake nodded.

"Maybe you had the right idea."

Shake held her breath. "Really?"

Ronnie nodded. "I've been thinking . . . maybe we do deserve a better life. All of us."

"All three of us?" Shake asked. She wanted to make sure they were talking about the same thing.

"Yeah," he said. "Mom's not . . . she's not that good for us."

Shake gave a little shiver of disgust. "She hates me."

"She doesn't hate you," Ronnie said. "She doesn't much think about you." He made a face, as if he knew he was being disloyal, but couldn't help it. "She only thinks about what's good for her. What makes her happy."

"You wouldn't miss her?" Shake asked. This was a big step, a huge step for Ronnie. She wanted to be sure.

"Naw." Then he reconsidered. "Well, maybe. At first anyway. But once we figured stuff out on our own, I think we'd be okay."

"I know we'd be okay," Shake said. Her voice dropped to practically a whisper and she asked, "When?"

"When you feel better," Ronnie said. "Maybe tomorrow. Maybe the next day."

"I feel good now," Shake said, snuggling closer to him.

"You have to rest," Ronnie told her. "Eat a little something, then sleep some more. You need to get your strength back."

But Shake didn't want Ronnie to go. "I was scared you didn't want us," she said. "That you didn't want to be a dad." She was having trouble wrapping her head around this new improved Ronnie, this seemingly more *responsible* Ronnie.

"We're a family," Ronnie said. "We'll do whatever we have to do." He stood up and smiled at her. "We'll run away. Live by our wits like Bonnie and Clyde."

"I like that." Shake had watched the movie on TV a few weeks ago and the notion that she could be a modern-day Bonnie Parker appealed to her.

"The three of us," Ronnie murmured, looking almost dreamy now.

"What about that other baby?" Shake asked. "What's going to happen to her?"

Ronnie's smile slipped a notch. "I think . . . Mom has plans for her."

MARJORIE was standing at the bottom of the steps, waiting for Ronnie.

"What the hell were you doing up there all this time?" she asked. She was wearing her pseudo-nun's outfit, but she was chugging a Budweiser straight from the can.

Ronnie shrugged. "I took her the food."

"Yeah? What else?"

"We were just talking."

"Just talking," Marjorie mimicked. "Talking about what?" She was afraid the baby might have given Shake a slight hold over Ronnie. Couldn't let that happen.

"Nothing important." Ronnie started to turn away. He'd felt good talking to Shake about the baby. He'd felt more grown-up, more like a man than he ever had before. Just talking about a new life together helped pull him out of his dark, scary places.

Marjorie leered at him. "You better get your head in the game, kid. There's gonna be some big changes around here."

Ronnie stopped in his tracks and swung around to stare at his mother. "What do you mean?" he demanded. "What are you talking about?"

"Forget about that girl upstairs," Marjorie hissed. "Forget about the baby. Your baby . . . and that other kid. They're going to be out of here first thing next week."

"Don't you dare . . . *do* anything," Ronnie growled. His mother thought there were going to be changes? Well, there certainly might be. Little did she know that *he'd* be the one making those changes.

"I do whatever I damn well please," Marjorie said. "Not that it's any of your business." She spun away from him and walked into her studio.

Ronnie stood in the hallway waiting patiently. Waiting for his mother to scream. It didn't take long.

There was an ear-piercing shriek followed by Marjorie's plaintive wail. "What have you *done* to my Glynnis doll? How could you? How *dare* you!"

Marjorie rushed back out into the hallway, her face white as a sheet, her jaw working frantically, teeth practically gnashing the air. In her hands she carried an eighteen-inch baby doll. The doll was dressed in a pale peach organza dress with a white Peter Pan collar and puffy sleeves. Where its little head used to be, a bloody fox head had been impaled.

"Have you gone completely loony!" Marjorie screamed. The fox eyes stared at her, hard and beady; the whiskers fairly twitched.

"Like it?" Ronnie asked.

"You fool. You imbecile," she raged. "I'll show you who's . . ." Her arm shot up and her hand clenched into a fist, ready to slug him.

Quick as a striking cobra, Ronnie grabbed Marjorie's wrist and pinched it tight.

"Let me go!" Her dark eyes, sunk into her putty face like raisins, blazed fiercely at him.

"What did you call me?" Ronnie glowered back at Marjorie, gripping her wrist tight, really digging in his fingernails. Then he hoisted her up slowly until she was standing on tiptoes, practically dangling. He decided she looked like a helpless old cow about to be slaughtered.

"Stop it, stop it!" Marjorie screamed, twisting in his grip, eyes rolling back in her head. "Put me down!"

Ronnie fixed her with a crooked, half-glazed smile. "Shut up, bitch," he whispered. "You shut up before I take you outside and lop your head off with an ax."

Marjorie snapped her mouth shut as a jolt of fear ripped through her. And for the first time in her life, Marjorie did exactly what her son told her to do.

37

WHO wants the last slice of pepperoni?" Max asked.

"Me," Bagin said. He gazed across the conference room table at Afton, put a hand to his mouth, and stifled a burp.

"Go ahead and take it," Afton told him. "In fact, you're welcome to it."

It was practically nine o'clock on Friday night. Afton, Max, Thacker, Jasper, Bagin, and a half dozen others had hung around police headquarters, talking nervously, waiting for Darden's phone to ring, finally ordering out for pizza.

Darden sat at the far end of the table, looking miserable. He didn't eat; he didn't talk to any of the others; he just stared at his cell phone as if willing it to ring.

It hadn't.

For the second time in two days, techs had attached a microphone and miniature tracking device to Darden's clothing. They'd debated at length about fitting him with a tiny camera, but had decided against it.

Privately, Afton feared that the kidnappers might have abandoned their original plan to collect a ransom. She worried that the Darden baby might have died, accidentally or otherwise, so there wasn't going to be a phone call. But here she was, just the same. Waiting, hoping to beat the odds, sweating bullets along with the rest of them.

"You should go home to your kids," Max said. He'd told her that twice already, as if she were the only person in the room who had kids at home.

"They're fine," Afton muttered. "Why don't you go home to yours?"

Max shrugged. "It's snowing outside, you know?" Four inches had filtered down this afternoon. More snow—an even larger and more dangerous weather system—was already barreling through the Dakotas and heading their way.

"Yeah," Afton grumbled. "It's snowing. Tell me something I don't know."

Max held her eyes for a few moments, and then broke off his gaze. He knew she was just as invested in this case as he was. Just as frustrated by the lack of inertia.

Another twenty minutes crept by. Detectives, FBI agents, and uniformed officers came and went. They made urgent, whispered phone calls, rattled candy wrappers, slurped coffee, and tried not to alarm Darden any more than they already had.

Darden, for his part, was not holding up particularly well. No longer looking like a male catalog model for Brooks Brothers, he was dressed in blue jeans and a droopy plaid shirt. He was also chewing his fingernails ragged, muttering to himself, and taking endless trips to the men's room.

Privately, Afton thought Darden might be ready to crack. It had been forty-eight hours since the first phone call had come in from the kidnappers. And there'd been nothing since. She suspected his nerves were pretty much frazzled.

Bagin tossed a half-gnawed hunk of crust into the pizza box, where it clunked loudly and bounced a few crumbs around. He flipped the lid closed, and then stood up slowly and stretched. Reached down and scratched his belly.

Max lifted an eyebrow. "You got a personal problem?" he asked.

Bagin slid a hand up and touched the area just below his throat. "I think that damn pizza gave me a case of heart—"

And that's when the phone rang. Not any sort of melodic ringtone, but a shrill, startling ring. A ring that said, *Okay, boys and girls, time to pull it together and get down to serious business.*

Darden stared at his cell phone as if he couldn't believe what was happening. As if an inanimate object had suddenly started speaking to him.

There was a flurry of officious footsteps and then Thacker's voice barked out, "Answer it."

Darden reached gingerly for his phone and pushed the On button.

"Hello?" he croaked. He sounded like a ninety-year-old man who'd lived in a cave for the last ten years.

Thacker snapped his fingers for everyone to shut up. He wanted Darden to answer the phone, listen carefully, and ask a few gently rehearsed questions. The cell phone had been adapted so that any conversation would be recorded. They would all hear the call in its entirety in a matter of minutes.

Darden bowed his shoulders forward and said, "Yes, I understand." There was more conversation on the other end of the line and he said, "Okay, but it's going to take me a while to get there." He listened some more, his mouth going slack. "Absolutely."

When he hung up, he looked like he'd been sucker punched in the gut.

"We gotta listen to the call!" Max boomed.

They all raced down the hall and crowded into a smaller room, which held a myriad of audio and video equipment. Dick Boyce, the tech guy, hit a button on a piece of equipment and the conversation crackled to life.

"Hello?" They were hearing Richard's voice, just as they had a few moments earlier.

"Listen carefully, Mr. Darden," came a male voice. "If you want to get your baby back alive, you are to drive to the corner of Sims and Weide in Saint Paul. Do you understand?"

Afton frowned. This wasn't what she'd been expecting. She'd thought that the doll lady or the pizza guy would be calling. This was a man, same as the other night, with a fairly cultured voice. What was going on?

"Yes, I understand," came Darden's voice.

"Bring the two million dollars," said the voice. "When you arrive, you will be given further instructions."

"Okay, but it's going to take me a while to get there," Darden said.

"Come alone. No police."

"Absolutely."

WAS this the same guy who called the other night?" Thacker asked. Everyone was clustered around Darden, staring at him as if he were a class biology project.

"I think so." Darden coughed and cleared his throat. "I'm pretty sure it was."

"This person sounds very controlled," Jasper said. "This is a guy who's thought things through rather carefully. He's not going to be easy to deal with."

"Shouldn't I get moving?" Darden quaked. He looked terrified, like a man about to face a firing squad. At the same time, he seemed anxious to be on his way with the ransom money. To get it over with.

That was when the mad scramble began. Everyone started talking at once while the tech guys double-checked the tiny tracking devices and microphones attached to Darden's clothing.

"I still think we should put a camera on his jacket," Thacker said. "Maybe stick it on his lapel?"

"You sure you want to do that?" Max asked.

"Positive," Thacker said. "We need eyes. We can't take any chances."

"We're already taking chances," Afton said. To her, job one was getting Elizabeth Ann back safely. After that, she didn't care if they shot the kidnapper with a high-powered rifle or dragged him to jail behind a fleet of squad cars.

But Thacker and Jasper were explicit in their plans. Darden had his tracking device, as well as a broadcast mike and a miniature camera. They wanted to know what was happening every second of the way. Vehicles carrying the FBI and two SWAT teams would follow Darden closely on parallel streets, and a helicopter would track his every move from overhead. The Saint Paul Police Department was standing by on alert, ready to jump in if needed.

Afton pulled Max aside. "What are we going to do?" In all the planning and furor, they hadn't received a definite assignment. In fact, they'd effectively been sidelined. Everything was now in the capable hands of the FBI and the MPD hostage and rescue professionals.

"We'll go, too," Max said in a low voice as they slipped down the hall. "We'll tuck in behind the FBI and SWAT guys."

DO you think the caller was the same guy from the other night?" Afton asked.

"Darden thought so," Max said. He was driving his Hyundai, following five minutes behind the dark, unmarked car that carried Jasper, Thacker, and Bagin.

"So who is he? I mean, it's not the doll lady and he's obviously not the kid I tangled with, the one we suspect is the pizza guy." Afton hung on for dear life as Max drove full bore down I-94. He was hitting speeds of almost seventy miles an hour, blowing past cars and trucks that crawled along tentatively on the snow-clogged freeway. Had they passed the unmarked car carrying Thacker and company? Maybe not. That car had been going like a bat out of hell, too.

Max's knuckles were practically white from his death grip on the steering wheel. "There must be three kidnappers, working in concert."

"Doesn't feel right to me." Afton fiddled with the radio equipment they'd been issued. Besides Max's police radio, they had a special radio that was linked directly to Darden's microphone. It would allow all parties concerned to listen in on any commentary that Darden made. More important, it would let them eavesdrop on his face-to-face confrontation with the kidnapper.

"Nothing feels right to me," Max said. "Turn up those radios, see if anybody's saying anything yet."

Afton did. But Darden remained silent. And the police radio just carried the usual squeal. She peered through the windshield. "Damn, this snow just keeps coming down."

"More tomorrow," Max said. "Weatherman is predicting some kind of superstorm. They're saying maybe eight more inches."

"Think this will all be over by tomorrow?" She meant a resolution to the kidnapping, not the bad weather.

Max stared straight ahead, fighting the wind that buffeted his car back and forth, trying desperately to stay in his lane. "I don't know."

As they swept through Spaghetti Junction, the multifreeway tangle that cut through downtown Saint Paul, Afton said, "Thacker and Jasper and the rest of those guys probably got off at Sixth Street, right?"

"Had to," Max said. "That would be the logical way. That's how we're going to do it anyway."

They circled around the off-ramp and popped out on West Seventh Street. A Super America station was straight ahead; a warehouse sat directly to their right.

"Where are they?" Max asked. He scanned both directions, sounding surprised that they hadn't bumped up on Thacker and Jasper's tailpipe.

"Maybe we passed them. You were driving pretty fast."

"Huh."

"Darden was instructed to drive to Sims and Weide," Afton said, consulting a hastily printed map. "In what's known as East Saint Paul. That would mean a left turn. Here on West Seventh. Then heading across a couple of bridges."

"I don't know," Max said. But he turned north anyway, heading toward Payne Avenue. They passed Red's Savoy Pizza on their left and shot across a freeway bridge.

Afton couldn't remember the last time she'd been over on this side of Saint Paul. The labyrinth of streets, the lack of sequential numbering, the lack of familiar landmarks made everything seem foreign. A former celebrity governor had once complained that Saint Paul's streets had been designed by "drunken Irishmen." His pronouncement—while crude and not terribly politically correct—wasn't all that far off base.

"Where the hell are we?" Max muttered. His windshield wipers were struggling to keep up.

"Careful," Afton cautioned. "We don't want to overshoot anybody." What she really meant was, *We don't want to overshoot Darden and blow everybody's cover.*

"Now what?" Max asked, clearly flummoxed. "You're the one with the map."

"Left. Hang a left right here. We need to go up Payne Avenue."

Max made the turn and swept north again, the whole of Swede Hollow Park, dark and deep, just off to their right. "Now what?"

"Now pull over," Afton said. "Because Darden just started talking."

Max pulled over to a curb that was delineated only by a huge ridge of plowed snow. "Hope we don't get stuck," he grumped. Saint Paul snow removal was often sketchy at best.

Afton goosed the volume on their communications equipment. "Shush. Listen up."

They put their heads together and listened.

Darden was talking now, his voice sounding low and cautious, giving a kind of play-by-play for the benefit of the FBI and SWAT teams.

"Okay, I just pulled up at the corner of Sims and Weide," Darden said. "There's not a living soul here that I can see. Just a few houses, not many lights on. One quadrant of the intersection leads off toward a playground, although it's covered with snow. I think maybe a ball field." He hesitated. There was the sound of his car door snicking open. "I'm getting out now." There were slight crunching sounds. "Nothing. I think this might be . . . Wait a minute." Now they could hear his breath sounds, hoarse and a little panicked. "I hear something." More crunching. "There's a phone ringing. A pay phone over there." Now there was wild excitement in his voice.

"Holy crap," Max said. "That must be the last pay phone left in existence."

"Kidnapper really plotted out the route," Afton muttered.

"Hello?" Darden had answered the ringing phone, his voice high and reedy. "Yes," he said. "I know where that is."

There was more crunching and then the sound of his car door opening and closing. When he was safely inside, Darden said, "Same voice. This time he told me to head over to that old nightclub by the Wabasha Street Caves. I'm supposed to look around the parking lot for a pop can. Inside is supposed to be another set of directions." He swallowed hard, and then said, "I hope you guys are listening in because this feels very dangerous. Like I'm walking into a trap."

"We're listening," Afton said, even though she knew Darden couldn't hear her.

Max shook his head. "This is like a bad scavenger hunt that . . . Oh, holy shit."

"What?"

"I'll bet the kidnapper is leading him toward those old beer and mushroom caves."

"It'd be hard for SWAT to follow him in there," Afton said.

Max pounded a fist against the steering wheel. "No, it's going to be damn near impossible. That's a terrible place. Those caves are dug right into the hillside. You've got a bluff that rises nearly eight hundred feet high above them and is nearly impossible to scale. And the Mississippi River dips within fifty yards of those caves. It's mostly dense woods along there. There are no streets . . . no lights . . ."

"And if those new directions send him farther back . . ."

"The farther back you go," Max said, "the more deserted it gets. Just a tangle of trees and underbrush. And if the kidnapper tries to lure Darden inside one of those caves, all bets are off 'cause it's dangerous as hell. There are drop-offs inside, noxious gasses."

"What are we gonna do?" Afton asked. She remembered that some high school kids had died in those caves a few years ago. They'd crawled in to drink beer and smoke pot, but ended up breathing deadly carbon monoxide.

Max worried his upper teeth against his lower lip. "I can't imagine what the SWAT team will do."

"Can we get over there somehow? I mean us, you and I?"

"We can't risk it. There's only that one narrow road in, past Harriet Island Park. If the kidnapper is watching, and I'm sure he is, we'll be spotted in a second."

Afton was almost frantic. "There has to be someplace we can go."

Max considered this for a few seconds. "There might be a spot up top. Way up on the river bluff."

38

AS Afton and Max careened across the Lafayette Bridge, the lights of Holman Field, where they'd jumped onto a helicopter just five days ago, shimmered dimly off to their left. At this late hour, traffic was almost nonexistent in this industrial part of the city where large, low warehouses stretched for blocks and sodium vapor lights lent an unnatural yellow glow.

All the while they listened to Darden's mutterings and the squeal on Max's police radio.

They could hear Don Jasper screaming at the SWAT guys to pull on their white coveralls and get into position fast.

But would they be fast enough, Afton wondered, even as sharpshooters were being dispatched?

Cruising down Plato Boulevard, Max made a couple of turns, and then headed up Ohio Street, barely slowing as he blew through a stop sign. It was a narrow, twisty street that climbed upward at a steep angle. It took them directly up the east bluff that loomed over downtown Saint Paul and the Mississippi River.

"Isn't there a park up here somewhere?" Afton asked as they popped out on top. "A place where we can see what's going on?"

"I think . . . this way," Max said, turning right.

He churned along unplowed streets, and then pulled to the curb at Cherokee Avenue, where they both jumped out. Wind and snow buffeted them as they ran through knee-deep snow to a small overlook on the edge of the bluff.

Downtown Saint Paul was spread out before them. At any other time the view would be spectacular, a twinkling wonderland of tall buildings interspersed with historic churches, ancient breweries, pocket-sized parks, turreted old sandstone buildings, and redbrick warehouses. But with the snow drifting down, the atmosphere was softened and fuzzed, as if a filter had been thrown across the entire city. Definition was hazy; lights were dimmed. On the opposite bluff they could barely make out the humped row of landmark mansions.

Looking straight down, they still weren't able to see the caves or the path that ran alongside them. The angle was too steep, and there was just too much forest and tangled brush.

"Nothing to see," Afton said, disappointed. She was hoping to get a glimpse of the main cave. Every time she'd seen the place, it had looked otherworldly. An enormous flat sandstone face set into a gigantic hill and fronted by a castle-like brick facade. Several rounded wooden doors, the kind a cadre of trolls might use, formed an entrance. Legend held that the caves had once been a speakeasy that entertained the likes of John Dillinger and Ma Barker. The natural refrigeration properties had also made it ideal for beer storage back when Saint Paul breweries had pumped out gallons and gallons of the amber suds. In the eighties someone had turned the cave's carved-out, rounded interior into a nightclub. Now it was some sort of event center.

Afton cradled the communications gear inside her parka and jacked up the dial up so they could hear what Darden was saying.

"Okay," Darden said. "I'm here outside the Wabasha Street Caves. There are a few cars in the parking lot and I can hear music playing inside." He sounded lonely and scared. "I just got out of my car and now I'm looking around for that pop can."

Darden's voice came to them fuzzy and laced with static. He sounded like a distant radio signal that faded in and out.

"This is awful," Afton said. She was actually feeling sorry for the man. He not only sounded terrified, but could be walking into an ambush. Yet he was willing to do whatever it took to rescue his daughter. His actions were definitely heroic.

"He's still hanging in there," Max said. "Doing the best he can."

Darden's voice crackled again. "There's a Mountain Dew can sitting here. Kind of propped up on a pile of snow. I'm going to take a look inside." The signal faded out for a moment and then he was back. "I think this is it. Yes, there's a note inside. I'm going to pull it out and read it verbatim." He cleared his throat. "It says: 'Drive toward Harriet Island and take the road south to Bauer's Recycling Plant. Leave the car and follow the hiking trail that leads past the old caves.'"

"That's a dead end," Max said.

"Holy shit," Afton said. "I wish we could . . ." She cocked her head toward Max and suddenly looked past him. Through far, heavy flakes she saw the faint outline of the High Bridge silhouetted behind him. She grabbed Max's sleeve and spun him around. "The High Bridge. We've got to get up there," she cried. "Maybe we can see what's going on."

"Maybe," Max said. They were scrambling back through the snow toward his car. "We'll give it a shot."

Cherokee Avenue led directly to the High Bridge. On Max's say-so, they left the car and walked out onto the bridge. It looked slippery and icy, and no cars were venturing across it. A panorama of city, river, and woods spread out below them. Since they were obscured by darkness and falling snow, it was doubtful that anyone would look up and be able to spot them.

"Do you see Darden down there?" Max asked. "Anything?"

"Not yet," Afton said. "But I'll tell you something. This kidnapper is a guy who knows Saint Paul. I mean, he either lives here or he grew up here."

"Why do you think that?"

"You take your average Minneapolis person. They hardly ever venture across the river into Saint Paul. You know why? Because they don't think it's worth it. Everything they're ever going to want is right there on the Minneapolis side."

"That's a pretty harsh assessment, don't you think?"

"But it's the truth. I'm telling you, this guy, the guy who set this up is from Saint Paul."

"But where is he?" Max asked. "And where's Darden?"

Afton scanned the distance. "I don't know. Wait . . . there's a pair of headlights bumping toward us. I think that might be Darden. Looks like he's about a half mile away."

Max squinted down. "Ah, he's pulling into that recycling place. Gotta be him."

Afton lay down on the bridge and peered out through the struts of the metal railing. She pulled the communication device out of her parka and listened. After two seconds Max crouched down to join her.

"The snow is almost knee-deep," Darden was saying. "And I'm not seeing any tracks at all, so I'm guessing nobody's been back this way for a while."

"He sounds scared," Afton said.

Max lifted a hand and brushed snow from his face, leaving wet streaks. "He should be scared."

"I don't know if this is a double cross or not," Darden continued in hushed tones. "Or if somebody is going to come in from the opposite direction."

Max studied the bluffs below. "Someone would have to skim down that cliff if they were approaching him from the opposite direction."

"Could be done," Afton said.

Max gazed at her for a moment. "Could you do it?"

"Maybe." She looked over and studied the bluff. "Probably."

ALL right," Darden said. "I'm still struggling through the snow. There's that enormous cliff to my left, and the frozen Mississippi River is just off to my right."

The microphone was working well now, and Afton and Max could hear the crunching of snow along with Darden's ragged breathing.

"He's getting tired," Afton said. She could just barely see him, a tiny dot moving far below, trying to wade through a narrow, open patch of snow, following what was an obliterated trail.

"I don't see anything moving out here," Darden said. "Of course, it's darker than shit. Jeez, I hope those SWAT guys are in place. This is getting weirder by the moment."

"This feels like an ambush," Afton said to Max.

"Can't see anybody else, though," Max said.

Darden continued to give his play-by-play. "I see a . . . I think it's a wooden shack up ahead. Anyway, it's all ramshackle and falling down. Maybe that's supposed to be the spot where we make the exchange?"

"Careful, careful," Afton murmured. When she craned her neck, she could see the faint outline of the shack, too, and wondered if the kidnapper lurked inside? Was Elizabeth Ann waiting in there, too, in the terrible bone-chilling cold?

"As soon as I make the exchange," Darden said, "I'm going to fall flat on the ground and stay down. Then you guys take your shots, okay?"

"Jesus," Afton breathed.

Darden moved closer to the shack. His raspy voice reflected his inner tension as he shook and shuddered in the freezing cold.

"Damn it, I still don't see anybody," Darden said. He paused. "Wait a minute, I think I hear something." He sounded both stressed and puzzled. "It sounds like something mechanical. Like an outboard motor or a chain saw."

Afton and Max heard it, too. An annoying buzzing sound, like some kind of giant, mechanized insect.

"What is that?" Max wondered.

Afton knew what it was, but before she could voice an explanation, a snowmobile jounced and roared along the riverbank far below them.

"Shit!" Max cried.

They watched as Darden caught sight of the snowmobile and stumbled. Then he flung his arms out wide and dropped to his knees.

"Don't hurt me, don't hurt me!" Darden screamed. "I've got your money, the full two million dollars. Please just give me back my daughter!"

Afton watched in horror at the tableau that was unfolding below them. The snowmobile buzzed around him in a wide circle and then stopped.

Darden hurled the duffel bag of money toward the snowmobile driver. "Here's your money!" Darden cried. "Take it."

The driver, wearing a black helmet, bubble facemask, and snowmobile suit, leaned sideways on his sputtering machine and swung one leg over. Then, in one quick motion, as if fearing a trap, he tossed down a small bundle and snatched up the bag of money.

Darden scrambled forward on his knees toward the bundle. "Elizabeth Ann!"

The snowmobiler jumped back onto his machine. The engine roared loudly as he kicked it into gear. Then, tossing up an enormous crest of powdered snow, he sped off in the same direction from which he'd come.

That's when it all went ka-pow crazy.

Darden scooped up the bundle, cradled it against his body, and suddenly screamed. "It's not her!" His voice rose up in a pitiful wail. "It's just a rolled-up blanket!"

"Dear Lord," Afton cried.

At the same instant, a volley of shots exploded from beneath the bridge. Thacker's sharpshooters were firing at the snowmobiler, the shots seeming to come from inside one of the caves as well as from a tangle of brush down near the riverbank.

Afton saw the snowmobiler swerve wildly, trying to take evasive action and escape the bullets that were intended to bring him down. As loud *pops* continued to ring out, the snowmobiler changed course and went screaming down the steep riverbank. Seconds later, he skittered out onto the flat, dull gray ice of the Mississippi River.

"He's on the river," Max shouted.

The snowmobiler was really pouring it on. Zigzagging back and forth, pushing his snowmobile's engine to the max.

He'd almost made it to the middle of the frozen river and Afton was starting to wonder what his escape strategy would be. Head down the river in the direction from which he'd come? Run straight across and ditch the machine on the opposite bank? Make a run for it and try to get swallowed up by the city? If she could keep the snowmobiler in her sights, she knew it would be a tremendous help to all the law enforcement personnel that had to be converging on the area right now.

All of a sudden there was another crack—a sound not quite as loud as a rifle shot but even more ominous.

"The ice," Afton said, pointing. "The river's not completely frozen over in the middle. Look there, it's breaking up."

"Must be a fast current," Max said. "So only a thin skim of ice was able to form."

Afton and Max watched as the snowmobiler throttled back. The ice was obviously unstable and he was struggling to find a safer route.

An enormous hunk of ice broke loose and suddenly jutted up like a slippery on-ramp. Jagged and dangerous looking, the piece of ice looked like an enormous broken windowpane.

The snowmobiler, far from being an expert with his sled, wobbled slightly as he tried to change direction yet again.

The slowing down was what did it, of course. A snowmobile running at top speed can practically skip across open water. But a hint of hesitation and it suddenly becomes a heavy piece of machinery, subject to the whims and principles of thin ice and basic gravity.

Two more enormous jagged cracks yawned open. Then an entire network of cracks, almost like a spider's web, spun out from around the snowmobile. The snowmobiler gunned his sled left in a last-ditch effort to save himself.

But it was too late.

From up above, from their bird's-eye perch on the High Bridge, Afton and Max watched in horror as the ice parted and a gaping black hole appeared. The snowmobile's skids teetered for one long moment on a snaggletoothed shard of floating ice, and then it plunged into the dark water.

The snowmobiler sank to his waist in the freezing water. Clearly having abandoned his sled and the duffel bag filled with ransom money, he struggled and paddled desperately amid a froth of bubbles. As hypothermia quickly set in, his arm motions slowed to a pathetic pace and he sank to his neck. Now only his round snowmobile helmet appeared to float on the surface like a dark bubble. He hovered there for another thirty seconds and then, with nary a sound or cry, disappeared completely.

BY the time Afton and Max raced back to their car and careened down the bluff, the scene had evolved into chaos. Thacker and Jasper were in the epicenter, shouting at a dozen officers, screaming into their radios.

"Now. *Now!*" Thacker cried. "Send a helo down the river to see if they can spot any sort of vehicle with a trailer. Our guy had to park and unload his snowmobile somewhere in the area." His eyes flicked across Afton and Max. "And get hold of the cops in Lilydale and Mendota. Shake 'em out of bed if you have to. I want a full-court press on this. Saint Paul PD is jumping in, too."

"If we can locate the vehicle," Max said to Afton, "we can trace the registration and ID the kidnapper."

Thacker continued to scream into his police radio. "Yes, check marinas. Especially check marinas. I don't care if they're closed. This shitbird had to park somewhere."

Sirens blasted and bright lights split the night as two enormous trucks thundered in. Saint Paul's Fire and Rescue Squad. A dozen men jumped down, manning ladders, ropes, and long poles with barbed hooks on the end so they could fish around in the murky water. Two men scrambled to pull on dry suits. It was the same frantic scene that was repeated dozens of times all over the frozen Midwest whenever a car, person, or snowmobile plunged through the ice.

"You think they can find the kidnapper?" Afton asked. "Pull him out?"

"If it even was the kidnapper," Thacker snapped as he came over to join them. He was hopping up and down, stomping his feet against the relentless cold. "For all we know, this snowmobile guy could've been a phony who was hell-bent on collecting the ransom money."

"He'd have to have some pretty decent inside information," Afton said.

Thacker grimaced as a TV van humped its way toward them. "It happens."

"Maybe this guy was just the errand boy," Max said. "Hired by the kidnapper."

"If that's the case, he's a bad luck errand boy," Afton said. "Because now all that money's at the bottom of the Mississippi." She wondered what two million dollars of waterlogged money looked like.

"This has been bad luck all around," Thacker said. He glanced over at Richard Darden, who'd since been retrieved from the woods. Darden sat shivering on the back end of an ambulance, a blanket wrapped around his shoulders. His head was bowed and he was weeping while one of the EMTs, a young African-American man with soulful eyes, tried to comfort him.

FINALLY, there was nothing left to do but regroup. Which was how Afton found herself sitting in Mickey's Diner in downtown Saint Paul, guzzling hot coffee with Max, Deputy Chief Gerald Thacker, Don Jasper, Harvey Bagin, and Andy Farmer.

"Nothing to show for tonight but a damn hole in the ice," Thacker said. His hair was plastered flat against his head from wearing a stocking cap and he looked beyond haggard. He seemed to be taking tonight's failure personally.

"Maybe the divers will have better luck in the morning?" Jasper asked.

"Maybe," Max said. "But it's going to be treacherous as hell. There's an even bigger storm rolling in."

"Does it ever stop snowing here?" Jasper asked. "In Chicago we get wind off Lake Michigan and a couple weeks of below-zero temperatures. But this much snow . . . it's almost apocalyptic. I mean, what's next? Frogs and locusts?"

"This year's snowfall is unusually heavy," Afton told him.

"That so?" He looked like he wanted to believe her.

"No. It's always like this," she said.

A faint smile creased Jasper's face. "You were just trying to make me feel better, is that it?"

"Did it work?" Afton asked. She liked this rangy FBI agent who was able to maintain his cool as well as his sense of humor.

"No," Thacker said in a tone that indicated their banter wasn't one bit welcome at the table.

Afton cleared her throat. "What happened with Darden?"

"Ambulance took him to Regions Hospital," Thacker said. "They thought he might be suffering from hypothermia." He placed his hands flat on the table and then pushed himself up. "Okay, everybody. Party's over. Go home and get some shut-eye. We start again first thing tomorrow." He pulled out his cell phone, scowled at it, and shuffled off to make another call.

"We're in limbo," Jasper said. "Still haven't located the dead snowmobiler's vehicle. Maybe when we fish him out, we can get a positive ID and work from there."

"Might have to thaw him out first," Bagin said.

"Hopefully the current hasn't carried his body all the way down to Hastings," Max said.

"If that's the case, there won't be a lot to go on," Jasper said.

Afton set her coffee cup down with a loud *clink*. "Then we start over, just like Thacker said. We go back to square one, review the case files, and try to get a fresh perspective."

Jasper, looking slightly bemused by her tenacity, hooked a thumb in Afton's direction. "Is she always such a pit bull?"

Max shook his head. "You have no idea."

39

MARJORIE was finishing a bowl of Grape-Nuts Flakes when the newsflash came across the morning show. She'd been watching *Wake Up with Terri and Tony*, which aired early each Saturday morning on Channel 7. Terri was showing Tony how to make a graham cracker piecrust, laughing her fake TV personality laugh and making a big show of slapping his hand whenever he did something wrong. Which was, of course, fake TV bumbling.

When the anchorman's face came on, Marjorie stood up and walked to the sink to rinse out her bowl. She turned on the faucet, tuning out the anchorman and the stupid, screaming red graphics that whirled about his head. But when the anchorman uttered the fateful words *Darden baby* and *bungled ransom*, her world suddenly tilted on its axis.

What?

The words crashed inside Marjorie's brain like a freight train careening off its tracks. She spun around and rushed to the TV. Frantically jacked up the sound.

She watched in horror as the anchorman, who cautioned viewers that this was, as yet, an unconfirmed report, laid out all the dirty details. He explained about the ransom call that had been received by Richard Darden, the mysterious directions that had led him to the Wabasha Street Caves, the bungled ransom, and how the kidnapper's snowmobile had plunged through thin ice. He closed his report by noting that the drowned man, whose body had just been recovered some forty minutes ago, was suspected to be that of Lars Torbert, a prominent Saint Paul attorney.

Marjorie's jaw dropped.

Ransom demand? Wabasha Street Caves? Saint Paul attorney?

None of that had remotely figured into her plan. So what the hell had just happened?

As her cold, reptilian brain strained to process this bizarre information, the realization of what had probably happened began to fall into place. And finally, the answer lit up like a cool blue neon beer sign hanging in the front window of a bar.

That asshole Torbert had rolled the dice and tried to pull an end run on her. He'd attempted to negotiate a phony exchange that would net him a big fat pile of money. Only it had worked out badly for him. And now he was dead, drowned like the filthy weasel he was, probably laid out on a cold slab in the Saint Paul morgue.

Marjorie walked into her doll studio and sat down so hard she practically jounced the fillings in her teeth loose. She needed to focus. She needed to think. Most important, she needed to weigh her *options*.

She picked up a Krissy doll and sat there stroking its silky blond hair. Studied its little girl lips, idly decided that they should be bolder, maybe even with a Hollywood pout.

Marjorie figured she had twenty-four hours at best before the net would begin to settle around her.

If the police tore through that scumbag Torbert's records, and surely they would, then sooner or later they were bound to find something—paperwork, phone records, whatever—that linked him to her.

That would be a disaster of epic proportions.

Of course, having that little hot potato asleep in the crib upstairs was fairly incriminating as well. Something would have to be done. New plans would have to be put in place. And fast.

Marjorie picked up a pair of scissors and started trimming the doll's hair. She snipped methodically at the long, flowing tresses, turning them into a shoulder-length bob. As her mood darkened, her anger and frustration grew, until it seemed to encompass her like a black, amorphous blob. She snipped away more hair. The doll's bob was becoming a pixie cut.

The police will be coming, she told herself. *And when they do, they're not going to show one lick of mercy. All they'll care about is what happened with the Darden baby and the Pink woman.*

She hacked aggressively at the doll's hair, making one side spikey and stubbly.

I'll be sent to prison. For life. I can't let that happen. I won't let that happen.

Marjorie threw down the scissors and watched them skitter across her worktable. Exhaling heavily, she bent sideways and slid open the bottom drawer of a metal filing cabinet. Pulled out a gun.

Better to settle this now, on my own terms.

She leaned back and caressed the dull metal of the gun. Thought about how easy it would be to shoot Shake and Ronnie. They were stupid and docile, like cows. They'd never see it coming, never think to defend themselves. She could pack up her good dolls and just get the hell away from here.

Maybe, just maybe, she could bundle up the two babies and take them along. She could dump them on the black market somewhere, maybe in Kansas City or Saint Louis. Someplace like that. She knew a few people. She'd been dabbling in this business long enough.

Kill them and then I'll drive down to . . .

Marjorie gazed out the window. Pulled herself out of her mad fantasy long enough to see that there was a winter storm raging outside. Icy crystals of snow *tick-ticked* at the window like ragged fingernails. She saw that the snow had drifted up and over the cars in the driveway, turning them into soft, white humps. With this much snow, the roads would be damn near impassable. Hell, their driveway was completely drifted in. Still . . . if she couldn't get out, then the police couldn't get in. That brought her some small degree of comfort.

I'll have to wait. But probably no more than ten or twelve hours. Don't want to push my luck any more than I have to.

As soon as the snow eased up, she'd call Ort Peterman, the farmer who was their nearest neighbor. He was a big old Norski who owned a big old snowcat. He'd come over and plow her out if she asked. Have to pay him forty bucks, but what the hell. It was a small price to pay for her freedom.

That was it then. That was her plan. Shoot and scoot. Marjorie's snarling expression turned into a grin as she began to hum tunelessly.

And make plans. Lots of plans.

Lately, she'd been nursing a secret fantasy. Make some kind of big score and then get the hell out of Dodge. Move somewhere where she could rent a little apartment and go on disability. Get that monthly mailbox handout. She'd seen an episode on *60 Minutes* about how, down in Kentucky, everyone and his brother-in-law was on disability. If those stupid hillbillies could work a decent con, why couldn't she? She was ten times smarter than they were. Besides, if she ever wanted to go back into business, there were probably plenty of dumb hillbilly girls with unwanted hillbilly babies.

40

SUSAN Darden was the last person Afton and Max expected to see this Saturday morning as they huddled at Max's desk. But here she was, pulling off a knit stocking cap, looking anguished and expectant.

"I just came from Regions Hospital," Susan told them. "Checking on Richard." After Darden had been transported to Regions Hospital, he'd been treated for overexposure and kept overnight. Some sedation had been involved, too.

"How's he doing?" Afton asked.

"Not too many ill effects," Susan said. "Aside from the fact that he's angry and bitter about what happened. And upset about the money." She glanced around the Robbery and Homicide squad room. "The doctors say he can be released later today."

"His actions were very brave last night," Max said.

Susan gave a shrug. "Redemption."

"Really?" Afton asked. She wondered if something like this could bring the two of them back together. Tragedies sometimes became the binding tie, the shared emotion, that pulled families back from the brink of separation. Of course, she would never take a scumbag like Richard back, but Susan might.

"No, not really," Susan said. "Nothing's changed between us. I'm still going to file for divorce. But it's nice to know that Richard finally grew a pair of balls."

"Huh," Max said.

Susan swallowed hard and seemed to fight for control of her emotions. "What I really came here for, what I really want to know, is do you still think we have a chance?"

"If we didn't believe that, we wouldn't be here," Max said. "We wouldn't still have an entire team working overtime to find your baby."

Susan touched a hand to her chest. "Thank you. I guess I needed to hear that directly from you." Her eyes glistened with tears. "I really do believe that my baby is alive and is coming back to me. I *have* to believe that."

"We're doing everything we can," Afton said. It was the first time she'd given her assurance to Susan when she didn't believe it one hundred percent.

AFTON and Max were halfway through their notes, everything spread out around them on the conference room table, when Thacker careened into the room. He was wearing khaki slacks and a maroon-and-gold University of Minnesota hoodie. It was the first time Afton had ever seen him in casual attire. She thought he looked decidedly untucked.

"Divers just recovered the snowmobiler's body along with the duffel bag of money," Thacker told them, sounding a little breathless. "Pulled out the whole damn sled, too."

"Holy shit," Max said. "Do we know who the guy is?"

"Was it a woman?" Afton asked.

"Not a woman," Thacker said. "That's the weird thing. Saint Paul just ID'd him and it turns out the guy's a lawyer."

Afton was confused. "Wait a minute, you mean Darden's lawyer? Slocum?"

"No, no. Oh, hell no," Thacker said. "This guy's ID says his name is Lars Torbert."

"Who's Lars Torbert?" Max asked. "I never heard of him. Wait, you said he's a lawyer?"

"Lawyer from Saint Paul," Thacker said. "A firm by the name of Scanlon and Torbert."

"No shit," Max said. "So what's his connection to the kidnapping?"

"We don't know," Thacker said. "The FBI is at Torbert's office right now. They're pulling it apart, top to bottom, trying to see if they can figure this thing out."

"Torbert has a partner?" Afton asked. "What was the other name you mentioned? Scanlon?"

"Right," Thacker said. "A woman. She's in custody right now. Over in Saint Paul. But she's not talking."

A woman, Afton thought. *Could it be the doll show woman?*

"Do you think this Scanlon knows anything?" Afton asked.

"Possibly," Thacker said. "But it's hard to say. She's not talking and she's asked for a lawyer."

"A double layer of lawyers," Max said. "Are you going to charge this woman with anything?"

"Yes, but it probably won't stick for very long unless the FBI uncovers a shitload of evidence."

"Still, you've got her for the time being," Max said. "Maybe she'll crack. Maybe we'll get some sort of confession."

"And maybe a bunch of daffodils will pop out of my ass," Thacker said, looking glum. "Hell, we don't even know if this Torbert had anything to do with the kidnapping or if he was just the negotiator."

"I wouldn't exactly call that negotiating," Afton said. "Grab the money and then try to punk Darden with a fake baby?"

"I say nail his ass," Max said.

"Except that he's dead," Thacker said.

I hate to say this," Afton said once Thacker had left, "but Torbert probably got what he deserved."

"Karmic justice," Max said. "In light of the slimeball move he pulled last night."

"The problem being, if the female partner wasn't involved, then we're back to square one."

"We're back to square one anyway."

Afton was studying the FBI's interview with Jilly Hudson when the phone rang. It was Dr. Healy, the director of the Medical Examiner's Office over in Hudson.

"Dr. Healy," Max said. "How's your brother-in-law?"

Afton stopped what she was doing to listen in.

Max listened for a moment and then said, "Good. Glad to hear he's doing so well. So what's up? You found something on the body?" He listened for a few more moments. "Uh-huh. Okay." He made a few quick notes and then thanked Healy.

"What?" Afton asked, once Max had hung up.

"Dr. Healy says they ran a number of tests on Muriel Pink using a mass spectrometer and have some preliminary results."

"Can he send them over to us?"

"He's e-mailing everything right now," Max said. "Grab my laptop and open the e-mail. It's probably being dumped into my in-box right now."

It was.

"Okay, this is interesting," Afton said as she scanned Dr. Healy's report. "They found tiny flakes of paint on Muriel Pink's body."

"Paint," Max said.

"Ho, wait a minute," Afton continued. "It also says that crystals of oxalic acid showed up."

"Same as the baby from Cannon Falls."

"What the hell?" Afton was mystified. "When I asked if there might be a connection, I was pretty much grasping at straws. But this . . . this almost confirms it."

"Not exactly," Max said. "We still don't know what this oxalic acid shit is used for. It could be a component in some common household product."

"Okay. Let me Google it."

Afton hunted around for a few minutes. "Well, crap. It says here there are all sorts of industrial uses."

"There you go."

"One of them is for pickling."

"Pickling what?" Max asked. "Pickling pickles?"

"I don't know," Afton said. "I'm still reading this shit." She mumbled to herself as she skimmed along. "Okay, here's something else. It also says that oxalic acid is used in taxidermy."

"Taxidermy?" Max said.

"For pickling and tanning hides. To stop bacterial growth and degrade the soluble proteins."

Max frowned. "No shit."

But Afton's brain had begun to spin. "Think about this," she said, starting to get excited. "If you look at this as a kind of hobby activity, taxidermy might not be all that different from creating reborn dolls. You're working with stuffing material, glass eyes, and animal hairs and fibers."

"Holy crap," Max said. "We gotta take this to Thacker."

THACKER was impressed. So was Don Jasper.

"We need to start looking at taxidermists," Jasper said, jumping on the information.

"We can make some calls," Max said. "Maybe go out and start canvassing, talking to area taxidermists."

"No, no, you two stick around," Thacker said. "Let the FBI take care of all that. They're the computer geniuses. They can run down a list of area taxidermists, start asking questions, and alert the various law enforcement agencies around the state. Maybe bring in the DNR people, too, since it could involve animal parts."

"This is good work," Jasper said. "This is actionable information."

BUT there wasn't nearly enough action for Afton and Max.

"The thing is," Afton said, "if this *is* somehow connected to taxidermy, it could be a taxidermist over in Wisconsin."

"So we alert Wisconsin taxidermists as well as state law enforcement officials," Max said.

Afton had continued her search on the Internet. "I found something else that's interesting."

"What's that?" Max asked.

"There's a company over in Menominee, Wisconsin. Burdick's Taxidermy and Supply. Besides doing actual taxidermy, they claim to be the Midwest's largest distributor of taxidermy supplies."

Menominee's just thirty minutes from Hudson," Max said.

"That's what I'm thinking, too. Hudson's become a sort of . . . what would you call it? A chokepoint for us."

"Problem. There are three inches of fresh snow on the roads and the National Weather Service is predicting seven more."

"So?" Afton said. "We'll take the Navigator."

41

THE accumulation of snow on the Interstate had made driving so treacherous that Afton and Max barely made it to Burdick's Taxidermy in Menominee.

"I was going to close early," Burt Burdick told them when, after a nerve-racking ninety-minute drive, they finally showed up at his door. "But then I got your call. Not many folks crazy enough to venture out on a day like this. Especially when you're coming all the way from The Cities."

Burdick was short, stocky, and wore a khaki shirt and matching stiff pants tucked into hunter green rubber boots. Afton thought he looked like a DNR guy who'd been defrocked of all his wildlife badges.

"We appreciate you staying open for us," Max said. "I hope you've got a vehicle with four-wheel drive. Conditions are seriously lousy out there."

"Drive a Jeep Grand Cherokee myself," Burdick said. "Should be okay if this conversation doesn't take too long." He stared at them through thick glasses that magnified his inquisitive brown eyes. "What is it you detectives are so hot to talk to me about anyway?"

Without getting into specific details, Max told Burdick about the crystals of oxalic acid that had turned up on two separate bodies. He didn't mention anything about a dead baby or about Muriel Pink's murder.

"We did some research," Afton said, "and discovered that oxalic acid is one of the main components in pickling and tanning agents."

"It is," Burdick said. "And I've got a funny feeling about the direction this conversation is headed. Two homicide detectives show up on my doorstep?" He shook his head. "I hate like hell to think one of my customers might be some kind of damn killer."

"Well, we already know they kill animals," Afton said.

Burdick shot her a wary, disapproving look. A look that said, *You're clearly one of those radical, delusional people who are dead set against hunting.*

Afton just fixed him with a cool smile. "Why don't you just give us a little background information about your store and its products." She nodded toward the interior, where glass counters glistened with bottles of degreaser, skull bleach, and tanners, and shelves held glass eyes, fleshing knives, scalpels, and modeling tools.

"Okay then." Burdick hitched at his belt. "We're one of the preeminent taxidermists in the state of Wisconsin. Besides myself, I employ two other full-time taxidermists." He waved a hand at a wall that was a rogue's gallery of stuffed animal heads. "We handle everything from jackrabbits to black bears. Last year we even did a Cape buffalo."

"Impressive," Max said.

"I understand you're also a supply house," Afton said.

"That's right," Burdick said. "We also wholesale materials to other taxidermists."

"How many taxidermy studios like you are there around here?" Afton asked.

Burdick shook his head. "There's nobody like me. I'm the largest tool and chemical supplier in the upper Midwest."

"Then how many other just plain taxidermists?" Max asked.

"In this local area? Not many. There's Hap Johnson over in Eau Claire, Wally Fitzler up in Hayward . . ."

"So a dozen or so?" Afton asked.

"More like a half dozen. Not that many indies left anymore."

"Hunters today aren't interested in having their game stuffed?" Max asked.

"Yes and no. The big thing is there are a lot more freelancers," Burdick said.

"Freelancers?" Afton's brows shot up.

"Sure," Burdick said. "There are lots of guys doing taxidermy down in their basements. It's caught on real big. So they come to me and buy all the chemicals, degreasers, and tools that they need. Then they go home and get their instructions off the Internet." He chuckled. "You can find step-by-step videos on YouTube."

"Do you have any kind of list?" Afton asked him. "Of freelancers from around here? From this immediate area?"

"I have a customer list," Burdick said. "A database on my computer." He tapped an index finger against his lower lip. "To pinpoint just the customers from around here, I could probably sort them out by zip code if you're interested. And it sounds like you are."

"We definitely are," Max said.

"Thank you," Afton said. "We really appreciate your help on this."

"Take me just a couple minutes to print that list," Burdick said.

"One more thing," Max said. His voice had taken on a slight edge and Afton knew where he was going. What he was about to ask.

"Of all your current customers," Max said, "is there anyone you can think of who might be a little dangerous, a little bit out there on the edge?"

Burdick gazed at him. "You mean, do I know anybody who might be a killer?"

"That's right."

"No, I don't," Burdick said. "At least I hope I don't."

AFTON studied the list Burdick had given them over burgers and hash browns at the Liberty Café in downtown Menominee. The café was an old-fashioned luncheonette-type place with red vinyl bumper car booths, a juke-box attached to the wall in every booth, and copper pans and kettles hanging on the wall. A thin skim of dust coated the copper pans and kettles.

"There's twenty-six guys on this list Burdick gave us," Afton told Max. "Which is way too many for us to investigate on our own. We're going to have to bring in Wisconsin DCI."

"That's what we probably should have done in the first place," Max said. He glanced out the café's front window, where the street was practically devoid of cars and the swirling wind was busy carving snow into drifts. "Bad out there."

A waitress was suddenly hovering at their booth.

"Everything okay?" she asked. She was motherly looking and wore a pink frilly apron and a plastic spoon-shaped name tag that said JANELLE.

"Fine," Afton said.

"Tasty," Max said. He had wolfed down his entire burger and was eyeing Afton's.

"Is there anything else I can get you folks? Piece of apple pie? The check?" She was obviously anxious for her shift to be over. Anxious to get home before the storm clobbered them with its full intensity.

"No thanks," Max said. "Looks like you're probably going to close this place early, huh?"

"We're planning to do exactly that," Janelle said.

"Then just the check," Max said.

Janelle peeled their check off her notepad and set it down on the table. "There you go, hon." And she was off to the next booth, trying to hurry them along like a mother hen. A frightened mother hen.

"If we don't get back across the river pretty soon, we're gonna be stuck here forever," Max said. "Hey, you're not gonna eat your pickle?"

Afton shook her head.

"Give it here."

THEY shrugged into coats and hats, wrapped scarves around their necks, ready to head back outside and brave the elements.

Max studied the bill, muttered to himself, and then pulled out a twenty.

"You want me to . . ." Afton asked. But Max shook his head. He'd be expensing it anyway.

Just as they were heading for the door, Afton pointed to a piece of taxidermy that sat on a wooden pedestal near the coatroom. It was a large brown wolverine posed on a twisted hunk of cedar. The animal was pulled back onto its haunches, snarling. Its eyes were fierce and bright, and its right front paw was raised up in front of it.

"This is really something," Afton said. "Who did this?"

Janelle gazed at her across the top of an old brass cash register. "A local kid by the name of Sorenson. He's pretty good."

"Yes, he is," Afton said.

"Is Sorenson on our list?" Max asked.

Afton pulled out her sheet of paper and checked. "Yup. And so are twenty-five other guys."

"Add that to the fifty-three taxidermy guys in Minnesota and that's a lot of ground to cover."

"Gonna take a while," Afton said.

A half mile out of town, when they slid down the entry ramp onto the Interstate, the situation had worsened.

"Has this even been plowed?" Afton asked. "I thought for sure they'd have been out plowing by now, trying to keep the freeway clear. I mean . . . there are trucks, truckers driving up from Chicago and Milwaukee . . ."

"The Highway Department has been plowing," Max said. "They're just not keeping up. This snow's coming down too fast." He frowned. "You okay? You sound rattled. Do you want me to drive?"

"No, I'm okay."

"Just take it easy and keep your eyes on the road. Hold your speed down and don't take any chances."

"You're a fine one to talk."

"Well . . . it doesn't matter how long it takes us to get back now. Once we're home, we won't be going anywhere for a while."

As they cruised down the hill outside Hudson and crossed over the Saint Croix River, Afton started to breathe a little easier. It felt like the halfway point now. Halfway home and halfway closer to Poppy and Tess. She knew exactly what they were all going to do tonight. She was going to make pigs in a blanket, Poppy's all-time favorite. Then they were all going to curl up together. Maybe play a game. Something old-fashioned and soothing, like Candy Land or Monopoly.

"There's open water here, too," Max said. His head lolled to one side, studying the river as they spun by.

"Because of that power plant upstream," Afton said. "Must disgorge a lot of hot water."

"Good for the ducks and geese that hang around all year."

"Unless somebody shoots them and stuffs them."

"You're in a mood," Max said. Then he chuckled. "You know how many snowmobiles go crashing through the ice every winter?"

"I don't know," Afton said. "But I bet you're going to cheer me up by telling me."

"There were something like a dozen snowmobiles last year, even more the year before. I tell you, it's an epidemic. And I'm not just saying that because of that Torbert guy last night. Guys tow their fish houses out onto a lake, hammer back a few shots, and then go blasting around on their 'bile, never even noticing the open spots."

"You should probably count ATVs, too."

"There you go, that'd up the number considerably."

"What are you gonna do?" Afton said.

"Not much you can do. Just fish out the idiots."

THEY were on the outskirts of Saint Paul, cruising past 3M. The three-lane highway had been reduced to just one icy rut when they got a call from Thacker.

"We might have discovered something interesting," Thacker said. "The FBI just got done tearing through that lawyer's office. Torbert's office."

"What'd they find?" Max asked.

"They discovered a file with a number of names in it. They think it might have something to do with illegal adoptions."

"They found something in Torbert's office that might pertain to illegal adoptions," Max told Afton.

"Holy smokes," Afton said. "That could be the break we've been looking for." She motioned with her hand. "Hurry up, put him on speaker."

Max hit the speaker button and Thacker's voice crackled out. "Don't get your undies in a twist yet, kids. All they found was paperwork on what looked like payments."

"Payments," Afton said. "Why do you think they relate to illegal adoptions?"

"Because it looks like that was Torbert's specialty. Adoptions. Private adoptions."

"No shit," Max said.

"What else do we know about these payments?" Afton pressed.

"There's receivables and payables," Thacker said. "The receivables, those may have come from adoptive parents, since they're all in the range of one hundred to two hundred thousand dollars. The payables are in far lesser amounts, but we don't know what those are all about. We haven't contacted Torbert's bank yet or tried to run down any of the names."

"Let us know when you do, okay?" Max said.

"Wait a minute," Afton said, feeling jazzed. "The payables, the smaller amounts. Do we know who those went to?"

"Um . . . yeah," Thacker said.

"What are the names?" Afton dug in her jacket pocket and pulled out the list Burdick had given her. She knew it was a long shot. "We got some names from that taxidermy distributor. Let's at least see if we can cross-reference something."

"We're going to end up with a pile of names," Max said. "Why don't we let the computer sort it out, wait and see if we get any kind of match?"

"I realize that's the protocol," Afton said. "But couldn't we at least get a jump start?"

"I guess it couldn't hurt," Max said.

"Okay," Thacker said. "Whatever. It's a short list."

"First name?" Max asked.

"Monahan," Thacker said. "Harold Monahan."

Afton scanned the list as she drove, veering off slightly toward the center median.

"Don't be doing that," Max crabbed at her. "You can't read and drive at the same time. Here, hand over that list before you slam this car in the ditch and cripple us both for life."

"Sorry," Afton said. She handed over the list.

Max scanned the list. "Mmn, Monahan's not here. What's the second name?"

"Adams," Thacker said.

"Nope."

It was the third name that sent the cherries spinning and the bells clanging like crazy.

"Sorenson," Thacker said.

This time, even though Afton had both hands squarely on the steering wheel, she once again swerved toward the center median. Because she recognized the name from Thacker's list. It was the name of the kid who'd stuffed the wolverine back at the Liberty Café.

42

WE have to turn around," Afton said through gritted teeth.

"What?" Max's head swiveled toward her. He clicked a button, taking the phone off speaker. "Hang on a minute," he told Thacker. Then he stared at Afton as she slowed the car to barely a crawl. "Are you crazy? In case you hadn't noticed, lady, we're on I-94 smack dab in the middle of the blizzard of the century. Our tire tracks are filling in behind us. We've already passed six cars in the ditch. If we play our cards right, we could be the seventh."

"Tell Thacker we have to go back. Insist on it."

"Why?"

"Sorenson. It's the same name. If this Sorenson guy has something to do with illegal adoptions and the wolverine taxidermy guy is named Sorenson, there could be a connection. No, there has to be a connection. Tell that to Thacker. Insist on it."

"I don't know," Max said. Still, he held the phone up to his mouth and related Afton's theory back to Thacker. Then he sat there and listened, his head bobbing silently. "I see," he finally said.

"What?" Afton asked. She was looking ahead, trying to figure out where she could turn off and double back. There. Century Boulevard was dead ahead. "Is something wrong?"

"Sorenson's not a guy," Max said. "It's a woman. Marjorie Sorenson."

"That's her then," Afton said. "She's the kidnapper, the doll lady who called herself Molly. She's the one who took Elizabeth Ann." She said it with an urgency and a solemn finality, as if she knew they'd finally arrived at the end stage of the hunt.

"You don't know that," Max said. "You're just cobbling together a few wild ideas."

"Is there a man living with her? A boy? Ask Thacker."

Max did that.

"He doesn't know," Max said. "Thacker says we'll have to contact Wisconsin State Revenue, see if she claimed any dependents."

"There's no time for that. We have to turn around and find that Sorenson woman right now. If we wait any longer, we risk not finding that baby. Ever again."

"We can't just go cowboying in there," Max warned. "We have to have a warrant. At the very least we need to get Thacker's approval."

"Then talk to him," Afton yelped. "Convince him."

IT wasn't easy. Thacker hemmed and hawed. He worried about jurisdictions and fretted about blowback for stepping on the toes of neighboring law enforcement agencies. He worried about bureaucratic issues. Like shouldn't they inform Don Jasper and his FBI team and give them an opportunity to investigate as well?

Finally, Afton grabbed the phone. "Please," she begged. "We think there's a strong possibility that this woman, Marjorie Sorenson, is the one who kidnapped the Darden baby. Her and the taxidermy kid. It all fits, the names, the animal hair, the bad odor. Give us the address so we can at least check her out."

"This is so not a good idea," Thacker said.

"She's in Wisconsin, right? We're already halfway there."

"Max said you were headed back here."

Afton set her jaw. "We just turned around. We've already passed the cutoff for 694. Her place probably isn't that much farther on. What? Maybe ten or twenty miles?"

"In a raging storm."

"Aw, it's not so bad," Afton said as she struggled to keep the Navigator on the road.

Thacker still resisted. "I've given you two way too much leeway already."

"After what went down last night," Afton argued, "this has the possibility of a home run."

"Afton . . ."

"Please, Chief. You have kids, don't you? If they were missing, wouldn't you want everyone to pull out all the stops no matter what? No matter if they stepped on a few toes or ruffled some feathers? No matter if they played their hunch and took a risk?"

There were a few seconds of dead air, and then Thacker finally said, "Okay, I'm going to let you do it. But for Christ's sake, be careful!"

EASIER said than done, of course. Because once they were back across the Saint Croix River, the roads were in even worse driving condition. The snow had compacted and frozen on the roadways, forcing semitrucks and trailers to pull into truck stops and rest stops all along the route.

"Your Navigator's a beast," Max said, "but it ain't no match for this storm."

"We're not turning around," Afton said. She checked the navigation screen for about the hundredth time. They'd plugged in the address Thacker had given them and had turned off onto County Road F. It was a narrow lane that snaked south, paralleling the Saint Croix River, yet set on top of a high glacial ridge. A ridge that seemed to be getting pounded by the full brunt of the storm.

"Shit," Max said. He was nervous about Afton's hunch, uneasy about the weather. "This lousy two-lane road hasn't even seen a plow. Plus we're on this stupid high ridge so there's nothing to stop all this snow from drifting like crazy."

Afton refused to agree with him even though she knew he was right. For the last ten miles she'd been powering her vehicle through five, maybe six, inches of snow. Up ahead, drifts and a curling wall of snow blocked their way. It looked like an impasse.

"We won't make it through," Max said. "Gotta turn around. I know it's a bitter pill to—"

Afton jammed on the brakes and slewed heavily to one side, barely avoiding a skid into the ditch. Then she carefully K-turned the Navigator back and forth, finally turning it completely around.

"Good girl."

She drove another half mile or so. Then, without warning, she hung a sharp left and dropped down a road that carried them down a steep incline.

"Whoa. Wait!" Max shouted. "What the hell do you think you're doing? This isn't the way home." His eyes were wild, and he was thrashing around, held only in place by his seat belt. "This isn't part of the program."

"Detour. According to the nav system, this road should take us right past the Sorenson farm."

"Do you not realize we're headed down a murderously steep grade?" Max said, grasping the dashboard for support. "It's gonna take us *below* the Sorenson farm. You better turn around right now."

"Can't." Afton stared straight ahead. "Road's too narrow."

"Then pull into the next driveway."

"No can do."

They passed two small farms that were hunkered into the hillside as the road continued to descend in a steep spiral. The snow was coming down so fast and heavy, they could barely see a hundred feet ahead of them.

"That's it for me," Max said, throwing his hands up. "Zero visibility and a lost cause. I'm calling Thacker and telling him to order you to turn around." He grabbed his cell phone and punched in numbers. "Shit!"

"Now what's wrong?" Afton asked.

"I can't get a connection." Max punched in the numbers again. "My calls keep getting dropped. This stupid storm must've knocked something out. The towers or the satellites or whatever these stupid phone carriers use now. Moonbeams."

Afton jammed her foot on the brake and they slid to a stop.

"What?" Max said. "You've finally come to your senses?"

"We're here."

Max leaned forward and peered through the windshield. "Here? There's nothing here but a cliff."

"That's right," Afton said. "And the Sorenson farm should be right at the top of this cliff."

"I don't exactly see an elevator or a flight of stairs, so how do you propose getting up there?"

"We'll climb up the rocks."

Max gaped at her. "Have you lost your freaking mind? This is, like, a ridiculously vertical mountain. It's a steep, badass mountain like in that movie *The Eiger Sanction*. You remember that? Because I'm sure you've seen it."

Afton was shaking her head. "This is your basic sandstone cliff. Not that big a deal. Come on, the Sorenson house is directly above us. If you squidge your head to one side, you can see smoke curling up from its chimney."

"You're crazy," Max said. "You know that? Certifiably." But he climbed out of the car with Afton and stomped through the snow to take a look. "Madness," he muttered.

Afton walked to the base of the cliff and stared up. Max wasn't sure if she was bluffing or if she seriously intended to scale the cliff.

Afton hoisted herself up onto a boulder. "I don't think it's going to be that difficult. This is basic bouldering. You use handholds and footholds and just proceed up one step at a time." She looked at him. "You give it a shot."

Max put a leg up and tried to gain a foothold. Just when he thought he'd gained a solid perch, his foot slipped off and he went down, banging his shin against a rock.

"I'm wearing desert boots," Max said. "With slippery rubber soles."

"Try again."

Max tried to climb again, but every time he kept slipping back.

"It can't be done," he said. "I'm sorry, but this isn't going to work. My feet are too clumpy and I don't know the first thing about climbing. We have to wait for the snowplows to do their thing up top and then we'll come back tomorrow." He started to tromp back toward the car. "I should have known this was a terrible idea. It's snowing like a bastard and we're barely going to make it back across the river. Hell, we might have to ditch in Hudson for the night."

"Can't you call Don Jasper and have him drop some FBI commandos in here or something?" Afton asked. "I mean, where are the guys in the black helicopters when you need them?" She was only half serious. Decided she had to do something to cajole Max out of his angry funk.

"That only happens in the movies," Max said. "Besides, I already tried calling and couldn't get a connection." He shrugged. "Sorry. That's all she wrote."

Afton walked to the rear of the Navigator and lifted the hatch. She dug around for a minute and pulled out a twist of rope.

"Oh no," Max said. "You're not going to try to scale that hill by yourself."

She pulled out a set of crampons and an ice ax.

He rubbed the back of his hand against his cheek. "On the other hand, maybe you are."

Afton slipped the crampons over her boots and snugged the straps tight. "I'm going up," she told him in a matter-of-fact voice. "I'm going to take a look around and try to determine if the Darden baby is in that farmhouse. I promise I won't do anything stupid."

"You're going to climb that big cliff. That's pretty stupid right there."

"No," she said. "It's risky. There's a difference between stupidity and risk."

"Now you tell me." Max stood back and watched as she continued to gear up.

When Afton was ready, she mustered a small smile. "Okay. Ready."

"I'm gonna drive back to that last farm we passed and call the cops in Hudson," Max told her. "They're the closest, so they can get here the fastest."

"If that farm even has a landline."

Max ignored her. "I'll have Hudson PD contact WisDOT and try to get the road up top plowed as soon as possible. Then we'll come in full force with the cavalry."

"Okay," Afton said. "Sounds like a plan."

"And I have to call Thacker and Jasper, too."

"Oops."

"I'll probably be forty or fifty minutes behind you, an hour at most," Max said. He gazed at her and turned even more serious. "Listen, you go in, grab that little baby if you find her, and then get the hell out of there. Wrap her up like a burrito in a dozen blankets and head out the front road. You got that? That's where we'll be coming in."

Afton nodded. "Got it." She was suddenly scared. And she knew that Max knew she was scared. "You think the baby's there, too, don't you?"

"I do, yeah. I hate to admit it, but you've got me convinced."

"Good," Afton said. "Anything else?"

"Ah, just one more thing."

"What?" Was he going to tell her to be careful?

Max handed her his Glock. "Try not to shoot yourself."

43

WE can't leave," Ronnie said.

Shake sat up in bed, instantly alert. "What's wrong?" Oh no, had Ronnie chickened out? Had he changed his mind? Had Marjorie gotten to him? Had she bickered and harassed and browbeat him to death?

"We're in the middle of a real badass snowstorm," Ronnie said. "Our driveway's completely drifted and the Interstate's closed."

"Oh." Shake glanced out the window at the snow and then relaxed against her pillows. Ronnie hadn't changed his mind after all. He was just being cautious about their safety. For some reason, this small gesture made her heart swell. Ronnie being thoughtful and mature. It was a whole new side to him. "So when do you think we can get out of here?"

"I don't know." His eyes bounced down to where the baby lay sleeping in her crib. "Maybe tomorrow. It depends on when our snowplow guy shows up."

Shake gave a little shudder. "It scares me to spend one more night under this roof."

"We'll be okay. I'll make sure of that."

"Your mother wants to get rid of our baby. Give it away or maybe even sell it."

"There's no way I'm gonna let that happen," Ronnie said. He gazed at

Shake and offered her an encouraging smile. He thought how funny it was that Shake had never played into his rape fantasies. Of course, that first time at Club Paradise, she'd pretty much attacked him. Pulled him into the dancers' dressing room and whispered into his ear how hunky he was. Said she wanted to be his girlfriend. He'd never forgotten that. Those might have been the kindest words that were ever spoken to him. Now something inside him made him want to protect Shake and the baby. Create a little bubble of safety for them. This feeling was new to him and he decided to proceed cautiously.

"I'm still worried," Shake said. "Your mother is getting freakier and freakier." She didn't want to bring up the subject of this past Tuesday night, when Ronnie had slipped out with his mother. Didn't want to pry too much. She might lift a rock and find something ugly and dirty wiggling around underneath it.

"How are you feeling?" Ronnie asked.

"Hurts," Shake said. She knew what Ronnie really meant. How are you feeling down there? "But I can still get to the bathroom okay. Probably could walk around if I really had to. I know I could make it down to the car."

"Good. I'm gonna put together a few things downstairs. You still got that purple duffel bag?"

"In the closet," Shake said. It was still half full from when she'd tried to run away before.

Shake's new, improved Ronnie gave a half smile. "Start thinking about what you want to bring with you. Tonight I'll help you pack."

44

SCALING the cliff was definitely not a piece of cake. With the relentless wind buffeting her and tiny snow crystals stinging her eyes and face like needles, Afton felt uneasy and clumsy. Still, she was moving from one rock to another with what she hoped was a degree of authority. Moving steadily upward, always gaining ground, digging in with her crampons, using her ice ax to find purchase.

Halfway up, the easy lower half, she snugged one end of her rope around an outcropping of rocks. She calculated the distance upward, and looped the other end around her waist in a sort of self-belay. Now if she fell, she might be able to arrest her fall if she could react fast enough. A small comfort, but not insignificant in the scheme of things.

The top half of the cliff was much more difficult. The angle she'd taken had led to a daunting wall of limestone that left her feeling exposed. Afton crab-stepped to her left, hoping to find a few decent handholds and toeholds. She was wearing thin climbing gloves and her fingers were starting to stiffen up in the cold. She forced herself to stop moving, laid her cheek against the frozen wall, and jammed her right hand inside her coat. She waited two minutes while her hand thawed out, and then did the other hand.

There. Much better.

Afton started climbing again, slowly and methodically, finding a lip of rock here, a nose of rock there. As she muscled herself upward, her entire body began to warm and she began to feel in sync with the climb.

Twenty feet from the top, the juts of rock flattened out even more. Now she was free climbing, searching for fingerholds instead of handholds.

But there have to be some good holds, right?

Not necessarily.

Gotta be a couple. Somewhere.

Afton flattened herself against the sheer rock face and peered up, half closing one eye. There they were . . . a few cracks and juts of rock. She knew that a successful ascent depended on strength, control, and finesse. She just prayed she had enough energy left to muster all three of these elements.

Twenty feet above her, now fifteen feet above her, she could see a cornice, a dangerous overhang of snow. That would be the tricky part, the part where she'd depend solely on her upper body strength and the sharpness of her ice ax.

She felt almost mechanical now. Climb, thrust, climb. Keep the rhythm going. She stretched an arm high above her head, swung her ice ax hard, and hoped for the best . . .

Whack!

The steel claw bit in securely.

TWENTY-FIVE minutes after beginning her climb, Afton hoisted herself up and over the lip of the cliff. She lay there in the snow, panting, trying to collect her wits, willing her chilled, overtaxed muscles to stop shaking. It had been touch and go near the top. And touch and go was never good, especially when you were free climbing all by your lonesome in the middle of a raging blizzard.

She lifted her head tiredly and stared straight ahead. Saw the faint outline of an old farmhouse shimmering like a mirage through sifting snow.

Okay, Afton told herself, *here comes the real test. This is where the game turns deadly serious.*

Crouching low to the ground, Afton plunged toward the house, battling her way through thigh-high snow. When she was ten feet from the farm-house, she stopped and gave it a quick perusal. The place looked weary and desolate. And not just because of the blizzard that raged around it. If a house could have a presence, this one reeked of desperation and unhappiness. As she moved toward the front porch, Afton tried to imagine this place in sum-mer. Would there be wild roses twining up the columns? Monarch butter-flies sipping nectar in the fields? She thought not.

When Afton still didn't see any movement inside, she covered the rest of the distance fast and clambered up onto the front porch. Slowly, care-fully, she peered through a frosted window.

She saw a kitchen. Pots and pans sitting on the stove, a refrigerator, lights blazing overhead. But nobody there.

But wait. Something was there. She tilted her head sideways and saw a playpen. A baby's mesh-sided playpen had been set up right next to the stove.

Afton sidled away from the window until she was facing the front door. She drew a deep breath, and then touched a hand to the doorknob and turned it slowly. When the door swung open, she stepped tentatively over the sill, nerves fizzing like mad, but grateful for the wall of warmth that suddenly enveloped her.

Now what? Find the baby. But do it fast.

Moving quietly through the kitchen, Afton glanced into the playpen as she went past it. A flash of pink caught her eye, causing her to hesitate. There, puddled in the bottom, was a pink blanket.

Afton bent down and gathered it up. The blanket felt soft to the touch. Exquisitely soft. She fumbled with the piece of fabric, turning it over until she found a label. One hundred percent cashmere. The Darden baby had been wrapped in a pink cashmere blanket.

Was the Darden baby being hidden away in this farmhouse? Or had some lucky person who lived here hit the jackpot at their baby shower?

Afton folded the blanket and tucked it under her arm along with her ice ax. Then she stepped out into a hallway. Way down at the far end of the house, probably in another room—the living room?—a television set blared loudly. It was an afternoon soap opera from the sound of the dialogue. Some woman with a high, chirpy voice haranguing a guy named Jeff. Calling him a lousy two-timer.

Good. Hopefully, all that noise would cover the sounds of her footsteps.

There was a narrow doorway directly to Afton's left. Slowly, carefully, she pushed the door open with the tips of her fingers and peered in. Her first impression was that of a Greek chorus of dead-eyed babies. But as she continued to stare in, she knew they were dolls, dozens of dolls, all posed on shelves. There were dolls with luxurious flaxen hair, dolls dressed in tiny little onesies, and dolls with arms and legs so pink and plump you almost wanted to reach out and pinch them. At the same time, the sheer number of them was eerie. One doll, okay. Four dozen of the strange little things, definitely disturbing.

Afton pulled the door closed and moved on to the narrow staircase that loomed just to her left. Were there bedrooms upstairs? Probably. And if there were bedrooms, there just might be a crib with a baby tucked into it.

Very slowly, very deliberately, Afton began to climb the stairs. The staircase was narrow—she could almost touch the walls with both elbows—and the treads were shallow. It was as if the house had been constructed in a much earlier era for smaller, more utilitarian people.

Afton hesitated when she reached the top of the stairs and looked around. There was a bedroom off to her right, the door standing wide open. She could see two more doors down the dim hallway ahead.

Was there a surprise behind door number one?

Afton chose the bedroom to her right. Tiptoed up to the doorway and poked her head in.

There was a girl sleeping in the bed, her face gone slack as she snored softly. From the looks of her, she was probably no more than eighteen or nineteen years old. But what made Afton catch her breath was the baby nestled in a homemade wooden crib right next to the girl's bed.

Stepping into the room, Afton's fingers twitched. She was ready to snatch up this baby and run like hell. She reached down, anxious, nervous, and caught herself just in time. Because, dear Lord, this was a *newborn* baby, not a three-month-old baby.

Was she in the wrong place? Her mind was suddenly in turmoil. She couldn't be. She couldn't have erred this badly. And there was the telltale pink cashmere blanket . . .

The girl under the covers stirred slightly. Then her eyes came open and she stared blankly up at Afton. Slowly, her mind seemed to process the fact that there was a woman standing by her bedside, dressed in snow gear and holding an ice ax. Her face convulsed with fear.

"Who are you?" Shake asked in a tremulous voice as she struggled to sit up. "What are you doing here?"

Afton said the first thing that popped into her head.

"I'm here for the baby."

Shake shrank back in terror. Then she seemed to muster her courage and flung an arm out as if to protect the baby sleeping beside her. "Please," she said, "I'm begging you, don't take my baby. I know I signed all the papers and everything, but I changed my mind. I really did." She hiccupped hard as tears welled in her eyes. "I made a terrible mistake."

"This is your baby?" Afton asked. She wasn't quite sure what this poor girl was babbling about.

Shake bobbled her head. "Me and Ronnie's, yes."

Afton peered into the homemade crib again, as if to make sure of what she was seeing. "This baby's a newborn."

"Please," Shake begged. "I only just had her last night. But I love her."

"You just gave birth to her? Here? Last night?"

Shake suddenly looked confused. "No, I think it might have been two nights ago." She pressed both hands against her face and peered through her fingers. "I don't know, you're scaring me. You're getting me all confused."

Afton knew she didn't have much time. "What's your name?"

"Shake. My real name is Sharice but everybody calls me Shake."

"How many people live here, Shake?"

"Um . . . three of us. Well, five if you count the babies."

Afton felt a kind of pop deep inside her brain. "There's another baby?"

Shake seemed to choke down her fear then. "Who are you?"

"I'm with the Minneapolis Police Department."

Now Shake was more flustered than fearful. "Oh shit, I knew there was something bad going on. You're here because of Marjorie, aren't you? She's crazy, you know. She brought that kid home and—" Shake stopped abruptly. "Wait a minute. You came here to get *that* baby?"

Afton's heart leapt. "That baby's still here?"

Shake nodded. "Yeah, sure she is. Well, I think she is. I've been sleeping and—"

"Where is she?" Afton knew she'd been at this too long. She was pressing her luck. "Where have they been keeping her?"

Shake curled a finger and pointed. "The room next to this one."

"You said the woman who brought her home was Marjorie. Marjorie who?"

"Sorenson?" Shake said in a small voice.

"And this is the same woman who creates and sells reborn dolls?"

Shake nodded. "Yeah."

"And she has a son."

"Ronnie," Shake said. "My boyfriend." She hiccupped. "My baby's father."

The pizza guy, Afton thought. She had to grab the Darden baby and get the hell out of here. Could she manage it? Holy shit, it felt like she was trapped in a den of rattlesnakes.

"Wait here," Afton said to Shake.

Shake pulled up the bedspread tight to her chin. "Where would I go?"

Afton tiptoed out into the hallway and paused. The TV was still blasting away downstairs, and so far nobody seemed to have heard her. Shake hadn't raised an alert. That was good. Maybe she could grab the Darden baby and get away without anyone being the wiser. Send help back for Shake and her baby.

That was the plan anyway.

But plans have a way of not working out. Because somewhere between peering into the Darden baby's crib and ascertaining that this was probably the missing Elizabeth Ann, Afton heard a ruckus going on downstairs.

Damn. Somebody must have heard her moving around up here on the creaky linoleum.

Afton had a split-second decision to make. Grab the baby and try to bull her way past whoever had just started screaming their head off downstairs? Or face them by herself and hope for the best?

She left the baby and dashed out into the hallway.

Downstairs, the screaming had intensified.

"We got big trouble, Ronnie!" came a woman's shrill voice. "Get up here and bring your knives!"

That was Marjorie. Calling for Ronnie. This is so not good.

Pounding footsteps shook the stairway. Like a bull on a rampage, Marjorie barreled up the narrow stairs, her faded housecoat billowing around her. When she got to the landing and saw Afton standing there, she stopped, a look of utter shock on her face.

Afton stared at the woman with cold, barely contained anger. This was the woman who'd caused everyone so much pain. "Hello, Molly," she said. "We've been looking for you."

"Who the hell are you?" Marjorie screeched. "Get out. Get out of my house." Her eyes glowed hard and beady, like a rat's.

"It's over," Afton said. "I know all about the baby. I know all about you."

"You don't know shit."

"I know you're going to prison."

"That ain't never gonna happen," Marjorie hissed as her right arm slowly emerged from the folds of her housecoat.

That slight motion kicked Afton's brain into overdrive. *Gun. Old lady's got a gun,* her brain screamed out as she caught the gleam of cold metal.

Afton had a gun, too, of course. Only it was stuck way the hell down in her jacket pocket. Feeling her insides turn to water, she started to fumble for the Glock, and realized she was moving way too slow. Marjorie had just about raised her gun to eye level and had closed one eye, sighting to take aim at her.

"Marjorie!" Shake suddenly screamed, her voice ringing out like the whine of a bandsaw. She stood in the doorway of her bedroom, looking terrified in a faded green nightgown.

Marjorie jumped, startled by Shake's earsplitting scream. In that split second, Afton hoisted her ice ax high above her head and brought it down hard across Marjorie's right forearm.

Marjorie let loose a horrific, high-pitched screech as she reflexively pulled the trigger. Afton's blow had been enough to knock her aim off and her shot went wild, crashing into the door frame, spewing shards of wood.

"You bitch," Marjorie seethed. With bloody blue murder in her eye, she jerked her injured arm up to shoot again.

As though her life depended on it—and it probably did— Afton swung her ice ax in a tight, practiced arc. Whistling like a missile, the deadly tip, honed meat-pick sharp for biting into rock and ice, caught Marjorie in the left temple.

The impact was deep, the result instantaneous. Marjorie yodeled a high-pitched scream, like an animal caught in a trap. Her lips slicked back over her upper teeth and her pupils retreated into tiny pinpricks in a sea of ghastly white. A geyser of blood spurted from her head wound, spattering both Afton and Shake. Marjorie's arm jerked sideways and the gun flew out of her hand, clattering down hard on the linoleum, then bouncing its way down the stairs.

Marjorie, who was still standing upright as bright red blood sprayed like a faucet, made a gurgling, underwater sound that sounded like *glub bluh*. Then she managed one shaky, tottering step backward. In her smooth cotton slippers, both heels slid back over the lip of the top stair and she teetered dangerously on the edge. Her arms flailed wildly as if she somehow sensed the precariousness of her situation. A split second later, her brain fully registered the trauma from the ice ax. Her arms dropped leadenly to her sides and she tipped straight over backward.

Bones cracked and splintered, blood painted a nasty Jackson Pollock as Marjorie tumbled down the narrow stairs. She made one final ass-over-teacup cartwheel and landed in an ungainly lump with one arm twisted behind her back and her leg practically cocked around her neck.

Oh my God, was Afton's first thought. *What have I done?*

"What just happened here?" Shake's frightened, ragged voice cried out as she shuffled forward to look. She gazed down at Marjorie, and then shrank back from Afton, as if fearing the same horrible fate.

"Everything's fine," Afton said even as she thought, *No, it's not fine. Nothing's fine. I just killed a woman.*

"What did you *do* to her?" Shake quivered. She bent forward and clawed at her nightdress, pulling it into a knot. "Is she dead? Did you *kill* her? My God, what did you do?"

Suddenly, without warning, another voice joined in with Shake's caterwauling. A male voice.

"Ma? Ma?" someone yelled from below. Footsteps pounded and a door banged open.

Someone running up from the basement? Afton wondered as she hastily wiped a mist of blood from her face.

"Holy shit, what happened?" the voice cried again. "What the hell's going on up here? Shake, did you—" The yelling ceased abruptly.

Afton finally thought to drop her ice ax and pull out the Glock. She gripped the heavy gun tightly, mentally girding herself in case she really had to use it.

"Get back in bed," Afton ordered Shake, who retreated sullenly to her room. Then she leaned forward and peered down the staircase.

A young man gazed up at her from the bottom of the stairs, pale and blond, unexpectedly youthful looking. His face was a contorted mix of shock and surprise as he regarded Afton. Then, almost as an afterthought, he stared down at his mother's dead body.

"You killed her," he mumbled in a strangled voice. Then, more forcefully, "You killed Mom."

Oh shit, Afton thought. *He's put it together all right. I'm up here and Mom's down there.*

On the plus side, she was the one holding the gun.

"Who are you?" Afton demanded. "Are you Ronnie?" Was this the kid she'd tangled with at the hospital? She aimed the gun directly at the midpoint of his body. At the greater kill area.

The boy didn't answer. Instead, he continued to stare at his mother.

Every joint in Marjorie's body was cocked at an unnatural angle, and a thin, white bone protruded from her upper thigh. Her housedress had popped open to reveal a ratty pink slip.

Muttering something under his breath, Ronnie took a step forward and suddenly kicked Marjorie's body with the toe of his boot. "Bitch," he snarled. "Stupid bitch." He kicked her again, harder this time, then pulled his mouth into a crooked smile and spit at her.

Stunned, wary at what she was seeing, Afton gripped her Glock tighter. Caught up in the throes of a deep psychological conflict, Ronnie seemed to be processing multiple streams of data. She didn't know if his brain was struggling to mourn his mother or break free from her. And she didn't care. All she wanted to do was to rescue the Darden baby and keep everyone safe.

Ronnie stood in place for a few moments, swaying slightly as if in a trance, still working the scene through his brain. Then, looking pale and stricken, he dropped to his knees. Afton assumed he was going to touch his fingertips against Marjorie's neck to feel for a pulse, for any sign of life. Instead, the boy thrust a hand under her body and felt around.

Oh no.

In one lightning-fast move, Ronnie swept up Marjorie's gun, wrapped his fingers around the pistol grip, and was suddenly back on his feet again.

Dear Lord, he's got her gun.

Ronnie bounced the gun in his hand, as if testing the heft and feel of it, then stared up at Afton. One watery blue eye fluttered, his lip curled in distaste. Finally he said, "You're the bitch who stuck me with the needle."

"You're under arrest," Afton snapped out. She had to stay calm and get on top of this kid. If she didn't, she knew she could die. "Set down your weapon and place both hands on top of your head."

"Sure thing," Ronnie said. His arm came up in one fast, fluid motion and he pulled the trigger.

Bang!

Plaster exploded above Afton's head as she flew backward, flattening herself against the wall.

"What the hell was that?" Shake screamed. She suddenly appeared in the doorway again, eyes wild, face contorted with fear.

"Get back inside," Afton warned.

Bang!

Another bullet zinged past them. Ronnie wasn't a great shot, but he knew how to crack them off just the same.

"Ronnie," Afton called out. "Put down the gun. Do you want to kill Shake? Do you want your own baby to get hit by a stray bullet?" Her body thrummed with fear. She wasn't trained for this sort of situation! She desperately needed help!

"Shut up," Ronnie screamed at her. "Just shut the hell up."

"The police are on their way," Afton shouted back at him. "They'll be here any minute."

"Ronnie!" Shake called out in an agonizing warble. "You gotta come get me. We have to get the hell out of here."

"Stop it," Afton hissed at Shake. "Don't you get it? That boy is *shooting* at us. He's in the middle of a breakdown."

"Ronnie wouldn't hurt us," Shake whined.

Ronnie fired another shot and Shake hastily backpedaled into her bedroom.

Afton drew a deep breath. Ronnie's uncontrollable violence, her realization that she was the only one who could keep the two babies safe, suddenly jolted her mind into a new place she'd never been before. A place that acknowledged her fear, but was also weirdly cold and rational. She knew she had to make her stand. She knew that, if pushed to the limit, she would have to kill him.

Afton counted to three and slowly eased herself around the corner, gun at the ready, finger on the trigger.

But Ronnie had disappeared.

45

AFTON gripped the Glock as she stood like a sentinel at the top of the stairs. Shake's baby had begun to cry, making mewling little kitten sounds. The baby down the hall was screaming its head off. And Ronnie had pulled a disappearing act. She didn't know if he would try to surprise her by charging up the stairs like a crazed animal, or if he'd retreated to the basement to take stock of things.

All of Afton's instincts screamed at her to defend this part of the house. And that was exactly what she planned to do.

Two minutes passed and then five minutes. The babies seemed to let up a little with their crying. Thank goodness. Then a door slammed downstairs.

Both hands gripping the Glock, Afton fairly quivered on the balls of her feet. Every nerve felt like it was being stretched to the point of breaking.

A shuffling sound echoed from down below, soft and faint, almost like rats scuttling across floorboards.

What the hell?

As if an unseen puppeteer was at work, Marjorie's body began to move. It slid slowly at first, then gradually picked up speed. Afton had only a narrow view as the torso and legs dragged past, leaving in their wake an ugly slick of brownish-red blood. Seconds later, Marjorie's bare feet disappeared, with only a single dirty cotton slipper left behind.

Afton tried to think. Ronnie had come back to collect his mother's body. But where was he taking her? Was this some sort of deviant behavior or was he trying to make a getaway? Or was this a trick to lure her downstairs, to stage an ambush?

Of course it was. It had to be.

"Ronnie?" she called out. "Just give it up."

No answer.

"Ronnie?"

That was when the lights winked out.

"Damn," Afton whispered to herself as darkness settled around her like an ominous cloud.

"Ronnie?" Afton called again. But there was still no answer.

The door to Shake's bedroom creaked open.

"The lights went off," Shake said.

"Yes," Afton whispered. "Do you know where the fuse box is?"

"Maybe . . . in the kitchen?"

When Shake opened her door, it offered a faint spill of light from her bedroom window. Afton could see that it was almost dark outside. Pretty soon, she wouldn't be able to see her own hand in front of her face. And in a big old spooky house like this, where she was the unknowing interloper, total darkness would put her at a terrible disadvantage.

Shake's eyes were drawn to the Glock in Afton's hand. "Are you gonna kill Ronnie?" she asked.

"Only if he tries to kill me."

"He wouldn't do that."

"He already did. Now be quiet and go back to bed."

Afton remained at the top of the stairs, never lowering her guard. She might not be able to see Ronnie coming, but she'd be able to hear him. And then she would shoot and shoot and shoot until she took him down. Yes, that was the plan. Because she figured she only had to hold out for another hour at best. That's when Max, God bless his soul, would come charging in with a cadre of state troopers and whoever else he could round up. The cavalry *would* come to the rescue.

It was only when Afton smelled the first whiff of smoke that her attention wavered and a tickle of panic started to seep in.

"Ronnie?" she called out when she was really thinking, *Holy shit. Is that smoke?*

Yes, Afton was pretty sure it was smoke. She fought down a rising tide of fear, but there was no way around it. Ronnie must have started a fire somewhere in the house.

But where? That was the big question, wasn't it?

Shake crept back out to the landing. "What the hell?" she whispered. "Is something burning?"

Afton ran back to the second bedroom and snatched up the Darden baby, along with all her bedding. She carried the fussing, fidgeting baby into Shake's room and handed her over. "You keep the two babies in here with you. Then I want you to close the door after me and wedge as many blankets as you can along the bottom of the door. Okay?"

"Okay," Shake said. She put a hand on top of her head as if this was all too much for her.

Afton eyed a battered wooden dresser that held a music box and a clutter of makeup. "Can you slide that dresser over a couple of feet and shove it up against the door? Barricade yourself in?"

Shake bent forward as if in pain. "I guess."

"Do that," Afton said. "And don't come out for anything."

Shake's eyes were twin saucers of fear. "Where are you gonna be?"

The left side of Afton's mouth quivered in a nervous tick. "I'm going downstairs."

SLOWLY, carefully, Afton edged her way down the narrow stairs. She kept her hip pressed firmly against the wall and her finger squarely on the trigger. If Ronnie meant to smoke them out, to burn down the house around them, then she would have to stop him. She would put herself on the offensive and hunt him down like the despicable monster he was.

For Afton, the worm had turned. The predator was now prey and she was coming after him. That is, if only she could keep her wits about her.

The smoke was much thicker once she reached the first floor. Afton dropped into a low crouch, pulled the neck of her sweater up over her mouth and nose, and slipped out of her boots.

Stay cool, she told herself. *Stay frosty*. She eased forward quietly, making her way in a kind of half crawl, half slide. She was headed for the kitchen, the source of all the smoke.

As she passed Marjorie's workroom, the door was partially open and she could see a few dolls staring out at her through wisps of smoke. No Ronnie in there, though. No fire either.

Okay. Keep moving.

Afton pushed forward, forcing herself to take shallow sips of air as she peered through the thick haze. The acrid smoke burned her eyes and sent tears streaming down her cheeks. Her heart pounded like a snare drum inside her chest. She was terrified that a single cough or sneeze might give away her position.

Visibility was reduced to almost nothing the closer she got to the kitchen. But the smoke was clearly coming from some sort of fire that Ronnie had started there.

Great gluts of smoke billowed toward her, like ugly, toxic clouds. The scent of charred garbage floated in the air. Afton prayed that this same smoke wasn't swirling upstairs via old air ducts or vents and that Shake and the babies weren't being forced to breathe these noxious fumes.

Afton had scuttled through the kitchen doorway and advanced a good six or seven feet when her right knee whacked hard against something.

Ouch. What was that? Table? Chair?

She couldn't see a damn thing in the swirl of smoke and she was feeling both light-headed and short of breath. She inched forward, trying to swallow back her anxiety and panic, and hit her knee again.

Damn, what *was* that? Part of the stove?

She reached out tentatively, fearing she would burn her fingers. Instead, the back of her hand knocked against something.

There was an immediate, metallic thud. And just like that, the smoke seemed to lessen. What had she done?

Afton scrambled to her feet, realizing she'd managed to cut off the source of the smoke. Something awful had been burning furiously inside the oven and she had unwittingly but mercifully banged the oven door shut.

Struggling forward another step, Afton tried to remember exactly where the kitchen door was located. She desperately needed to find fresh air or she was afraid she'd lose consciousness. Air first, and then track down Ronnie.

The room was still filled with dark smoke as she ran her fingertips lightly along the edge of the stove. To her left, something soft brushed up against her—curtains maybe?—as she lurched along. She managed another ten feet, holding her breath, blinking furiously. Still gripping the Glock, she batted blindly and smacked into one of the glass panes in the door.

Lucky, lucky, lucky, she thought as she fumbled lower. Turning the doorknob, she slammed her foot against the door in her best kung fu kick.

The door flew open and Afton somersaulted outside, lurching across the front porch, landing on her hands and knees in the soft snow. *Plop*. She tilted her head back and sucked greedily at the clean, icy air, thankful she'd finally made it out in one piece. Even though wind and snow lashed all around her, her head was beginning to clear and her brain fog had started to lift. Eyes that felt like burning coals just moments ago were slowly beginning to see more clearly. She blinked, trying to orient herself. Gazed about, almost surprised at the tremendous mountains of snow that had built up, and saw . . . Ronnie.

He was ten feet ahead of her, dressed head to toe in a black snowmobile suit and shiny black helmet. He was hunched over, working furiously to strap his Pac boots into a pair of homemade wooden snowshoes. Afton peered through the swirl of blinding snow and was able to make out the snowshoes' leather laces and heavy coats of varnish. A pair of metal ski poles were stuck in the snow next to him.

Ronnie was trying to escape.

Afton hefted the gun and pointed it at him. "Ronnie!" she shouted.

With the howling wind and the heavy helmet on his head, Ronnie couldn't hear her.

Afton scooped up a handful of snow, mashed it into a hard snowball, and rocketed it at him.

Ronnie straightened up like he'd been poked with a hot wire. He spun around in a blind panic, almost losing his balance. When he saw Afton kneeling there, pointing a gun at him, his eyes hardened like twin nickels and spit flew out his mouth. He fumbled a hand toward a pocket in his nylon suit.

"Don't!" Afton cried out.

Ronnie pulled out his gun and fired anyway. Except the only thing that happened was a dull click. He was out of bullets.

Bellowing like an enraged bull, Ronnie fumbled for one of his ski poles. He pointed the sharp end directly at Afton's face and charged.

Afton shot him in the leg. A no-hesitation shot that drove the slug directly into his upper left thigh, shattering his femur instantly.

Ronnie screamed like a stuck pig, a sharp, high-pitched scream that rose like steel wheels skidding against metal. The ski pole flew from his hand as he leapt a foot into the air, kinked his entire body around, and then collapsed in the snow. His ungainly landing on his wounded leg made him scream again, and he struggled to roll over and right himself. He couldn't do it. Crumpled like a squashed bug, he howled wildly as damaged nerves and tendons telegraphed excruciating pain to his brain. He threw his arms above his head and thrashed around, his arms batting the snow as if he was desperately trying to make a snow angel.

Afton was on top of Ronnie in a flash. She pressed the Glock firmly against his forehead and grabbed his gun. It was a piece of shit, an old Rossi revolver, but she wasn't taking any chances.

"You shot me!" Ronnie frothed at the mouth and he'd bit his lip so blood streamed down his chin. "I'm gonna kill you," he shrilled. "I'll skin you alive. I'll slit open your belly open and—"

"That's enough, Ronnie," Afton said tiredly. "Just shut the hell up."

She walked back to the house. With the door standing wide open and the wind howling, most of the smoke had cleared from the kitchen.

Which, Afton decided, wasn't necessarily a good thing.

Because she finally found the missing Marjorie.

Hanging upside down, her feet tied neatly to a heavy metal light fixture, Marjorie dangled above the battered kitchen table. With her toes pointed toward the ceiling and her housecoat fluttering in the breeze, she looked like an upside-down ballerina twirling a macabre dance of death.

In the oven, Afton found the melted, smoking remains of several dolls.

46

IT took Wisconsin's Department of Transportation two hours to finally get through. In the dying light of the afternoon, the bright yellow glow of a snowplow's high beams heralded the procession. Following right behind the enormous plow were two Wisconsin State Patrol cruisers, an ambulance, and Max driving the Navigator.

When Afton heard the roar of the dozer and the whoop of the police sirens, she stepped outside and met them all on the front porch. The pink cashmere blanket was draped around her shoulders.

The two State Patrol guys were the first of the first responders to flounder through the snow to reach her.

"You okay?" one of them asked. He had kind eyes, a droopy walrus mustache, and his name tag said WENDORF.

Afton nodded. "I'm okay. We're all okay." Then she reconsidered her words. "Well, there is a dead woman hanging in the kitchen. And the man I shot is lying in there, too." Ronnie had managed to pull himself back inside the house, where he collapsed. Afton had secured his wrists, wrapped a tourniquet around his leg, and covered him with a blanket. She'd also located the fuse box and restored the lights.

Two EMTs followed as the troopers rushed in. Carrying black medical bags and tugging a collapsible gurney over the snow as if it were a bobsled, they scrambled up the unshoveled steps to the porch.

"You've got casualties?" one of the EMTs asked. She was a young woman bundled in a navy blue parka and looked nervous.

"One casualty and one gunshot victim," Afton said. "Plus we've got a newborn and her mom and another three-month-old baby." Her words felt dry and rough in the back of her throat. "It's the Minneapolis baby who was kidnapped."

I had to shoot the boy," Afton told Max as they stood in the overheated living room. "He was trying to slap on a pair of snowshoes and take off over the fields."

"The pizza guy," Max said. "He drew on you?"

"He shot at me a couple of times, then tried to shish-kabob me with a ski pole." She hugged herself tightly as if she'd just endured some great natural disaster and had come out the other side, banged up but still alive. "Ronnie Sorenson. He's probably the one who murdered Muriel Pink."

"Even if he got away, he wouldn't have gone far," Max said. "Thacker didn't just give us the go-ahead; he also notified the governor of Wisconsin, who hit the panic button and put the entire state on high alert. They were gathering an army of law enforcement, from sheriff's departments to state troopers to Fish and Wildlife guys."

"The black helicopter with the guys sliding down the ropes," Afton said with a half smile.

"Something like that, yeah." Then, "How's the baby?"

"Elizabeth Ann," Afton said. "She seems fine. No ill effects that I could see. But I'm glad the EMTs are checking her out."

"How are you?" Max asked.

"I'm hanging in there," Afton said. "Obviously a little shell-shocked."

"Yeah, you've got that thousand-yard stare."

"I'm sorry, I probably could have handled things differently."

"You didn't shoot the old lady?" Max asked. "Marjorie?"

Afton shook her head. "She was the one firing at me. The only reason she missed was because I smacked her with my ice ax."

"And then she came at you again?"

Afton looked nervous. "That's when I hit her in the head and she tumbled down the stairs."

"So you never used the gun on her? That's all you used to defend yourself with? That stupid ice ax?"

Afton started to nod, then shook her head. "Not so stupid. Saved my life." Tears seeped into the corners of her eyes. "But the boy. He just kept coming at me."

"You did just fine," Max said. He put his arms around her gently. "No, better than fine. You did exactly what was called for in the line of duty."

47

ELIZABETH Ann Darden was suddenly not one bit sleepy as she snuggled in Afton's arms. Her eyes were wide open as she focused on Afton's face with a good deal of curiosity.

"Hello there," Afton said, speaking softly to her. "A lot of very worried people have been looking for you for a long time. Your mommy and daddy miss you very much. Are you ready to go home?" Afton smiled faintly at Max. There was only one thing left to do.

"You want me to make the call?" Max asked. "Get Susan Darden on the line?" He held up his cell phone. "It's working okay now."

"I think I'd like to talk to her myself."

Elizabeth Ann waved her little arms with enthusiasm. She'd been fussy earlier, but one of the EMTs had warmed a bottle for her and the feeding had settled her down. Now she seemed as content as any baby could be.

"But you dial the number," Afton said.

Max heaved himself down onto the couch and dialed the number. When someone answered, he said, "Yeah. This is Montgomery. Everything turned out real good. That's right, we recovered the kid." He listened for another couple of moments, and then said, "Okay, I'll hang on." He gazed at Afton. "Officer Drury went to get her. Said she was upstairs, taking a nap." He handed the phone to Afton.

Susan Darden came on the line a few seconds later. "Detective Tangler," she cried. "You found Elizabeth Ann? You've really got her?"

"She's right here in my arms," Afton said.

"And you're sure she's okay?" Susan asked. "What if there's something wrong with her?"

"The EMTs already checked her out and pronounced her as healthy as can be," Afton said. "Now she's wiggling around and gurgling like a happy baby. But you know what? I should probably let Elizabeth Ann tell you herself." She held the phone down to the baby's face. "Talk to your mama, sweetheart."

"Elizabeth Ann!" Susan Darden's excited cry burst across the phone lines.

Elizabeth Ann, whether flattered by all the attention, amused that Max had just tickled her tummy, or alerted by the sound of her mother's voice, suddenly let out a hearty giggle.

"That's her!" Susan cried. "I can hear her. That's my baby. Oh, thank you, thank you!"

Afton jiggled her knee. "Go ahead, Elizabeth Ann. Talk to your mama all you want."

Elizabeth Ann opened her mouth, promptly blew a bubble, and said, *"Fweee!"*

"My baby," Susan crooned as Max took the phone from Afton's hand so he could give Susan a timeline on when they'd be bringing her back.

"That's a good girl," Afton whispered to the little baby who snuggled in her arms. "You're safe now. I promise you with all my heart that you're forever safe."

Afton lifted her eyes and stared out the side window. The headlights from five different vehicles cast bright beams that pierced the darkness. She saw a black body bag lying in the snow. Marjorie. She saw a figure lying in the back of the ambulance. Ronnie.

Afton smiled a thin, cool smile and cut her gaze away. She had more important things to worry about. Like her own kids.

She had to call Poppy and Tess the minute Max was off the phone. Had to tell them she was on her way home. Had to promise them that, as long as she was watching over them, they'd be forever safe and loved.

MOM Chao Cherry hunched forward in a broken wicker chair and stared anxiously across the Mississippi River toward the University of Minnesota campus. Almost unrecognizable as a wealthy *khunying* from Bangkok, she wore a polyester blouse and baggy pants, cheap rubber flip-flops, and carried an eight ball of cocaine in her handbag. Only her red lacquered nails, edged in twenty-four karat gold, hinted at her ridiculous wealth.

"Time?" Mom Chao Cherry asked in an accent that probably sounded Thai or Chinese to a Westerner, but to a linguist's ear, clearly betrayed her American heritage.

"Paed nalika," Narong replied. Eight o'clock.

The corners of Mom Chao Cherry's mouth crinkled faintly, giving her aging face the appearance of a patient but ravenous crocodile. *"Di yeiym,"* she said. Most excellent.

She hadn't been back to America in more than sixty years, ever since her missionary parents had dragged her off to Asia to bring the word of Jesus to the impoverished, war-ravaged people of China. But this homecoming felt incredibly sweet. Like sweet revenge. Now, relaxing slightly, she reached into her bag and pulled out a cigarette. Lit it with a hissing lighter and inhaled deeply. She would have preferred to imbibe her drug of choice, cocaine, but that would have to wait. Right now there was wild work to be done.

Narong, who was old beyond his years at twenty-four, lifted the PF-89 rocket launcher onto his right shoulder and braced himself. Two years of compulsory service in the Royal Thai Armed Forces and another two years in the private employ of Mom Chao Cherry had taught him to truly love all forms of weaponry. He was in awe of their cold precision and the impersonal way in which they delivered death. Narong, whose name literally meant "to make war," hungered for the moment when he could sight a potential target in his crosshairs, gently squeeze the trigger, and feel the pulse-pounding rush of total destruction. For close-up work, he was an expert in *awud mied*, or Thai knife fighting.

They'd come to this third-floor room above the Huang Sheng Noodle Factory some two hours earlier, right after they'd received the call from their hospital contact. Entering through the back door, eyes downcast, they'd pushed past the cooks and dishwashers that toiled in the hot, humid, clattering kitchen where bean sprouts littered the floors and orders were barked out in green grocer Cantonese.

Up to the top floor they'd been led by the nervous owner, and then down a long hallway lit with bare bulbs. They'd ghosted past small cramped dormitory rooms that held two and three sets of narrow bunk beds, finally emerging in this end room with a lumpy bed and the smell of rancid cooking oil and mouse droppings. A room with a single window that afforded the perfect prospect of the slow rolling Mississippi River and, beyond it, the University of Minnesota Hospital Medical Center complex.

THE helicopter swept in from the north, decelerating to approximately five knots. Two pilots in a Bell 407 who'd made this run a hundred times before. They'd just dropped out of an indigo blue sky scattered with bright stars, like jacks strewn haphazardly across a lush cashmere blanket. A mile to their right, Minneapolis skyscrapers twinkled in the night—the IDS tower, Capella Tower, and the Wells Fargo Center, as well as a dozen high-rise luxury condominiums. Closer still was the newly constructed football stadium, raking the skyline with its harsh, unforgiving wall of reflective glass.

The chief pilot, Captain Sam Buell, had his hands on the cyclic stick, his feet working the rudder pedals. He was carrying no emergency patients tonight, just medical cargo he'd picked up in Madison, Wisconsin. So, an easy run for Buell, who was looking forward to spending the night with his girlfriend, who lived in a nearby North Loop condo. She was an assistant producer at a TV station, a hot chick with a killer body and a healthy appetite for experimental sex. She had no clue that Buell had a pregnant wife waiting for him back home. Or if she'd figured it out, she didn't much care.

Buell's feet worked the pedals as he swung the helo around in a wide arc over the turgid Mississippi. He was preparing for their final approach. All he had to do now was coast in slowly and drop the skids. The landing zone, with its sixteen green perimeter lights, shone like a Christmas tree. No problem there.

"Looking good," his copilot, Josh Ansel, said. "Ten-degree angle, LZ dead ahead. Almost there." Ansel was young and unmarried, so he might be hitting the clubs tonight. First Avenue, where Soul Asylum and Prince had gotten their starts. Like that.

Buell hovered the Bell 407 over the dark ribbon of river as easily as if it were a giant bubble floating on a summer breeze. He was just about to throttle back and adjust his airspeed and pitch when a tiny flash, no bigger than a lightning bug, caught his eye.

Buell frowned, concerned that someone might be aiming a laser pointer directly at his windshield. There were dormitories close by, jammed right up to the edge of the towering riverbank, so there was always the chance some dumb-ass kid would pick him out as a target.

But dumb-ass kids were the least of Captain Buell's problems at this moment. The rocket slammed into his helicopter with an angry hiss, piercing the metal skin, pulverizing the gearbox, sending the bird into a perilous and lethal spin. In the darkened cockpit, with the hydraulics gone, sensor gauges, warning lights, and control switches all went crazy. Ansel screamed in fear, or maybe it was pain from the raging inferno that suddenly engulfed them.

And when the big explosion came, a riotous event of incandescent shrapnel, Ansel was already gone, bones and flesh sizzled into an unrecognizable carcass. Buell had maybe a split-second longer, time for a fleeting regret about a baby he'd never see.

TWO students walking back from Stoll's Bar in Stadium Village witnessed the eruption overhead. A raging, pulsing beacon that looked as if a big-ass rocket had just blown up in space.

"Holy shit!" one of the men cried as the remains of the flaming bubble jerked and throbbed in the air and then, like an angry demon cast out of the bowels of hell, hurtled downward in a furious arc, screaming directly toward them. The two men had just enough presence of mind to dive beneath a bus shelter before sheets of fire and twisted hunks of metal rained down upon them.

Nearby, on Washington Avenue, a bus was hit by an enormous fireball of white-hot metal that shattered the windshield and sent the vehicle crashing into a light standard. A rotor spun free of the plummeting debris and carved its way into the side of the chemistry building. More debris rained down as students returning from Walter Library, a Chekhov play at Northrop Auditorium, and a French film festival at the Bell Museum, all began to shriek in terror. A minute later, a dozen sirens cranked up to join the unholy cacophony.

Gerry Schmitt is the *New York Times* bestselling author of more than thirty-five mysteries, including the Afton Tangler Thrillers as well as the Tea Shop, Scrapbooking, and Cackleberry Club mysteries, written under the pen name Laura Childs. She is the former CEO of her own marketing firm, has won dozens of TV and radio awards, produced two reality TV shows, and invests in small businesses. She and her professor husband enjoy collecting art and traveling, and they have two Shar-Peis.

Find out more at gerryschmitt.com or become a friend on Facebook.